LIGHTS OUT

Collected Stories

DOUGLAS CLEGG

ALKEMARA
PRESS

Praise for Douglas Clegg's Fiction

"Clegg's stories can chill the spine so effectively that the reader should keep paramedics on standby."
—Dean Koontz, *New York Times* bestselling author.

"Douglas Clegg has become the new star in horror fiction."
—Peter Straub, *New York Times* bestselling author of *Ghost Story* and, with Stephen King, *The Talisman*

"Douglas Clegg is the best horror novelist of the post-Stephen King generation."
— Bentley Little, *USA Today* bestselling author of *The Haunted.*

"Clegg gets high marks on the terror scale…"
—*The Daily News (New York)*

For Raul, of course.

CONTENTS

Also by Douglas Clegg

STAND-ALONE NOVELS

Afterlife

Breeder

The Children's Hour

Dark of the Eye

Goat Dance

The Halloween Man

The Hour Before Dark

Mr. Darkness

Naomi

Neverland

You Come When I Call You

NOVELLAS & SHORT NOVELS

The Attraction

The Dark Game (Two Novelettes)

Dinner with the Cannibal Sisters

Isis

The Necromancer

Purity

The Words

SERIES

THE HARROW SERIES

Nightmare House, Book 1

Mischief, Book 2

The Infinite, Book 3

The Abandoned, Book 4

The Necromancer (Prequel Novella)

Isis (Prequel Novella)

THE CRIMINALLY INSANE SERIES

Bad Karma, Book 1

Red Angel, Book 2

Night Cage, Book 3

THE VAMPYRICON TRILOGY

The Priest of Blood, Book 1

The Lady of Serpents, Book 2

The Queen of Wolves, Book 3

THE CHRONICLES OF MORDRED

Mordred, Bastard Son (Book 1)

COLLECTIONS

Lights Out: Collected Stories

Night Asylum

The Nightmare Chronicles

Wild Things

BOX SET BUNDLES

Bad Places (3 Novels)

Coming of Age (3 Dark Novellas)

Dark Rooms (3 Novels)

Criminally Insane: The Series (3 Novels)

Halloween Chillers

Harrow: Three Novels (Books 1-3)

Harrow: Four Novels (Books 1-4)

Haunts (8 Novel Box Set)

Lights Out (3 Collection Box Set)

Night Towns (3 Novels)

The Vampyricon Trilogy (3 Novels)

With more new novels, novellas and stories to come.

Get the Newsletter

Get book updates, exclusive offers, news of contests &
special treats for readers—become a V.I.P. member of
Douglas Clegg's long-running free newsletter at:

DouglasClegg.com/newsletter

Foreword

The first time I heard the term "lights out," was in summer camp. An entire world went dark at once. The environment changed. Rules fell apart.

The others in the camp who had been well-behaved might suddenly run amok in the dark. You could get in trouble. You could sneak out. The unlit hours were filled with adventure. No one was around to stop you.

Terrible things could happen.

Wonderful things could happen.

Coincidentally, it was also the time that I discovered a larger world of dark fiction than I had known existed.

This was a basketball camp. We slept in college dormitories. We played on the courts of Davidson College in North Carolina. I learned every dirty joke and cuss word I'd missed out on during my first 12 years of life — and most of them came by way of the coaches. The other kids were all a great group. Some of them had been playing basketball since the age of four, training to become star athletes once they got to high school and college. Others — like me — were there because we just loved playing basketball.

I loved and hated that camp in equal measure at the time; looking back, I wouldn't have traded those weeks for the world. What an experience.

The workouts were grueling. There was very little in the way of a break during the long day. You arose sometime after 6, showered, ate a quick breakfast — and then you were on the court doing dozens of physical training and coordination exercises until lunch. After lunch, there was usually a long practice game, then dinner, followed by strategy films of other games.

And then, lights out.

After lights out, you could sneak away if you weren't utterly exhausted — or, if you happened to have a paperback, you might flick on a flashlight under the covers and start reading.

At this camp, in the middle of the day during lunch hour, you'd take a few minutes to go drop off — or pick up — the previous day's gym clothes at the laundry.

The laundry service seemed a huge luxury. You'd drop off your duffel bag full of smelly socks and shorts and pick them up later, all bright and clean.

That day, I was in a hurry. I'd forgotten to drop my laundry off the day before, and so I skipped lunch to drag two days' worth of gym clothes over to the receivables window at the front of the laundry room.

The woman who worked at the counter was absorbed in a book at just that moment; she probably didn't expect boys to show up for another half hour. I felt bad interrupting her, but I needed to get that laundry done. She looked up, smiled, listened to my tale of woe, and said it could possibly be done but to make sure I had gym clothes for the next practice.

I asked her about the book in her hand. She told a bit about the story in it, which had to do with murder and a hitchhiker.

"You like dark stories?" this magnificent laundress asked me.

I nodded.

Did I like dark stories. I'd been raised on Poe and Hawthorne, among other writers of classic short fiction.

This angel of basketball camp offered me an entire suit-case full of paperback anthologies of dark mystery stories and horror — including six H.P. Lovecraft collections with skulls and weird stuff on the covers. She promised that when I finished the one suitcase, I was to empty it and keep the books I wanted but return the suitcase.

And then, she said, she'd fill it again.

Reader, I went to town.

After lunch, I'd race back to my room and open this magical suitcase to find a new anthology beneath the pile of others I'd already read through. If I got caught in a story and couldn't finish before afternoon practice began, I'd make up the rest of the story in my head as I dribbled and took shots. I was more inside those stories than on the court. When playing in the weekly big game, I imag-ined these tales projected on the movie theater of my mind.

Late at night, I'd turn on my flashlight and get right back into it, no matter how exhausting the workout had been that day.

The smell of those paperbacks! Musty or fresh, didn't

matter to me. The feel of the pages, which turned themselves as I swam the currents of those stories!

There were these great *Mystery Writers of America* anthologies of crime and suspense stories (*Tales for a Rainy Night* being such a standout I remember every story in it even to this day, proving mystery stories can be scary as hell). Tale after tale that caught me in its trap, its net, its undertow — making me forget the world around me and the passing of time. There is no time in story; there is only "what happens next." I discovered tales from M.R. James and Arthur Machen, too, and then there was Ray Bradbury's *The October Country* and *The Illustrated Man,* each turning my world inside out with its dusky beauty.

Finally, I walked with H.P. Lovecraft along his mountains of madness, shivered beneath the shadows over Innsmouth, visited Dunwich and Arkham, and imagined the strange model who sat for an artist named Pickman.

I devoured these paperbacks in a frenzy of late nights and stolen hours. I could not get enough of them.

I fell head over heels in love with the dark tale.

And I felt I'd been given the key to the most amazing world, where pulp met literary, imagination soared against a backdrop of twilight, where anything could happen, where night creatures roamed, and where human nature met its mythological match.

The fiction of "lights out."

Now, as an adult, there is nothing so ordinary as the moment when the lights go out. These things happen. Sometimes, you forgot to pay the electric bill, or a storm comes through and your entire neighborhood has gone dark. Perhaps you're in bed and you turn out the lamp but are unable to sleep as you face the dark.

But there are times when more dangerous things occur and you're not safe in your home or in a place surrounded by familiar faces. You might be in the woods; as you leave the main path, branches overhead seem to converge and block out the sun — and you find yourself in the dark even at midday. Or you explore a cave and the flashlight dies in your hand. Or you're on an isolated road in the middle of nowhere after a moonless midnight, out of gas, and your battery dies just as the wind picks up.

I could play out other scenarios of fears we all have, night visions, strange dreams in the pitch black, the illusions we create, the mind movies we unleash.

This is the realm where nightmare logic rules, where wondrous and unearthly creatures can emerge — or where the worst human impulse shows itself as the mask slips down and we bear witness to the genuine face of the dark.

On the other hand, there's nothing like your imagination when the world has vanished and you're living in a dream. That's the moment when magic carpets soar and a secret wish reveals itself and the thing you're most afraid of becomes your own reflection in the mirror of night.

Come along with me. I've brought together three previously published volumes of my short fiction — including the Bram Stoker Award and International Horror Guild Award-winning collection *The Nightmare Chronicles*, with *Night Asylum* and the collection *Wild Things*. To these, I've added the previously uncollected novelette (first published in *Dark Discoveries #27* in its April 2014 issue) *Funerary Rites.*

Included are the novelettes *The Dark Game, White Chapel* and *I Am Infinite, I Contain Multitudes* as well as stories of quiet dread, dark fable, outright horror, mythological madness, and chilling suspense. This enormous collection represents the majority of my past short fiction (excluding all works of novella-length or more) from sometime around the year 1990 and into early 2014. I'll continue to write stories, novelettes, novellas and novels as long as I have breath (and mind).

I hope you'll continue to read them.

— Douglas Clegg
July 20, 2014

LIGHTS OUT

Funerary Rites

A NOVELETTE

WHAT RUBY SAID

When the foreigners first came, they rented the old Dunwoody place with its rundown barn at the back.

"Coppery people," is how Ruby began her description of them. "The women wear these yellow and blue robes draped like this," she drew her hand over and across her shoulder. "They set everything in straw baskets gently, like putting babies down to sleep. You should have seen the look I got from Jean Marie when I helped them. My *goodness*, you'd have thought I was passing nuclear secrets to the Rosenbergs."

We walked home from her father's store where my wife took afternoon shift three days a week while our son spent time with his aunt. It was one of those warm, unhurried summer evenings from which we stole ten trouble-free minutes together, headaches calmed, hand in hand like kids.

"They say much?"

She shook her head. "Just pointed at things. Held out cash for me to pick and choose from. They've got a smell." Realizing how ugly this sounded, she added, "not unpleasant at all. But unlike anything I've smelled before. Wonder what it is?"

❧

RUBY, whose family went back two hundred years in our village, had never seen three women who looked so different from anyone else in her world.

My wife had grown up within the village terrarium. In some ways, it's why I loved her, particularly after the war, when everything else changed so much. Ruby had retreated in some respects and become more of a small town, old fashioned girl than she'd been when we met.

This is not to say she was ignorant or backward — or even shy. She got her education — a good one — having studied history and art in a local college of pastoral setting, with an ambition of moving *to New York City or even Paris and working in a little gallery or maybe the Metropolitan Museum of Art*, she said within the first twenty minutes of our inaugural conversation, surrounded by a dome of chatter and music.

Who could not fall in love with her?

What a momentous night that was for me:

Imagine if that busload of college girls had not arrived from the state's outer reaches to crash the October tri-colle-

giate party at Oyster River where dancing went all night
and lights were strung like the Milky Way from beam to
beam in a barn-sized boathouse.

There, I — morose and undone by my first full month
away from home — approached this most compelling girl
who stood alone at the edge of everything. She, of soft dark
hair and narrow brown eyes hidden beneath the kind of
glasses you'd draw off just before you'd kiss her. She was
dressed in what looked like her grandmother's cocktail dress
with the pelt of a long blue cardigan draped across one
shoulder, a magnificent misfit, clutching a bottle of Coca-
Cola in one hand as if ready to crack heads with it, a permanently unlit cigarette in the other, not giving a damn about
dancing or drinking or whether she looked foolish or not.

"Look around, the world's coming apart at the seams
but in here it's all fun and games — and I'd avoid the punch
if I were you," Ruby said to me. "I had to be dragged here.
What's your excuse?"

"I think I came here to meet you," I said.

RUBY PROBABLY WOULD HAVE LEFT with me after college
— and headed off for New York, Paris, or just plain old
Boston — had not history both large and small cut short
the path.

War intervened the following winter, during which I
mainly saw the inside of safe, dusty corridors packed with
bespectacled and exacting old men nearly as boring as the
work. Flat-footed, four-eyed, color-blind, with a slight hand
tremor from birth and an aptitude for numbers and memo-

rization, I was deemed fit more for paperwork than for fighting; I cataloged the missing and the dead.

It became my unenviable job to connect names with numbers and home addresses so that — eventually — a doorbell would be rung and some family stateside given the bad news.

I ran across the names of college friends who had fallen, neighborhood sons who'd been lost in the Pacific, and those possibly dead in the rubble of Europe. I grew to hate the larger world and dream of the kind of village where nobody knew much about what went on out there.

During the first year or two of the war, Ruby and I wrote constantly to each other. The news came from the Pacific that her beloved brother died in combat. In fact, I saw his name on the lists and felt a jab in my heart when I thought of how Ruby would take the news.

Later, when her mother grew sick the letters trickled and then stopped entirely.

She had become moored to her home by that point. Her father needed her, she wrote in her last letter, her sisters couldn't keep the store running, it looked grim for her mother, and Ruby couldn't shake the thought of her older brother dying like that.

And then, the silence.

As soon as I could, I returned, terrified I'd lost my girl to someone else. After I'd located her and spent days in her company, I proposed marriage, imposed pregnancy, and then there was no getting her to up-and-go anywhere else.

For me to be with Ruby, I had to give up the outside world.

At the time, it was how I wanted it. Her hometown remained locked in a dream of what a New England village had always been. The milk was fresh, the air clean, the trees thick with leaf, the streams ice-cold in summer, the neighbors a bit dull, distant yet companionable, friendly in an untrusting way.

After several months, the long lists of the dead vanished from my dreams. I loved my wife and child, I disagreed affably with my father-in-law; we worked, we loved, we played, we ignored; we kept shutters closed in winter and opened our doors wide when spring finally came.

We nestled into village life.

There we were, fairly typical among the locals, more than a decade after our wedding, me at the bank counting other peoples' money and her at the afternoon shift, not ten minutes' walk from where she'd been born, our only child — named for her dead brother — eleven years old the summer that the Smiths arrived.

On that particular walk home, within the first few days of our foreign invasion, I grew inordinately happy.

My wife glimpsed a new horizon in the foreigners and hadn't shrunk from it. In fact, she'd become curious about the newcomers, because "sometimes I feel like a stranger here, too. I don't really think like my father, do I?"

"No," I said. "Not your sisters, either. Or anyone we know. Thank god."

"I think maybe we should travel more," Ruby said on that particular evening, "now that Caleb's older. Aren't you a little bored with things the way they are? I know I am. We could use a breath of fresh air, maybe a change of scenery."

The time had come. We'd hidden too long. Perhaps we'd buy a Chevrolet and drive out west; or do a southern trip; maybe go see Manhattan and tour around a little.

I welcomed the arrival of outside influence in our lives in the form of the Smiths.

At least, I did for awhile.

❧

ABOUT THE SMITHS

❧

THE GENERAL SCUTTLEBUTT went that they were a pack of gypsies, then Hindu, Amazonian tribesmen, possibly deposed Mongolian royalty, exiles from Borneo or the Sudan or Burma, terrible Barbary Coast people, islanders of some ruined South Sea paradise — and finally something else entirely that most of us had never heard of.

You might assume we were not the friendliest of villages, but many in town were worried based on the news reports. Immigrants packed Boston, Portsmouth bulged with foreigners, and Manhattan to the far south became a different country entirely.

We never thought outsiders would make it so far inland.

First there were maybe six of them.

Within a week or three, we could count at least fourteen on Main Street on a morning so bright you had to shield your eyes from the sun to make out their crowd hanging around the butcher shop.

Tom Raleigh, who worked the register, told us the foreigners always asked for cuts of meat that nobody ever ate.

"You mean like marrow bones?" Ruby asked.

"Heads," I guessed. "Or hooves."

"No," he said. "I'm not even sure these parts got names. We usually throw that stuff out."

I looked at my wife and she at me, with a crooked, slight smile breaking the calm of her face.

In the pause, Tom added, "it's a little disturbing."

"Well, it's not exactly the end of the world," I said. "I mean, these people seem okay, don't they?"

"Sure," Tom said as he weighed and wrapped up the pork loin we'd have for supper. "I got nothing against them. Nothing at all. I just don't think it's normal. But what do I know? I mean, to each his own."

"I'm going to be up all night wondering what those cuts are," Ruby said on the way out as I held the door open. "It's not like they're cannibals or anything."

"He made it up," I said when we got to our car.

"Now, why would Tom do that?"

I opened the car door for her; she slid in. Once I'd gotten in on the other side, I said, "He's like everyone else. He's got to put his two cents in, have a story about them, spread a little dirt. This town's too damn small."

After that, other strange and unsavory Smith stories began cropping up. Lois Abbott, who ran the library, said Smiths had been stealing books. Paul Lockwood said he caught some of their men peeping through windows at night when most people were asleep. May Peters, at the coffee shop, swore on her father's grave that they went through the trash early in the morning "like a gang of raccoons." Even Helen Cooper — usually less gossipy than most — told my wife she didn't like the way the Smith men eyed teenage girls in town, "like they're sizing up which ones to kidnap as brides."

The Smiths, it was said, held strange celebrations out in

the autumn woods accompanied by ghostly chanting and drumbeats "like in *Tarzan*." Two Smith women were seen bare breasted down at the stream, washing sheets against the rocks.

And then some idiot spread the rumor that some Smiths had been caught out at the cemetery "doing voodoo."

You could attach any cockamamie story you wanted to the name Smith, and nine times out of ten, it would stick.

WE CALLED our foreigners the Smiths because nobody could pronounce their names. "Smith" became a joke that we'd never in a million years mention to their faces. Little Smith, Smith Junior, Uncle Smith, Big Smith, Old Smith, Pretty Smith, Ancient Smith — that kind of thing.

Most of their clan grabbed the lowest rung mill jobs. They never complained these were beneath them or that they were made for better things. They took them happily, and by all accounts, turned the mills around.

We'd see Smiths wandering around on weekends or sometimes early Monday morning. They'd arrive to town in packs of four and five to pick up sundries and fabric or when a big brown trunk arrived from the old country to our post office.

The Smiths didn't drive cars. They used ox-drawn wagons and bicycles. The older ones walked into town clutching hand carved staffs like Biblical shepherds. The elder Smith ladies carried groceries on wooden crossbars at their shoulders or in baskets balanced perfectly on their heads. They'd slowly trudge back — barefoot in summer —

to their rented rundown farm, a two mile walk on a blistery afternoon.

You couldn't even offer them rides — I tried once or twice but just got nods and dismissals from the Smith crowd, along with that chattering sound they made when trying to be polite.

At first, we were all proper with the Smiths and respected their customs. You could say — despite the gossip about them — that there existed peace in the land.

But then there was that incident at the cider mill.

The Battle of Dunwoody Farm

The rowdier boys in the village claimed a Smith started it.

The boys who raised the flag and ran up the hill mainly came from the Crocker family, six tawny-haired scoundrels between the ages of 12 and 17, all of them destined for prisons in some distant future, all of them getting away with their crimes (stealing a few sawbucks from a till, spying on a local Venus in her bath, egg-fights along Main Street, a window shot through, the murdered parakeet incident, the famous joyride in a jalopy ending in a crash and tumble, whisperings of girls-in-trouble leaving town under mysterious circumstances).

There were others, too, the sheep-boys who followed the bad ones. These little disciples were as guilty; and yes, I counted my own son in that. Caleb had turned twelve at the time with just enough rambunctiousness in his blood to do the wrong thing.

The boys of the village first threw hard, green apples like grenades; then the warm pies sitting out along cooling shelves; finally rocks and marbles and anything that could gain velocity between fist and back-of-head.

The Smith boys — most of them under the age of fifteen — fought back, of course, but with less dumb luck.

A skirmish ensued, war declared. What began at the cider mill ended with a chase out to the Dunwoody farm. Cows fled their pen, chickens flew, windows smashed, a threshold trespassed.

A flaming arrow made it into a barn window and someone — I suspected Paul Lockwood's kid — dumped manure in the well.

After the whuppings — and there were several — we all made our sons apologize.

It was quite a spectacle: twenty boys of varying shape and size, prodded forward by their fathers in a kind of Death March through town, out along the little bridge over the stream that went to the Dunwoody place.

Their heads hung low, they scratched at imagined itches, some hands clasped in droopy prayer or slow hand-wringing, some (mainly those Crocker boys) cast sidelong glances to the fields beyond the stone walls as if plotting escape routes.

My boy Caleb bowed his head and said he was sorry to every single Smith, though he only marginally participated in the fracas and received not a single belt to his behind. Still, I gave him a good talking to and there'd be no privileges for a good long while.

He had, I told him, better damn straighten up before he ended up like a Crocker.

The kids cleaned up their mess. An offering of cash for repairs. A calf given as a gift. A fence mended. We — of the Selectmen — got out and repaired the barn.

The Smiths themselves quickly offered the olive branch, spoke slowly and formally in a language none of us understood but I guessed was their way of telling us to put it in the past and leave them alone and please — in their eyes a sliver of fear — *don't ever bother us again.*

A cloud came over our town that day and remained.

We felt ashamed of our sons' behaviors. We didn't like the idea that we'd become the bad neighbors. We preferred to think of foreigners as a kind of benign tumor to be watched for signs of malignancy.

We were not arrogant people. We liked to live in peace. We didn't nurture disagreements, though they existed. We didn't want to get involved in conflicts with any foreigners. We'd heard that some towns created battle lines with their own versions of the Smiths and sometimes this ended in terrible consequence for everybody.

TURNS OUT, in their exuberant and uncalled-for attack, our boys managed to desecrate some sacred cow or other.

Young Smith — one of the eldest of their boys — explained the whole thing to me in halting English without actually naming our sacrilege.

A blasphemy had occurred. Our boys had no idea what they'd really done. Young Smith told us that their women stopped eating because of it. Two middle-aged Smiths had to leave at once — at great expense — for the journey to the motherland to offer propitiation. Offerings were being burnt even as we were informed of this.

We had crossed into the territory of taboo and Young Smith warned us that the older men of his tribe wept with this injustice, a strong-hearted young man lost his left hand in a mill accident and a young wife miscarried twins with misshapen limbs, among other signs of tribal apocalypse.

"This house is no longer holy," Young Smith told us. "It is a place of darkness to us now. We must avoid a war."

A war?

Foreigners! Invaders! War!

All the things we didn't want in our little off-the-beaten-track borough.

Later, at our town meeting, we scratched our heads and came up with possibilities of which line had been crossed. Was it the hay that burned in the barn? The well? The escaped cow? Someone even suggested it might be that apples were sacred to whatever hundred gods and goddesses the heathens worshipped.

Or the pies?

We never figured it out, but nobody wanted to start a war — "their word not ours" — with the Smiths because "nobody knows where that'll end."

The lowest of our minds — and we had more than our share — imagined machetes, spears, little knives, or shrunken heads all in a row.

The Smiths moved a little further out of town.

For their new tribal home, the Smiths grabbed the big house at the edge of the marsh.

MALVERN HOUSE — enormous and colonial and crumbly — was somewhat hidden from an untrammeled dirt road behind high stone walls and jagged trees. The marsh stench was impossible to avoid. Who else would choose to live there but outsiders?

My friend, Cormac Danielson, their landlord and a man who owned several dilapidated properties in the deep woods, took some heat over this rental, a few nasty looks by the harsher folk in the village, but most of us didn't care. Few ever traveled that road, no one hunted at the marshes anymore, it was a dead end off an out-of-the-way half-past a nowhere. The place came surprisingly cheap and held a good twelve bedrooms — perfect for the Smiths — and not a single indoor toilet.

By then, there were at least twenty of them living at Malvern, all loosely related, most coming down the matriarchal side from the old lady we called Ancient Smith.

Twenty became forty. More Smiths arrived over a two year period.

One winter, they bought Malvern House for what was reportedly a tidy sum. Well of course, some people said, they could buy it and the damn marsh and even the fields around it when they lived forty to a house and they all took the mill jobs away from more deserving people. They'd been moving up in their jobs, and rumor went that one of them was about to make an offer on the paper mill.

"They're going to own us all soon enough, just watch," Paul Lockwood said, though we all laughed at the time.

Local boys — expressly warned to never bother the Smiths again — reported strange goings-on out there. Wild animal cries. Smells of strange spice and odd bonfires along the marsh. Music played on weird drums, screechy fiddles that sounded like mating cats and oddly shaped clarinets that produced even odder whines. Lights in the sky. Bizarre sounds of strangulation that might pass for singing.

Paul Lockwood began calling Malvern House the city of foreign relations by the time my boy turned fifteen. People eventually forgot that it was ever called Malvern House and instead, it became known as Smithville.

By then, they owned the paper mill and had bought one hundred fifty acres of woodland along the river, including the old Shalcross farm. A much larger Smith settlement arose, and the boundaries of Smithville continued nudging out along the county line.

We pretty much stayed away from them, and they — in turn — kept their distance.

Until something happened to change it all.

The Coffee Shop Debate

One summer morning, the oldest Smith boy came riding his bicycle to town.

He was tall and scrawny and wore only a cloth at his waist. He dropped the bike in the street and went running up to Dr. Knowles' office, across from the bank where I worked. The kid shouted so much that we all went to the windows to watch as the doctor stepped out and exchanged a few words with the boy. Then, Dr. Knowles went back inside.

The boy paced, striking the air with his fists. He glanced

over at those of us watching. The look on his face was devastating — tears streamed down his face, his mouth open and sagging, his eyes pleading.

"Something bad's happened with those people," one of the bank tellers said.

Dr. Knowles came out to the street, spoke with the boy, put his hand on the boy's shoulder. They left together in the doctor's sleek Chrysler.

It was the first time — to any of our knowledge — that a Smith sat in a car seat.

This became a topic of interest down at the coffee shop where several of us watched the Chrysler return and park across the street, just after the work day had ended.

Dr. Knowles, noticing our stares as he got out of his car, came striding over.

Once inside the coffee shop, he called an informal meeting of the Selectmen.

This was easily accomplished because we were all sitting around with half-drunk cups of coffee in our hands.

"THE OLD LADY'S so sick, I wanted to put her out of her misery," Dr. Knowles told our group when we'd pushed tables together and gathered with our lemonades and coffees and pastries. "They don't believe in hospitals. And it doesn't matter — she won't make it to one. I got her as comfortable as anyone can be in that condition."

He stirred his coffee and looked down into it as if it were a crystal ball. "She'll be dead by tomorrow."

"Terrible," I said.

Ruby sat opposite me, next to Helen Cooper, whose

husband Josh — my closest friend in town — was to my left. Paul Lockwood sat to my right, while Dr. Knowles had squeezed in between Willie Crocker and Dave Neary at table's end.

"Awful," Ruby said. "I feel as if I just saw her at the store last Wednesday. She's old but I didn't think…"

"As weepy as this is," Paul Lockwood said. "What's it got to do with any of us?"

"They need to perform funerary rites," Dr. Knowles said.

"Sounds heathen," Paul grumbled.

"Well, everybody has customs," the doctor said. "And they have a particular way they bury their dead in that country."

"But they're not in that country."

Dr. Knowles laid out the basics:

"The boy told me his family fasts for three days. There's some holy man of theirs in Manhattan who will come up. Preparations may take a full week. The body stays above ground. They say prayers night and day. The women cover themselves in ash and the men will wear nothing but a plain cloth around their waists. No one washes until after a customary period. The children won't speak during sunlit hours. There are a few less savory aspects to the customs, but there's no need to talk about it here. By week's end, they'll have a feast — and even games."

"I assume this won't be like the Olympics," Willie Crocker joked.

"Sounds heathen," Paul Lockwood groaned. "I mean, I'm not saying it's wrong. I hate to judge people, but it sounds so damn heathen."

We all looked across the table at him.

"Never seen you in church," I said.

"Church is for hypocrites and sinners," Paul said.

Dr. Knowles continued, "The son took off immediately. There's a larger community of his mother's relatives over in Boston. They have a whole process to this. It's very regulated, I suppose. Now, I may not agree with it but I know these people. I know how hurt — and angry — they'll be if we can't accommodate this one night."

I shrugged. "Let them do whatever they want out there."

The doctor offered an inscrutable look. "It's more involved than that."

A few among us muttered things, but I kept my eyes on Dr. Knowles' face.

"Drop the other shoe," I said.

He rubbed his eyes. The man was exhausted.

"They need to parade her through our streets," he said.

"That's necessary?" Paul Lockwood jumped in. "A *parade*?"

"This was their matriarch," the doctor said. "She's sort of — well, I suppose you'd call her a queen of their tribe. She gets a royal procession."

"Like Fourth of July?" Dave Neary said.

"Maybe we should roll out a red carpet," Paul Lockwood said. "Bow down. Pray to their gods."

"Damn Smiths," Willie Crocker said. "They should just take the boat back to where they come from."

Dr. Knowles sighed. "This is no different than our funerals. You go along the streets, the hearse, all that. If this were our President, or even the Governor..." He looked around at the rest of us. Then at me, as if I might help convince the others.

"Sure," I said to our group. "It's a little unusual. But it's not like we didn't go all out when Vernon Browne kicked off a few years back."

"Not the same thing," Willie Crocker said. "He was an American war hero."

"I don't see why we need to let them bring their customs here," Helen said, avoiding all our looks.

"We were here first," Willie Crocker said. "When those Smiths have lived here for two hundred years, then they can have some say in this."

"I have nothing against them. Honestly," Helen said. "But they don't live in the village."

"They buy from us," Ruby said. "They bank here. I mean, I'd hate to lose their business, Helen. Wouldn't you? The store's grown because of them. They could just as easily go to Remington or Hazelford if they had to, and I'd hate to think of the money we'd lose, if nothing else."

"I'm telling you, it's heathen," Paul Lockwood said for the umpteenth time, and on went the arguments.

"Here's the part that'll be a tough sell for our neighbors, I'm sure," Dr. Knowles interrupted our debate. "They have rules to this procession. No one can look at them. We have to draw curtains, close shutters. Not a single person in town — man, woman, child or dog — can be on the street. It's that sacred."

We all took this in.

"How long's this shindig going to last?" I asked.

"It'll start right at sundown and run until dawn I think. He told me it's involved. It'll be noisy, too."

"Primitives," Paul Lockwood said. "Wailing, caterwauling, no doubt chanting."

"It's a cult," Josh Cooper said. "I don't mind them, but I

don't really like the idea of this." He leaned in to me. "I mean, do you? Why do they even need to come through our village? Can't they stay out on their own land?"

The table went silent.

May Peters brought the coffee pot over and refilled our cups. She apologized for eavesdropping, "but whenever I hear about the Smiths, I just can't help it."

"May?" I asked.

"I've never liked them," she said.

"You ain't alone, sister," Willie said.

"They're not so bad," Ruby said. "If you give them a chance."

Truth was, they weren't bad at all; and yet, in my deepest self, I had to admit that I'd never been quite comfortable around the Smiths. They'd kept themselves so separate over the years that it was as if our own culture had been rejected by them as not worthy. I wasn't smart enough to explore why this bothered me, but it *did* bother me. This seemed at the root of all our unease.

They had never quite accepted *us*.

As if we hadn't heard her the first time, May repeated, "I've just never liked them and I'm not afraid to say it out loud."

Dr. Knowles looked up at her. "It's not a matter of 'like'. They're part of our town. They've hurt no one. They deserve our respect — and compassion — in this situation."

"They smell different," May said. "They cook strange stuff, too."

"My wife cooks strange stuff," I said, and Ruby reached over to swat the air in front of my face in mock anger.

"Close our curtains? That's ridiculous. I won't do it," May said as she receded into the coffee shop while her voice grew louder. "What are we supposed to do? Not go outside, not even look at the stars? Skip any kind of night out we might have planned? Who does that? Is everything supposed to shut down at nine o'clock for them? For those people?"

After May mumbled away, Dr. Knowles lowered his voice. "A lot of people are going to feel like that. Look, we must convince everyone to do this. The Smiths believe that if even one outsider sees the funeral parade, terrible things will happen. World-changing things, he said. For all of us."

"Like what?" Willie asked, a kind of backwoods challenge in his voice.

Dr. Knowles shrugged. "We really want to find out?"

"Maybe they'll set us on fire," Paul muttered. "They like their fires, those heathens."

"This *is* their Queen. And frankly," Dr. Knowles tilted his head slightly as if convincing himself, "they outnumber us."

There, someone had finally said it. More than three hundred Smiths occupied farmland and woodland, and our little village didn't quite hit that number. If you needed any kind of factory job, you probably worked *with* or *for* at least one of the Smith clan. If you worked over in Hazelford, where the great jobs tended to be, you had to drive twenty miles across Smith land to get there.

Dr. Knowles had said the one thing that none of the rest of us wanted to examine:

We didn't really run things in quite the same way as we once had. Oh, we ran the village, no doubt, and we were like the villages in all directions, but in terms of population, the Smiths had us beat.

At the table, we chewed the subject a bit more, but

agreed with Dr. Knowles in the final minutes before heading home.

We'd call an emergency town meeting to make this happen.

Then, after a night of shouting matches in the old meeting hall that went late into the night, we exhausted opponents of this proposal into offering just this one summer night to the Smith family and to no one else.

It was in the town's best interest.

One night we heard the sound of a strange horn — deep and sonorous — and knew that the funeral had begun.

The Funeral Parade

Sunset brushed the trees with a rusty haze. Within an hour or two, we all should've been heading to bed anyway but...well, who could sleep once they thought of the entire Smith clan and some strange priest of their cult walking down Main Street?

We anticipated some unavoidable indecency in the request to close our eyes to their dark celebration. It gave a little thrill to the quiet summer night.

Before drawing the final curtain in the front hall, I glanced out into the shadowed street and saw that all the neighboring homes were shuttered.

The village — from what I could see —shut down tight as a clam.

I closed the curtain.

THE INSIDE of our home became toasty to the point where we'd all stripped down to shorts and undershirts and my wife wore only a slip once we'd sent Caleb up to his room.

Josh Cooper kept calling me: had they come 'round yet? Did anyone see them?

And I kept telling him to forget it and just go to bed.

I sat in the living room watching Ruby pace back and forth as if expecting a guest at the door. Now and then, she'd look over and say, "I don't know why I'm so keyed up," or "you'd think I'd just read a book and go to bed, but I'm almost afraid."

"It's the heat," I said. "Look, if you'd just sit. Drink some lemonade. You'll cool down."

"It's not the heat," she said, "although my god, these fans do nothing without the windows open."

I pointed out the three windows that were in fact open, particularly the ones facing the garden. "And we have six fans going. It's not that bad."

"And the noise. Someone should invent a quiet fan. It's like living inside a beehive," she said. "I'm hoping they come through fast. I can maybe take an hour of this. Maybe not even an hour."

"Take a cool shower," I said.

"It is *not* the heat," Ruby said. "And I don't need a shower."

Caleb, expressly forbidden to look out his shuttered window, had gone to bed — reluctantly — early, with a book he'd been supposed to read all summer, although my wife and I heard his radio on upstairs playing rock n roll over the hum of fans.

"Any other night, I'd yell for him to turn it down," I said.

Ruby ignored my comment.

"You think anyone will look?" Ruby asked. "I mean, how will they not? You're told not to do something, you do it. It's human nature."

"God, I hope not."

"It's not as if the Smiths'll notice," she said. "Jeanne Marie told me she was going to peek. But only a little. There's that dormer window with a little bit of the shutter missing and she said she and Bill would sit up just for a look."

"They shouldn't risk it," I said. Then I swore. "Everybody promised they wouldn't look. I hope Jeanne Marie was just pulling your leg."

"Well it's not as if the Smiths'll see them. And that's all we need to do. Make sure they don't see us looking."

"Is it so hard to just not look outside for one night? How often do we come home, have supper and then not even glance out the open window?"

"This is different."

"How so?"

"It's like being in prison," she said. "Or a coffin."

Ruby stopped pacing. She went and sat on the rug by the coffee table. She picked up a copy of *Reader's Digest* and read off all the article titles in a droning voice and then put it down again. She drew her knees to her chin, reminding me of a girl I once knew. Her long tan legs, the silky slip, the way her shoulders shrugged and her hair swept across half her face. She had never looked more appealing to me. Where was that girl with the Coke bottle in one hand, the cigarette in the other, the glasses and old-fashioned dress that I'd first met? Replaced now by this siren, a dream of slip and girl and desperation.

"Come here, you," she said.

"Honey?"

"Come here." She held her arms out. I went over and crouched down in front of her.

She drew me into the cradle of her body. We were sweaty and there was something filthy about her wanting me like that. I felt as if I were taking advantage of her.

I pulled back, and we sat there staring at each other.

"I know, I know," she moaned. "I just wanted to get away from all this. Can't we get away?"

I felt confused by this state she was in.

"It's okay," I said. "We can go upstairs if you want."

"No," she said. "It's like I want a pill or a drink."

"What a compliment."

"You know what I mean. I just want to block it out."

I returned to the chair and she stood up and began pacing again.

"I didn't think I'd feel like this," she said. "All jittery. It's like the world's going to end or something."

"I promise you the world won't end."

"I mean, they could've picked Hazelford. They've got that farm by the river. Why us? It's strange. It's just too strange."

She stomped her feet, just a little, a spoiled girl instead of a woman in her thirties.

"What's gotten into you?"

"I don't know," she said. "I don't know. But all I think is, you go along in life the way you're supposed to, you do all the right things, all the things that make a good life.

"You marry, start a family, raise your kid, work a job, go

to church, honor your father, be nice to everybody, and then one night you're in a closed up house with every door locked up and you can't even look outside because you're somehow not good enough.

"It's how I feel right now, and I know it sounds crazy, but when I think of my brother Caleb dying on some foreign island and my mother dying in her bed and thinking I'd lost you until you came back and then how things changed so quickly here and how I've been afraid to…"

I had to catch my breath as she went on and on. I'd never heard my wife talk like this.

She dug up tales from her childhood, from our own past, some argument we had, the miscarriage after Caleb, the fact that I hadn't fought in the war but pushed papers while her brother had given the ultimate sacrifice, the idea of wifedom and what it meant, and sisterdom and daughterdom and motherhood and how fathers expected so much and how she'd given up chances because of the stupid war and all these women in town who made comments about your house and wallpaper and how much your husband made and how you dressed and all the stupid things she'd had to do because it was like following a rule book.

Her nose ran and spit flew in the middle of this rough waterfall of words and she stood over me flailing her arms around.

I felt somehow responsible.

She didn't shout, she just let this stream flow from her. She grew all teary-eyed. Sweat burst along her forehead. She went off on me and the world and everything she'd never mentioned before in her life.

I wondered if she might be having a nervous breakdown.

Only then did I notice that our son's radio had gone silent upstairs.

My wife and I stared at each other in the buzz of many fans. I patted my lap. Calming, perhaps exhausted, she sat down and we cuddled, but I could tell that this wasn't enough. We were sweaty, uncomfortable, dissatisfied.

Just get through this one night, I thought. *She feels boxed in. It's the heat. It's the idea that we're not as free as we thought we were. That's all. She'll be fine in the morning.*

"You do everything right," she whispered as if in a confessional. "But it doesn't matter. You give up dreams. You do things so other people will think you're fine. You don't take risks because if you risk things, you lose. People you love might die. The world might fall apart. But nothing you do adds up. None of it makes sense."

I thought about how maybe we should've taken those trips we'd planned — to the Grand Canyon or to St. Augustine or even just to Manhattan to see the museums.

We'd let life get in the way.

The phone rang. She got out of my lap.

"Where you headed?"

Ruby glanced back at me and for a second I thought she wouldn't answer.

"Honey?" I said.

"I think I'll take that shower."

I reached for the phone.

"THAT YOU?" It was Josh.

"Who else?"

"Hear the music yet?"

"No."

"It'll get louder when it gets to your side. Believe me."

A pause on the line.

"You better not be looking," I said.

"I just snuck a peek out the attic window. Over the rooftops to where the road veers into town. And you wouldn't believe it."

"I don't want to hear about it. Just shut the curtains, go to bed, or go work in your basement or something."

"Hell with that. You should see it. Torches lighting everything up like it's the middle of the day practically. And Elephants! Camels! A wagon — no, more like a golden chariot, drawn by tigers! It's like the circus — or Cleopatra — coming to town. There must be a hundred or more of them — not all of them Smiths, either — waving incense around, twirling sabers and dancing. The men in robes, the women wrapped up like mummies but some of them — hold on to your hat — don't got nothin' on from the waist up."

"Quit looking," I said.

"All of 'em moving this way and that, a big guy blowing this bull's horn and a bunch of women playing some kind of flute. Bunch of little boys running around smashing cymbals together. Two guys wearing big antlers, some of them painted all in gold and silver. And then there's Mr. and Mr. Smith…"

"Wait, you're *still* watching?"

"Pretty much."

"Stop it."

"Look, you've got to see this — they have crowns on. Golden crowns with glittering jewels. Like it's the sultan and his queen or something. And that oldest boy of theirs? He's got this big pole and at its top it looks like a golden snake all wrapped around it. He has flowers all over him, head to toe, and maybe a dozen half-naked girls following after him like he's the catch of the day."

"Shut it," I said.

"You've just got to look out a window. Wait, they're going around, over near your place," he said. "I'm telling you, you have never in all your days seen something like this and I'm guessing you never will again. You miss this, you miss everything."

I hung up the phone.

I argued with my better nature: we promised, this is their ritual, this is their custom, honor them, they're good neighbors, Josh exaggerated anyway, how could camels and elephants and tigers be all together here?

They weren't even from a country of camels and elephants and tigers after all, why would they have them?

Had they raided a zoo? Rented from Ringling Brothers?

But it drove me a bit crazy.

I went over to the living room window. *I might just move the curtain slightly. Just a quarter inch. Just enough to see out.*

I began to hear the music. The cymbals, the flutes, the beat of the drums, the strange string instruments that whined and screeched. If I stepped away from the curtains, our fans drowned out the sounds. But right up next to the window...

The Smith noise grew louder in my head.

My fingers brushed the curtain's edge.

Don't do it, I thought. *What if they see you?*

Josh Cooper already risked a possible skirmish by spying from his attic. How many more in town would break their promise?

❦

"YOU'RE LYING. OR JOKING," I said when I called Josh back.

"No," he said. "You need to look out there. They'll never see you. They're too involved in their…well, their spectacle. I saw three little girls riding some kind of large wild pig. I've never seen anything like it. And all these banners. And colored paper. And blankets with spirals and things all over them. And lights, these amazing lights."

"What about the coffin?"

"Coffin? What? Oh, no, it's not like that. They must not believe in that. Ancient Smith. The Queen. You should see. It's as if she's still alive. They have her raised up in this silver chair of some kind and she's dressed like she's going to a wedding, all bright scarves and bracelets. It really is something to see, you should just look, just for a second."

I went silent. I'd heard a noise from upstairs.

"Got to go." I hung up. I bounded up the stairs, thinking I'd check on Ruby in the shower. Halfway up, I saw Caleb crouched in the hall by the narrow window, his head beneath the shade.

"What do you think you're doing?"

He bumped his head on the glass. The paper shade slapped him as he ducked back from under it.

When Caleb turned around he couldn't look me in the eye.

"Sorry, dad."

"Go to your room."

"But dad, you got to see it. There's this…"

"Stop right there, young man." I pointed at him as if throwing a lightning bolt. "You know the rules tonight."

"They'll never see me," he said. "And there's this bird — I think it's a bird — it's huge and clomping around. And one of the Smith kids is riding it just like a horse."

"Really?" I asked, losing my fatherly power for a moment.

"Just look for a second," my boy said.

"We promised we wouldn't."

"They'll never know."

"It's *honor*, Caleb," I said and then shooed him to his room at the back of the house.

I wanted to peer under the shade, but resisted.

Instead, I went to check on Ruby. I knocked on the bathroom door and heard her say, "just a minute," so I waited on the landing. I kept glancing over at the shade, wondering if my sense of duty was getting in the way of seeing something truly remarkable.

After awhile, the water still running — Ruby loved her long showers — I went to our bedroom. I lay down in the dark and listened to the strange music outside.

I closed my eyes.

At some point in the night, I heard our front door slam shut.

I got up and went downstairs, thinking someone might be breaking in.

The door wasn't completely closed.

Someone had gone outside.

Who?

I peered out the front window, nearly trembling, thinking that I was doing something awful.

The parade was still going but the drums had stopped their incessant beating. I saw flashes of it: large bears walking on hind legs, a woman riding a chariot drawn by tigers, several children carrying sparklers, wide hoops being tossed in the air and caught again as they landed effortlessly in young men's hands, the colorful robes, the elephants, the dancing women, the children playing cymbals and flutes, a long chain of dancers as the Smiths performed their rites all night through our village.

Among them, I caught a glimpse of my son.

Caleb was shirtless and had painted his chest in bright colors as he danced around with various young Smiths. Helen Cooper — with silk of various shades drawn over her — rode atop the elephant with others from our village, and there was Young Smith and Child Smith and Girl Smith and Middle-Age Smith, and then wonder of wonders, Paul Lockwood, too, part of this strange procession.

Running after them, grabbing the hand of one of the Smith uncles, May Peters leapt up to a platform carried by several Smiths and began dancing.

I worried about the idea of feuds and bad blood and thought of terrible futures for us, for the Smiths, for our village and its mostly placid surface.

I felt a sudden urge to join in the festivities, but I remained worried: what would become of us? Would the Smiths forgive those who did?

Or would we pay a heavy price for breaking this rule?

World-changing things, Dr. Knowles had said.

I couldn't run out there. I couldn't just go grab Caleb. I'd cause more of a problem, create a greater sacrilege.

Better just to leave it. Pretend you saw nothing.

These are the things I considered in my three a.m. weariness.

I wasn't even sure if I might actually still be in bed dreaming. I had that half-awake, half-somewhere-else feeling the whole time.

When I went back to bed, I noticed that Ruby was not there, on the other side. There wasn't even an indent in the pillow where her head would have rested.

Probably sleeping downstairs in the den, I thought. Sometimes she did. Sometimes I snored. Sometimes, she told me, she couldn't stand my heat when we lay there together in the middle of the night.

I woke up later than usual.

I checked Caleb's room. My unease turned to panic when I went downstairs and could not find my wife.

Damp footprints went from the bathroom to the front door, which was open wide to the street.

When I stepped out onto the front porch, I noticed several of the other houses across from us with their doors open wide, too.

By the end of the day, those left in town could only guess what happened.

"Dr. Knowles said we'd been warned," Josh said, when I stopped by his hardware store. "And they shouldn't have looked."

"I doubt that's all that happened," I said. "I mean, we both looked. We didn't join in."

"I didn't even think Helen so much as peeked," he said. "She was going a little crazy last night. It was so hot. She got angry that any of us agreed to their terms. But I didn't think..."

"Yeah, Ruby was sort of like that, too," I said.

I imagined Ruby, watching from the bathroom window. *The long cold shower, walking out, dancing, being lifted up onto one of their chariots.*

"Why *them* and not us?" Josh said on another day when we'd gotten used to what happened the night of the parade. "Why'd Helen run out there like a kid heading for the ice cream truck? I mean, I saw it happen and I knew — I just *knew* — that if I stepped outside the door, I'd end up with the Smiths, too."

"Maybe they were missing something over here," I said, looking down into my hands. "Who knows?"

And another afternoon, work day done, in the coffee shop:

"Don't worry. They'll come back," Josh said, patting me on the shoulder. "I mean, living in Smithville? It's not what they're used to. The weather'll turn. It won't seem so exciting. They'll miss comforts. They'll wake up and wonder, *what the hell was I thinking?* I mean, I can't even imagine Helen without modern plumbing. I doubt she'll make it to October.

And then they'll return home, tails between legs, the village'll get back to its business and we'll forgive and forget. We'll all look back on this summer as one of those odd things, like when the Crash happened, or when Pearl Harbor got hit, like we think it'll never be normal again, but you know, after awhile, it just goes back to being what it always was."

"Sure," I said. "They'll come back."

RUBY SIGHTINGS

A NEW FEAR of the Smiths overtook our village.

What else might they take?

What further revenge would they exact? How much did we really know about them and what they were capable of?

We had weapons — some of us said — we can go free our children and husbands and wives at gunpoint; but no one picked up a gun because on some deep level we feared that the Smiths held a power greater than even bullets.

Or worse, that our loved ones wouldn't want to return to the lives they'd had. They might prefer instead the many hearths of Smithville.

Now and then, those of us who remained behind would drive out to their settlements to catch a glimpse of someone we'd lost.

I saw my boy Caleb — by then, seventeen — standing at a window at the old Malvern place. His face was painted in streaks of whitewash and blue. He wore a mottled blue and green robe wrapped over his shoulder like a toga. He held a little baby in his arms.

When I waved, he didn't seem to recognize me.

Caleb had their look — that Smith gaze, a strangely placid expression, a kind of flat affect as if he were living in a different world beneath his skin.

I tried to trap my son once or twice. He became docile when I locked him up. He wouldn't eat. He'd start chanting in that foreign language — a doleful bleating.

I had to let him go. What was the use? I didn't want to take the risk that he'd starve to death in his father's house or that I'd end up causing something worse to happen.

I watched as he rode his old bicycle back to Smithville.

I began to stay indoors, mostly. I shuttered the windows every night, stopped listening to the news, went to bed early, woke up late, did my job, said the expected things, and hoped for the best.

Others ran into Ruby now and then.

I'd ask them not to speak of her so much, not to me, not anymore. "She's not who she was," I'd say or else, "She's made her choice," or "I guess I never really knew her at all. How well do we really know anyone?"

If only, I'd think.

If she'd just stayed inside, just kept the curtain closed, just done what was asked.

Friends told me about how good Ruby looked, but also how strange, how different, how similar, as if Ruby had been copied by the Smiths and the real Ruby no longer existed, not the Ruby they'd known their whole life, anyway.

How she didn't seem to recognize them at all when they

tried talking to her. How she refused their offers of lifts or escorts or their whispered pleas to come back to town.

How Ruby would move past them, after a Saturday morning's errand, her hair long again, sometimes braided, her skin a deep rich summer tan, a crossbar yolk on her shoulders, carrying baskets of groceries or piles of colored fabric.

She walked barefoot — they said — and not too far behind a few of the other Smith ladies.

The Stain

Jason hunted for the T-shirt just outside the walls of the hotel compound.

He haggled over the price of a particular shirt — the kind Kyle would love. It was boiling hot out; the sea breeze did nothing to cool down the market stall.

After an extended back-and-forth with the seller, Jason got a sweet deal: the shirt, flip-flops, plus a few knickknacks for his son's collection.

The guy selling souvenirs under the plastic awning lived — no doubt — among the squalor of hut and shack that ran the length of road between hotel and airport. The man's teeth were a mess. Bright-eyed but malnourished, he sweated in the sauna of noon.

Jason felt a twinge of guilt, having bargained so aggressively just to shave off a buck or two. He recalled his wife's phrase, spoken on their honeymoon a decade earlier, at a coastal resort in that kind of country: "The misfortune of being born in the wrong place."

Still, Jason closed the deal with American dollars.

The seller chattered in the universal language of pissed-ness to the short woman who wrapped the items and slipped them into a brown paper bag.

Jason gave the shirt to Kyle the minute he got home from the airport that night.

※

"Look what it says," Jason told his son.

Kyle, who was nine, read it out loud.

"Wow," his son said, after. "Wow."

"Wow is right," Jason said. "When you're a little older, I'll take you there. It's got cool cliffs and these islands out in the ocean that you can actually swim to. Your dad para-sailed. It's like flying."

Over dinner at the sushi place in town, his wife Amy said, "Don't I get a T-shirt?"

"Maybe next time. I brought in three new clients, one trip."

"And that means…"

"Well, we can probably put an offer on the beach condo."

She took a sip of her soda, picked up a chopstick and jabbed it at the air. "Do we really want to do that? We may take a hit for it."

"It's for Kyle, too."

"I think we should just save the money. Invest some more," she said and reached over to harpoon a piece of dragon roll off his plate. He crossed chopsticks with hers and knocked it back in his court.

"Yeah but a condo, just think," Jason said. "Income

property, plus vacations. It'll pay forward. Add a little to our investment portfolio."

"But can we make a business of it?"

"It's a start," he said. "You never know where it might lead."

When they got home, Jason drove the nanny back to her little apartment, paying her double for the extra time.

After Amy fell asleep, Jason went to look in on Kyle.

☙

IN BED, Kyle's head was nearly covered by the blanket. Jason drew the cover down a little, kissing his son on the back of the scalp.

Kyle wore the T-shirt. A slight discoloration ran along the collar where the manufacturer tag had turned upward.

Jason turned on the flashlight of his cell phone to look.

A brown-red stain.

He checked the back of Kyle's neck, but there was no cut.

He wondered if the stain had been there when he'd bought the shirt.

A few weeks later, Jason — at home, contacting potential clients — was interrupted by a call from Kyle's school.

☙

JASON MET with the headmistress that afternoon. Her office looked out over the vast grounds with its soccer field and swimming pool. She mentioned Kyle's moods, his disruptive behavior among the other boys, his outbursts.

"But that's why he's here. You're handling it," Jason said.

Then, she mentioned the T-shirt.

"I still don't understand," Jason said.

The headmistress, her eyes a bit too kind, said, "He wears it under his school shirt every day."

"That against the rules?"

"Of course not," she said. "Our nurse suspected he was using it to hide something. We've seen this before."

Earlier that day during recess, one of the teachers noticed some bruises at Kyle's neck. Boys got bruised all the time, but these seemed odd. Sent him to the school nurse. The nurse noticed that the bruise disappeared down behind the collar of his T-shirt. Kyle told her about having problems sleeping. Waking up in the middle of the night. A scratchy feeling on his back. She asked him to take the T-shirt off. He wouldn't. She had to physically draw it off. He became uncontrollable.

"That's when she saw it," the headmistress said.

"Saw what?"

"The blood. The markings."

Before four, Jason wrangled an appointment with Kyle's pediatrician, who examined the bruises and sores on his back.

❧

"IT'S NOTHING — LOOK." The doctor wiped the trace of blood away and smoothed out the faint scars with his fingers. "I don't think this is anything serious. Just a skin thing."

"How could it happen?" Jason looked from the doctor to his son.

His son looked down at his feet.

"Kyle?" Jason asked.

His son looked up at him. "I told you. I don't know. Maybe I fell. I don't remember."

"Yep, that's probably it," the doctor said. "Probably scraped himself a little. It's not as bad as it looks. See? Might have brushed against something, scratching it. That would account for any blood."

"You sure it's not something worse?" Jason asked.

The doctor would run some tests. He took a little blood, gave an overdue booster shot, suggested a specialist of some kind if it kept up.

"I'm okay," Kyle said. He looked at his father.

"Did anyone hurt you?" Jason asked.

Kyle shook his head. "I already told you a million times."

That weekend, Jason and Amy set up camcorders all over the house.

⁂

THEY HID THEM AMONG SHELVING, behind hanging plants.

Every night, they watched video of the nanny and Kyle from the previous day.

The nanny —from Ecuador — proved efficient for the most part but did push Kyle away when he went to grab a second cookie after he got home from school.

Jason didn't quite like Maria that much after this, but it was hardly cause for firing her.

When asked — frequently — Kyle denied any knowledge of the origin of the bruising and sores.

The bruises faded in a few days.

"My brothers were always bruising themselves," Amy said in bed one night. "Boys play rough. You must've been in a few fights as a kid. That alcoholic school nurse just over-reacted."

The next afternoon, while doing laundry, Jason drew the T-shirt from the hamper.

❧

THE STAIN WAS STILL THERE, right near his son's side. Jason saw a new stain at the collar and another down along the lower part of the shirt, and yet another by the sleeve edge.

He scraped at the stains with his fingernail.

Little dried flecks came up.

He remembered how — as a boy — he once or twice scraped up his side falling off his bike. He'd bruised himself all over after accepting a dare to jump from a boulder. Suspended over a bridge, he'd burned and blistered his hands. No one had ever thought — in those days — to mention it.

Jason bleached the shirt three times, but the stains wouldn't quite come out. He kept seeing them, faint as they'd become.

He threw the shirt out in the trash.

When Kyle discovered it was missing, he slammed his bedroom door and told his father he didn't love him.

Jason and Amy both laughed at this over a drink before bed.

❧

"I'm pretty sure I said that to my mother half a dozen times before I was fourteen. Maybe after that, too," she told him. "Don't worry, he still loves you. He's being silly. Maybe we spoil him too much. Your mother thinks so."

Jason didn't respond. He did spoil Kyle, but when he thought of his own childhood, he didn't want Kyle to ever feel the way he felt as a boy — going without when it came to things every boy wanted.

In bed, finishing up the last of several spreadsheets on her laptop, Amy clicked over to a travel site to book their flight to Costa Rica.

"There. We're set," she said.

"When?"

"Two weeks from now. Sun, sand, sea — and vacation home hunt."

In the days leading up to the trip, Jason felt coldness from Kyle — still angry at the loss of his favorite shirt.

Just before hugging his son goodbye, Jason promised he'd bring back a bunch of "T-shirts, sunglasses, sandals. Cool stuff."

When the airport limo drove off, Jason looked back, waving from the open window.

Kyle stood in the driveway with Maria.

His son turned away a little too quickly, grabbing Maria's hand, tugging her back to the house.

❧

In Costa Rica, Jason and his wife spent mornings checking out dozens of condos and houses on the coast. Their afternoons and evenings became bouts of windsurfing, sailing — and drinking a bit too much.

"I don't think I ever want sex again," he laughed after their second go-round in one afternoon.

Every night at seven, they had video chats with Kyle on the laptop. Jason spent a half hour asking him about his day, what he'd done and what friends he'd seen.

They'd play a brief game of Turtle Races on the computer before shutting it down. He always let Kyle win.

"You miss him already?" Amy asked.

"Yep. Next time, we'll bring him. It'll be fun. I want to teach him how to wind surf."

"I'll be worried he might drown. You know me. He's too young."

"Plenty old enough to go out on the water — with me there to catch him. Maybe kayaking, too. That'd be fun."

Amy leaned into him. "Remember when it was always like this? Just the two of us?"

He put his arm around her. "Okay, one more time before shut-eye. Just one more and then this old man's got to sleep."

❧

They settled on one of the condos in a colorful complex called *Cabeza del Mar*.

The property management company was first-rate. A handful of laborers worked on the floors as Amy stepped around them, inspecting their work, suggesting the kitchen appliances.

The agent told them that if they signed the contract soon, they could decide all the upgrades, including the *en suite* bathroom.

"We'll take a few weeks down here a year, rent it out the rest of the time," Jason told Amy over margaritas at their new favorite watering hole. "By the time we're fifty and taking early retirements, it'll be paid off, and maybe we'll spend winters here,"

"Or sell it when the market revives," Amy said. "I bet it'll be worth a million then. Maybe more."

"Given what we're going to be paying, it better be more."

They had a goal of reaching eight million dollars in savings and investments — minimum — by the time they were fifty. They looked for new business opportunities whenever they could; that's where Amy's market research skills came into play.

Jason was certain they'd make more than their goal if they were careful. They weren't doing too badly, although they had friends who were doing much, much better.

"Still," Amy said, "Not bad for two kids from the suburbs."

On their last day in Costa Rica, Jason remembered the souvenirs for Kyle. One of the cute little shops near the beach had several T-shirts.

❦

"Very cool," Jason said as he sifted through the mountain of shirts, all with printed sayings on the front or back, most of them about the beach and islands and surfing.

"You know, the whole T-shirt industry isn't a bad one," Amy said. "At the company, we've seen growth in this kind of stuff."

"T-shirts? But they're so cheap."

"You'd be surprised. High volume, low costs, high sales. Resorts like this. I'll bet millions of people come through here annually. And every one of them buys a tee or a beach blanket. A memento, gifts for friends."

"But we're not exactly up on this kind of business."

"One of our clients is in textiles — they have a varied industry, but making cheap clothes is big for them."

"In Malaysia?"

"Various countries," she said, rattling off several, some of which he'd never heard of.

"These are made here, there and everywhere," the shop owner said.

Jason looked over at the wizened old American with mottled skin.

"Little factories," the man said. "Nice clean places, each one of 'em."

"You're from the states," Jason said.

"New York," the man said. "I own this shop and three others down the beach. Run them during high season, on my vacation. I'm in Manhattan most of the year. Started in boxer shorts and went to tees. My wife — died five years, November — used to tell me I'd moved up in the world. Underwear always does well. Resort business is on the upswing."

He went on: in America, in summer, T-shirts were huge.

Tourist resorts in Central and South America, year-round profits. Big profit margin, low overhead. "Most people can afford to buy a T-shirt — a great way to pull in cash. Souvenirs are big. We had shops in Cancun, Mazatlan, Cozumel, along this coast, of course. Miami and San Diego, too. Used to have three shops in Tokyo. Closing most of these, year by year."

"Really," Jason said, looking at the shirts in his hand. "Must be a boatload of work."

"Not these days," the man said. "Overseers run the factories. The accounts are pretty basic. You don't need to have an American down here — or anywhere. You get a local who knows the laws, knows how to crack the whip, so to speak. Here, China, Africa even, India, other parts of Asia, too. Big production, cheap, and a ton of sales. Even online. We've had the biggest growth online. Used to be, I had to fly all the hell over the world to check on factories. Now I just hire these overseers who run these places independently. Throw a rock in any port city, and you'll hit some guy just waiting to start up a factory. They take a percentage off the top, including production costs — I don't ever have to worry about it. Everything shows up, inventoried, and everything sells to the point where I don't even discount it. Nothing ever *doesn't* sell."

After buying several of the shirts, they took the old man out for lunch. Jason and Amy shot a barrage of questions at him from across the table.

LATER, in their hotel suite before checking out, she said, "You really think this is worth doing?"

"Well, we can research it a bit. But I always see people buying souvenirs — and those cheap shirts are popular."

"Everybody has at least one," Amy said.

"And you're always making up funny sayings and stuff."

"True," she said. "It's my one dumbass talent outside of corporate bullshit."

"And we're always talking about diversifying our income."

"Yeah, but there'll be start-up costs."

"Maybe instead of buying a condo, we should create a company. Just a little one."

"Aw, but I loved the condo."

"Sure, but maybe in a year, we'll buy ten condos. Think about it that way."

"But there's a hell of a lot of T-shirts out there."

"We'll differentiate," he said. "We'll do T-shirts just for kids. Or something."

"Sure. We can test it."

"Then, we get them out there," he said. "Get the process going and if it breaks even, fine. If it takes off, we sell it for a big payday within three years. Or less. Who knows? Then, we're not around when it crashes."

❦

KYLE SEEMED THRILLED to get the shirts from Costa Rica. He fell in love with one that had a picture of a palm tree and said, "Fun, Meet Sun."

The boy wore it everywhere.

❦

WITHIN FOUR WEEKS, Amy and Jason got their prototypes up and out. They launched some small online stores with various names, took out banner ads and made a few deals with established vendors.

Jason kept up with the old man on business trips to Manhattan, frequently taking him to lunch and sometimes drinks and dinner, asking him questions, getting advice, until finally, the old man said, "When is enough *enough*? Now's the time. The market's down, but T-shirts are up. If not now, when? Get this going. You'll expand into other areas, once it's running smoothly."

"You don't mind competition?"

"Please. I'm getting out of the business. I'm too old. Time for me to go to my little shops in Costa Rica year-round. Just enjoy the sun and my grandchildren."

He recommended various regions around the world for the factories but settled on one or two as sure bets. "You'll get your best bang for your buck, and you'll never have to see it if you don't want."

"Are you kidding? I'd love to see the place where they make our shirts."

"I can't advise that," the old man said. "Let them do their thing, you just do yours."

Still, Jason got on a plane within a week, heading to a small, obscure country the old man recommended.

§

THE FACTORY WAS a large warehouse thirty miles from the coast.

Jason met the overseer — a local with an unpronounceable name, in his late thirties, smart, educated, confident.

The overseer pointed out the factory floor where the workers would go at it, the bathrooms, his own office, and the machines.

"You'll never have to worry about a thing," the overseer said. "I take care of it all. You'll check spreadsheets and run sales and marketing. And think of this: all the people you're giving jobs to. I thought my little factory would go under, but you're saving it."

Jason had a good trip.

"Production's already begun," he told Amy.

A FEW WEEKS LATER, a problem cropped up.

Kyle.

The nanny was upset because a woman had come to the door one afternoon demanding things, bothering her, bothering Kyle when he got home from school.

A neighbor, it seemed, had called the local social service agency.

The next morning, Jason met up with the caseworker.

"WE GOT A REPORT," she said, after checking her computer. "Someone noticed your son had scarring around his throat."

Jason stared at her. "*What?*"

She glanced up from her desk. "We didn't find anything wrong with him. We spoke to him. He showed us his neck. It was fine. Still, we had to follow up."

There was a procedure, she told him. She passed him some paperwork. He filled it out.

Jason wondered if he needed to call his lawyer.

He wondered which neighbor had done this.

That night, Jason sat on the edge of Kyle's bed as his son got into his jammies.

❧

KYLE KEPT THE T-SHIRT ON. Jason asked him to take it off and put on his pajama top.

"But I like to sleep in it."

"I need to wash it. Sleep in another one."

"But this is my favorite," Kyle said.

"Come on, Kyle. Just change into another one. That one's filthy. *Stinky*." He tried to make the word "Stinky" sound funny so that Kyle would loosen up. But the boy didn't.

"You're being stubborn."

"I sleep good in it," his son said.

Jason got up, pulled out the middle drawer in the pine dresser by the bed, and reached for a T-shirt.

"This is a cool one."

"No."

"Kyle," Jason said. "Just change."

A strange look — one Jason had never seen before — a kind of *dread* brushed across his son's face.

The boy looked frightened and embarrassed in a much deeper way than Jason thought he would be.

"Kyle, what's going on? What are you hiding?"

"Nothing."

"*Kyle.*"

His son began crying.

"You're being a baby about this. You have other things to sleep in."

"I don't want to take my shirt off."

"Why not?"

Kyle looked down at his hands. "I just don't. Don't ask me to."

"Look, one way or another, that shirt's coming off your back. My advice is: just forget all this nonsense. Take it off. *Now.*"

Jason did his best to remain patient. He spoke with a gentle tone to his voice with warmth in his glance despite the direct order. He was, after all, a loving, understanding, and patient father — for the most part.

"Please, Dad. Don't make me take it off. *Please.*"

Jason caught his breath. He felt a strange power rising up in his throat. He coughed it back. *Breathe. Just breathe. Don't get angry.*

"Kyle, look," Jason said, calming. "I'm your best friend, right? And I'll never hurt you. *Never.* But this is important. I think you know why."

"Please," his son whimpered.

Reluctantly, Kyle raised the shirt over his head.

The boy didn't look at his father when he grabbed the other T-shirt.

"Stop. Freeze." Jason said, just as Kyle began drawing the new shirt down over his neck.

His son stood still.

Jason flicked up the bedside lamp to its highest setting and lifted off the shade.

The room lit up.

Kyle's side and chest looked bruised. Jason grasped his son's shoulders lightly, turning him around.

The boy's back had a series of crisscross scars raised up in a pattern that made him think of…a *whipping*.

"Holy shit," Jason said. He felt kicked in the gut. "Kyle, what happened?"

Kyle closed his eyes as if he'd dreaded this moment. When he opened them, he looked down at his feet.

"Who did this to you? Was it someone at school?"

Kyle glanced up at his father. He whispered something.

Jason couldn't hear him. He crouched low in front of his son, looking at the scars and bruises.

"Just tell me who did this," Jason whispered. "I'll take care of it. It won't ever happen again."

"I don't *know*," Kyle whispered. "I don't *know*. It just happens."

IN BED WITH AMY, Jason told her.

"Holy shit," she said.

"Exactly what I said."

She wanted to bolt out of bed and check it out for herself.

Jason told her that would only embarrass Kyle more. "I washed his back. Put some lotion on. He said it doesn't hurt."

"You think it's psychosomatic or something?"

"We'll get him to the doc tomorrow. Don't worry."

"Who the hell is doing this?" she asked.

"It's not Maria, obviously."

"Maybe we need to change schools," Amy said. "If

they're not doing something about this, it may be time to lawyer up. Maybe they're protecting some fucked-up little sociopathic bully."

In the morning, when Jason helped get Kyle ready for a trip to the doctor's, he noticed that some of the bruises had faded.

By the time they got to the doctor's office — and waited another forty minutes for Kyle's pediatrician — the bruises were mostly gone.

❧

THE CRISSCROSS PATTERN on the boy's back was barely visible when the doctor had Kyle undress.

"Sure, I've seen this sometimes," the pediatrician said. "We don't quite know what it is. Sometimes kids are allergic to stuff. We can test him."

"Allergies?" Jason said. "To what?"

"Maybe it's the material. What's this made from?"

Jason shrugged, touching the edge of the material at Kyle's shoulder. "Natural fibers, I think."

"Where's it made?"

"Does that matter?" Jason asked.

The doctor nodded. "Sometimes these factories have other things going on in them. You never know. I've certainly seen this before. Cheap goods, lower standards."

Before he left the doctor's office, Jason set up two more appointments — one with the child psychiatrist recommended by the social worker — and one more to double check the bruises the following week.

After Kyle's session with the psychiatrist, Jason was handed a prescription.

"He seems stressed," the psychiatrist said. "We'll get him on a couple of good meds and see how it goes. He may be a little sleepy after the first dose. If you notice erratic behavior, call me."

"Did he talk about anything I should know?" Jason asked.

"Don't worry about this," she said, ignoring the question. "It'll pass. Get those pills. They'll kick in within a week. I'll bet this clears up by the weekend. I'll call social services about the other thing."

"That's it?"

The psychiatrist nodded. "Bottom line, your son is fine. Kids go through phases. He's not in pain. He's not being bullied. My only concern is that he gets some rest."

That night, Jason called the overseer of the factory, who swore up and down that the factory was clean. The workers weren't sick. The fibers were not only natural but had been tested for allergens.

"Don't worry," his overseer said. "I make shirts for a ton of suppliers. Hell, we make sheets now, we make towels, place mats, scarves, purses — you name it. I've got deals with a lot of great places. You'd be surprised all the stuff we make here."

He mentioned several brands to Jason, who noticed — as he went through the house later — that in fact, most of the upholstery was from that region, and the 750 count sheets on the bed were exclusively from this particular factory.

❨❩

UNABLE TO SLEEP THAT NIGHT, Kyle crawled in bed with his mother and father.

Given the rough week and the new course of pills that Kyle was on, Jason decided to allow this bending of the rules.

In the morning, after Amy left for her commute, Kyle still snoozed, head on his mother's pillow. He wore the T-shirt that Jason had just thrown out the night before.

Looking at his son's back under the shirt, Jason saw a crisscross of faint scars, bloodstains along them.

He reached out to touch one of the scars. It was slightly raised. His son flinched, waking up.

"Daddy?" Kyle turned around to look at him. "It happened in my dream again."

"Again?" Jason asked. "What do you mean 'again'?"

Kyle nodded. "That's when I see him."

"Who?"

"The boy. The one who's hurt." Kyle said. "I dream about him. He says he dreams about me. He likes seeing where we live."

"Bad dreams?"

Kyle nodded. "They beat him."

Thoughts raced through Jason's mind:

Kyle was going to tell him the truth. He was going to tell him it was a dream, but it was really and truly the truth. His son was going to tell him now who had done this.

It was no allergy. No psychiatric problem.

Some other boy was hurting him. A boy in the city. A boy in school. A boy in the neighborhood.

"Who beats him?" Jason asked.

"Others."

"Who are the others?"

His son squinted, tilting his head to the side.

"You can trust me," Jason said, almost frightened of what his son might say. "Have these 'others' threatened you?"

Kyle shook his head, slowly.

"Tell me what happens in the dream."

"The boy gets hurt. The others make him hurt."

"And who are they?"

"People," Kyle said.

"Do they live near us?"

Kyle shook his head.

"Please, son. This is important. Tell me more about the boy."

"He's not fast enough."

Jason remembered all the bullies in gym class from his own childhood, the boys who just liked to pummel other kids who were slow or less athletic or seen as weak by them.

"Is the boy not a fast runner? Or good at basketball?"

"Not fast enough," Kyle said. "They make him bleed. They make him cry. Sometimes he can't sleep for days. He's afraid they might kill him. He thinks they've killed someone he knew. Someone who's not around anymore."

Unable to control himself, Jason nearly leapt for his son, grabbing him in a bear hug.

"Daddy? Are you okay?"

"Nobody's ever going to hurt you. Nobody," Jason whispered. "You just need to tell me. You need to trust me. I'm your father. I love you. I love you no matter what you do, no matter who you are. You could do the most terrible thing in the world, Kyle, and I would love you anyway. I will love you until the world comes to an end. Even after that, I'd still love you."

Kyle struggled against his father's embrace, but then he began crying, too.

"You're scaring me," he said.

Jason let go. He took a few heavy breaths, calming.

After a minute, Kyle told him more about the boy and what he remembered from the dreams — the bruises on the boy, the scars and welts on his back and shoulders, even the name.

"I think it's his name. I'm not sure he told me. But I think this is his name."

After pulling Kyle into another school — a better, more expensive one — Jason banned all T-shirts from the house.

KYLE EXPERIENCED minor side effects from his medication but slept through most nights. He seemed better behaved and more alert during the day.

The bruising and scarring became a distant memory.

The dreams of the boy hurt by others no longer happened, according to Kyle.

The side business of T-shirts took off. Within two years, a buyer approached Jason and Amy about buying the whole operation from them.

Amy felt the offered price was too good not to sell.

Before the sale, they'd take one last trip down to the shirt factory, give a big fat bonus to the overseer and the office workers, and then a great "goodbye" bonus to every single worker on the floor.

❧

IT WAS a big day at the factory, which had grown into three large buildings.

Amy *oohed* and *ahhed* over the operation. Jason marveled at the ambitious production schedule; the blocks of apartments for the workers; the canteen; the offices. The overseer and his secretary took them to the little area where their shirts were manufactured.

The line workers remained busy, down on the floor, a humming hive moving in and around a variety of machines. There were several older women, some middle-aged, at least one expectant mother among them. The men were younger, some of them in their teens.

Jason was surprised to see children there, too, running errands, sewing, cutting fabric, rolling it out.

He knew this was the standard of the country, and even children needed to bring money home to their poor families. He didn't love seeing it and mentioned it to the overseer.

"Only fourteen and up in my factory," the overseer said with pride. "The laws here allow for much, much younger. Children need work, just like anyone else, but some of these boys come from families with nothing. Absolutely nothing. It's a pleasure to find some kind of work for their children."

"They look way too young." When Jason said this, he felt Amy's elbow in his side.

"We're short, young-looking people," the overseer's secretary said. "Not tall and strong like you people."

All of this did little to reassure Jason. He and Amy exchanged glances.

They went around to the happy and grateful employees, many of whom wept when they were handed cash.

The boys — they seemed not much older than Kyle — came up, grinning, thanking, speaking the few words of English they could manage. The girls at the machines kept their eyes downcast but thanked both of them for the money with nods and closed-mouth smiles.

One little boy — *could he have been fourteen? Looked younger.* He was Kyle's height, but much thinner. He ran up and hugged them both, speaking bad English, thanking them but not daring to look up at their faces.

Jason felt an unexpected tug at his heart. He gave the boy double the amount.

The boy wore one of their T-shirts, the one that Kyle had loved back when he was allowed to wear it.

As the boy turned to run back to his station, Jason saw the crisscross bloodstain marks along his back where the shirt had been torn. He remembered seeing a long strip of thick cowhide hanging above the door of the overseer's office. When Amy had mentioned it, the secretary remarked that it was hers "so I can whip the boss into shape when he gets lazy," and they all had a good, polite laugh at this.

"You gave him too much," the overseer said, mentioning the boy by name as he ran off among the aisles of machinery. "He's a daydreamer. Never fast enough, never on top of his work. I don't know why I keep some of them on."

"You have a big heart," his secretary said.

Jason recognized the name of the boy.

꙳

JASON FELT LOST for the rest of the tour through the factory. He could not look Amy in the eye, nor did he manage much in the way of conversation with the others.

He canceled dinner but nodded when Amy said she wanted to go as a final thank you to the overseer and his secretary. She was sorry he felt ill.

Jason went to lie down in their hotel room.

Amy returned from dinner, very excited, and woke him at midnight.

꙳

"OH MY GOD, Jason, you wouldn't believe it," his wife said, her voice rising with excitement. "I think we can make a killing with high-end sheets and pillowcases. We all crunched numbers tonight. They showed me some print-outs regarding the competition. He can bring it in under budget. He told me that our business made him rich enough to keep expanding product lines and now…"

She kept talking about the millions they could make and maybe even attach products to a celebrity and market them through some big box stores to appeal to middle-class people who wanted great bedding at low, low prices.

He felt as if he were gasping for air with every word she spoke.

He ran his fingers along bruises at his throat and felt the skin of his back rise slightly to meet the edge of the whip.

Underworld

We were subletting the place on Thirty-Third Street, just down from Lexington Avenue—it was not terribly far from my job across from Madison Square Garden where I was an ink-stained drudge by day before transforming into a novelist by night.

Jenny was getting day work on the soap operas; nothing much, just the walk-on nurses and cocktail waitresses that populate daytime television, never with more than a word or two to say, so it was a long way to her Screen Actors Guild card.

She made just enough to cover the rent. I made just enough to cover everything else, plus the feeble beginnings of a savings account that we affectionately named *The Son'll Come Out Tomorrow*, because at about the time we opened the account, Jenny discovered that she was pregnant.

This worried the heck out of me, not for the usual reasons such as the mounting bills. and the thought that I might not be able to pursue writing full-time, at least not in this life.

The worry came from Jenny's habit of sleeping with other men.

It will be hard to understand this, and I don't completely get it myself, but I loved Jenny in a way that I didn't think possible. It wasn't her beauty, although she certainly had that, but it was the fact that in her company I always felt safe and comfortable.

I did not want to ever be with another woman as long as I lived. I suppose a good therapist would go on and on about my self-image and self-esteem and self-whatever, but I've got to tell you, it was simply that I loved her and that I wanted her to be happy.

I didn't worry if I was inadequate or unsatisfying as a lover, and she never spoke openly about it with me. I was just aware she'd had a few indiscretions early in our marriage, and I assumed that she would gradually, over the years, calm down in that respect. I felt lucky to have Jenny's company when I did, and when I didn't, I did not feel deprived.

I suppose that until you have loved someone in that way it is impossible to understand that point of view.

So I wondered about the paternity of our child, and this kept me up several nights to the point that I would slip out of bed quietly (for Jenny often had to be up and out the door by five a.m.), and go for long walks down Third Avenue, or down a side street to Second, sometimes until the first light came up over the city.

During one of these jaunts, in late January, I noticed a curious sort of building—it was on a block of Kip's Bay that began in an alley, and was enclosed on all sides by buildings.

Yet there were apartments, and a street name (*Pallan Row*, the sign said), and two small restaurants, the kind with only eight or nine tables, one of them a Szechwan place, the other nondescript in its Americanized menu; also, a flower stand, boarded up, and what looked like a bit of a warehouse. The place carried an added layer of humidity, as if it had more of the swamp to it than the city.

I am not normally a wanderer of alleys, but I could not help myself—I had lived in this neighborhood about a year and a half, and in that time had felt I knew every block within about a mile and a half radius. But it was as if I had just found the most wonderful gift in the world, a hidden grotto, a place in New York City that was as yet undiscovered except by, perhaps, the oldest residents. I looked in the windows of the warehouse but could see nothing through the filthy windows.

All day at work, I asked friends who lived in the general vicinity if they knew about Pallan Row, but only one said that she did. "It used to be where the sweatshops were—highly illegal, too, because when I was a kid, they used to raid them all the time—it was more than bad working conditions, it was white slavery and heroin, all those things. But then," she added, "so much of this city has a history like that. On the outside, carriage rides and Broadway shows, but underneath, kind of slimy."

On Saturday, I convinced Jenny to take a walk with me, but for some reason I couldn't find the Row; we went to lunch. Afterward, I remembered where I'd led us astray, and we ended up going to have tea at the Chinese restaurant. The menu was ordinary, and the decorations vintage and tacky.

"Amazing," Jenny said, "look, honey, the ceiling," and I glanced up and beheld one of those lovely old tin ceilings with the chocolate candy designs.

The waitress, who was an older Asian woman, noticed us and came over with some almond cookies.

"We're usually empty on weekends," she said. She glanced up at the tin ceiling, having noticed Jenny's interest. "Nice, huh? This was part of a speakeasy in the twenties— the cafe next door, too. They say a mobster ran numbers out of the back room. Before that, it was just an icehouse. My husband began renting it in 1954."

"That long ago?" Jenny said, taking a bite from a cookie. "It seems like most restaurants come and go around here."

"Depends on the rent." The woman nodded, still looking at the ceiling. "The owner hasn't raised it a penny in all those years."

She glanced at me, then at Jenny. "You're going to have a baby, aren't you?"

Jenny grinned. "How'd you guess?"

The woman said, "I can see it in your face. You'll have a boy, I bet."

After she left the table, we finished the tea, and just sat for a while. The owner's wife occasionally peeped through the round porthole window of the kitchen door, and we smiled at her but shook our heads to indicate that we weren't in need of service.

"When the baby comes," she said, "Mom said she'd loan us money to get a larger place."

"Ah, family loans," I warned her.

"I know, but we won't have to pay her back for a few years. Can you believe it? Me, a mother?"

"And me, a father?" I leaned over and pressed my hand against her stomach. "I wonder what he's thinking?"

"Or she. Probably, 'Get me the hell out of here right now!' is what it's thinking."

"Babies aren't 'its.'"

"Well, right now it is. It has a will of its own. It probably looks like a little developing tadpole. Something like its father." She gave my hand a squeeze. I kissed her. When I drew my face back from hers, she had tears in her eyes.

"What's the matter?"

"Oh," she wiped at her eyes with her napkin, "I'm going to change."

"Into what?"

"No, you know what I mean. I've been living too recklessly."

"Oh," I said, and felt a little chill. "That's all in the past. I love you like crazy, Jen."

"I know. I am so lucky," she said. "Our baby's lucky to have two screw-ups like us for parents."

Now, it could be that I'm just recalling that we said these words because I want her memory to be sweeter for me than perhaps reality will allow. But we walked back up Second Avenue that Saturday feeling stronger as a couple; and I knew the baby was mine, I just knew it, regardless of the chances against it.

We caught a movie, went home and made love, sat up and watched Saturday Night Live. Sunday we took the train out to her mother's in Stamford, and then as the week was just getting under way, I walked through the doorway of our small sublet to find blood on the faux Oriental rug.

YET THE DOOR had been locked. That was my first thought.

I didn't see Jenny's body until I got to the bathroom,

which is where her murderer had dragged her, apparently while she was still alive, and then had dropped her in the tub, closed the shower curtain around her. It wasn't as gruesome as I expected it to be—there was a bullet in her head, behind her left ear, and she was lying face up, so I didn't see the damage to the back of her scalp. She didn't even look like Jenny anymore. She looked like a butcher shop meat with a human shape. She looked like some dead woman with whom I had no acquaintance. I was pretty numb, and was thinking of calling the police, when it occurred to me that the killer might still be in the apartment. So I went next door to Helen Connally's and knocked on the door. Helen, in her sweats, saw my panic, let me in, and made me some tea while we waited for the police. I hated leaving Jenny there, in the tub, for the ten minutes, but if the murderer was still lurking, I had no way of defending myself.

After the police and the neighbors and Jenny's mother had picked my brain about the crime, it hit me.

I had not only lost my partner and lover, but also my only child. I cried for days, or perhaps it was weeks— it was like living, for a time, in a dark cave where there was no hour, no minute, no day, only darkness.

When I emerged from my stupor and weeping, the police had arrested a suspect in my wife's murder, and then the mystery unraveled: we had been subletting an apartment from a man who had several such places around the city, and each one was used, occasionally, by the man's clients as a place of business on certain weekdays for drug dealing.

The dealers' assumption had been that on a given day of the week, no one was home. Best the detectives could tell,

Jenny had come home too early on the wrong Tuesday, a drug deal was in progress, and one of the men had killed her as soon as she'd come in the door.

I was devastated to think that strangers could be in our apartment; but of course, it wasn't really ours. The renter of the apartment was arrested; he pointed the finger at a few associates; within a year, the guilty were behind bars, and I was living in a place off Houston and Sullivan Street, over in the SoHo area.

I eventually began seeing Helen Connally, my former neighbor, on a friendly basis.

It was almost as if the tragedy of my wife's death had given us a basis on which to form a friendship. Helen was thirty-two to my twenty-eight, and, while I knew I would never love her the way I loved Jenny, she was a good friend to me through a most difficult time.

We spent a year being slightly good friends, and then we became lovers.

I SHEPHERDED some out-of-town friends of ours on an informal sightseeing tour of the Big Apple one Sunday. With noon approaching, I brought them down to little Pallan Row.

I thought the Szechuan place would be good for lunch, but when we entered the alley, both it and the cafe were closed; windows were boarded up.

"Jesus," I said, "just a year ago, the woman running it told me that they'd had it since the fifties."

Helen took my elbow. "C'mon, we can go get sand-wiches up at Tivoli. Or," she turned to the couple we'd brought, "there's a great deli on Third. You guys like pastrami?"

Their voices faded into the background as I looked through the section of the restaurant's window that was clear, and thought I saw my dead wife's face back along the wall, through the round glass window of the door to the kitchen.

"Oliver," Helen said, looking over my shoulder, "what's up?"

"Nothing," I said, still looking at Jenny, her dark hair grown longer, obscuring all but her nose and mouth.

"It must be something."

"It's just an old place. It was once a speakeasy, back in the twenties. Think of all that's gone on in there," I said.

Jenny's face, in that round window, staring at me.

"Cool," Helen said. She was originally from California, so "cool" and "bummer" had not yet been erased from her vocabulary of irony. She stood back, and her friend Larry whispered something to her.

I watched Jenny's face, and noticed that when her hair fell more to the side of her face, there were no eyes in her eye sockets.

"Let's go," Helen whispered. "They want to take a ride on the ferry before it gets dark."

"Okay, just a sec," I said.

Jenny moved away from the round window.

My heart was beating fast.

I assumed that I was hallucinating, but the thought of spending the rest of the afternoon escorting this couple around town when I had just seen my dead wife was absurd.

I made an excuse about needing to be by myself—

Helen always took this well, and I caught an understanding look from Anne, who nodded.

I knew they would go on to a late lunch and talk about how I still hadn't quite recovered from Jenny's death; and I knew Helen would act the martyr a bit, because it was so hard to play nurse to me over a woman who had cheated constantly behind my back.

I adored Helen for her care and caution around my feelings; I wished them a good afternoon, and stood there, along the Row, watching them, until they had rounded the comer and were out of sight.

After a few minutes, I took off my shoe and broke the window glass, and tugged at one of the boards until it gave. Within half an hour, I stepped in through the broken window and walked across the dusty floor to the kitchen.

THE KITCHEN WAS ALL LONG, shiny metal shelves and drawers, pots and pans still piled high. But it was dark, and I saw no one. I walked across the floor, back to the walk-in freezer, and looked through its frosty pane of glass. Although I could see nothing in there, I found myself shivering, even my teeth began chattering, and I had the sudden and uncomfortable feeling that if I did not get out of that kitchen, out of that boarded up restaurant right then, something terrible would happen.

It didn't occur to me until I was on the street again that there should've been no frost on the glass pane at the walk-in freezer; that, in fact, there was no electricity to the entire building, perhaps to the entire block.

HELEN NOTICED, over the next few days, that I was becoming nervous. We sat across from each other in our favorite park, me with the Times, and her with a paperback; I looked up, and she was watching me. Another day, we went to a coffee shop, and she mentioned to me that my knees, under the table, were shaking slightly. She said this with some seriousness, as if shaking knees were an indicator of some deeper problem. But I doubted myself then, and I did not want to talk about seeing my dead wife in the Chinese restaurant kitchen on Pallan Row. Finally, my restlessness turned nocturnal, and I tossed and turned in my sleep. Helen, sleeping over, finally sat up in bed at four in the morning and flicked on the bedside lamp. Her eyes were bloodshot.

"You haven't slept a full night for two days," she said. "Tell me what's going on."

I spent about an hour dodging the issue, until finally, as she pushed and pushed, I told her about seeing Jenny.

"She was blind," Helen said, speaking to me like I was a lying twelve-year-old.

"Not *blind*. She had no eyes. I felt she could see me, anyway. She was staring at me. She just had no eyes."

"So you went in there and no one was there, right?"

"But that freezer," I said. "Why would it be running?"

Helen shrugged. "I'm going to make a drink. You want something?"

At five-thirty a.m., she and I had vodka martinis. I followed her out to the fire escape while Manhattan awoke and the sky turned several shades of violet before becoming the blank light of day.

We sat side by side.

"I don't believe in ghosts," I said, sipping and feeling drunk very quickly. "I don't believe that the dead can rise or any of that."

"What do you believe?"

I watched a burly man lift crates out of the back of his truck down in the street. "I believe in what I see. I saw her. I really saw her."

"Assuming," she said, "that it was Jenny. Assuming that the freezer was running on its own energy. Assuming you saw what you saw. Assuming all those things as givens, what does it mean?"

"I have no idea. I thought at first maybe I was just crazy. If I hadn't seen the frost on the freezer window, I don't think I would've believed later on that it had been Jenny at all. Or anything but an hallucination."

Helen was obstinate. "But it's got to mean something."

"Why?" I asked.

I slept through the next day fairly peacefully, and when I got up, Helen was gone. I watched television, then called a few friends to set up lunches and dinners for the following week.

Helen walked through the door at six-thirty in the evening, and said, "Well, I found that alley again. I pulled back one of the boards."

❧

WHEN SHE SAID THIS, I felt impulsively defensive—it was my alley, it was my boarded-up restaurant, I felt, it was my hallucination.

"I can't believe you did that," I said.

She halted my speech with her hands. "Hang on, hang on. Oliver, the windows are bricked up beneath the boards."

"No, they're not."

"Yes," she said. "They are. You couldn't have gotten in there."

We argued this point; we were both terrific arguers. It struck me that she hadn't found the right alley, or even the right Pallan Row. Perhaps there were two Pallan Rows in the city, near each other, perhaps even almost identical alleys. Perhaps there was the functional Pallan Row and the dysfunctional Pallan Row.

This idea seemed to clutch at me, as if I had known it to be true even before I thought it consciously.

The idea took hold, and that night, on the pretext of going to see a movie that Helen had already seen twice with friends, I took a cab over to Pallan Row.

IT WAS colder on Pallan Row than in the rest of the city. While autumn was well upon us, and the weather had for weeks been fairly chilly, down the alley it was positively freezing. My curiosity and even fear took hold as I peeled back one of the window boards, the very one I had pulled down on my last visit. Helen had been right: the windows were bricked up beneath the boards. But then, I had to wonder, why the boards at all?

I touched the bricks; had to draw my fingers back quickly, for they seemed like blocks of ice. I remembered the owner of the Chinese restaurant telling Jenny and me that it used to be an ice house. I touched the bricks again, and they were still bitingly cold—it hadn't been my imagination.

I walked around the alley but saw no way of getting into the buildings again, for all were bricked up.

And then I heard it.

A sound, a human sound, the sound of someone who was trapped inside that old icehouse, someone who had heard me pull the board loose and who needed help.

I am no hero, and never will be. For all I knew, there were some punks on the other side of that wall torturing one of their own, and if I walked into the middle of it, I would not see the light of day again.

And yet I could not help myself.

I found that if I kicked at the bricks, they gave a little. The noise from within had ceased, but I battered at the bricks until I managed to knock one of them out. It seemed to be an old brick job, for the cement between the blocks was cracked and powdery. After an hour, I had managed to dislodge several.

To my surprise and amazement, there was light on within the old restaurant. I looked through the sizable hole I'd made and saw the former proprietress of the Chinese restaurant standing behind the bar, dressed in a jade-colored silk gown, talking with her barman. A few people sat at the tables, eating, laughing. None of them had noticed my activity at the window.

As I put my face to the hole, I breathed in air so cold that it seemed to stop my lungs up.

I moved back and stood up. I was sure that this was a delusion; perhaps I needed some medication still, for immediately after Jenny's death, I had begun taking tranquilizers to help blot out the memory of finding her dead. Perhaps I still needed some medical help and psychological counseling.

I crouched down again to look through the opening and noticed that at one of the tables, facing the other way, was a woman who looked from the back very much like Jenny.

I noticed the ice, too. It was a shiny glaze along the walls and tables; icicles hung down from the chocolate-patterned tin ceiling. I watched the people inside as if this were a television set. I lost my fear entirely. All my shivering came from the arctic breezes that stirred up occasionally from within.

I thought I heard someone out in the alley behind me, and turned to look.

HELEN STOOD THERE in a sweatshirt and jeans, my old windbreaker around her shoulders. She held a sweater in her arms.

"I figured you'd be here. Look, it's getting chilly," she passed the sweater down to where I sat on the pavement.

She glanced at the bricks beside me, and the light from within the building. "I see you've been doing construction. Or should I say deconstruction."

"You see the light?" I asked her.

She squatted down beside me. "What light?"

"I know you see it," I said, but when I glanced again through the hole, the place within had gone dark.

"What is it about this place for you?" she asked. "Even if you did see Jenny here, or her ghost, whatever—why here? You and she only came here once. Why would she come here?"

"I think this is Hell," I said. "I think this is one of those corners of Hell. I think Jenny's in Hell. And she wants something from me. Maybe a favor."

"You really believe that?"

I nodded. "Don't ask me why. There is no why. This is a corner of Hell that maybe shows through sometimes to some people. I don't even think 'maybe'. I know that's what this is."

"I know you're joking," Helen said.

"I wish I were."

She stood up, stretched, and offered me her hand to help me get up. I took it.

Her hand was warm, and I felt a rush of blood in the palm of my hand as if she had managed to transfer some warmth to me.

And then, the sound again.

A human voice, indistinct, from within the walls.

Helen looked at me.

"You heard it too," I said.

"It's a cat," she said. "It's a cat inside there."

I shook my head. "That's no cat. Maybe Jenny can only show herself to me. Maybe Hell can only show itself to me, but you heard it."

"Wouldn't Jenny's ghost be in your old apartment where she died?" Something approaching fear revealed itself in the tremble of Helen's voice.

She was beginning to believe something that might be dreadful. It made me feel less alone.

"I don't think it's her ghost. A ghost is spiritual residue or something. I think she's in here, it's really her, in the flesh. I need to go back in and find out what exactly she wants from me."

The noise again, almost sounding like a woman weeping.

"Don't go in there," Helen said. "It may not be anything. It may be something awful. It may be somebody waiting in there the way somebody waited for Jenny."

I took her face in my hands and kissed her eyelids. When I drew back, I whispered, "I love you, Helen. But I have to find out if I'm crazy. I have to find out."

We went and sat in an all-night coffee shop talking about love and belief and insanity. Because I was beginning to convince myself that Pallan Row was a corner of hell, I waited until the sun came up to investigate further within its walls. Helen returned with me, and between the two of us, we managed to break enough bricks apart and away from the wall so that the hole grew to an almost-window-sized entrance.

I asked her to wait outside for me, and if anything happened, to go get help. I went in through the window, scraping my head a bit. The room on the other side was empty and dark, but that unnatural ice breath was still there, and, through the kitchen portal window, there came a feeble and distant light.

Helen asked every few seconds, "You okay, Oliver? I can't see you."

"I'm fine," I reassured her as often as she asked.

I walked slowly to the kitchen door, looked through the round windowpane. The light emanated from the freezer at the other end of the long kitchen. I pushed the door open (informing Helen that this was my direction so that she wouldn't worry if I didn't respond to her queries every few minutes) and walked more swiftly to the walk-in freezer.

The freezer door was unlocked. I opened it, too, and stepped inside.

The light was blue and as cold as the air.

THROUGH THE ARCTIC fog I could make out the shapes of human beings, hanging from meat hooks, their faces indistinct, their bodies slowly turning as if they had but little energy left within them. I did not look directly at any of these bodies, for my terror was becoming stronger—and I knew that if I were to remain sane as I walked through this icehouse of death, I would need to rein in my fear.

Finally, I found her.

Jenny.

Ice across her eyeless face, her hair, strands of thin, pearl necklace icicles.

She hung naked from a hook, her head drooping, her arms apparently lifeless at her side.

Her belly had been ripped open as if torn at with pincers, the skin peeled back and frost-burnt.

I stopped breathing for a full minute, and was sure that I was going to die right there.

I was sure the door to that freezer, that butcher shop of the damned, would slide shut and trap me forever.

But it did not.

Instead, I heard that human sound again, closer, more distinct.

I heard my heart beating; my breathing resumed.

The sound came from beyond the whitest cloth of fog, and I waved my hands across it to dissipate the mist.

There, lying on a metal shelf, wrapped in the clothes

that Jenny had been buried in, was our baby, his small fingers reaching for me as he began to wail even louder.

I lifted him, held him in my arms, and wiped the chill from his forehead.

Someone was there, among the hanging bodies, watching me. I couldn't tell who, for the fog had not cleared, neither had the blue light increased in intensity. I could not see to see. I felt someone's presence, though, and thanked that someone silently. I thanked whoever or whatever had suckled my child, had warmed his blood, had met his needs. The place no longer frightened me. Whatever energy the freezer ran on, whatever power inspired it, had kept my child safe.

I took my son out into the bright and shining morning.

"This was why I was haunted," I told Helen upon emerging from the open window. "This is what Jenny wanted to give me."

I can only describe Helen's expression, through her eyes, as one approaching dread. She said, "I think you should put it back where it belongs."

"Babies aren't 'its,'" I said, and recalled saying this to Jenny once, too, at this very place. Or had Jenny said it to me? We had been so close that sometimes when she said things, I felt I'd said them too. I glanced down at my boy, so beautiful as he watched the sky and his father, breathing the vivid air.

Across his forehead, I saw a marking, a birthmark, a port-wine stain, perhaps, which spread across his skin like fire until he became something other than what might be called flesh.

White Chapel

A NOVELETTE

✥

You are a saint," the leper said, reaching her hand out to clutch the saffron-dyed robe of the great man of Calcutta, known from his miracle workings in America to his world fame as a holy man throughout the world.

The sick woman said, in perfect English, "My name is Jane. I need a miracle. I can't hold it any longer. It is eating away at me. *They* are."

She labored to breathe with each word she spoke.

"Who?" the man asked.

"The lovers. Oh, God, two years keeping them from escaping. Imprisoned inside me."

"You're possessed by demons?"

She smiled and he saw a glimmer of humanity in the torn skin.

"Chose me because I was good at it. At suffering. That is whom the gods choose. I escaped but had no money, my friends were dead. Where could I go? I became a home for every manner of disease."

"My child," the saint said, leaning forward to draw the

rags away from the leper's face. "May God shine His coun-tenance upon you."

"Don't look at me, then. My life is nearly over," the leper said, but the great man had already brought his face near hers. It was too late. Involuntarily, the leper pressed her face against the saint's, lips bursting with fire heat. An atten-dant of the saint's came over and pulled the leper away, swatting the beggar on the shoulder.

The great man drew back, wiping his lips with his sleeve.

The leper grinned, her teeth shiny with droplets of blood.

"The taste of purity," she said, her dark hair falling to the side of her face. "Forgive me. I could not resist the pain. Too much."

The saint continued down the narrow alley, back into the marketplace of what was called the City of Joy, as the smell of fires and dung and decay came up in dry gusts against the yellow sky.

The leper woman leaned against the stone wall and began to ease out of the cage of her flesh.

The memory of this body, like a book, written upon the nerves and sinews, the pathways of blood and bone, opened for a moment, and the saint felt it, too, as the leper lay dying, *my name is Jane*, a brief memory of identity, but had no other past to recall, her breath stopped, the saint reached up to feel the edge of his lips, his face, and wondered what had touched him.

What could cause the arousal he felt.

❧

"HE RESCUED five children from the pit, only to flay them alive, slowly. They said he savored every moment, and kept them breathing for as long as he was able. He initialed them. Kept their faces."

This was overheard at a party in London, five years before Jane Boone would ever go to White Chapel, but it aroused her journalist's curiosity for it was not spoken with a sense of dread but with something approaching awe and wonder, too.

The man of whom it was spoken had already become a legend.

Then, a few months before the entire idea sparked in her mind, she saw an item in the Bangkok Post about the woman whose face had been scraped off with what appeared to be a sort of makeshift scouring pad.

Written upon her back, the name Meritt.

This woman also suffered from amnesia concerning everything that had occurred to her prior to losing the outer skin of her face; she was like a blank slate.

Jane had a friend in Thailand, a professor at the university, and she called him to find out if there was anything he could add to the story of the faceless woman.

"Not much, I'm afraid," he said, aware of her passion for the bizarre story. "They sold tickets to see her, you know. I assume she's a fraud, playing off the myth of the white devil that traveled to India, collecting skins as he went. Don't waste your time on this one. Poor bastards are so desperate to eat they'll do anything to themselves to put something in their stomachs. You know the most unbelievable part of her story?"

Jane shook her head.

He continued, "This woman, face scraped off, nothing

human left to her features, claimed that she was thankful
that it had happened. She not only forgave him, she said,
she blessed him. If it had really happened as she said, who
would possibly bless this man? How could one find forgiveness for such a cruel act? And the other thing, too. Not in
the papers. Other parts of her, mutilated. She didn't hold a
grudge on that count either."

❧

In wartime, men will often commit atrocities they would
cringe at in their everyday life. Jane Boone knew about this
dark side to the male animal, but she still weathered the
journey to White Chapel, because she wanted the whole
story from the mouth of the very man who had committed
what was known, in the latter part of the century, as the
most unconscionable crime, without remorse.

If the man did indeed live among the Khou-dali at the
farthest point along the great dark river, it was said that
perhaps he sought to atone for his past. White Chapel was
neither white nor a chapel, but a brutal outpost that had
been conquered and destroyed from one century to the next
since before recorded history. Always to self-resurrect from
its own ashes, only to be destroyed again.

The British had Anglicized the name at some sober
point in their rule, although the original name, *Y-Cha-Pa*
when translated, was *Monkey God Night*, referring to the
ancient temple and celebration of the divine possession on
certain nights of the dry season when the god needed to
inhabit the faithful.

The temple had mostly been reduced to ashes and fallen

stone, although the ruins of its gates still stood to the southeast.

Jane had already written a book about the camps to the north, with their starvation and torture, although she had not been well reviewed Stateside.

Still, she intended to follow the trail of Nathan Meritt, the man who had deserted his men at the height of the famous massacre.

Meritt had been a war hero, who, from those court-martialed later, was said to have been the most vicious of torturers. The press had labeled him, in mocking Joseph Campbell's book, *The Hero With A Thousand Faces*, "The Hero Who Skinned A Thousand Faces."

The war had been over for a good twenty years, but Nathan was said to have fled to White Chapel. There were reports that he had taken on a Khou-dali wife and fathered several children over the two decades since his disappearance. Nathan Meritt had been the most decorated hero in the war.

Children in America had been named for him.

But then news of the massacre surfaced, the stories of his love of torture, and his rituals of skin and bone.

It was the most fascinating story she had ever come across, and she was shocked that no other writer, other than one who couched the whole tale in a wide swath of fiction, had sought out this living myth.

While Jane couldn't get any of her usual magazines to send her *gratis*, she had convinced a major publishing house to at least foot expenses until she could gather some solid information.

To get to White Chapel, one had to travel by boat down a brown river in intolerable heat. Mosquitoes were as plentiful as air, and the river stank of human waste. Jane kept the netting around her face at all times, and her boatman took to calling her Nettie.

There were three other travelers with her: Rex, her photographer, and a British man and wife named Greer and Lucy.

Rex was not faring well. He'd left Kathmandu in August, and had lost twenty pounds in just a few weeks. He looked like a balding scarecrow, with skin as pale as the moon, and eyes wise and weary like those of some old man. He was always complaining about how little money he had, which apparently compounded for him his physical miseries. She had known him for seven years, and had only recently come to understand his mood swings and fevers.

Greer was fashionably unkempt, always in a tie and jacket, but mottled with sweat stains, and wrinkled; Lucy kept her hair up in a straw hat, and disliked all women. She also expressed a fear of water, which amazed one and all since every trip she took began with a journey across an ocean or down a river. Jane enjoyed talking with Greer, as long as she didn't have to second-guess his inordinate interest in children. She found Lucy to be about as interesting as a toothache.

The boatman wanted to be called Jim because of a movie he had once seen, and so, after morning coffee (bought at a dock), Jane said, "Well, Jim, we're beyond help now, aren't we?"

Jim grinned, his small dark eyes sharp, his face wrinkled from too much sun. "We make White Chapel by night, Nettie. Very nice place to sleep, too. In town."

Greer brought out his book of quotes, and read, "'Of the things that are man's achievements, the greatest is suffering.'" He glanced to his wife and then to Jane, skipping Rex altogether, who lay against his pillows, moaning softly.

"I know," Lucy said, sipping from the bowl, "it's Churchill."

"No, dear, it's not. Jane, any idea?"

Jane thought a moment. The coffee tasted quite good, which was a constant surprise to her, as she had been told by those who had been through this region before that it was bitter. "I don't know. Maybe Rousseau?"

Greer shook his head. "It's Hadriman the Third. The Scourge of Y-Cha."

"Who's Y-Cha?" Rex asked.

Jane said, "The Monkey God. The temple is in the jungles ahead. Hadriman the Third skinned every monkey he could get his hand on, and left them hanging around the original city to show his power over the great god. This subdued the locals, who believed their only guardian had been vanquished. The legend is that he took the skin of the god, too, so that it might not interfere in the affairs of men ever again. White Chapel has been the site of many scourges throughout history, but Hadriman was the only one to profane the temple."

Lucy put her hand to her mouth in a feigned delicacy. "Is it... a decent place?"

Greer and Lucy spent their lives mainly traveling, and Jane assumed it was because they had internal problems all their own that kept them seeking out the exotic, the foreign, rather than staying with anything too familiar. They were rich, too, the way that only an upper class Brit of the Old School could be and not have that guilt about it; to have inherited lots of money and be perfectly content to spend it as it they so pleased without a care for the rest of mankind.

Greer had a particular problem that Jane recognized without being able to understand: he had a fascination with children, which she knew must be of the sexual variety, although she could've been wrong. It was just something about him, about the way he referred to children in his speech, even the way he looked at her sometimes, that made her uncomfortable.

She didn't fathom his marriage to Lucy at all, but she fathomed very few marriages. While Greer had witnessed the Bokai Ritual of Circumcision and the Resurrection Hut Fire in Calcutta, Lucy had been reading Joan Didion novels and painting portraits of women weaving baskets.

They had money to burn, however, inherited on both sides, and when Greer had spoken, by chance to Jane at the hotel, he had found her story of going to White Chapel fascinating; and he, in turn, was paying for the boat and boatman for the two-day trip.

Jane said, in response to Lucy, "White Chapel's decent enough. Remember, British rule, and then a little bit of France. Most of them can speak English, and there'll be a hotel that should meet your standards."

"I didn't tell you this," Greer said to both Jane and Lucy, "but my grandfather was stationed in White Chapel for half a year. Taxes. Very unpopular job, as you can imagine."

"I'm starved," Lucy said, suddenly, as if there were nothing else to think of, "do we still have some of those nice sandwiches. Jim?" She turned to the boatman, smiling. Lucy had a way of looking about the boat, eyes partly downcast, which kept her from having to see the water, like a child pretending to be self-contained in her bed, not recognizing anything beyond her own small imagined world.

He nodded, and pointed toward the palm leaf basket.

While Lucy crawled across the boat—unbalanced and in terror that the entire thing would tip and throw her into the water—Greer leaned over to Jane and whispered, "Lucy doesn't know why you're going. She thinks it's for some kind of National Geographic article," but he had to stop himself for fear that his wife would hear.

Jane was thinking about the woman in Thailand who claimed to have forgiven the man who tore her face off. And the children from the massacre, not just murdered, but obliterated. She had seen the pictures in Life. Faceless children. Skinned from ear to ear.

She closed her eyes and tried to think of less unpleasant images.

All she remembered was her father looking down at her as she slept.

She opened her eyes, glancing about. The heat and smells revived her from dark memories. She said, "Rex, look, don't you think that would be a good one for a photo?" She pointed to one of the characteristic barges that floated about the river, selling mostly rotting meat and stuffed lizards, although the twentieth century had intruded, for there were televisions, on some of the rafts, and a hibachi barbecue.

Rex lifted his Nikon up in response, but was overcome by a fit of coughing.

"Rex," Lucy said, leaning over to feel his forehead, "my God, you're burning up," then, turning to her husband, "he's very sick."

"He's seen a doctor, dear," Greer said, but looked concerned.

"When we get there," Jane said, "we'll find another doctor. Rex? Should we turn around?"

"No, I'm feeling better. I have my pills." He laid his head back down on his pillow and fanned mosquitoes back from his face with a palm frond.

"He survived malaria and dengue fever, Lucy, he'll survive the flu. He's not one to suffer greatly."

"So many viruses," Lucy shook her head, looking about the river.

"Yes, so many ways one might die," Greer said in such a way that it shut his wife up completely, and she ate her sandwich and watched the barges and the other boatmen as though she were watching a television show.

"Are you dying on me?" Jane asked, flashing a smile through the mosquito net veil.

"I'm not gonna die," Rex said adamantly. His face took on an aspect of boyishness, and he managed the kind of grin she hadn't seen since they'd first started working together several years back, before he had discovered needles. "Jesus, I'm just down for a couple of days. Don't talk about me like that."

Jim, his scrawny arms turning the rudder as the river ran, said, "This is River of Gods, no one die here. All live forever. The Great Pig God, he live in Kanaput, and the Snake God live in Jurukat. Protect people. No one die in paradise of Gods." Jim nodded toward points that lay ahead along the river.

"And what about the Monkey God?" Jane asked. Jim smiled, showing surprisingly perfect teeth, which he popped out for just a moment because he was so proud of the newly made dentures. When he had secured them into his upper gum again, he said, "Monkey God trick all. Monkey God live where river goes white. Has necklace of heads of childs. You die only once with Monkey God, and no come back. Jealous god, Monkey God. She not like other gods."

"Monkey God is female," Jane said. "I assumed she was a he. Well, good for her. I wonder what's she's jealous of?"

Greer tried for a joke. "Oh, probably because we have skins, and hers got taken away. You know women."

Jane didn't even attempt to acknowledge this comment.

Jim shook his head. "Monkey God give blood at rainy times, then white river goes red. But she in chains, no longer so bad, I think. She buried alive in White Chapel by mortal lover. Hear her screams, sometime, when monsoon come, when flood come. See her blood when mating season come."

"You know," Greer looked at the boatman quizzically, "you speak with a bit of an accent. Who did you learn English from?"

Jim said, "Dale Carnegie tapes, Mr. Greer. *How to Win Friends and Influence People.*"

Jane was more exhilarated than exhausted by the time the boat docked in the bay at White Chapel. There was the Colonial British influence to the port, with guard booths, now mainly taken over by beggars, and an empty customs house. The place had fallen into beloved disrepair, for the great elephant statues, given for the god Ganesh, were overcome with vines, and cracked in places; and the lilies had all but taken over the dock. Old petrol storage cans floated along the pylons, strung together, with a net knotted between the cans.

Someone was out to catch eels or some shade-dwelling

scavenger. A nervous man with a straw hat and a bright red cloth tied around his loins ran to the edge of the dock to greet them; he carried a long fat plank, which he swept over the water's edge to the boat, pulling it closer in.

The company disembarked.

*

REX, the weakest, had to be pulled up by Jim and Jane both.

Lucy proved the most difficult, however, because of her terror of water. The boatman pushed her from behind to get her up to the dock, which was only four rungs up on the ladder.

Then, Jane didn't feel like haggling with anyone, and so, after she tipped Jim, she left the others to find their ways to the King George Hotel by the one taxicab that existed in White Chapel.

Jane chose instead to walk off her excitement and perhaps get a feel for the place.

She knew from her previous explorations that there was serendipity to experience. She might, by pure chance, find what she was looking for. But the walk proved futile, for the village was dark and silent, and except for the lights from the King George, about a mile up the road, the place looked like no one lived there. Occasionally, she passed the open door to a hut through which she saw the red embers of the fire, and the accompanying stench of the manure that was used to stoke the flame.

Birds, too, she imagined them to be crows, gathered around huts, kicking up dirt and waste.

She saw the headlights of a car and stepped back against

a stone wall. It was the taxi taking the others to the hotel, and she didn't want them to see her.

The light was on inside the taxi, and she saw Rex up front with the driver, half asleep. In back, Lucy, too, had her eyes closed; but Greer, however, was staring out into the night, as if searching for something, perhaps even expecting something. His eyes were wide, not with fear but with a kind of feverish excitement.

He's here for a reason. He wants what White Chapel has to offer, she thought, like he's a hunter. And what did it have to offer? Darkness, superstition, jungle, disease, and a man who could tear the faces off children. A man who had become a legend because of his monstrosity.

After the car passed and was just two sets of red lights going up the narrow street, she continued her journey up the hill.

When she got to the hotel, she went to the bar. Greer sat at one end; he had changed into a lounging jacket that seemed to be right out of the First World War.

"The concierge gave it to me," Greer said, pulling at the sleeves, which were just short of his wrists, "I imagine they've had it since my grandfather's day." Then, looking at Jane, "You look dead to the world. Have a gin and tonic."

Jane signaled to the barman. "Coca-Cola?"

When she had her glass, she took a sip and sighed. "I never thought I would cherish a Coke so much. Lucy's asleep?"

Greer nodded. "Like a baby. And I helped with Rex, too. His fever's come down."

"Good. It wasn't flu."

"I know. I can detect the D.T.'s at twenty paces. Was it morphine?"

Jane nodded. "That and other things. I brought him with me mainly because he needed someone to take him away from it. It's too easy to buy where he's from. As skinny as he is, he's actually gained some weight in the past few days. So, what about you?" She didn't mean for the question to be so fraught with unspoken meaning, but there it was: out there.

"You mean, why am I here?"

She could not hold her smile. There was something cold, almost reptilian about him now, as if, in the boat, he had worn a mask and now had removed it to reveal rough skin and scales.

"Well, there aren't that many places in the world... quite so..."

"Open? Permissive?"

Greer looked at her, and she knew he understood. "It's been a few months. We all have habits that need to be overcome. You're very intuitive. Most women I know aren't. Lucy spends her hours denying that reality exists."

"If I had known when we started this trip ..."

"I know. You wouldn't have let me join you, or even fund this expedition. You think I'm sick. I suppose I am. I've never been a man to delude himself. You're very—shall I say—liberal to allow me to come even now."

"It's just very hard for me to understand," she said. "I guess this continent caters to men like you more than Europe does. I understand for two pounds sterling you can buy a child at this end of the river. Maybe a few."

"You'd be surprised. Jane. I'm not proud of my interest. It just exists. Men are often entertained by perversity. I'm not saying it's right. It's one of the great mysteries..." He stopped mid-sentence and reached over, touching the side of her face.

She drew back from his fingers.

In his eyes, a fatherly kindness. "Yes," he said, "I knew. When we met. It's always in the eyes, my dear. I can find them in the streets, pick them out of a group, out of a schoolyard. Just like yours, those eyes."

Jane felt her face go red, and wished she had never met this man who had seemed so civil earlier.

"Was it a relative?" he asked. "Your father? An uncle?"

She didn't answer, but took another sip of Coke.

"It doesn't matter, though, does it? It's always the same pain," he said, reaching in the pockets of the jacket and coming up with a gold cigarette case. He opened it, offered her one, and then drew one out for himself. Before he lit it, with the match burning near his lips, he said, "I always see it in their faces, that pain, that hurt. And it's what attracts me to them, Jane. As difficult as it must be to understand, for I don't pretend to, myself, it's that caged animal in the eyes that—how shall I say—excites me?"

She said, with regret, "You're very sick. I don't think this is a good place for you."

"Oh," he replied, the light flaring in his eyes, "but this is just the place for me. And for you, too. Two halves of the same coin, Jane. Without one, the other could not exist I'm capable of inflicting pain, and you, you're capable of bearing a great deal of suffering, aren't you?"

"I DON'T WANT to stay here," she told Rex in the morning. They had just finished a breakfast of a spicy tea and shuvai, with poached duck eggs on the side, and were walking in the direction of the village center.

"We have to go back?" Rex asked, combing his hands through what was left of his hair. "I don't think I'm ready, Janey, not yet. I'm starting to feel a little stronger. If I go back…and what about the book?"

"Not back, no," she said. "I just meant I don't want to stay here. At the hotel. Not with those people. He's a child molester. No, make that child rapist. He as much admitted it to me last night."

"Holy shit," Rex screwed his face up. "You sure?"

Jane looked at him, and he turned away.

There was so much boy in Rex that still wasn't used to dealing with the complexities of the adult world; she almost hated to burst his bubble about people. They stopped at a market, and she went to the first stall, which offered up some sort of eely thing. Speaking a poor version of Khoudali, or at least the northern dialect that she had learned, Jane asked the vendor if there might be another hotel – not an English one, but one run by locals.

He directed her to the west and said a few words.

She grabbed Rex's hand and whispered, "It may be some kind of whorehouse, but I can avoid Greer for at least one night. And that stupid wife of his."

Rex took photos of just about everyone and everything they passed, including the monkey stalls. He was feeling much better, and Jane was thrilled that he was standing tall, with color in his cheeks, no longer dependent on a drug to energize him. He took one of her with a dead monkey. "I thought these people worshiped monkeys."

Jane said, "I think it's the image of the monkey, not the animal itself." She set the dead animal back on the platform with several other carcasses. Without meaning to, she blurted, "Human beings are horrible."

"Smile when you say that." Rex snapped another picture.

"We kill, kill, kill. Flesh, spirit, whatever gets in our way. It's like our whole purpose is to extinguish life. And for those who live, there's memory, like a curse. We're such a mixture of frailty and cruelty."

The stoop-backed woman who stood at the stall said, in perfect English, "Who is to say, miss, that our entire purpose here on Earth is perhaps to perform such tasks? Frailty and cruelty are our gifts to the world. Who is to say that suffering is not the greatest of all gifts from the gods?"

Her Khou-dali name was long and unpronounceable, but her English name was Mary-Rose. Her grandmother had been British; her brothers had gone to London and married, while she, the only daughter, had remained behind to care for an ailing mother until the old woman's death. And then, she told them, she did not have any ambition for leaving her ancestral home. She had the roughened features of a young woman turned old by poverty and excessive labor and no vanity whatsoever about her. Probably from some embarrassment at hygiene, she kept her mouth fairly closed when she spoke. Her skin, rough as it was, possessed a kind of glow that was similar to the women Jane had seen who had facelifts. This may have been from living in White Chapel with its humidity.

Something in her eyes approached real beauty, like sacred jewels pressed there. She had a vigor in her glance and speech; her face was otherwise expressionless, as if set in stone. She was covered in several cloths, each dyed clay red, and wrapped from her shoulders down to her ankles; a purple cloth was drawn about her face like a nun's wimple. It was so hot and steamy that Jane was surprised she didn't go about as some of the local women did, with a certain discreet amount of nakedness.

"If you are looking for a place, I can give you a room. Very cheap. Clean. Breakfast included." Mary-Rose named a low price, and Jane immediately took her up on it. "You help me with English, and I make coffee, too. None of this tea. We are all dizzy with tea. Good coffee. All the way from America, too. From Maxwell's house."

Mary-Rose lived beyond the village, just off the place where the river forked. She had a stream running beside her house, which was a two-room shack. It had been patched together from ancient stones from the ruined Y-Cha temple, and tar paper coupled with hardened clay and straw had been used to fill in the gaps. Rex didn't need to be told to get his camera ready: the temple stones had strange images scrawled into them. He began snapping pictures as soon as he saw them.

"It's a story," Jane said, following stone to stone. "Some of it's missing."

"Yes," Mary-Rose said, "it tells of Y-Cha and her conquests, of her consorts. She fucked many mortals." Jane almost laughed when Rose said "fucked," because her speech seemed so refined up until that point. No doubt, whoever had taught Rose to speak had not bothered to separate out vulgarities. "When she fucks them, very painful, very hurting, but also very much pleasure. No one believes in her much no more. She is in exile. Skin stolen away. They say she could mount a believer and ride him for hours, but in the end, he dies, and she must withdraw. The White Devil, he keeps her locked up. All silly stories, of course, because Y-Cha is just so much lah-dee-dah."

Jane looked at Rex. She said nothing.

Rex turned the camera to take a picture of Mary-Rose, but she quickly hid her features with her shawl. "Please, no," she said.

He lowered the camera.

"Mary-Rose," Jane said, measuring her words, "do you know where the White Devil lives?"

Seeing that she was safe from being photographed, she lowered the cloth. Her hair spilled out from under it; pure white, almost dazzlingly so. Only the very old women in the village had hair even approaching gray. She smiled broadly, and her teeth were rotted and yellow. Tiny holes had been drilled into the front teeth. "White Devil, he cannot be found, I am afraid."

"He's dead, then. Or gone," Rex said.

"No, not that," she said, looking directly into Jane's eyes, "you can't find him. He finds you. And when he finds you, you are no longer who you are. You are no longer who you were. You become."

꿔

JANE SPENT the afternoon writing in her notebooks:

Nathan Meritt may be dead. He would be, what, fifty? Could he have really survived here all this time? Wouldn't he self-destruct, given his proclivities? I want him to exist. I want to believe he is what the locals say he is. The White Devil. Destruction and Creation in mortal form. Supplanted the local goddess. Legend beyond what a human is capable of. The woman with the scoured face. The children without skins. The trail of stories that followed him through this wilderness. Settling in White Chapel, his spiritual home. White Chapel, where Jack the Ripper killed the prostitutes in London. The name of a church. Y-Cha, the Monkey God, with her fury and fertility and her absolute weakness. They say the river runs white at times, like milk, it is part of Y-Cha. Whiteness. The white of bones strung along in her necklace.

The white of the scoured woman, her featureless face covered with infection.

Can any man exist who matches the implications of this?

The Hero Who Skinned A Thousand Faces.

And why?

What does he intend with this madness, if he does still exist, if the stories are true?

And why am I searching for him?

And then she wrote:

Greer's eyes looking into me. Knowing about my father. Knowing because of a memory of hurt somehow etched into my own eyes.

The excitement when he was looking out from the taxi.

Like a bogeyman on holiday, a bag of sweeties in one hand, and the other, out to grab a child's hand.

Frailty and cruelty. Suffering as a gift.

What he said, two halves of the same coin. Without one, the other could not exist. Capable of great suffering.

WHITE CHAPEL, and its surrounding wilderness, came to life just after midnight. The extremes of its climate: chilly at dawn, steamy from ten in the morning till eight or nine at night, and then hot, but less humid, as darkness fell, led to a brain-fever siesta between noon and ten o'clock at night. Then families awoke and made the night meal, baths were taken, love was made; all in preparation for the more sociable and bearable hours of one a.m. to about six or seven, when most physical labor, lit by torch and flare, was done, or when hunting the precious monkey and other creatures more easily caught just before dawn. Jane was not surprised at this. Most of the nearby cultures followed a similar pattern based on climate and not daylight. What did impress her was the silence of the place while work and play began.

Mary-Rose had a small fire going just outside the doorway; the dull orange light of the slow-burning manure cast spinning shadows as Mary-Rose knelt beside it and stirred a pan. "Fried bread," she said as Jane sat up from her mat. "Are you hungry?"

"How long did I sleep?"

"Five, six hours, maybe."

The frying dough smelled delicious. Mary-Rose had a jar of honey in one hand, which tipped, carefully, across the pan.

Jane glanced through the shadows, trying to see if Rex was in the corner on his mat.

"Your friend," Mary-Rose said, "he left. He said he wanted to catch some local color. That is precisely what he said."

"He left his equipment," Jane said.

"Yes, I can't tell you why. But," Mary-Rose said, flipping the puffed circle of bread and then dropping it onto a thin cloth, "I can tell you something about the village. There are certain entertainments that are forbidden to women which many men who come here desire. Men are like monkeys, do you not think so? They frolic, and fight, and even destroy, but if you can entertain them with pleasure, they will put other thoughts aside. A woman is different. A woman cannot be entertained by the forbidden."

"I don't believe that. I don't believe that things are forbidden to women, anyway."

Mary-Rose shrugged. "What I meant, Miss Boone, is that a woman is the forbidden. Man is monkey, but woman is Monkey God." She apparently didn't care what Jane thought one way or another. Jane had to suppress an urge to smile, because Mary-Rose seemed so set in her knowledge of life, and had only seen the jungles of Y-Cha. She brought the bread into the shack and set it down in front of Jane. "Your friend, Rex, he is sick from some fever. But it is fever that drives a man. He went to find what would cool the fever. There is a man skilled with needles and medicines in the jungle. It is to this man that your friend has traveled tonight."

Jane said, "I don't believe you."

Mary-Rose grinned. The small holes in her teeth had been filled with tiny jewels. "What fever drives you, Miss Jane Boone?"

"I want to find him. Meritt. The White Devil."

"What intrigues you about him?"

Jane wasn't sure whether or not she should answer truthfully. "I want to do a book about him. If he really exists. I find the legend fascinating."

"Many legends are fascinating. Would someone travel as far as you have for fascination? I wonder."

"All right. There's more. I believe, if he exists, if he is the legend, that he is either some master sociopath or something else. What I have found in my research of his travels is that the victims, the ones who have lived, are thankful of their torture and mutilation. It is as if they've been—I'm not sure—baptized or consecrated by the pain. Even the parents of those children—the ones who were skinned—even they forgave him. Why? Why would you forgive a man of such unconscionable acts?" Jane tasted the fried bread; it was like a doughnut. The honey that dripped across its surface stung her lips; but it wasn't honey at all; it had a bitter taste to it. Some kind of herb mixed with sap?

It felt as if fire ants were biting her lips, along her chin where the thick liquid dripped; her tongue felt large, clumsy, as if she'd been shot up with Novocain. She didn't immediately think that she had been drugged, only that she was, perhaps, allergic to this food. She managed to say, "I just want to meet him. Talk with him," before her mouth seemed inoperable, and she felt a stiffness to her throat.

Mary-Rose's eyes squinted, as if assessing this demand. She whispered, "Are you not sure that you do not seek him in order to know what he has known?" She leaned across to where the image of the household god sat on its wooden haunches. Not a monkey, but some misshapen imp. Sunken into the head of this imp, something akin to a votive candle. Mary-Rose lit this with a match. The yellow-blue flame came up small, and she cupped the idol in her hand as if it were a delicate bird.

And then she reached up with her free hand and touched the edges of her lips. It looked as if she were about to laugh.

"Miss Jane Boone. You look for what does not look for you. This is the essence of truth. And so you have found

what you should run from, the hunter is become the hunted," she said, and began tearing at the curve of her lip,
peeling back the reddened skin, unrolling the flesh that
covered her chin like parchment.

Beneath this, another face. Unraveling like skeins of
thread through some imperfect tapestry, the sallow cheeks,
the aquiline nose, the shriveled bags beneath the eyes, even
the white hair came out strand by strand. The air around
her grew acrid with the smoke from the candle, as bits of
ashen skin fluttered across its flame.

A young man of nineteen or twenty emerged from
beneath the last of the skin of Mary-Rose. His lips and
cheeks were slick with dark blood, as if he'd just pressed his
face into wine. "I am the man," he said.

The burning yellow-blue flame wavered, and hissed with
snowflake-fine motes of flesh.

Jane Boone watched it, unmoving.

Paralyzed.

Her eyes grew heavy. As she closed them, she heard
Nathan Meritt clap his hands and say to someone, "She is
ready. Take her to Sedri-Y-Cha-Sampon. It is time for
Y-Cha-Pa."

The last part she could translate: Monkey God Night.

She was passing out, but slowly. She could just feel
someone's hands reaching beneath her armpits to lift her. I
am Jane Boone, an American citizen, a journalist, I am Jane
Boone, you can't do this to me, her feeble mind shouted
while her lips remained silent.

*

TWO YEARS LATER, the saint lay down in the evening and

tried to put the leper he had met that day out of his mind. The lips, so warm, drawing blood from his own without puncturing the skin.

Or had it been her blood that he had drunk?

Beside his simple cot was a basin and a pitcher of water. He reached over, dipping his fingers into it, and brought the lukewarm droplets up to his face.

He was, perhaps, developing a fever.

The city was always hot in this season, though, so he could not be certain. He wondered if his fear of the leper woman was creating an illness within his flesh. But the saint did not believe that he could contract anything from these people. He was only in Calcutta to do good. He was revered as a great teacher.

The saint's forehead broke a sweat.

He reached for the pitcher, but it slipped from his sweaty hands and shattered against the floor.

He sat up, and bent down to collect the pieces.

The darkness was growing around him.

He cut his finger on a porcelain shard.

He squeezed the blood and wiped it across the oversized cotton blouse he wore to bed.

He held the shard in his hand.

There were times when even a saint held too much remembered pain within him.

Desires, once acted upon in days of innocence and childhood, which now seemed dark and animal and howling.

He brought the shard up to his lips, his cheek, pressing.

In the reflecting glass of the window, a face he did not recognize, a hand he had not seen, scraping a broken piece of a pitcher up and down and up and down the way he had seen his father shaving himself when the saint was a little boy, the way he himself shaved, the way men could touch themselves with steel, leaning into mirrors to admire how close one could get to skin such as this. Had any ever gone so far beneath his skin?

The saint tasted his blood.

Tasted his skin.

Began slicing clumsily at flesh.

JANE BOONE SENSED MOVEMENT.

She even felt the coolness of something upon her head. A damp towel?

She was looking up at a thin, interrupted line of slate-gray sky emerging between the leaning trees and vines; she heard the cries of exotic birds; a creaking, as of wood on water.

I'm in a boat, she thought.

Someone came over to her, leaning forward. She saw his face. It was Jim, the boatman who had brought her from upriver. "Hello, Nettie," he said, calling her by the nickname they'd laughed about before, "you are seeing now, yes? Good. It is nearly the morning. Very warm. But very cool in temple. Very cool."

She tried to say something, but her mouth wasn't working; it hurt to even try to move her lips.

Jim said, apparently noticing the distress on her face, "No try to talk now. Later. We on sacred water. Y-Cha carry us in." Then he moved away. She watched the sky above her grow darker; the farther the boat went on this river, the deeper the jungle.

She closed her eyes, feeling weak.

Ice-cold water splashed across her face.

"You go back to sleep, no," Jim said, standing above her again. "Trip is over."

He poled the boat up against the muddy bank. When he had secured it, he returned to her, lifting her from beneath her armpits.

She felt as if every bone had been removed from her body. She barely felt her feet touch the ground as he dragged her up a narrow path. All she had the energy to do was watch the immense green darkness enfold about her, even while day burst with searing heat and light beyond them.

When she felt the pins-and-needles feeling coming into her legs and arms, she had been set down upon a round stone wheel, laid flat upon a smooth floor.

Several candles were lit about the large room, all set upon the yellowed skulls of monkeys, somehow attached to the walls.

Alongside the skulls, small bits of leaf and paper taped or nailed or glued to the wall; scrawled across these, she knew from her experience in other similar temples, were petitions and prayers to the local god.

On one of the walls, written in a dark ink that could only have been blood, were words in the local dialect. Jane was not good at deciphering the language.

A man's voice, strong and pleasant, said, "'Flesh of my flesh, blood of my blood, I delight in your offering.' It's an incantation to the great one, the Y-Cha."

He emerged from the flickering darkness. Just as he had seemed beneath the skin of Mary-Rose, Nathan Meritt was young, but she recognized his face from his college photographs. He was not merely handsome, but he had a radiance that came from beneath his skin, as if something fiery lit him, and his eyes, blue and almost transparent, inflamed. "She is not native to this land, you know. She was an import from Asia. Did battle in her own way with Kali, and won this small acre before the village came to be. Gods are not as we think in the West, Jane, they are creatures with desires and loves and weaknesses like you or I. They do not come to us, or reveal themselves to us. No, it is we who approach them, we who must entertain them with our lives. You are a woman, as is the Y-Cha. Feelings that you have, natural rhythms, all of these, she is prey to, also."

Jane opened her mouth, but barely a sound emerged. Meritt put his finger to his lips. "In a little while. They used it to stun the monkeys. What that bread is dipped in. It's a drug called *hanu* and does very little harm, although you may experience a hangover. The reason for the secrecy? I needed to meet you, Miss Boone, before you met me. You're not the first person to come looking for me. But you're different from the others that arrived here."

He stepped farther into the light, and she saw that he was naked.

His skin glistened with grease, and his body was clean-shaven except for his scalp, from which grew long dark hair.

Jane managed a whisper. "What about me? I don't understand. Different? Others?"

"Oh," he said, a smile growing on his face. "You are capable of much suffering, Miss Boone. That is a rare talent in human beings. Some are weak and murder their souls and bodies, and some die too soon in pain. Your friend Rex suffers much, but he's of the garden variety. I have already played with him. Don't be upset. He had his needles and his drugs. In return, he gave me that rare gift, that…"

Meritt's nostrils flared, inhaling, as if recalling some wonderful perfume, "That moment of *mastery*. It's like nothing else, believe me. I used to skin children, you know, but they die too soon, they whine and cry. They don't understand, and the pleasure they offer…"

"Please stop," Jane said.

She felt strength seeping back into her muscles and joints. She knew she could run, but would not know to what exit, or where it would take her. She had heard about the temple having an underground labyrinth, and she didn't wish to lose herself within it.

But more than that, she felt no physical threat from Nathan Meritt.

"You're so young," she said. "You look like you're twenty. I never would've believed in magic, but…"

He laughed. When he spoke again, it was in the measured cadences of Mary-Rose. "Skin? Flesh? It is our clothing, Miss Jane Boone, it is the tent that shelters us from the reality of life. This is not my skin, see."

He reached up and drew back a section of his face from the left side of his nose to his left ear, and it came up like damp leaves, and beneath it, the chalk white of bone. "It may conform to my bones, but it is another's. It's what I learned from her, from the Y-Cha. Neither do I have blood, Miss Boone. When you prick me, I don't spill."

He seemed almost friendly and came closer to sit beside her.

"You mustn't be scared of me," he said in a rigid British accent. "We're two halves of the same coin."

Jane Boone looked in his eyes and saw Greer there, a

smiling, gentle Greer. The Greer who had funded her trip to White Chapel, the Greer who had politely revealed what a monster he was and how he accept his own horror.

"I met them both in Tibet, Greer and Lucy," Meritt said, resuming his American accent. "He wanted children. We had that in common, although his interests, oddly enough, had more to do with mechanics than with intimacy. I got him his children, and he paid his price with flesh. Two days of exquisite suffering, Jane, along the banks of a lovely river. Greer did not quite expect it. I had some children with me, bought in Bangkok at one hundred dollars each. I let them do the honors. Layers of skin, peeled back, like some exotic rind. The fruit within was for me. Then the children, for they had already suffered much at Greer's own hands. I can't bear to watch children suffer more than a few hours. It's not yet an art for them. They're too natural."

"And Lucy?"

He grinned. "Ah, Lucy. I could crawl into Greer's skin, but I enjoyed the game. But poor little Lucy couldn't tell the difference because she didn't give a fuck about him or anyone. Our whole trip down the river, only Jim knew that I was within Greer. Old Jim's a true believer. Sweet Lucy, the most dreadful woman from Manchester – and that's saying a lot. I'll dispose of her soon, though, but she won't be much fun. Her life is her torture—anything else is redundant."

Jane wasn't sure how much of this monologue to believe.

She said, "And me? What do you intend to do?"

Unexpectedly, he leaned into her, brushing his lips against hers but not kissing. His breath was like jasmine flowers floating on cool water. He looked into her eyes as if he needed something that only she could give him.

He said softly, "That will be up to you. You have come to me. I am your servant."

He pulled away, stood, and turned his back to her. He went to the wall and lifted a monkey skull candle up. He held the light along the yellow wall.

"You think from what I've done that I'm a monster, Miss Boone. You think I thrive on cruelty, but it's not that way. Even Greer, in his last moments, thanked me for what I did. Even the children, their life forces wavering while stains along their scalps spread darker juices over their eyes...Why, they whispered praise with their final breaths that I had led them to that place."

He held a light up to the papers stuck to the wall. His shadow seemed enormous and twisted as he moved the light in circles. He didn't look back at her, but moved from petition to petition.

"These are all blessings and praises and prayers from the locals, the believers in Y-Cha," he said. "And I, Miss Boone, I am her sworn consort, and her keeper, too. It was Nathan Meritt and no other, the Man Who Skinned A Thousand Faces, who is her most beloved and to whom she has submitted herself, my prisoner. Come, I will take you to the throne of Y-Cha."

Jane followed Nathan down winding corridors, their walls covered with dried animal skins.

THEY ARRIVED to a pool of water, a perfect circle, filled with koi and turtles, at the center of a chamber. The area itself was poorly lit, but there was a fire in a hearth at its far end. She heard the sound of rushing water just beyond the walls.

"The river," Nathan said. "We're beneath it. She needs the moisture, always. She has not been well for hundreds of years."

He stepped ahead, toward a small cot.

Jane followed, walking around thin bones that lay scattered across the stones.

There, on the bed, head resting on straw, was Lucy.

Fruit had been stuffed into her mouth, and flowers in the empty sockets of her eyes.

She was naked, and her skin had been brutally tattooed until the blood had caked around the lines: drawings of monkeys.

Jane began to scream, and knew that she had, but could not even hear herself.

When she stopped, she managed, "You bastard, you said you hadn't hurt her. You said she was still alive."

He touched her arm, almost lovingly. "That's not what I told you. She did this to herself. Even the flowers. She's not even dead, not yet. She's no longer Lucy."

He squatted beside the cot, and combed his fingers through her hair. "She's the prison of Y-Cha, at least as long as she breathes. Monkey God is a weak god, in the flesh, and she needs it, she needs skin, because she's not much different than you or me, Jane, she wants to experience life, feel blood, feel skin and bones and travel and love and kill, all the things animals take for granted, but the gods know, Jane. Oh, my baby," he pressed his face against the flowers, "the beauty, the sanctity of life, Jane, it's not in joy or happiness, it's in suffering in flesh."

He kissed the berry-stained lips, slipping his tongue into Lucy's mouth.

With his left hand, he reached back and grasped Jane's hand before she could step away. His grip was tight, and he pulled her toward the cot, to her knees.

He kissed from Lucy to her, and back, and she tasted the berries and sweet pear.

She could not resist—it was as if her flesh required her to do this, and she began to know what the others had known, the woman with the scraped face, the children, Greer, even Rex, all who must worship

Y-Cha.

Nathan's penis grew erect and dripping and she touched it with her hand, instinctively.

The petals on the flower quivered.

Nathan pressed his lips to Lucy's left nipple and licked it like he was a pup suckling and playing. He turned to Jane, his face smeared with Lucy's blood, and kissed her, slipping a soaked tongue, copper taste, into the back of her throat.

She felt the light pressure of his fingers exploring between her legs, then watched as he brought her juices up to his mouth.

He spread Lucy's legs apart, and applied a light pressure to the back of Jane's head.

For an instant, she tried to resist.

But the tattoos of monkeys played there, along the thatch of hair, like some unexplored patch of jungle, and she found herself wanting to lap at the small withered lips that Nathan parted with his fingers.

Beneath her mouth, the body began to move.

Slowly at first, then more swiftly, bucking against her

lips, against her teeth, the monkey drawings chattered and spun.

She felt Nathan's teeth come down on her shoulder as she licked the woman.

He began shredding her skin, and the pain would've been unbearable, except she felt herself opening up below, for him, for the trembling woman beneath her, and the pain slowed as she heard her flesh rip beneath Nathan's teeth, she was part of it, too, eating the dying woman who shook with orgasm, and the blood like a river.

A glimpse of her, not Lucy.

Not Lucy.

But Monkey God.

Y-Cha.

You suffer greatly. You suffer and do not die. Y-Cha may leave her prison.

She could not tell where Nathan left off and where she began, and seemed beyond the threshold of any pain she had ever imagined in the whole of creation.

She ripped flesh, devouring, blood coursing across her chin, down her breasts, Nathan inside her now, *more* than inside her, rocking within her, complete love through the flesh, through the blood, through the wilderness of frenzy, through the small hole between her legs, into the cavern of her body, and Y-Cha, united with her lover through the suffering of a woman whose identity as Jane Boone was quickly dissolving.

Her consciousness: taste, hurt, feel, spit, bite, love.

IN THE MORNING, the saint slept.

His attendant, Sunil, came through the entrance to the chamber with a plate of steamed vegetables. He set them down on the table and went to get a broom to sweep up the broken pitcher.

When he returned, the saint awoke.

The servant stared at his master's face as if he were seeing the most horrifying visage in all of existence.

The saint took his hand to calm him, and placed his palm against the fresh wounds and newly formed scars.

Sunil gasped, because he was trying to fight how good it felt, as all men did when they encountered Y-Cha.

His mouth opened in a small *o* of pleasure.

Already, his body moved. He thrust, gently, at first. He longed to be consort to Y-Cha.

He would beg for what he feared most, he would cry out for pain beyond his imagining, just to spill his more personal pain, the pain of life in the flesh.

It was the greatest gift of humans, their flesh, their blood, their memories. Their suffering. It was all they had, in the end, to give, for all else was mere vanity.

Words scrawled in human suffering on a yellow wall:

FLESH OF MY FLESH, blood of my blood
*   I delight in your offering*
*   Make of your heart a lotus of burning*
*   Make of your loins a pleasure dome*
*   I will consecrate the bread of your bones*
*   And make of you a living temple*
*   To Monkey God.*

THE SERVANT OPENED himself to the god and the god enjoyed the flesh as she hadn't for many days – the flesh, blood and beauty. It was known among the gods that a man was most beautiful as he lay dying.

The gift of suffering was offered slowly, with equal parts delight and torment.

As she watched his pain, she could not contain her jealousy for what the man possessed.

The Skin of the World

"I gotta go, anyway," my brother Ray said.

He had a look on his face that I only now understand, a look of wanting to do something without regard to
consequences. He had a face like a raccoon, dark-encircled
eyes, and a need to get into things he wasn't supposed to. I
remember that face with fondness, not for his smile or his
wildness, but for what came after.

It was 1969, and a man had landed on the moon the
day before which is why we'd been staying at my uncle's. My
uncle had a color television set and my father didn't believe
in them until the day a man walked on the moon.

It had been an unpleasant family outing, and my
brother was giving my father some lip. We drove past the
sign that said Vidal Junction, and my father turned to my
older brother, Ray, and told him to just keep it shut tight or
he'd be walking from there back to Prewitt. As if to show he
meant it, my father slowed the car to ten miles an hour, and
pulled off on the shoulder.

My mother was quiet. She kept facing forward, as she always did, and I pretended I wasn't even there.

Vidal Junction was just a sliver of a gas station and maybe an old diner off the railroad tracks, but it had been abandoned back in the thirties.

When I was much younger my mother and I had stopped there to collect some of the junk she took to her junkshop dealers, like old telephone pole insulators and bits from the gas pumps. It had looked the same since I was four, that junction, a ghost place, and that sign just sitting up there: *Vidal Junction,* as if it would continue, lifeless, into infinity.

"It's damn hot," my father said, parking the car so we could all look at the old gas station, and my brother Ray could get good and mad about my father's threats to make him walk.

"Look at that big heap behind the pumps."

My mother was trying to remain silent, I could tell. But she wanted to say something; she ground her teeth together so as not to let anything out.

"What do you boys think it is?"

"I don't know," I said. It looked like a piece of a car, but I didn't know cars too well, and it could just as easily have been a piece of a rocket. I smelled something from my cracked window, something sweet like candy.

"Maybe you can sell it to one of your junk shops," my father said to my mother.

"Antique stores," she said.

"This place is strange," my father said, "you'd think somebody would plough it over and put up some stores or maybe grow something. Maybe that thing's from outer space. Or Russia. Or maybe it's like space trash. Everything's space-*something* these days. Right, Ray? That's right, Ray? You think it's from Mars?"

I heard a click, and there was my brother Ray opening the door on his side of the car.

"Maybe I will walk from here," Ray said. "Just maybe."

"Just maybe my ass," my father said. "It's a sure thing."

Ray got full out of the car and left the door hanging open.

"Coop," my mother said. She reached over and touched my father gently on his shoulder. He shrugged. "Coop," she repeated, "it's twenty miles home."

"Only fifteen, by my estimate," my father said. "He's old enough. Or is sixteen still a baby?"

My mother was silent.

Ray walked across the steamy asphalt on the highway, over to Vidal Junction and I wondered if he was going to burn to a crisp. As if he sensed this, he took his shirt off and rolled it up and stuck it under his right armpit. He was so bony that kids at school called him Scarecrow, and I swear you could read the bones of his back, line by line, and they all said *Up Yours*.

My father started up the station wagon.

"Coop," my mother said. Coop wasn't my father's name, but it's what Ray used to call him before I was born and my father was a Corporal and wanted to be called Corporal but Ray could only say Coop. My mother had called him Coop since then. To my father it must have been the kind of endearment that reminded him that he was a father after all and no longer a Corporal. My mother probably figured it would soften him, and it probably did.

"He wants to walk, let the boy walk," my father said. "I didn't make him walk. I didn't. His choice."

That was the end of that, and my father started up the car, and as we drove off toward Prewitt, I looked out the back window and saw Ray just sitting down by one of the old gas pumps and lighting up a cigarette because he knew he could get away with it.

We crossed the railroad track, and the road became bumpy again because nobody in the county much bothered to keep up this end of the highway, and it would stay bumpy until we got out of this side of the valley.

§&

"FIFTEEN MILES," my mother said. We sat on the front porch, just sweating and wondering when Ray would be home.

"Daddy said he used to run fifteen miles every Saturday."

My mother looked at me, and then back to the road.

"Used to," she said under her breath.

"Ray walked ten miles in the rain last March."

My mother stood up and said, "oh." I thought at first it was because she saw Ray coming up the road, but there was nothing there. We had four neighbors, back then, before the development came through, and the nearest house was a half-mile down the road. Across the road was a pond and some woods, and beyond that the mountains and the Appalachian Trail. It was pretty in the summer, if the temperature dropped, to sit on the porch and watch the light fade by slow degrees until the sun was all but gone by nine-thirty and it was past my bed time.

My father looked out through the screen door.

"They still teach math?" My father said. "At a slow pace,

given the sun and other factors, you can figure on maybe three miles an hour, and that's only if he keeps a moderate pace. So he won't be home 'til eleven. Maybe midnight. Ray's stubborn, too. Got to factor that in. He may just sleep out back of Huron's, or by the river."

"Mosquitoes'll eat him alive if he does," I said.

"He's done this before," my mother said, more to herself than to anyone.

"He can go to hell for all I care," my father said.

A brief silence followed this. I thought about my parents and my brother who seemed to ruin any peace we had as a family; I thought of the pain my mother felt; I was already tired of the fights between Ray and my dad.

"Huron said he might carry some of your junk," my father said, softly.

"Oh," my mother said. She walked out into the yard and called for the collie to come in for the night.

I wondered what Ray was thinking right now, or if he was sneaking a beer at Huron's, or if he was just out of sight but almost home.

SEVEN DAYS LATER, I was fairly sure we would never see Ray again, and we eventually moved, when I was twelve, to Richmond, where my father got a job that actually paid, and where I was sure we had arrived because it was so different from Prewitt. I thought of Ray often, and what our family would've been like if he had ever returned from his walk that day when I was ten and a half.

I have to admit that our family was the better for his loss. My father became a tolerable man, and the violence that I had known from early childhood transformed into a benevolent moodiness, an anger that took itself out on, not his family, but his employer, or the monthly bills, or the television set. No longer did he throw furniture against the wall when he and my mother argued, and never again did he raise his voice to me. I missed my brother somewhat, but he had never been kind to me, nor had he been my protector. Ray had always dominated things for me, and had even gone so far, once, to piss on my leg when I was five (and he was just about eleven) to prove that he was the brother with the power.

Although my mother suffered greatly for a few years after Ray disappeared, I think even she finally blossomed, for Ray was a difficult child, who, according to her, since birth had been demanding and unreasonable and quick of temper. I think that Ray did a great service by walking the other way from Vidal Junction, or wherever I assumed he had marched off to, for my mother had the tragedy of loss, but over the years she drew strength from the thought that Ray was, perhaps, living in some rural Virginia town, and functioning better without the burden of his family.

Perhaps he was even happy.

Never once did it cross anyone's minds that Ray was dead. He was a cuss, and cusses don't die in the South. They become the spice of the land, and are revered in the smaller towns the way unusually beautiful women are, or three-legged dogs.

❧

WHEN I GREW UP, I moved around a bit, raised a family, and then got divorced.

When my son was five, I decided we'd take a trip to his grandma's for a belated visit. I had custody of Tommy for six whole days, which was generous of my ex-wife

I took the surface roads through all the small towns in the mountain valley. It would be nice to drive to Prewitt and show my kid the failed horse farm.

But my memory of the area was bad, and I was too proud to stop at gas stations for directions.

We got a little lost.

Tommy wanted lunch, and I pulled off at a coffee shop that looked like it was made of tin and was shaped like an old-fashioned percolator.

The waitress was cute and told Tommy that he was the red-headiest boy she had ever seen. The place smelled like rotting vegetables, but the ham biscuits were good, and I taught my son the lost art of *see*-food with the biscuits and some peanuts thrown in. His mother would hate it when he returned to Baltimore and kept opening his mouth when it was full of food.

"You know which way to Prewitt?" I asked the waitress.

She went and got a road map for me, and I moved over so she could scootch in next to me and show me the route down past Grand Island, and off to the south of Natural Bridge.

"All these new highways," I said, "got me confused."

"I know what you mean," she said. "They just keep tearing the hills up. Pretty soon it's gonna look like New York."

Because I wanted to keep flirting with her, I began the story of my missing brother, which never ceased to interest Tommy whenever I told him. While I spoke, I watched the girl's face, and she betrayed nothing other than interest. She was years younger than me, maybe only twenty, but it was nice that she enjoyed my attentions at least as much as I enjoyed hers. I ended, "…and to this day, we don't know where he went."

She looked thoughtful, and reached over, combing her fingers through Tommy's hair to keep it out of his eyes. "Well, I've heard about that place."

Tommy asked for more milk, and the girl got up to get him some. When she returned I asked her what she'd meant.

"Well," she said, her eyes squinting a bit as if trying to remember something clearly from the back of her mind, "they don't call it that, anymore, Vidal Junction, and the railroad tracks got all torn up or covered over. But it's still there, and people have disappeared there before."

"You talk like it's a news story," I said.

She laughed. "Well, it was one of those boogeyman kind of stories. When I was a kid."

You're still a kid, I thought. It struck me then, that she reminded me in some way of Anne, my ex. Not her looks, but the girl in her.

"What's a boogeyman?" Tommy asked.

"Someone who picks his nose too much," I told him.

The waitress looked very serious, and she spoke in a whisper. "There was a girl in Covington who ran away from home. My cousin knew her. She got to that place and she didn't get further. My aunt said she was taken by her stepfather, but my cousin said that was just to keep us all from getting scared."

"It's one of those stories," I said, but then I started to feel uneasy, as if the child in me were threatening to come out. "You know, like you hear from a friend of a good friend about a dead dog in a shopping bag that these punks steal, or the hook in the back of the car."

"What's a hook in the back of the car?" Tommy asked.

"Fishing hook," I said by way of calming him. His mother had been telling me that he had severe nightmares and I didn't want to feed them.

But the girl went ahead and scared him anyway, by saying, "well, folks around here I grew up with think it's something like the asshole of the universe."

I paid our bill, and I raced Tommy to the Mustang, because the girl had finally given me the creeps and convinced me that Tommy would have more nightmares—for which I would be rewarded with fewer and fewer weekends with him.

But, instead, Tommy said, "I want to go there."

"Where?"

"The asshole."

"Never say that word again as long as you live."

"Okay."

"She was weird, huh."

"Yeah," he said. "She was trying to scare you."

"I think she was trying to scare *you*."

He shrugged. "I don't scare."

I DIDN'T hunt Vidal Junction down intentionally, but we happened to come upon it because of my superb driving which, at the rate we were going, would set us down at my mother's in Richmond at midnight. It was only five-thirty. I didn't recognize the Junction at once. It had changed. The sign was gone, and the old gas pumps, while they were still there, were surrounded and almost engulfed by abandoned couches, refrigerators, and old rusted-out clunkers along the roadside.

I would've just driven by the place if it were not for the fact that Tommy told me that he had to pee. He could not wait, and what I had learned in my five years of fatherhood was that my son meant he had to go when he said it.

I pulled over and got out of the car with my son, and told him to pee behind one of the couches. I didn't stand near him just because I was afraid of the waitress' apocryphal warning, but because I worried about copperheads and perverts.

I glanced around the junction and noticed that the girl in the coffee shop had lied: the railroad tracks were very much in evidence.

"Lookit," Tommy said, after he had zipped up. He grabbed my hand and pointed to the bottom of the torn up old couch.

"It's asphalt," I said. *Or oil*, I thought.

Or something.

"Don't touch it," I told him, but I was too late. Tommy stooped over and put his fingers right into it. "I hope it's not doggie doo."

I pulled him up and away, but as I did he let out a squeal, and then I saw why.

The skin of his fingers, right where the pads were, appeared ragged and bleeding. The top layer of skin had been torn off.

"Owee," he said, immediately thrusting his fingers in his mouth.

The asshole of the universe is right, I thought.

"Hurts bad?" I asked.

He shook his head, withdrawing his fingers from between his lips. "Tastes funny."

"Don't eat it, Tom, for God's sakes."

He began crying as if I had slapped him — which I never did — and he went running across the drying field of junk.

I called to him.

I heard a door slam.

I WENT TOWARD THE SOUND, behind the old gas station, and there stood a man of about forty, with long hippie-style hair, and a white cotton T-shirt on and jeans, covered head to toe with dirt. "Tried to stop him," the man said. "He went in, and I tried to stop him."

"Tommy!" I called, and heard something that sounded like him from inside the gas station. The man blocked my way to the doorway, which had, in its last life, been the gas station restroom. It was odd that it had a screen door, and it seemed odder that this man standing there didn't move as I came rather threateningly towards him.

He wore a puzzled look, briefly. Then, he nodded to me as if he'd sized me up in a matter of seconds. "It's a kind of attraction they smell. I don't smell it much now, but at first I did. The younger you are, the more you catch it."

From the restroom, I heard my son cry out.

"You don't want to go in there," the man said. He remained in front of me, and I felt adrenaline rush through my blood as I prepared for a fight. "I tried to stop the boy, but it's got that smell, and kids seem to respond to it best. I studied it for three years, and look," he said, pointing to his feet.

And then I understood why he stood so still.

The man had not feet, but where his legs stopped, his shins were splinted against blocks of wood. He squatted down, balancing himself against the wall of the building, and picked up a small kitchen knife and a flashlight, and then slid up again.

"Be prepared," he said, handing me the knife, "I was smart, buddy. I cut them off when it started to get me. Cauterized them later. It hurt like a son-of-a-bitch, but it was a small sacrifice."

Then he moved out of the way, and I opened the screen door to the restroom, and was about to set foot inside when he shined a flashlight over my shoulder into the dark room. I saw the forms, and the beam of light hit the strawberry-blonde hair of my son, only it was not my son but something I can't even give a name to, unless it can be called skin, skin like silk and mud, moving slowly beneath the red-blonde hair, and from it the sound of my boy as if he were retreating somewhere, not hurting, and not crying, but just like he was going somewhere beyond imagining, and was making noises that were incomprehensible. Skin like an undulating river of shiny eels, turning inward, inward.

Knife in my hand, I stood on the threshold, and the man behind me said, "they go in all the time. I can't stop them."

"What in god's name is it?"

"It's a rip in the skin of the world," he said. "Hell, I don't know. It's something living. Maybe anything."

I felt something against the toe of my shoe, and instinctively drew back, but not before the tip of my Nike was torn off by the skin. The toes of my left foot were bleeding.

"Living organism," he said, "I don't know how long it's been here, but it's been three years since I found it. Could've been here for at least a decade."

"Maybe more," I said, remembering my brother Ray and his cigarette in front of the gas station, and his words, "I gotta go, anyway." He would've gone around back to take a leak, maybe smelled whatever you were supposed to smell, and then just went in.

The skin of the world.

"Does it hurt them?" I asked.

The man looked at me, startled, and I wondered for a moment what I had said that could startle a man who had cut his own feet off.

And it dawned on me, too, what I had just asked.

Does it hurt them?

The man didn't have to say anything, because he knew then what I was made of. That I could even ask that question. And what that question meant.

He looked like he was about to tell me something, maybe advise me, but he knew and I knew that only a man who had given up would ask that question.

Does it hurt them?

Because, maybe if it doesn't hurt, maybe it's okay that my son went in there, and got pulled through the seam of the world, the asshole of the universe. That must be what a man like me means when he has to ask.

"How would I know?" the stranger said, and hobbled across the grass, moist with the sweat from the skin of the world.

❧

I STOOD IN THAT DOORWAY, and could not bring myself to call to my son.

I shined the flashlight around in that inner darkness, and saw forms rising and falling slowly, as if children played beneath a blanket after lights out.

Soon, the evening came, and I was still there, and the man had gone off somewhere into the field of junk.

I thought of Tommy's mother, Anne, and how worried she would be, and perhaps the need she would have that I could respond to.

I began to smell the odor that the man had spoken of: it was gently sweet and also pungent, like a narcissus, and I remembered the day after my brother Ray had not come home, and how my mother and father held each other so close, closer than I had ever remembered them being before.

I remembered thinking then, as now, *it's a small sacrifice for happiness.*

Belinda in the Pool

S itting just in front of Michael and his daughter, the woman — white of hair and coat — lifted her card.

"Three hundred!" the auctioneer said. "Number 17!"

"If she'd just quit bidding," Belinda said, under her breath.

Michael — Number 5 — glared at the back of the annoying whiteness of Number 17. Belinda gave him a nudge. He held up his card.

Twenty people in sweaters and coats sat on hard plastic chairs crammed into the cold, dusty little shop.

Belinda squeezed his arm. "You can get it, Dad."

Nobody's going much over 500 dollars for this, Michael thought. It wasn't even worth three hundred to anyone in the market for antique watches with silver bands.

In that second between his most recent bid and the auctioneer's next mouthing, Michael tasted something bitter at the back of his throat.

After years of searching, here we are, he thought. *In a junk shop with Belinda, a twenty-minute drive door-to-door, the watch right there in front of us.*

"Your mother's not going to be happy," he said. "I wasn't even supposed to go over two-fifty. Holy cow."

"But we're almost there," Belinda said. "And it's just money. You'll make more. You always say that."

His daughter — verbally expressive beyond her fourteen years, curious, inquisitive, advanced in her thinking — constantly surprised him.

Belinda of the dark hair, slightly bowed shoulders, fresh-faced, the last of summer's freckles still faint on her cheek, green pond-water eyes, unremarkable nose, barest hint of mascara, vanishing dimple at her chin, most of the baby fat gone now, at the beginning of her swan years, a little silver crescent moon on a slim chain around her neck, fog-gray wool sweater pulled over orange T-shirt above blue jeans, fake tattoo — the Eye of Horus — at the back of her hand; she of the swim team, of the annual Charlotte Russe, made with the flourish of a great chef abandoning messy pans and spattered bowls in her wake, of sweet crushes on pretty male pop idols with wavy hair who posed in posters tacked up around her bedroom, of the little squeal of delight in sampling gelato at a shop on the *Via di San Simone*, of the amusement park obsession, of the junior debate team, of the long chess games with her old man where they talked endlessly of the world and school and how things used to be and how they were now, of the trips to Spain and England and Italy, of the bruised knees made better by a father's kiss, of the treasure hunts, of the late night movie marathons with stove-hot popcorn dripping in butter and parmesan; so much like her mother and so much unlike her, too.

And Belinda in the pool, Michael thought, suddenly cold.

"Dad, don't let anyone else get it. It's meant for you. I can feel it."

The woman in white raised her arm again, yellow card in hand.

င❦

WHEN THE AUCTION WAS OVER, Michael and his daughter remained in their chairs, waiting out rush hour traffic.

Belinda passed him a mint from the small flat tin she kept in her pocket.

"Sorry, Dad."

"Sometimes ya win, sometimes ya lose," he said.

"That's what losers say."

"Very funny."

He thought he might tell her, right then, about why that watch meant so much.

But why should she be burdened with his reasons?

Belinda was still a baby in his eyes, despite her womanly form emerging, *oh god,* he thought, here come the breasts, her waistline narrowing as hips curved and legs lengthened; and the way her hair sparkled after she'd brushed it; the strange silences during which he imagined her a captive in some newly-minted cell of that hormonal prison called adolescence, unable — suddenly — to talk openly about private feelings.

It came back to him as he sat there, a thud at his heart, the nightmare moment — those dreadful few seconds earlier that week when the reality hit him.

Somehow, it made the search for the watch that much more important.

⸲❧

HE'D DRIVEN over to pick her up at the YMCA. Tired of waiting in the parking lot, Michael went inside. He passed through the men's locker room, pushed the door into the swimming area.

He stood by the folded bleachers.

Belinda emerged from restless water and ascended the metal ladder at the edge of the pool. She wore a midnight blue bathing suit, her skin glistening. She'd only just drawn off her bathing cap, unleashing a cascade of thick, shiny hair that curved along her still-tanned shoulders.

Michael became aware of the boys. All those seventeen and eighteen-year-olds standing by the edge of the pool, towels flung over shoulders, their tell-all Speedos, mouths agape, eyes burning with intensity, an electrical, musky charge in the chlorinated air as they watched his daughter in a way that disturbed Michael to no end.

The kind of boy he had once been.

Oh god, Belinda. Not yet.

He could feel her slipping from his grasp. She'd be under the waves, carried by dangerous currents to some distant shore he'd never reach. No more gelatos with dad, no more squandering of Saturdays in junk shops, no more buttery, cheesy popcorn, no more *Michael-Belinda Misadventures*.

He tried to push the moment from his mind.

⸲❧

MICHAEL LOOKED down at his yellow card with the number 5 scrawled on it in magic marker. He passed it to her.

"A souvenir."

"Yee-haw." She folded up the card until it fit in the palm of her hand.

"Come on, it's been fun," he said. "Not a bad way to spend an afternoon off."

Belinda slumped further down in her chair. "There's absolutely no other watch you want in the entire world?"

"Sounds silly when you put it like that."

The shopkeeper's son began sweeping the floor around empty chairs. The boy — roughly fifteen, Michael guessed — glanced at Belinda and smiled.

"He's not very smart," Belinda whispered, leaning in close. She smelled of French soap and raspberries. "Look. He's doubling his work. You clear chairs first, then sweep."

"You should tell him."

"Like I care."

Belinda moved her legs to the right to avoid the broom. She didn't look at the boy. She swiveled in her chair. Her knees brushed against her father's. Instinctively, Michael pulled his legs away.

"Makes me angry," she said, after a full minute. "That lady just grabbed what's supposed to be yours."

"I was outbid."

"No, she grabbed it. It can't possibly mean as much to her — not like it does to you. Just look at her."

He turned his attention to the far right, beyond the chairs.

る

THE COUPLE that ran the shop sat on one side of a long narrow table. The lucky bidders took the chair directly across, one at a time, signing checks and paperwork.

Passed across the table: a 19th century painting of the mill stream with its chipped ornate frame, a little bronze art deco nude, two giant blue and green glass globes, the small cast-iron table with pink marble top, a doll with its face pushed in and dollhouse without doors that went with it, a mangy full-length mink, a small cardboard box filled with what Belinda had called "old lady jewelry," and a few other things that Michael mostly considered crap.

And then, the woman of white, taking a little square box from the owner.

He couldn't see what she did — her back was toward him — but guessed that she opened the box and drew out the watch.

Belinda arched her back, stretching out. "You could've bid more."

"Your mother would kill me."

"But this was the one time we found it," she said.

"It's just a watch. It doesn't really matter."

"If you want it, it matters."

"Sometimes it's good to want something but not get it."

"Yeah, except you never get what you want," she said. "Remember Italy? All your meetings were over. You wanted to go to Florence. Mom wanted two more days in Rome. We stayed in Rome."

"Well, we had a good time," Michael said. "And we can always go back."

"But we won't. You only go where work sends you. You never take a vacation just for you. And you won't ever see the Uffizi. Let's just write that little dream off."

"Well, I say we'll go again," he said. "Someday. Florence ain't going anywhere."

"You never know," she said. "A war. A tsunami. A world cataclysm. Things happen. I'm betting a couple thousand years ago somebody put off a summer trip to Pompeii and then — well, that's that."

"You're a little too smart for your old man."

"It's just that things only come around once. Sometimes."

Belinda crossed and uncrossed her legs. She tapped her foot against the empty chair in front, kicking it just enough that the chair moved forward.

"I don't know if I want to live in the same universe where that lady gets the watch, and you don't," Belinda whispered as she glanced around. "It's...It's an injustice."

He wasn't sure, but it looked like her eyes shone with tears.

He reached over and hugged her. She pressed her face against his shoulder.

"Aw, come on," he whispered. "Sometimes the hunt's better than the treasure."

Belinda drew back, a glint of tear at her cheek. She wiped it away. The Eye of Horus, now a smudge on the back of her hand.

"I wanted you to get it," she said.

"Me, too."

"It's not fair."

"Life's never fair." He kissed her on the forehead. "And it's not all about me, anyway. But you've got to be the sweetest kid on the planet to stick up for your old man. We'll find that watch someday."

"And someday you'll see the Uffizi Gallery," she said, with a slow drip of cynicism.

The shopkeepers' son began clearing chairs away. Again, the boy glanced over at his daughter.

"See? He's going to have to sweep all over again," Belinda said, momentarily distracted from her mood. "If he'd done it right the first time…"

Michael closed his eyes. *Don't think of the pool.*

"Dad, Dad — look, quick," Belinda said as if she were waking him up to an emergency.

Michael opened his eyes.

❧

BELINDA TURNED HALFWAY and pointed toward the front window of the shop.

The woman of whiteness stood out at the street, glancing one way and then the other, waiting for a gap in the heavy traffic. She stepped off the curb only to be chased back to the sidewalk by a car.

"They need to put more traffic lights downtown," Belinda said.

The shop was on a strange corner, jutting out like a peninsula into a choppy sea of streets.

"She won't get across any time soon," Belinda said. "She should walk down to State Street and then go over. Or wait it out in here. Someone should tell her."

Michael watched the back of the woman of white.

"Dad, remember how you're always saying I should take fate into my own hands?"

"Of course. Seize the day."

"You can still get the watch."

"It's too late," he said.

"She's standing right there. You could offer her fifty bucks more."

Michael stood up to get a better look out the window.

Belinda slipped outside and went to stand just behind the woman. She glanced back at her father through the shop window, motioning for him to follow.

❦

"Excuse me," Michael said. "Miss?"

The woman of white didn't look his way at first.

"Hello?" he asked.

She glanced over. Younger than he'd expected, given the white hair.

Belinda stepped up. "My dad just wants to see if he can buy that watch off you."

"I'm sorry," the woman said. "You bid on it, too?"

"We sat right behind you." Belinda brought out the yellow card from the back pocket of her jeans, unfolding it. "See? Number 5."

The woman looked from Michael's face to his daughter's.

"My daughter, Belinda."

Then, he introduced himself.

The woman of white smiled at Belinda.

"I'm Carolyn. What a beautiful sweater." Then, she looked over at Michael, her smile fading. "I could never give this watch up. You could pull out five thousand dollars cash right now. I wouldn't be able to hand it over. And I'm not rich. I could use five thousand. Couldn't we all."

She held up her wrist, drawing the coat sleeve back. The

silver and turquoise gleamed in the moody slant of November's dimming light.

"It's really a man's watch. Seems old-fashioned to say it. As if watches could be male or female." The woman dragged her sleeve down again.

"My dad's been looking for that exact watch for years," Belinda said.

The woman looked from Belinda to her father. "I'm sorry. Maybe you'll find another one."

Belinda walked behind the woman's back. She mouthed a word that Michael thought might be: "fate," or perhaps, he thought: "hate." Or "wait."

"Sure I can't change your mind?" Michael asked.

The woman held her hand up, a stop sign. "Please leave me alone."

Carolyn turned and looked back toward the shop.

Michael wondered if she might run inside and claim he was harassing her. He had to be sensitive. He took a step back.

"No," he said. "I understand. Honestly…"

Belinda, on the other side of the woman, made a rolling motion with her hands, which Michael interpreted as *keep talking, Dad*.

"Just name a price," he said, worried that the woman might throw out some astronomical figure and then he'd have trouble saving face in front of Belinda.

"Look," the woman said. "Fuck off."

She stepped into the street.

Something about Belinda caught his eye.

His daughter darted to the edge of the curb, a blur of motion reaching for Carolyn's white coat.

In the same second that Belinda did this, a truck came

out of swift traffic, brakes squealing and slammed into the woman of white at the dead center of her body.

Belinda stepped back to the curb. Instinctively, Michael nearly leapt for his daughter, and they both crumpled down to the sidewalk in each other's arms.

Carolyn flew like a great white bird to the truck's windshield, reaching upward.

The woman of white slid down across the hood and then fell to the street.

MICHAEL RODE with the woman in the ambulance, after making sure that the police would give Belinda a ride home.

He felt responsible. He wondered if he'd scared the woman a little, making her want to get out into the street, away from him.

Michael noticed that the sleeves of her coat had torn, but her arms were pristine. The watch seemed to have survived perfectly well.

AT THE HOSPITAL, Carolyn opened her eyes.

Michael told her where she was, who he was, and why she couldn't move.

The nurses flitted around the gurney, doctors chattered, someone called for a specialist, someone else called for someone named Bobby, and Michael felt a thud in his chest knowing he had a few seconds before anyone might see.

He thought of Belinda, all those times they'd scoured

auctions and shops, looking for a watch he was certain they'd never find.

And then, found.

And lost.

Right here, inches away.

Carolyn's eyes opened, watching him.

He slipped the watch off her wrist and into the pocket of his jacket.

She'll forget this. After the anesthesia, it'll all be a weird dream to her when she recovers.

Later, he called his wife and told her what happened — accident, hospital; nothing about the watch. His wife snarled at him for abandoning Belinda; for riding with some stranger in an ambulance.

"Who does that?" she kept asking as if he'd been unfaithful.

He managed to get Belinda on the phone.

"You okay?"

"I'm fine, don't worry," she said.

He was just about to hang up when Belinda asked, "Did you get it?"

❧

MICHAEL ARRIVED HOME LATE. He slept in the den on the couch, the watch cupped in his hands.

He woke up several hours later in the dark.

He remembered a dream: the woman of white, her face a bloody mess, rose from the depths of a swimming pool to strangle him.

He took Belinda to the city hospital the next afternoon.

"I STILL DON'T SEE why we're here," she said as they sat in the waiting area. "I mean, we don't actually know her."

"I want to make sure she's okay."

"You're giving it back, aren't you?" Belinda glared at him, then picked up a magazine and began flipping through pages, breathing heavily, making her disapproval known with little grunts and sighs.

CAROLYN LAY ASLEEP in her room in the midst of a labyrinth of tubes, hook-ups, and machines.

Michael set the wristwatch on the dresser by the bed.

HE BROKE out in a cold sweat in the hallway, just beyond the double doors.

Belinda looked over at him from her seat at the end of the corridor.

WHEN HE REACHED HER, she stood up.

"I need to use the bathroom."

"Over there," he pointed.

Michael sat down and closed his eyes. A headache came on. He pressed his hands over his eyes, leaning forward. A throbbing pain, suddenly, a build up of tension; guilt; the poor woman of white; a memory in the past that meant so much to him; the moments of loss in his life; the damned vision of Belinda in her bathing suit rising from the waters of the YMCA pool with all those boys.

After a minute or two, Belinda returned and put her arm over his shoulder.

"Dad, it's okay. I'm not mad at you or anything," his daughter whispered.

A month later, closing in toward the holidays, Michael got a letter from a law firm claiming he'd stolen — from their client, Miss Carolyn Hoskins — an expensive wristwatch.

❧

THE FIRM PRICED the watch at fifty thousand dollars.

"The value may be higher," the letter stated. "Our client believes the item is priceless."

He could only guess what had happened.

"That's ridiculous," Belinda said after he showed her the letter. "She didn't even pay six hundred for it."

They were both in the warm kitchen, a Saturday leaning toward noon. They shared a grilled cheese on rye and a bowl of tomato soup at the breakfast counter by the window overlooking the patio, which was covered with snow.

"Besides, you didn't take it," Belinda added after she'd read the letter a second time.

"Someone else — a nurse, maybe a relative — must have stolen it. After I put it back," Michael said, pausing to take a sip of orange spice tea, one of Belinda's winter concoctions. "Of course she thought I did it. She saw me pick it up."

"Oh come on," Belinda said. "Nobody's going to

remember that after they get hit by a truck. Her lawyer probably got your name and address from the cops. She just *thinks* you did it. What a greedy little piggy she turned out to be."

"Not sure what the next move'll be," he said, setting the letter down by his plate. "I guess I'll need to shoot a note back about that damn watch."

"Why'd you even take it back in the first place?" Belinda asked.

"I was wrong to steal it."

"If she died, she wouldn't have cared."

"But she didn't die."

"But she might've."

Michael cocked his head to the side, looking at his daughter's face.

"Is this the kind of stuff the debate team argues about?" He waved his spoon in the air as if making a point.

Belinda ignored the question. She picked up a paper napkin and leaned over, wiping up some of the soup spatter on the front of her father's shirt. She frowned slightly at the result.

"Listen, when I die, I don't care if someone takes my red shoes," she said. "And I love those shoes. I'd fight for those shoes."

"But wouldn't you care who'd get them?"

"Not if I'm dead."

Michael narrowed his eyelids. "Carolyn Hoskins isn't dead."

"She's seriously injured, Dad. She may slip into a coma or something. Anything could happen. And you're out your watch."

He bit down on his lower lip. He should've told her by

now why they'd hunted for that watch. It seemed too late. What was the point?

"It's not my watch," he said. "It never was."

"It *is*," his daughter insisted. "You want it. As long as I've known you, we've been looking for it. She doesn't need it. Not if she dies, anyway."

"Belinda, I don't like this kind of talk."

"It's not like you didn't think about it. If she died, what'd she need a watch for? She wouldn't care."

There was more to his little girl than Michael had ever realized.

He wondered if she had misinterpreted all those little chats and negotiations while they sought their treasures — the coins on the beach, the sulfite marbles, the amethyst glass bottles, the onyx elephant, and *the watch, the watch, the watch.*

"So, now it's okay to steal?"

She shook her head. "No, that's obviously *wrong*. If someone's *alive*. But I'm talking about if she died. A watch would be pointless to her. What's a wristwatch going to matter to someone who's out of time?"

"But could you live with that?"

She shrugged. "Maybe. If I'd been hunting for that watch since the world began. Like you have."

"Stealing from the *dead*, Belinda?"

"Listen," she leaned in, twirling her spoon lightly in the soup bowl. "Remember that red granite lion? The one in the British Museum. And all the other stuff. Did Lord Carnarvon really care that he was raiding tombs?"

"Well," Michael hedged a little. "It was a long time after King Tut died. Maybe if you give someone a few thousand years, a little thievery's forgivable."

"In fact, isn't it true that Lord Carnarvon and Carter and their team of thieves did the mummies good? They made King Tut famous all over again. We all love Egyptian history because of thieves. And don't even get me started on the Elgin Marbles."

"You might want to consider the legal profession," he told her.

They joked back and forth about the various museums built on theft from one group or another, the wonderful kingdoms built on extortion and skullduggery, the terrible De Medicis and the fantastic Renaissance (with Belinda reminding him yet again that he would never see the Uffizi), about auctions themselves being a kind of tomb plunder.

"I bet that watch shows up at auction again," Belinda said. "Maybe we can get it, after all."

"You miss the part where I'm being sued?"

His daughter shook her head slightly as if he were being an absolute fool of a dad.

"It's not a lawsuit," Belinda said. "It's a shakedown. She's lying there in the hospital. She got some ambulance chaser to send it. Don't be afraid. What can she prove? Who'll believe her? Who's going to even back her story?"

A week or so later, days away from Christmas, Michael saw the obituary in the newspaper.

"Carolyn Hoskins," he said the name three times.

"Who?" His wife asked as she went to grab her purse from the coffee table.

He glanced up. "Oh, that poor woman. The one who got hit."

"The one who's suing you?" Belinda asked.

"She died," Michael said.

"You're being sued?" His wife stopped in the middle of the room.

"Not anymore," Belinda said.

His wife glanced at their daughter with a mysterious expression. "I'm always the last to know in this house."

"She was in her late thirties," Michael said. "Single. New to the area. They'll do the funeral back in Chicago."

"Long way from home," Belinda said. "Does it say what she died from?"

His father looked over at her. "I'm sure it was the accident."

"Poor thing," Belinda said. "How awful. We should send flowers, Dad. We really should."

After her mother went upstairs, Belinda settled down beside Michael on the sofa. She tugged the newspaper from his hands.

"Such a dinosaur, still reading papers," she said.

"I like the feel of newsprint."

"Like I said. *Dinosaur.*" Belinda folded the paper in half and read the obituary silently.

"It's sad," she said.

She reached over and picked up Michael's cup of coffee. Lifting it to her lips, she checked to see if he disapproved. Took a sip, made a face, put the coffee back down on the coaster.

"You must feel a little better, Dad."

"Not really."

"I mean, because of the lawsuit."

He thought a moment. "I guess that's all in the past."

Belinda leaned back, one leg over the other, head on the cushion as she flipped through the rest of the paper.

"Isn't it weird, Dad? We spend years looking for this particular watch, right?"

He nodded.

"It's something you really, really want. Ever since I can remember, you talked about the watch."

"It was a little crazy, I guess."

"So we find out about the auction for some old stuff, and — *voila* — here's the exact watch. Right nearby. And then this woman outbids you. Only she gets hit by a truck. And then you take the watch when she's in the hospital, but you feel bad about it. So you return it the next day. And sometime after that, someone else steals it."

Belinda took a deep breath. "It's almost like she wasn't meant to have it."

"I guess we weren't meant to have it, either."

Belinda laughed. "That's not what I'm getting at. What I mean is, maybe the watch didn't want her. *Fate*."

"Well, poor Carolyn. Not a great fate."

"Yeah, if only she'd sold you the watch in the first place. She'd probably still be walkin' around with her white coat on."

Michael thought no more about this until Christmas day, when Belinda pulled him aside after all the presents were opened, after stuffing themselves on eggnog and pie, and after his wife took the dog out for a walk in the snow.

Belinda drew him into her bedroom.

&

SHE PATTED the edge of the bed. Michael sat down.

She wore her Christmas red sweater and gray sweat pants. Her feet were bare, toenails painted frosty pink.

He noticed — for the first time — that no pop star posters remained on the walls.

Belinda shook her hair out and drew it behind her ears so it wouldn't flop in her face. She wore the small diamond earrings they'd given her that morning.

From behind a pillow, she brought out a wrapped box.

"More Christmas?" he asked.

"I didn't want mom to see it."

"A secret?"

"Kind of." She shrugged.

Belinda passed him the box.

Michael looked down at it. He undid the knot of silver string and tore the neatly folded paper with its red and green snowflakes.

"Dad, remember how you once said to me how fate doesn't just happen — you have to make it?"

Opening the slats of the cardboard box, he saw a gently curved glimmer of silver.

Oh, Belinda, he thought, looking at her intensely. Eyes like pond water, faint freckles, barely-perceptible dimple in her chin. He felt as if someone kidnapped his child and put this girl — a replica, a changeling, almost Belinda but not quite — in her place.

"You stole it," he whispered as he held the watch in his hands.

"No guessing," she said.

But several other guesses began streaming through his mind as he thought of the events — of fate — of the woman in white so hesitant to step out into busy traffic,

Belinda with that rolling motion of her hands standing behind Carolyn Hoskins and mouthing a word — *Fate? Hate? Wait?* — reaching out to pull the poor woman back at the last second before she went into the path of the truck.

But had Belinda really tried to save her?

Michael imagined his daughter stepping forward and pushing the woman of white into traffic.

Impossible.

He looked at his daughter — really studied her face as if he'd never taken the time to see her. Not as a little girl but as an adult slowly emerging from some outer sheath of innocence as boys in speedos watched her and as a woman in a hospital bed looked up to see her pick up a watch from the dresser.

Had she returned to the hospital later, after the letter arrived? Had she pushed a pillow on Carolyn's face, unplugged machines or done any of the dozen things you could do to stop the life of someone who couldn't move much, who went in and out of consciousness, who lived on a morphine drip?

No, she wouldn't. *Ridiculous. She's smart and stubborn, and she can make your head spin with those moods of hers, but she'd never murder someone. What kind of father are you to even think it?*

But that memory of Belinda in the pool, the way she stopped near the top of the ladder as she let her hair fall from the bathing cap to her shoulders. He'd seen her glance at the boys — for just a second. As if she knew what she was doing to them.

Who was she? Who had she become?

"Belinda," he whispered, holding the watch in the palm

of his hand. He could barely get the words out. "How'd you get it?"

"I'll tell you. After you tell me something."

"All right," he said, breathing slowly, trying not to imagine.

She slid back, up against the headboard, drawing her knees toward her chest.

"It's something I've never understood — all these years."

"And then you'll tell me how you got this," he reminded her, the sense of an undertow in the room.

"Sure. Right after."

Belinda rested her chin in her hands, her elbows atop her knees, looking up at him with that sense of wonder she'd never quite lost from childhood.

"So, Dad," Belinda said. "What's this watch really mean to you?"

The American

Quested's, a cafe in the old Fire District, looked out on a triangle of park lined with sculptures and trees.

The barman brought out an espresso, tinged with lemon, on a small round tray. He set the cup down in front of the latest arrival.

The American stared at the small cup for a moment as if deciding whether or not to order something else.

"I tried to kill myself tonight," he announced to the couple at a nearby table.

HE SIPPED his drink and glanced out into the night, not caring if they listened.

"I smoked every cigarette I could find. Drank everything. I swam in the filthy river and then went to a brothel where the whores were shapeless and ancient."

"Now, that's the way to do it," one woman said, from the table nearest his. "Good for you. Bon voyage."

"So you come to a dark little cafe like the rest of us," said the Italian gentleman beside her, his face lit by candle glow from the table's center. "More drinks, good sir. This time, two shots. I feel lucky tonight."

The barman stood by, a small white towel draped across his arm, an emptiness in his gaze. "We're closing in a half hour."

"Why's that?" the tourist from Scotland asked.

"I have a life, that's why," the barman said.

"It's a lovely night," the Italian said, and then began singing, lightly, a beautiful old song in a reedy voice. The handful of ex-pats and tourists, all of them, smiling; with the exception of the American, who glanced face to face, table to table.

The slender branches of nearby trees, full of summer leaf, waved slightly, then, the breeze died.

The American began laughing.

"What's the joke?" said the woman.

"I want to obliterate myself. Somehow."

"Why's that?"

"I am one of the great unloved."

"You can't be more than twenty-three. You can find love next year."

"I don't think that's how it works. I think it begins at birth and goes from there. Then, one day you just recognize it. You're outside the joke that others get. You're not in on what they seem to connect with."

"You're just inexperienced," she said. Then, turning to her the man beside her, she whispered a few words in Italian.

He whispered back.

She said to the American, "Come sit with us. Would you like a cigarette?"

In a minute or two, he'd changed seats and sat across from the woman and her friends.

She introduced the young man to the others: the Italian gentleman, and a young couple from Bristol who were only in Rome for a week.

One of the Scottish tourists at the next table began whispering to one of the others as if he knew something about the American.

The woman said, "You look familiar to me."

"I'm here a lot, sometimes. I come late at night. I suppose I drink too much," the American said.

The woman looked at the older Italian man and smiled. "We like Quested's. So many people come here who speak English. My Italian is still a little rough, but I'm getting better, aren't I, Dario?"

The Italian nodded, "Yes. Every day you mispronounce a new word in my language."

"Oh," she said, nudging him with her elbow. She offered a sorrowful smile to the American. "I'm sorry you're not feeling yourself tonight. But that's what drinking's for."

"Have you ever burned for anyone?" the American asked. "Burned? I have. I do."

"Someone must've broken your heart," the woman said. "Here in Rome?"

"A whore," the American said.

"if you really mean 'whore,' you might be smart not to

give your heart where you put your wallet," the Italian said. "But I suspect you exaggerate."

"Well, a whore in spirit."

"All of us should be whores in spirit," the Italian said.

"Darling," the woman said, placing her hand on the Italian's wrist. "Give him a little space to grieve for his lost love. Don't all men call women whores when they've been thrown over?"

"It's a man, not a woman," the American said.

"*Aha,*" the woman said. "That explains it. Men are all whores. No exaggeration there."

"*I'm* not a whore," the Italian said.

"Of course you're not. Darling, go get us another drink. The barman's too surly."

After the Italian left the table, the woman — who seemed to the American like every British woman he'd met — leaned over and whispered, "You're gay, then. What's that like?"

The American grinned. "Here we go."

"No, I mean, what's it like to feel the way we — women — always feel, and yet have the same instincts as any man?"

The other woman at the table laughed. "It's true. It must be terrible."

"It's exactly the same," the American said. "Nobody feels differently. We're all looking for love, and we're all messed up at the same time. Some people are meant to be loved. I am not."

"That's ridiculous. Utterly ridiculous. Everyone is meant to be loved. Is this about your mother?"

"What?"

"Well, in my experience, men get screwed up by their mothers because mummy wanted a perfect little husband in the perfect little son. It's incestuous. I see it all the time. Especially with you American boys."

"My mother died when I was three, so I suspect that's not the issue."

"That destroys my theory," the woman said. "Do you really want to kill yourself? I mean, honestly, kill yourself?"

He thought a moment but did not answer. He leaned back, looking up at the tree branches. "It's impossible to see the stars through these trees."

"No, it's not. I see them."

"I can't."

The Italian returned with a round tray of small glasses filled with greenish-brown liquid.

"Here we are," the woman said. "Do you like absinthe?"

"Absinthe-*lootly*."

No one laughed.

He added, "I like everything that's bad for me."

"Maybe that applies to the men you pick. Tell me about this recent love."

"Recent one? My only love."

"Wait. You're joking."

"No, I'm not," the American said. "Before him, I hadn't been with a man."

"With a woman before?"

"A few times. In my teens."

"But this was your first real love. That explains a lot," the woman said. "First loves are dreadful unless you're the one who dumps him. So this was just your learning experience."

"No. He was the only one until he had me do things. But that was all for his benefit. It's over. My life."

"Don't be ridiculous," the woman said. "Here, drink.

You'll feel better. You'll burn away those feelings along with a few brain cells tonight."

The Italian began speaking to the barman who stood by.

"He wants to close up," the Italian said. "He has a sick child at home."

"Just one drink to go," the woman said. She raised her glass and sipped. "Do you feel it yet?"

"I feel too much," the American said.

"I mean the absinthe. They say it's terrific for destroying the brain."

"And hallucinating," said the Italian.

"I need hallucination to do what I need to do," the American said. "Here's the thing." He took a few sips. "Here's the thing. He told me he loved me. He made me do things that I wouldn't ordinarily do."

"Like?"

"I'd rather not say."

"I see," the woman said "*Sexual* things."

"And other things. He had me…do things. With others. He says it's what will bind us. I was stupid. I don't know who I am sometimes."

The American drank down his glass of absinthe too quickly. "I must be a terrible person. I've done things that I never thought I'd do. I've humiliated myself. I've crossed boundaries I thought I would never cross. For him."

"You'll get sick if you go at it like that," the woman said. "Sip. That stuff'll give you the biggest headache of your life by dawn. And dawn is coming up soon enough."

The Italian took his glass and set it down in front of the American. "For you."

The American glanced up at the Italian. He picked up the glass and took a sip. He kept his nose near the drink as if inhaling something delicious. He watched the Italian as he drank.

"This is a fine drink."

"It's terrible for you. This is really the way to kill yourself," the Italian said. "If you're going to do it. This, or perhaps gelato — or pastries."

The American looked at the glass and swirled the green liquid around in it. "How beautiful."

"This man of yours sounds terrible," the woman said. "Just awful."

"He sounds unusual, that's true," the Italian said. "But why do these things? Why do what he asks?"

"I love him. I loved him. I still do."

"Love means hurting yourself?"

"Sometimes."

"Did you enjoy any of this wickedness?" the woman asked.

"Enjoy?"

"Well, it sounds like a dirty movie. There must be some fun to it. You were asked to do things you wouldn't ordinarily do. You must like the authority of it. Being told what to do. And doing it."

"I suppose I do like it. And I hate that I like it."

He drank the rest of the Italian's absinthe.

"You've just lost some brain cells," the woman said. "Well, as terrible as that love affair sounds, there are others in the world for you. You're just starting out. There may be dozens of men you'll love before you find that elusive right one."

"I can't do that," the American said. "There's only one man for me. I am not going to live that life, from one to another. I've known people who did that. It is awful. It turns love into a machine."

"But what did this man do to you?" she asked. "He didn't care for you. He used you. No matter how you would like that to be, that's not love. That, my friend, is a machine of some kind. That love of yours." A slight laugh. "It may be fun. It may be a good memory for when you're old and gray and want to think of misspent youth. But it's not love."

"You don't understand," the American said. "Love is about giving yourself up. Body and soul."

"Is it? I thought it was an action. I love Dario," she leaned into the Italian and gave him a squeeze. "But by love, I mean, I do things with him, for him, we have fun, we think about life together. But if he asked me to do something I couldn't do, I'd draw a line."

"Would you?" the Italian began laughing. "Well, I guess I know the limits of our love life now."

"Ha ha," she said.

"No, truly," the Italian said, kissing the top of the woman's scalp and watching the American. "I would draw no line for you. If you wished me to sleep with others, I'd do as you wished."

She swatted at the Italian. "Oh, you. This young man is serious." She leaned across the table and touched the top of the American's hand. "Love is when you trust each other. Like good friends. Best friends."

"I don't think that's love. That's complacency," the American said. "Love is a lot more extreme. It's everything or nothing. I'm not sure trust is part of it."

"That's because you're young."

"You're not old. How old are you?"

"Nearly thirty."

"I bet at twenty you felt differently."

"Perhaps I did. But you grow up." Then, seeing the stricken look on his face, she added, "I think sometimes in life, to learn about love, you have to break at first. You can't have those illusions you have when you're a child. And you will break, first, before you find out what love is. You break and are hurt. As you are now. But then you mend and grow stronger, and you come to realize what love is and what it isn't. And you avoid what looks like love, but is really just some wild animal that has no love in its soul."

"I want to burn from love," the American said.

The woman took a sip from her glass and then lit up a cigarette. "This is such a serious topic. We should talk of lighter things."

"All right," the American said. "How about the war?"

"Oh, no, let's go back to your sex life."

The American, his eyes glazing a bit from the drink, looked at his glass as if he could see the past in it.

"He had me sleep with soldiers, several at a time. Then, with the wife of a friend."

"A woman?"

"Yes. Then, one night, a man of seventy. He had me steal from people. Just to see if I would obey him."

The woman inhaled deep from her cigarette. "You're taking the piss now. This sounds made up."

"It's not," the American said. "I did it for him. I'd do anything for him."

"Well," the woman said, glancing at the others. "Then you need to separate from this person forever. You need to go get some help."

"Did he make you kill anyone?" the Italian asked.

THE AMERICAN DIDN'T ANSWER.

The woman and the Italian glanced at each other. The other couple began to talk about going home for the evening, back to their flat that was a quarter mile away.

After they left, the Italian said, "I think you're troubled. I think this love you talk of is very disturbing for you. Perhaps you just need to sleep."

"Who can sleep?" the woman asked. "I can't. Not until I put myself out with these." She lifted her glass, then noticed that the American's was empty. "More? Look, Tina's left some in her glass. Have it."

She passed the glass over to the American.

"You asked me if I ever killed anyone for him," the American said. He drank the absinthe down. "'Not yet' is my answer. But I would."

"Would you? That's terrible," the woman said.

"I know. I'm lost. That's why I tried to kill myself tonight. I want to end it. I am never going to be loved. I am not going to ever have him again. I know it. I know it."

"Did he ask you to kill someone?" the Italian asked.

The American glanced at the woman, then at the Italian. "He's out of my life."

"But he did ask you?"

"Yes. But I don't think I can."

"Why not?"

"Dario!" the woman said, giggling as if she had drunk a bit too much. "Of course he wouldn't kill anyone."

"I'm just asking. It sounds like a fantasy anyway. Who would have this young man sleep with an old man — or with soldiers — who loved him? Who would do that?"

the Italian said. "What kind of man? I don't believe he exists."

"He does," the American said. "And I'd do everything I did again. And then some."

"But not kill, I hope."

"I might. I might. I think everyone is capable of killing someone."

"I'm not," the woman said.

"You just haven't met the right person who needed killing," the American said.

"Why do this? For *love*? What does that mean?"

"It means I have no other choice."

"How are you going to kill?" the Italian asked. "If you decide to do this. Hand to hand?"

"That's what he wants. He told me who. He told me where and when. He wants me to use my bare hands."

"You don't seem that strong," the Italian said. "You don't look like you could kill a man."

The American glared at him and slipped a cigarette between his lips.

The Italian leaned forward with his lighter and lit up the American's cigarette.

The woman glanced at the two of them as if she were capturing the moment in some mental photograph. The way the American cupped his hand around the Italian's hand, encircling the heart of the flame as it touched the tip of his cigarette.

"Who did he ask you to kill?" the woman asked, a slight anxiety in her voice.

"Someone I don't know. Someone I don't care to know very well."

The Italian closed the lighter and drew back in his chair.

He glanced out into the dark morning. "What I love about the night is that we're all alone in it, even if we're together. Like this."

The woman went silent for a bit. Then, after a minute or two she said, "You should get away from this man completely. You should leave Rome. Go to Paris. Go back home if you need to. Stop drinking. Stop taking whatever drugs you take. Go discover life. There's more to life than love, anyway. You don't need to burn from love, or even burn from liquor. You need some rest and to get away from this terrible human being."

"I don't think I can live without him," the American said.

The woman glanced at the Italian, who still looked out at the night. Then, at the American. Then, to her empty glass.

The barman came out and told them that he was closing up whether they stayed at the tables or not. "I don't have this endless night that you people have."

"All right, all right," she said. "Let's go."

"We can't leave this young man here," the Italian said.

"Oh yes, we can. Do you need a taxi?"

The American stared at her but didn't answer.

She stood up and reached into her purse for money. "You need sleep is all." She said this indirectly. It could've been to anyone — the Italian, the American, the barman, or even to herself.

The Italian remained in his chair but looked up at her. "We can walk down to the fountain."

"No," she said. "Let's go home. Back to my place."

"Let's go to mine," he said.

The American stared at them both, and the woman was

nearly certain that tears rolled down his cheeks. She drew a tissue from her purse and passed it to him. "It'll be all right. Whatever it is."

The American took the tissue, swiping it around his eyes. "I've never killed anyone before."

"And you don't have to. Don't talk nonsense. Please."

The Italian finally rose, pushing his chair back. "You shouldn't have been drinking the absinthe," he said. "It's not good."

"Let's go," the woman whispered, loudly enough for the American to hear.

"All I'm saying," the American said. "All I'm saying is that I'm thinking of killing for him. That's all. I don't know why he drives me to this. I don't know what he wants. I only know I have to do what he wants."

The Italian stepped back from the woman and nodded. "Love is a cruel thing, sometimes. It needs proof. These are dangerous times in the world. We've met an assassin over drinks at Quested's."

As she passed by the American on her way out, the woman said, "Just go home and go to sleep. It'll seem different when you wake up."

She nearly touched him on the shoulder as a way of comforting him but withdrew her hand at the last second.

The woman and the Italian gentleman left Quested's, walking out under the trees, through the park.

As she stepped into the path between some thin sculptures, she shrugged off the touch of the Italian as if she were annoyed with him.

AFTER A MINUTE, the American got out of his chair, as well. The lights of Quested's shut off and the barman went home.

The American stepped into the park and moved through the shadows to catch up with the couple.

Subway Turnstile

✿

Walks through the turnstile, dropping tokens, grasping the boy by the elbow.

"Pull through," he says, but the little boy won't budge.

Glances at the others, behind them, waiting.

A friendly woman behind him suggests they hurry.

"The train's coming. Please," she says.

"Come on," he says, and again grasps, and again, the boy manages to stiffen.

"Are you scared?" he asks, and glances up at the others. "He's not usually scared."

Gets a kind look from the woman behind him.

She is wrapped up in a thick tan winter coat. A large handbag over her shoulder.

"Come on," he says, and this time reaches around and places his fingers against the child's throat.

"Davy," he says. "People are waiting."

"Let's go," the woman says, on the edge of polite.

The train comes and sounds of annoyance rise from a

low grumble behind the woman who stands at the back of the man with the boy.

"Just push him," someone says.

The heat of the train against his face.

Davy looks up at him. Shakes his head.

"I know what to do," the wrapped woman says, and steps beside the man.

SHE LOOKS at Davy and smiles sweetly.

She lifts him up in her arms and carries him through the turnstile.

"See? Not scary at all."

The boy whispers against her ear, "He's not my daddy. I don't know him."

She feels a shock go through her. Lowers the boy to the platform.

The man has come through, and takes the boy's hand.

"Thank you for that," the man says.

The little boy looks up at her.

"Come on, Davy," the man says.

The boy looks back at her as the man tugs at his hand.

They board the train.

The woman watches them, nearly about to do something. She glances at the others on the platform.

At the face of the boy through the smudged window of the train.

The train leaves the station.

She picks at her coat, unwrapping herself.

She finds a place on a bench and waits for the next train, but the heat of his whisper remains.

Becoming Men

A match struck; its tiny yellow flame illuminated the circle of boys, casting their faces in flickering.

Ralph went first, his breath coming slowly because he still hadn't recovered from the way they'd held him down; his asthma had kicked in slightly and they'd taken away his inhaler so he had to be careful.

Slow, deep breaths. His eyes hurt just from the memory of the interrogation's bright lights and then the bitter tears that followed his confession. Was he still crying? Even he wasn't sure, but he tried to hold it in as much as possible, to hold in the little boy inside him who threatened to burst out and show the others that he was what he'd always feared himself to be: a weakling.

The darting light of the match slapped yellow warpaint on all of their features.

He closed his eyes and began, "I had just barely gotten to sleep — halfway in a dream and it was all kind of like a dream when I heard all the shouting, it was my dad, he was shouting like crazy."

Jesus de Miranda, the smallest boy of thirteen that Ralph had ever seen, said nothing but his eyes widened and he had a curious curl to his lips like he was about to say something, even wanted to, but could not. There was something compelling to his face, something withdrawn yet very proud.

Ralph tried not to only look at him, because it made him feel little and ready to break down crying again, so he laughed like it didn't matter, "And my dad is such a loud son of a bitch."

Jack jumped in, "My dad didn't say a word. The bastard."

Hugh coughed. "My dad went nuts, he was just shouting, and my mom was crying, but even when the big guy grabbed me—"

"The big black guy," Jack added, then glanced at the others. The match died. Another one burst to life immediately; Ralph and his matchbook again.

"A big white guy," Marsh said, slapping Jack across the top of the head.

"Yeah, a big white guy, wearing camouflage shit and his face was all green, it was freaky, I tell ya," Ralph said, holding the piss-colored fire in his hands like a delicate small bird in front of the others so they could all see their own fear. "And I was so scared I pissed myself and my dad, when I saw him, he was practically crying but since I could tell they weren't beat up I knew somehow that they had something to do with this, and it had something to do with that thing with my cousin from three days before and maybe with the fire that burned down this old shack, but I never really thought they'd do something like this, I mean, shit, this kind of Nazi bullshit—"

"It's scary," Marsh said, and his voice seemed too small for his six-foot tall frame. He grasped his elbows, leaning forward on his knees. "I just smoked some pot. That was it. Not half as much as my friends."

"What did you do that got you sent here?" Ralph asked Jack.

A silence.

Match died.

"Ralph," someone said in the dark.

Ralph wasn't sure who it was, but he waited in the dark for a moment because the ghosts of their faces still hung there, photographed by the last light of the match.

Scraped another one against the matchbook. The little flame came up.

Marsh continued. "With me, I thought they'd killed my folks and my sister and they were gonna do something terrible to me. And then I wished it was a dream. All of it."

"They hit you hard?" Hugh asked.

Marsh shrugged. "Yeah. They hit me. That's all. I barely felt it by then. I just figured they were gonna kill me. I figured if I just concentrated or something it would all happen and then it would be over. I thought it was because of the time I bought pot and got more than I paid for. That's what I thought. I didn't even think. I just figured that was it. It was over."

"And it's worse than that," Jack said. "You know what I heard my mother say when they put the blindfold on me? I heard her say—"

"No one cares," Ralph said, too wisely. "They all lied."

The boys fell silent for a minute.

"I thought it was gonna be like tough love or something."

"They sold us up a river."

Jesus opened his mouth as if to speak, but closed it again. Fear had sealed his lips.

"They did it because they love me," Jack said, but he was crying, he was fourteen and crying like a baby and Ralph decided then and there that he didn't care what the others thought. He leaned over and threw his arm over Jack's shoulder. It reminded him of when his little brother got scared of lightning or of nightmares, and even though Jack was his age, it seemed okay, it seemed like it was the only thing to do.

Jack leaned his head against Ralph's neck and wept while the others watched.

Jesus de Miranda wept, too. Ralph asked him why, and he said it was because he was afraid of the dark.

Ralph gave him one match to keep.

"For an emergency," he said, and all the boys watched as the little de Miranda boy put it in his pocket, as if the match were hope and someone needed to keep it.

Ralph kept lighting his matches as other boys gathered around in the darkness and told their stories of woe, and wept, and gave up what fight they had in them.

By the time Ralph's last match died, morning had come, and with it, silence until the foghorn blasted its wake-up call.

TO BE A MAN
   YOU MUST KILL THE CHILD
   YOU MUST BURY THE CHILD
   YOU MUST GROW UP

YOU MUST ACCEPT RESPONSIBILITY FOR YOUR ACTIONS

YOU MUST TAKE ON THE RESPONSIBILITIES OF OTHERS

YOU MUST BURN

YOU MUST FREEZE

YOU MUST GIVE YOURSELF TO US

The words were emblazoned on the side of the barrack wall, and every morning, Ralph knew, he would see those words, every morning, no matter how hard he tried to resist them, they would enter his soul. In the line up, they had to shout out the words, they had to shout them out loud, louder, I can't hear you, louder, over and over until it seemed as if those words were God.

"Number one!" the big man named Cleft shouted so loud in rang in their ears, pounding his chest hard as if he were beating it into his heart, "I am your priest, your father, your only authority, understand? I am Sergeant Cleft, and my colleagues and I, your superiors in every way, are here to drill you until you break. We are not interested in bolstering your gutless egos. We are not interested in making men out of you. You are the worst kinds of boys imaginable, every one of your families has disowned you, and we intend to break you down as far as is humanly possible to go. Then, if you have what it takes, you will build yourself up from the tools we give you here. Right now, this is Hell to you. But when we are through grinding your bones and spirits, this will be heaven. I don't want any quitters, either. You never give up, do you understand me, grunts? Never ever give up! This isn't a camp for sissies and pansies, and you aren't here because you been good little boys! You got sent here because you are headed for destruction! You got sent here because

you couldn't cut it like others your age! You got sent here
before someone sent you to jail! Before you destroyed your
families! Before you could keep up your stupid antisocial
ways!"

His barks sailed over them, for by dawn, even the terrified ones were ready to put up some resistance, even Ralph's
tears were dry and he spent the time imagining how to
escape from this island in the middle of nowhere, how to
get a message out to the authorities that he'd been
kidnapped against his will, and then he was going to sue his
parents for kidnapping, endangerment, and trauma.

He looked at Cleft with cold eyes, and wished the big
man dead. Cleft was muscle-bound, large, a baton in his
belt strap, pepper spray too, and something that looked like
a stun gun looped at his back. Ralph glanced around at the
others, the twenty three boys, all with dark-encircled eyes,
all looking scrawny from a night of no sleep and dreadful
fear, and he shouted inside his mind.

*How could they do this? How could all these parents do this
to their children? What kind of world was this?*

Morning had come too soon, and they'd been roused
and tossed in the open showers (like the Jews, Ralph
thought remembering the show on the History Channel,
like the Jews being thrown in showers and gassed, or hosed
down before they started on their backbreaking labor,
treated not like people but like cattle), and then they all had
been given uniforms, and the boys had complied. It struck
Ralph as strange how everyone accepted it all; as if this was
the Hell they were all consigned to, and there was no way
around it. The uniforms were brown like shit, that's what
Cleft had told them, "Like you, you are shit, and you will
look like shit until we make men out of you!" Then no

breakfast, but barrels of water just outside the showers, and each boy, if thirsty, had to stick his head in the barrel like an animal and drink. Some didn't, but Ralph did. He wanted water badly, he wanted to drink the entire barrel despite the other boys' spit he saw floating in it, and the insects that had fallen in. The bugs were everywhere, from sucking mosquitoes to huge winged beetles that flew at the screen door on the barracks. And what kind of island was it? Where? Was it the Caribbean? Ralph thought it might be off the coast of Mexico somewhere, something about the light of the sky, something about the water, but his experience was limited. He knew the island was flat where they stood, raised like a plateau. There were cliffs diving down to the sea, he'd seen them when the helicopter had brought him in the night, when the blindfold had slipped slightly and he'd glimpsed the rocky cliffs and the crashing waves far below.

"Grunt!" Cleft shouted, and Ralph looked up. Cleft pushed his way through the front line of boys in their shit-colored uniforms, and found him. Cleft looked like a parody of a marine, a steroid joke, a pit bull-human love child, and when he stood right in front of Ralph, Ralph wished he would wake up. Just wake up, he told himself. It's a dream. It has to be a dream. Piss your pants. Roll out of bed.

Cleft barked, "You worthless sack of owl dung, you keep your eyes on me, you understand? I seen a lot of boys come through here, and you are the sorriest ass piece of shit I ever saw. You hear me?"

Ralph kept his gaze forward, staring at a place just below Cleft's eyebrows, not *in* the eyes, but between them.

"I said, you hear me?"

Ralph trembled slightly, feeling his knees buckle. Hunger grew from a place not in his gut, but in his extremities, his fingers, toes, the top of his head, it was like a spider tingling along his skin, squeezing his nerves. His mouth felt dry.

"I hear you like to set fires, Pig Boy," Cleft almost whispered, but a whisper that boomed across the heads of all the other boys. "I hear you did something really nasty to another boy back home. I heard you—" Ralph shut his eyes for a second and in his mind he was flying over all the others, he was going up to the cottony clouds. He felt hunger leave him, he felt tension leave him, he felt everything fly away from his body.

With a sickening feeling, he opened his wet eyes.

Then Cleft glanced down from Ralph's face to his chest, then his crotch. Cleft laughed, a nasty sound. "Baby Pig Boy here has pissed his panties!" Cleft clapped his hands together. "He's pissed his panties like a big Baby Pig Boy, haw! You can put out a lot of fires with that piss, can't you Pig Boy?"

Then, Cleft shoved him hard in the chest, so hard Ralph fell backwards on his ass. He looked up at the big man, the bulging muscles, the sharp crew cut, the hawk nose, and gleaming teeth. "Let me show you how to put out a fire, men!" Cleft laughed as he spoke, unzipping his pants and Ralph screeched at first — like an owl — as the piss hit his face. Cleft continued shouting, telling him that to be a man, one had to first prove himself worthy of manhood, one had to accept humiliation at the hands of one's superior, one had to take what one deserved whether one liked it or not, one had to know one's place—"You like to set things on fire, grunt, but you need a man to put out the fire inside you!"

Just kill me, Ralph thought. *Just kill me.*

We are just like the Jews in the concentration camps, Ralph thought, glancing to the others who still had their eyes forward, their lips drawn downward, looking scrawnier and weaker than boys of thirteen to sixteen should look, looking like they would all have been happy to not have Cleft pissing on *them*, happy that Ralph was the first sacrifice of the day, happy to die.

Just die.

IT BECAME a routine that they neither looked forward to, nor complained about, and the others who had sat up with Ralph the first night never spoke together again. Ralph would give Marsh a knowing look, and Marsh would return it, but for a millisecond before his eyes glazed over in what Ralph came to think of as "Clefteye." It was the zombie-like way they were all getting, Ralph included. When he lay asleep in his lower bunk, he could hear Hugh weeping in his sleep, then whimpering like a puppy, and sometimes Ralph stayed up all night listening for Hugh to cry, and it would help him fall asleep if only for an hour or two. Food got better, but not good. From the first two days of water only, they went to bread and water.

By the end of the first week, they were having beans, rice, water, bread, and an apple. By the second week, it was beans, rice, water, bread, milk, apple, and some tasteless fish.

Ralph noticed that his diarrhea had stopped by the third

week, as did most of the boys'. The labor was grueling, but Ralph didn't mind it because while he hacked at the logs, or while he chipped at stone with what seemed to be the most primitive of tools, he remembered his family and home and his dog, and it was, after awhile, almost like being with them until the workday was over.

The maneuvers began at night.

Cleft, and the six others who ran the camp, had them running obstacle courses in the stench of evening when the mosquitoes were at their worst, when the mud was hot and slick, when the sweat could almost speak as it ran down his back. Wriggling like snakes beneath barbed wire, climbing ropes to dizzying heights, leaping from those heights into mud, running across narrow, stripped logs, piled end to end, it all became second nature after the initial falls and screams.

Foghorn, as they called a large boy in Hut D, fell and broke his leg the first day of the obstacle course, and Jesus, the little boy that Ralph had never heard say so much as a word, got cut on the barbed wire, badly, across his shoulders, and then got an infection when it went untreated.

After the third week, none of the boys saw Jesus anymore. Some said he'd been sent back home. Some said he'd died. Some said he'd run off. Some said it was all bullshit and he was probably back with his dad in New York City, lucky bastard, with a scar on his shoulder, and an excuse for not being in Camp Hell.

Rumors circulated that Jack and Marsh had been caught jacking each other off. The next time Ralph saw them, he also noticed bruises around their eyes and on their arms.

Boys had ganged up on them, but Ralph didn't want to know about it. He was somewhere else. He didn't need to be among any of them, he was in a place of family and fire in his head, and although his muscles felt like they were tearing open when he lay down in his bunk at night, he knew that he was growing stronger both inside and outside.

And then, one day, Jack came to him.

"Got any more matches?"

Ralph opened his eyes. It had to be four a.m., just an hour or so before First Call.

The shadow over him gradually revealed itself in the purple haze of approaching dawn.

"What the—"

"Matches?" Jack asked again. "You're like the fireboy, right?"

"No."

"Liar. Come on, wake up. We have something to show you."

"I don't care. Leave me alone." Ralph turned on his side, shutting his eyes.

"He pissed on you. Don't you hate him?"

Ralph kept his vision dark. If he didn't open his eyes, it might all go away. "I don't care."

"You will care," Jack said. The next thing Ralph knew, it was morning, the horn blasted, the rush of ice cold showers, the sting of harsh soap, the barrels of water and then chow. Out in the gravel pit, shoveling, someone tossed pebbles across Ralph's back. He looked over his shoulder.

"Leave me alone," Ralph spat, the dirt sweat sliding across his eyes; he dropped his shovel, looking back at Jack.

"You set fires back home, I know that," Jack whispered.

"We all know it. It's all right. It's what you love. Don't let them kill that. We need you."

"Yeah, well, we all did something. What did you do to get you sent here?"

Jack said nothing for a moment.

"We found Jesus," Jack said, and tears erupted in his eyes. Ralph wanted to shout at him not to cry anymore, there was no reason to cry, that he was weak to cry, just like Cleft said—

Ralph asked, "Where is he?"

"Dead," Jack said. "They killed him. They killed him and they hid him so we couldn't find him. Did you know he was only ten years' old?"

"Bullshit," Ralph gasped. "He's thirteen."

"Ten years' old and his father sent him here after he left his mother. His father sent him because his father didn't give a damn about him. You, Ralph, you set fires. And me, I maybe did some stuff I'm not real proud of. But Jesus, all he did was get born in the wrong family. And they killed him."

RALPH CLOSED HIS EYES.

Tried to conjure up the vision of his family and home again, and the beautiful fires he had set at the old shack in the woods, the fires that had made him feel weak and strong all at once and connected with the world. But only darkness filled his mind.

Opened his eyes.

Jack's face, the bruises lightening, his eyes deep and blue, the dark tan bringing out the depth of the color of those eyes, a God blue.

"Dead?"

"Yep." Jack said.

"How?"

Jack glanced over at Red Chief and Commodore, the two thugs disguised as soldiers who stood above the gravel pit, barking at some of the slower boys. "Keep digging, and I'll tell you, but do you know what I think we're digging?"

Ralph cocked his head to the side, trying to guess.

"Our own graves."

JACK CONTINUED. "Me and Marsh been trying to find a way out every single night. We wait till three thirty, when the goons are asleep with only one on watch, and we get mud all over us, and we do the snake thing and Marsh and me get away from the barracks until we go out on the island, and we see that there's no way anybody's getting off this island without killing themselves, that's why security ain't so tight. It's a nothing island, maybe two square miles at the most, with nothing. The thugs' huts are in the east, and between those and ours and the work pits, there ain't a hell of a whole lot. But we find this thin crack opening between these rocks just beyond the thug huts, and we squeeze in—that's all the bruises—"

"I thought you got beat up."

Jack held his temper. "That's what we said, dumbshit, so nobody would know."

"I thought you two…"

Jack cut in. "We spread that story, fool. So we squeeze through the opening, and it's too dark to see, and this cave that we're hoping will take us out ends within six feet of entering it, only we feel something there in the dark, we feel something all mushy and stinky and only when Marsh falls on it and screams does he realize it's a body."

❦

IT WAS JESUS DE MIRANDA, the littlest boy at camp, dead not from an infection but from something that smashed his hands up and his knees, too. Ralph heard the rest, tried to process it, but it made him sick.

"Where are we?" he whispered, leaning against Jack.

"All I know is, I think we're all dead."

"All?"

"I think," Jack said. "I think they're going to just kill all of us. I don't think any of us are leaving."

Jack stuck four small rocks in Ralph's pockets.

"Later. They'll be useful," Jack said.

"Just like the Concentration Camps," Ralph whispered, and then Commodore shouted at him, and he returned to shoveling while the blistering sun poured lava on his back.

❦

"I SAID GET UP HERE, you worthless Pig Boy!" Commodore yelled.

By the time Ralph made it up from the pit, crawling along the edges, he scraped his knees up and was out of breath.

"Something you want to share with the rest of us?" Commodore said, his eyes invisible behind his mirrored sunglasses. "I saw you chattering down there, Pig Boy."

"Don't call me that," Ralph coughed.

"Something wrong?"

Ralph covered his mouth, hearing the balloon hiss of air from his lungs.

"Asthma," he gasped. "I don't have…my inhaler…"

"It's all in your tiny brain, Pig Boy, you don't need some inhaler like a mama's boy, you just need to focus. You need to be a man, Pig Boy," Commodore laughed, and shoved Ralph down in the dirt. Ralph felt his windpipe closing up, felt his lungs fight for air. He could not even cough. His eyes watered up, and he opened his mouth, sucking at air.

Commodore lifted him up again, bringing his face in line with Ralph's. Eye to eye, Commodore snarled, "Breathe, damn you!"

Ralph gasped. He knew he would die. He knew his lungs would stop. His vision darkened until all he could see were the man's brown eyes. He thought of little Jesus, dead, his hands smashed into bloody clay. Dust seemed to fill his mouth.

"Breathe!" Commodore continued, and reached over, pressing his hand down hard on Ralph's chest. "You want to be a man, Pig Boy, you breathe like a man, open up those lungs, make 'em work," and suddenly, air whooshed into Ralph's mouth.

The darkness at the edge of his vision erased itself into the light of day.

Ralph sucked at the air like he was starving for it.

"There," Commodore said, and pushed Ralph back down in the dirt. "You boys, you think you can create the world in your own image. That's your problem. You think you can keep from growing up. Well, growing up means accepting the burden just like the rest of us. Accept it, accept the truth, and you'll thrive. Keep doing what you've been doing, and you'll die."

Ralph sat on the ground, staring up at the man. The air tasted pure. He gulped it down, feeling his lungs burn.

TO BE A MAN
  YOU MUST KILL THE CHILD
  YOU MUST BURY THE CHILD
  YOU MUST GROW UP
  YOU MUST ACCEPT RESPONSIBILITY FOR YOUR ACTIONS
  YOU MUST TAKE ON THE RESPONSIBILITIES OF OTHERS
  YOU MUST BURN
  YOU MUST FREEZE
  YOU MUST GIVE YOURSELF TO US

They shouted it in the morning, still shivering from the icy waters that erased their dreams, standing in the shimmering day, a mirage of day, for in their hearts, they never felt dawn.

At night, Last Call, the bells ringing three times, running for a last cold shower, running for the latrine, and then Light's Out.

"He's under the hut," Jack said.

He'd gathered Hugh, Marsh, a boy named Gary, a boy named Lou, and Ralph wanted to see, too, to see if they were telling the truth about Jesus. At three a.m., they all hunkered down, crawling like it was another maneuver under barbed wire to get out of the hut unnoticed; then under the hut's raised floor, down a narrow tunnel that might've been dug out by jackals.

Jack and Marsh had dug an entrance that led down into a larger hole, and there, in the dark, they all felt Jesus' body, smelled it, some vomited, others gagged.

Ralph reached into the dead boy's pocket and drew out the last match, the one he'd given the little boy the first night they'd met to keep him from the dark.

Ralph struck the match against a rock, and it sputtered into crackling light.

They all looked at Jesus, at the rotting, the insects already devouring his puffy face, the way his hands were bloody pulps, his kneecaps all but destroyed.

"Holy—"

"—Shit"

"They did it," Jack said.

"Mother—"

"Yeah—"

"Holy—"

"Is that really him?" Gary asked.

"It has to be," Marsh said.

"Who else?" Ralph said, and then the last match died.

Sitting in the dark, the stink of the boy's corpse filling them, Ralph said, "If we let this go, we'll die. Right here. You all know about concentration camps in World War II. You all know what happens. This is just like it."

"Yeah," Lou said. "They killed him. Man, I can't believe it. I can't believe my mom would send me here. I can't believe…"

"Believe," Jack said. Ralph felt Jack's hand give Ralph a

squeeze. "Maybe our folks don't know what they do here. Shit, I doubt Jesus' father even knows."

"I can't believe it either," Ralph said. "They're monsters."

"They aren't human, that's for sure," Marsh added.

"What are we gonna do?" Jack asked the darkness.

"What can we do?" Ralph countered.

"Someone should so something," Gary moaned.

Then, they crawled out of the ground, up to their hut. The diffuse moonlight spattered the yard, lit the barracks and huts and showers and the boy's faces were somehow different in the night, flatter, more alike than Ralph had remembered them being. Before they went inside, Jack turned to Ralph and said, "Too bad you wasted that match. We could've set fire to this place with it."

Ralph said almost to himself, "I've never needed a match to set a fire."

❧

IN THE MORNING, a quiet permeated the camp, and when the boys trooped out to shout their pledge of allegiance to the dawn, their mouths stopped up as if their tongues had been cut off.

On the side of the barrack wall, the words:

TO BE A GOD
YOU MUST KILL THE ENEMY
YOU MUST BURY THE ENEMY
YOU MUST NEVER GROW UP
YOU MUST BURN THEM
YOU MUST FREEZE THEM
YOU MUST GIVE YOURSELF TO THE CAUSE
OF JESUS

There, besides the hastily scrawled revision, written in rough chalk, the body of Jesus de Miranda, held up by barbed wire twisting like vines around his limbs and torso.

Ralph glanced at Jack, who laughed, and then to Marsh who had a tear in his eye. Behind them, Cleft came striding, whistle in his mouth, wearing a green baseball cap and green fatigues. "Into the showers, you pansy ass bitches!" Cleft shouted, blowing the whistle intermittently.

Then the whistle dropped from his mouth. He saw the writing. He saw the boy's body.

Cleft reached up and drew his baseball cap off, letting it fall to the ground. He let out a whisper that sounded like, "Holy."

And then the rocks.

Jack had made sure there were enough, just enough, for ten of the boys, Ralph included and they leapt on Cleft, stronger now, their own biceps built up from weeks of labor.

Cleft tried to reach for the pepper spray, but he had to raise his hands defensively to ward off the blows. Cleft was like a mad bull, tossing them off to the side, but the rocks slammed and slashed at his face, tearing his hawk nose open, a gash above his eye blinding him with blood flow, and as the red explosions on his face increased, Ralph felt something overpowering within him.

He became the most ferocious, ramming at Cleft with all his weight, cutting deep into Cleft's shoulder with the sharp edge of a rock, bringing the big man to his knees.

Ralph grabbed for Cleft's belt, tearing it off the loops, holding up the pepper spray and stun gun and baton.

Ralph lifted the baton in the air and brought it down hard on Cleft's skull.

And then all of the boys leapt upon Cleft.

❧

"Yes!" Ralph shouted, high-fiving Jack, running with the others — a pack of wolves — across the muddy ground, through the steamy heat, rocks held high, Cleft's pepper spray in Ralph's left hand.

Jack held the stun gun, and Marsh, the fastest runner of them all was in the lead, waving the baton that still had Cleft's fresh blood on it.

They shrieked the words of rebellion they'd written on the Wall. Several of the boys had taken down the body of Jesus de Miranda and hoisted it like a battering ram between them as they flew to the sergeants' barracks.

They caught the masters in their showers, mid-coffee, shaving, cutting at them with their own razors, scalding them, beating them, until two more were dead, and the others unconscious.

Later, Ralph remembered the feeling of all of them, all the boys together, moving as one, storming the island, like lava overflowing a volcano.

❧

When it was mostly finished and night covered them, Ralph leaned toward Commodore; the man was tied to a chair, his great muscles caught in wire. Ralph held out a cigarette lighter, a souvenir from a downed sergeant.

Stepping forward, Ralph struck the lighter, the flame coming forth.

"Arsonist, murderer," Commodore said, his eyes blood-shot, his face a mass of bruises.

"Shut up or I'll cut out your tongue," Jack laughed. Ralph looked back at him, and wondered if, like Jack, he was covered with blood as well. He heard the shouts of the other boys as they raided the food supply.

"We didn't kill that little boy, you dumbfuck," Commodore said.

"Okay, here goes the tongue," Jack said, coming up to the bound man, clippers in hand.

"Liar," Ralph said, twisting the lighter in front of Commodore's face.

"One of you must've done it, "Commodore spat, but it was the last thing he said, for Jack had the clippers in his mouth. Ralph couldn't look, it wasn't something he enjoyed, but Jack had that glow on him, his whole body radiated with his joy.

The man didn't even try to scream.

Ralph looked at the blood on Jack's hands.

"Jesus, Jack," Ralph said, feeling the spinning world come back to him, the world of sanity that had somehow gotten out of control. "Jesus, Jack."

"What?" Jack laughed, dropping the clippers, clapping his red hands together.

Ralph looked back at the man, his mouth a blossom of bright red.

The man's eyes did not leave Ralph's face.

Ralph was amazed that the man didn't cry out in pain, that he kept his eyes forward, on Ralph, not pleading, not begging, but as if he were trying to let some truth up from his soul.

"Jack," Ralph went over to his friend, his blood-covered

friend, his friend who had helped him get through this time in Hell. "Was he lying?"

"Yep," Jack said, averting his gaze. The blood ran down his face like tears. "He's one of them. They always lied to us."

"You sure?"

Jack closed his eyes. "Yep."

Then, "Did you and Marsh kill Jesus?"

Jack opened his eyes, staring straight at him. "If that were true, would it change anything? Jesus is dead. He came here. They did all this."

Ralph felt his heart stop for a moment, and then the beating in his chest became more rapid.

"We're just like them," Ralph whispered, mostly to himself.

"No," Jack grinned, blood staining his teeth, "They're weak. We're strong. They're time is up. Ours is just beginning."

"What did you do that got you sent here?" Ralph asked for the last time.

"Nothing," Jack said. "Nothing that you need to know about."

"You killed someone, didn't you?"

"It was nothing, believe me," Jack smiled. "And you've done some killing yourself today, haven't you?"

"I wouldn't have if—"

"You'll never know," Jack slapped Ralph on the back. "But it's okay. I understand."

Later, the man they called Commodore died.

❦

JACK FOUND Ralph in the dark, sitting on a bench outside the barracks. He put his arm over Ralph's shoulders and whispered, "Now we can go home. We can go home and make them all pay."

"Are we men yet?" Ralph asked, feeling an icy hand grab him around the chest, under his skin, closing up his throat until his voice was barely a whimper.

"No," Jack said. "We're better than men. We're gods. Come on, let's play with fire. You'll feel better after that, won't you?"

He stood, drawing Ralph up by the hand. "You're good at fires, Ralph. We need you. I need you."

"I don't know," Ralph said. "Yesterday it was one thing. It seemed different. Jesus was dead. They were like the Nazis."

"I need you," Jack repeated, squeezing Ralph's hand tight, warm, covering Ralph's fingers in his. "You as you are, Ralph. Not what they wanted. As you are. I want you."

Ralph felt his fingers curl slightly under the weight of Jack's. He looked down at their hands and then up at Jack's face. "I can't."

"No shame," Jack said, "Let's set it all on fire. Glorious fire. Let's make it burn all the way up to the sun."

"That's my dream," Ralph whispered, a shock of recognition in Jack's words, a secret between the most intimate of friends. "How did you know my dream? My first night here, I saw it in my mind, a fire going all the way to the sun."

They stood there, frozen for a moment; then, Jack slowly let go of Ralph's hand, leaving in his palm a new silver lighter. "Go set fires across the land."

BEFORE THE SUN rose from the sea into an empty sky, the fires got out of hand.

Ralph realized — putting aside other considerations — that it was the most beautiful thing he had ever seen in his young life, the way fire could take away what was right in front of his eyes, just burn it off with no reason other than its own hunger.

Jack said it was the best day he'd ever had, and when the burning was done, the boys ran off to the showers, all except for Ralph who went in search of something new to burn.

A Madness of Starlings

W hat possessed me to retrieve the little fledgling, I
can't say for sure. I rescued the baby bird from the
jaws of the tiger-striped tomcat that had been stalking it. I
wanted to show my boys that the smallest of life sometimes
needed protection from the predators.

I brought it into the house, hoping to wait out the cat's
bloodlust. My two boys came out to look at it. I warned
them not to touch the bird just then. "The less contact it
has with people, the better."

After an hour, I took the bird outside again. My kids
watched from the living room window.

It hopped in the tall summer grass that I had not gotten
to with the mower. Its mouth opened wide, up to the skies,
expecting its mother to come with food.

I stepped back onto the porch and scanned the area to
make sure no cat returned. I hoped that the bird's mother
would return and feed it so that the balance of nature could
be restored and I'd have no more responsibility.

An hour later, the fledgling continued to hop and

squawk and open its mouth to heaven. No mother arrived. I had lost my own mother when young, and did not like remembering this when I saw the bird I came to call Fledge. Loss was the bad thing in life. I hated it, and didn't wish it on a baby bird.

I took the little guy in, and my wife, Jeanette, and the boys (little William and tall Rufus) helped me build a cage for it as part of our "Saturday Family Project." At first, Fledge would not eat from my hand — or from a straw. But we picked up some mealworms and crickets from the pet store in town, and soon enough, the little guy hunted them up on the floor of his cage.

Devouring fifty worms a day and perhaps ten crickets, Fledge grew fast.

&.

WITHIN FIVE DAYS, the little guy had full feathers and the boys and I took him into the rec room from flight training. He flew from Rufus' fingers to the bookcase.

I had to put a stepladder up to rescue him from the highest shelf.

"We have to let him go," I told the boys. "He's ready to fly. He's eaten a lot and knows how to catch crickets and peck for worms on his own."

"Isn't he a pet?" William pleaded. "He's ours now."

Rufus, the elder at nine, added, "He can't survive out there, Dad. He can't. He's too used to us."

"It's only been a week," I said. "He belongs out there."

"I heard birds only live a couple of years out there," Rufus said. "I bet in his cage, he'd live a long time."

"He's a wild bird, he's meant to be out there. Besides,

when we go to Florida in February, who's going to take care of him?

Will you clean the cage for the next twelve years if he lives that long? Every day that cage needs cleaning," I said.

Rufus looked very sad, and William's eyes glistened with the easy tears of a little boy who won't accept loss. "But Daddy," he said. "Daddy, I love Fledge."

"I know," I said. "But don't you want Fledge to be happy?"

William nodded. "I want him safe."

"He's happy here," Rufus said. "Now. He won't be happy when a cat gets him. Or when an eagle gets him."

"We don't have eagles around here."

"Or when he gets some disease and nobody takes him to the vet."

"I'm going to miss him," William said. "So long, Fledge."

"Look, he'll be around the yard. He's a starling. They're always here. He'll probably fly around and make a nest under your bedroom window."

William's eyes brightened. A smile crept across his face.

Noticing that I had turned the corner on William's emotional rollercoaster and now things were heading upward, I said, "And whenever you see him hurt, you can run out and bring him in and we'll take him to the bird doctor, if you want."

Rufus had begun to scowl. "I saw a dead bird out by the curb. That's what's going to happen to him if we let him go."

"Roof," I said. "Roof, look. When you grow up, we're going to let you go. You're going to fly away. And as much as I'd like to put you in a cage here so I can always see you, I know that's going to be wrong."

Of course, he didn't understand this. Rufus felt he'd never leave the house or his parents or the protected world of childhood.

But *I* knew he would.

I knew the bird needed to get out and live just like my kids would one day need to get out and spread their wings. Even when the tomcats of life got them.

The shelter of childhood was temporary, at best.

The boys put up more protests, with Rufus cataloguing the bleak prospects of a bird in our suburban world. I countered his arguments with tales of birds flying over the treetops, or Mother Nature, or how Fledge saw us as giant monsters that were not like his parents or brothers and sisters. "Starlings have to fly twenty miles a day to really enjoy life."

Finally, I let the discussion die down. When the boys were out playing with friends, I took Fledge onto my fingers, and leaned out the second floor window of our house.

The bird flew off.

Just as it got up into the air, clearing an overgrown azalea bush, another bird came down and began attacking it mid-air.

I felt panic and genuine terror.

I worried about the little guy, trying his wings out for the first time. Fledge continued flying toward a crabapple tree in the front yard. Fledge turned, almost as if he were looking at me. His mouth opened wide as he squawked like a baby. In that moment, I didn't see the bird; I saw my boys.

I HAD a premonition of a moment of terror in life when I would let go of my sons' hands and they would go off and the world would do its own version of attack on them. My imagination went haywire as I imagined Rufus in his early twenties in a foreign land, felled by bullets in a war; and William, injecting heroin into his arms, surrounded by lowlife friends in some crack house.

As I watched Fledge, he fluffed up his feathers and spread his wings wide and flew over the rooftop. I raced to the bathroom window, and saw Fledge flying over other houses, off through the neighborhood.

Fledge had made it past the attacking bird. Past the trees. We had done it, I thought. We helped Fledge get strong and healthy and become an adult, and he was going to live his life the way he was meant to live it. My brief insanity, those split-second visions of my boys, the dreadful futures I imagined for them — all of it dissipated and I laughed at myself and the way my mind worked.

Later, I told the boys that Fledge had flown off, and that he was fine. They moped a bit, but the more we talked about Fledge and Fledge's life, the better my children seemed to understand why Fledge had to go.

That first night, I went and sat in front of Fledge's empty cage. Beyond the cage, a window looked out on trees. I opened the window and lifted the screen. Part of me felt that Fledge might come back, or if he was hurt, he might show up for food again.

I kept the window open for three days, and then shut it.

I missed the bird.

We had kept the little guy for five days, but it was enough for me to begin to think about life and nature and to wake up each day hoping Fledge had not died in the night. Out the window, other starlings and robins and mockingbirds flew around, but I kept watch for Fledge. I brought out the old binoculars from the cabinet in the garage, and, early in the morning — before even my wife awoke — I went to the window and looked out. I whistled sometimes when I was in the yard, thinking Fledge might hear my voice.

Then, at twilight, I spoke to my wife, Jeanette, about the bird.

"It's a starling," she said. "They're nuisances. I bet the state would've paid you to kill it."

"Stop that," I said. "It needed help."

"I know. I'm kidding. Really. I'm kidding. But the bird's fine. Believe me. You protected it. You got the boys to think about nature a little. And now that bird's off doing what birds do."

"I never really noticed starlings before," I said. "I mean, I knew they were out there."

"God, in the fall they just swarm. Freaks me out sometimes. Like the Hitchcock movie."

"I was out in the yard this morning," I said. "I couldn't stop looking in the trees. And on the roof. I just figured he'd stick around."

She gave me a funny look, as if she were trying to figure out if I were joking or not. "Honey? It's a bird. You really want a bird, we'll get a cockatiel. But I don't really want a bird," she said.

"I don't want a bird, either," I said. Then, I laughed at

myself, and she giggled, too. We had some coffee and went out on the patio. We sat in the old deck chairs that were gray from years of neglect. "But it's funny."

"What's that?"

"Loss. All of life is about loss."

"No, it's not." She laughed and told me I had better not get depressed on her.

"Life has loss in it," she said, when she saw that I was a little hurt by her laughter. "But look, we both have great jobs, the kids are great. We're building to something. We have love. There's a lot in life besides loss."

"Someday, we'll lose everything. I mean it. I'm not sad about it. I guess I'm wistful."

"Wistful is sad."

"No it's not. Someday, the boys will go out into the world. Not everyone survives it. God, maybe I'll get heart disease. Or some…some accident will happen."

"You're getting morbid," she said. "I hate this kind of stuff. You shouldn't say it. It's too dark."

"I'm trying to grasp this thing. I'm nearly forty, and I want to be prepared. I want a good mindset."

"That bird," she said. "It got you thinking like this."

"It's nuts, I guess," I said.

"Not nuts, honey. But it's…it's useless. We have a good life. Bad things don't always happen. That bird. That bird is probably off flying around, happy as hell to be out of the cage and back in its natural environment. It's probably flocking with other starlings, devouring someone's grass seed or chasing off squirrels from a nest that it's building with a mate. It's an adult by now. It's fine. That's how life goes."

"Did you hear that?" I asked, startled as I glanced over at her.

She held her coffee mug near her lips, watching me. "What?"

"That sound. Was that Fledge?"

I heard it again. The bickering squawk of a starling. Somewhere among the trees.

"No. Wait," she said. "No."

Then, I heard a chirp at the rooftop. I looked up — it was a sparrow.

"Come here," Jeanette said.

I glanced over at her. She had raised her eyebrows ever so slightly, her version of close-up seduction.

"What for?"

"Just come here." She set her mug down on the little table, and scooched back in her chair. "Sit with me."

"We'll break the chair."

"Throw caution to the wind."

I went over, and she put her arms around me. Kissed me on the forehead. "My big baby who loves birds."

Deftly, she slipped her fingers to the buttons of my shirt, and opened them, her hands going to my chest, combing through the patch of hair. I kissed her, and she whispered, "The boys won't be back from the Nelson's 'til nine. Nobody can see us."

We made love in that uncomfortable deck chair, in that desperate way that old marrieds do, trying to recapture the wildness of premarital sex. Somewhere in the rapture of it all, I heard the chattering of starlings in the trees, and glanced up.

"What is it?" she asked. "Why did you stop?"

"I thought..." I didn't want her to know what I was thinking, so I kissed her on the lips. "Maybe we should do this later."

"Why?"

"I feel funny. What if someone sees us?"

"Nobody can see us."

"I feel like someone can," I said.

"So, we give 'em a show. Greatest show on earth."

"Naw," I said, trying to sound warm and cuddly and friendly, but I drew my underwear and pants back up, and buttoned my shirt. She left hers open, but drew her knees together.

"Since when do you turn down outdoors sex?" she asked.

"We've never had outdoors sex till now."

"I remember a certain hot August night on a lake in a little boat with life preservers as pillows," she said. "August 18th."

"You remember the date?"

"Sure. We were out at the lake. It was when we..."

She didn't have to finish the thought. It was the year before we conceived Rufus. It was to be our first child, the one who came from sex in the boat out on the lake at midnight. But she had lost the baby within four months. Eight months later, she was pregnant with Rufus.

I didn't like to be reminded of the first child.

THAT NIGHT, after my wife fell asleep, I went out to the patio for a cigarette. My first in three years. I kept the pack of Gitanes in an old backpack I'd had since college. It hung on a nail in the garage. Inside the pack, besides the French cigarettes I'd learned to smoke on a post-graduate trip to Paris, there was a bottle of Grand Marnier that had never been opened, a T-shirt with various obscenities written on it, and a pair of swimming trunks I had not been able to fit into since my twenties.

The cigarette tasted great, and I followed the first with a second. I thought of Fledge, up in one of the trees, his little leg hidden under his feathers, with the other leg down, small claws clutching a tree branch.

*

THE FOLLOWING SATURDAY, I took the boys for a hike. First, to a drug store to get some candy, and then up to the unincorporated area of town where there was a bike trail by the old railroad tracks. The boys seemed to have fun, running ahead of me, climbing rocks, finding a penny or quarter, balancing on the railroad ties. But I had begun hearing the birds. I heard more and more of them as we got deeper into the woods. Starlings, certainly, but also the caws of crows; the songbirds, too, with their chirps and whistles. I felt like I would hear Fledge's distinct squawk, but did not, and even while I told the kids to watch out for broken glass on the trail, or not to touch the poison ivy, part of me had blocked even my own children out.

I had never noticed so many birds before. Most of them were unseen, but their voices seemed loud, even annoying. Bickering in the skies, chattering in treetops, their language must have meant something to them. They must be communicating with each other. Mating. Attacking. Flocking.

Twilight came, and back at home, Jeanette made it bath time for the boys because of the dirt all over their faces.

I went to the second floor bedroom window, and

climbed out onto the ledge, and sat on the roof. Smoked a cigarette. Leaned back, and looked up at the veiled sky and the darkening clouds in the distance.

Distinct voices of the birds. Not just the usual cacophony. I felt as if my ears had begun to notice precisely how one sparrow chirped, how the swallows spoke to each other, and those starlings — their nastiness, their territorial voices that spoke of battle and ownership. I began to hear something in the world I'd never really heard before.

❧

"ARE YOU ALL RIGHT?" Jeanette asked that night. We lay in bed. Lights on. She had just put down the book she'd been reading.

"Of course."

"You're staring at the ceiling."

"I'm thinking. You know, there must be something weird about life. We took that little guy in for five days, and now I just notice birds. I've never noticed them before."

"What's that called?"

"What do you mean?"

"It's called something. When you didn't notice something. Then you do. Then you notice it's all around you all the time."

"Crazy?"

She grinned. "No. No. And it's not about something being ubiquitous, either. It's something else. Like when you've never heard a word before, and suddenly, once you've heard it, it's everywhere you look."

"I keep listening for him."

"For who?"

"Fledge."

"Honey," she said. "Aw. Poor baby. I miss the little guy too. You should be proud of yourself. You rehabbed a bird and set it free. That's what life should be about."

"I read about starlings. Online. They're non-native. They were brought here by a guy who released a hundred of them in Central Park in 1890. He wanted to introduce birds that were in Shakespeare's plays. So he brought starlings, among others. I read that in the wild they don't live all that long. In captivity, they can live up to twenty years."

She lay down and turned to me, her eyes like warm muddy pools. "I would rather have a few years among my own kind, with a life of mating and birth and, yes, even death, than twenty years alone in a cage."

"He wouldn't have been alone," I said. And then, "Aw, this is silly. I'm silly."

"Yes, you are. It's not about the bird, is it?"

"I told you before. It's about loss."

"I know. Life does have a lot of loss in it. You're almost forty. You'll probably start buying sports cars and chasing blondes."

"No. I'm not that guy," I said. "I just hate how life takes everything away."

"That's ridiculous. Think of all the people in the world and what they don't have. Now, think of all that you have. And tell me how life takes everything away from you."

"Not from me, personally. From everyone. Nobody really tells you that when you're Rufus' age. We protect our kids from it. But it's there."

"God. That fucking bird," she said.

She turned away from me, and reached over to flick the light off.

THAT WAS ORDINARY LIFE, but the extraordinary had entered my life through the voices of birds. Whenever I went outside, or opened a window, I heard them. Too many of them. The voices all going on about food and shelter and war and children and work and flight and anger and joy. I could tell that much from the tones of their voices. I noticed that when a storm came, the gulls from the bay — a good hour from us — suddenly were on our rooftop. But then, I began to hear the voices of the birds change when a storm was predicted, as if they knew, many hours before a thunderstorm reached us, that it was going to descend. Any changes in their voices, or the amount of bickering, heralded nestlings. I began to hate crows, for I saw them dive for the babies, and heard the awful wailing of the mother birds at the death of a child.

Then, one evening we watched a TV show on a Wednesday night; it was still light out; I began to hear the birds squawking and thought I heard Fledge, so I went to the window, opening it.

"WHAT'S UP?" Jeanette asked.

"I heard something."

She turned the television's volume down, and listened. "I don't hear anything. What was it?"

"Nothing," I said. I had begun to lie to her about hearing the birds outside. Listening for Fledge, trying to see if there was a message I should be hearing. That's what I had begun thinking: there was a message that might be delivered to me. Delivered unto me — it had begun to seem religious to me. Birds brought omens. God might speak through birds. I knew that was just my imagination, but something spiritual had entered my life through the sounds of the birds.

I took a day off from work, but didn't tell my family. Instead, I took some binoculars and spent the day up in my sons' tree fort, which nearly went into the thick woods behind our house.

I took water and sandwiches and soda; when I had to pee, I just peed off the tree. I listened all day to the birds, and I began to feel a change within me — toward nature. It made me sad in some way, because I began to see my wife as someone who would never truly understand me, and with whom I might never genuinely communicate what was within me. I loved my boys, but I knew they had other lives to live.

They, too, would develop their own secret languages and matings and lives.

I might never understand them fully as I could never fully comprehend my wife.

I began to take personal days off from work, and just wander the woods, or walk along the bike trail. I'd get lost for hours at a time in the deep forest that should not have been there — for there was a shopping mall two miles away, and a town on either side. Yet, a forest existed, and I could lose myself in it for half a day without seeing another human being.

There were arguments at home that escalated into shouting matches.

I became less tolerant of the boys' behavior when they crossed a line. At work, I just didn't deal with others much and spent most of my time pretending to be buried in projects that I knew I'd never finish. On my lunch break, I'd go out to the park and sit and listen to pigeons and yet more starlings, and watch as they flew and stole bits of food from near the trash cans and dive-bombed someone who sat too close to a hidden nest.

On a bitter day of bad reports at work, and a wife who didn't even want me to come home, I walked along the bike path in the woods, and could not stand the voices of the birds anymore.

I wept in my wife's arms that night, and told her I had some kind of madness in me. She cooed into my ear and told me she loved me and that it would pass, whatever it was, and if it didn't, we'd get help.

"It's all the loss," she said. "You didn't cry when we lost the baby. You didn't cry when your mother died. That bird did it. It reminded you of loss. It got to you."

The bird had changed me. The bird had never left me. I longed for the kingdom of birds rather than the kingdom of men. The voices of birds seemed, to me, to be more about life than the voices of mankind.

❧

A CALL CAME in to work for me, but I didn't pick up. I just let my voice mail get it, and it wasn't until my wife messaged me on the cell phone that I paid attention.

She wrote:

Emergency Room.

When I got there, she was trembling and pale. I held her, and she whispered, "William."

Strangely, I noticed a man nearby who looked as if he

had just done something terrible. He spoke to a nurse and mentioned "birds."

I suppose that was why I noticed him at all. Later, I learned that he had been the one driving the car.

DURING THE SIX months after my son's death, I began to listen only to the birds. I barely acknowledged Jeanette, and though I loved Rufus dearly, I could not bear to look at him for he reminded me too much of his little brother. I smoked my Gitanes in the open now, for my wife could not chide me during this time.

I spent long afternoons and evenings out on a lawn chair, beneath the sycamores and maples, my eyes skyward as I watched the dark flocks of starlings readying for winter. Their words comforted me, and took me elsewhere as they spoke of distant places of warmth and insects. Though I often thought of William's warm fingers in my hand or his soft whisper at bedtime, the birds told me about life and death and loss and continuations and how the spring brought hope and summer brought plenty. I also heard about the deaths of birds, of sorrow, of a mate shot down by a thoughtless boy with a gun, of marriages and the ends of marriages, of wounds that never healed, and feuds between siblings that continued to the end of life.

Laid off from my job by October third — in a massive layoff that left thousands without work — I came home to an empty house. By empty, I mean, bereft, without human voice. Jeanette and Rufus had left a couple of weeks earlier to stay at her sister's in the next town over, but they would be back (so my wife promised) or things would change or something. I wasn't clear on the details.

In the early morning, I went out in my boxers and sat on the back lawn. The earth had turned hard and cold, and the wind was strong. I listened for the birds, and leaned back, my arms crossed behind my head. Still sleepy, I began to doze when a voice brought me up from sleep.

What the voice had said, I am not sure. It seemed like my name or a name. The sound was nearly like a child's voice. Perhaps I had been dreaming that it was my dead son's voice.

I opened my eyes. There, on a slender leafless branch above me, a starling. Dark, and mottled with the yellow stars of adulthood, and — I was sure — it was Fledge himself. Watching me.

"Fledge?" I asked, but then laughed at my foolishness for asking a bird its name.

The bird cocked its head to the left and the right, and then hopped down to the ground. It fluttered over and hopped up on my chest. It began squawking and making a whistling sound that was a fairly good mimic of my own whistle.

Then, it hoped closer to my face.

Instead of a whistle, it spoke to me. "William," said the bird.

As I lay there, stunned by this hallucination, the bird flew away.

Now, of course I thought I had lost my mind, but I had to

know something I didn't know before. Something I'd never really asked or followed up on.

I went to visit the man whose car had hit and killed my little boy.

❦

"Yes?"

The door opened, and the man, who I guessed was about fifty, opened the door to his apartment. He lived in a rough neighborhood near the city, but had not lived there at the time of the accident. He had lived, the day when my son stepped off the curb, in a nice house, larger than my family's place, but the death of my son had changed him as much, if not more, than it had changed us. His own life had fallen apart. His wife and he had divorced. He had a grown daughter who blamed him, though it had been apparent that he had been driving the speed limit and had done what he could to avoid hitting my son and several children who had stepped into the street in heavy traffic. He had only hit my son, but four children's lives had been spared, including my eldest, Rufus.

Yet, his life had spiraled downward.

I saw it in the apartment building, which was dark and filthy.

I saw it in his eyes, as well. "Oh," he said, recognizing me. He didn't ask the next question, but it hung there as if he had: What do you want?

"You said something. I barely heard it. I guess I wasn't listening."

He opened the door a bit wider, but looked at me with

a kind of anticipation as if I might swing a punch at him. "I'm sorry," he said. "I really am."

"You said something about birds," I said.

"Oh." He looked over my shoulder as if expecting others to be with me. "The birds."

"What was it about birds. I overheard it. We were standing there, at the hospital. But I just caught the tail end of it. I didn't even know who you were at the time."

"I can't remember," he said.

"It's important. To me." Without realizing it, I had begun sobbing, and I suppose my body heaved with each exhalation of grief.

He came out into the hallway, and put his arm around my shoulder. "Come in. I'll get you some water."

§.

INSIDE THE APARTMENT, on a green, worn couch, I sipped from a glass. Vodka, not water. It tasted good.

He sat across from me. Behind him, the television was on, but the sound had been muted. "I don't remember about birds. Look, I'm sorry. I have nightmares about what happened. I see his face."

"Me, too."

"I see all their faces. If I had only…if I had only stopped for the ice cream my wife wanted. If I had just taken the short cut instead of driving down Apple Valley Road."

"I know. I think if I had just made him stay home from school. If I had just told Rufus not to play after school. 'If only' drives you nuts. I'm weary from it."

"Yeah."

"You said something about birds. At the Emergency Room. You were speaking to a nurse."

"Oh," he said. A shadow passed over his face. "Oh. The birds. I saw them. Blackbirds. I think that's what the kids were doing. There was a bird in the street. I saw it, too. Just sitting there, and I thought it was going to get hit by somebody. I think that's why the kids went in the street. Maybe I'm wrong. I don't know." He emptied his glass, and sighed. "Does it matter? I'm sorry. I'll be sorry for the rest of my life."

"It was an accident," I said, and then rose, setting my glass on the glass table.

&

I waited for Rufus after school. When he saw me, he looked at me as if I were the enemy. He walked cautiously to the car, and leaned into the open window.

"Come on, I'll drive you to Mom's."

"She's gonna be mad."

"She'll be mad when she sees me. At least she won't be mad at you."

Driving him to his mother's place — which really was his aunt's large home where they were staying for a few weeks until everything somehow either worked out or didn't — I said, "You doing okay?"

He remained quiet.

"I want to ask about something."

Again, no response from my boy.

"All right. Look. That day. That *day*. Was there a bird? Or a flock of birds?"

He looked at me, his eyes seeming to flash with anger.

Then, back to the road ahead. Then, he blurted, "Don't ever talk to me about that day again. I mean it. I never want to think about it."

As I dropped him off at his aunt's house, he slid out of his seat and had not yet swung the door shut. I said, "Just tell me. Why did you go in the street at all? There was traffic."

"Ask William," Rufus said, his face a mask of childhood fury, which was both pale and burning. "He's the only one who knows. I was trying to stop him. I was trying to stop him. Nobody believes me. I was trying to stop him!"

MY WIFE CALLED me on the cell phone ten minutes later and yelled at me for making Rufus upset. She said he had gone all fetal and wouldn't talk to anybody and that if I showed up at his school again she didn't know what she'd do, but she'd do something.

I barely heard her — the birds were talking outside, and I went out to them and tried to decipher what they were saying.

Winter had not quite come 'round the bend, but autumn had exploded briefly like a firecracker and stripped the trees bare.

On the twisted branches, the dark swarms of starlings began chanting.

I STOOD THERE, in awe of them, their beauty and their language and their flight.

They spoke of journeys to sunlit lands, and of love among them, and of the legends of their ancestors and of the anger and fury at the deaths of those they raised up from birth. I wandered back through the yard, into the woods, and followed them.

I, earthbound, watched as they danced tree to tree to sky to telephone wire to rooftop.

I began speaking in the tongues of birds and all else fell away, the whistles and warbles from my throat seemed perfectly natural. The starlings told their secrets to me.

I knew my son's final moments. The starlings told me what they had seen, what my boy William had done. It was in their songs, their exaltations, their chattering squawks as they surrounded me, a cathedral of dark birds.

They shared with me the love I had taught him for even the smallest bird, the tiniest creature, in the road, to be rescued from the traffic of human monsters. I heard his footsteps on the street as he raced into traffic.

The birdsong grew deafening. I clutched my hands to my ears, for I could not take what they told of my little boy.

I pressed my fingers deep into the skin of my ears — and deeper still to the wax — to plug them up and keep the sound of the last moment's of my boy's life from entering my brain. The pressure was enormous as I pushed my fingers deeper still.

And yet, I heard his voice as he shrieked, and the thud of the car against him — they warbled each note of his last moments of life so that I might feel I was there with him. I begged them to stop, but the birds continued their praise of my little boy. They mimicked his cries and the wheezes of his lungs and throat until he breathed his last.

I felt as if I were there, with William, in the street, his

head upon my lap, his eyes turned upward, his small body shivering.

As if I held his small body and looked up to God in the sky, but only saw the birds that had witnessed his death. The birds that had lured him into the street. The birds that had begun to drive me to madness with their terrible words and sounds.

Their voices, telling me of other secrets, of those who had died in the past, and the deaths to come.

Where Flies Are Born

The train stopped suddenly. Ellen watched her son fill in the coloring book with the three crayons left to him: aquamarine, burnt sienna, and silver.

She was doing this for Joey. She could put up with Frank and his tirades and possessiveness, but not when he tried to hurt their son. *Her* son. She would make sure that Joey had a better life.

Ellen turned to the crossword puzzle in the back of the magazine section to pass the time. She tried not to think of what they'd left behind.

She was a fairly patient person, and so it didn't annoy her much that it was another hour before anyone told the passengers it would be a three hour stop — or more.

Or more, translated into *overnight*.

Then her patience wore thin and Joey began to whine.

THE TOWN WAS a quarter mile ahead, and so they would be put up somewhere for the night.

So this was to be their Great Escape. February in a mountain town at thirty below. Frank would find them for sure; only a day's journey from Springfield. Frank would hunt them down, as he'd done last time, and bring them back to his little castle and she would make it okay for another five years before she went crazy again and had to run.

No. She would make sure he wouldn't hurt Joey. She would kill him first. She would, with her bare hands, stop him from ever touching their son again.

Joey said, "Can't we just stay on the train? It's cold out there."

"You'll live," she said, bringing out the overnight case and following in a line with the other passengers out of the car. They trudged along the snowy tracks to the short strip of junction, where each was directed to a different motel or private house.

"I wanted a motel," she told the conductor. She and Joey were to be overnight guests of the Neesons', a farm family. "This isn't what I paid for," she said, "it's not what I expected at all."

"You can sleep in the station, you like," the man said, but she passed on that after looking around the filthy room with its greasy benches. "Anyway, the Neesons run a bed-and-breakfast, so you'll do fine there."

❧

THE NEESONS ARRIVED in a four-wheel drive, looking just past the curve of middle age, tooth-rotted, with *country* indelibly sprayed across their grins and friendly winks.

Mama Neeson, in her late fifties, spoke of the snow, of their warm house "where we'll all be safe as kittens in a minute," of the soup she'd been making. Papa Neeson was older (*old enough to be my father*, Ellen thought) and balder, eyes of a rodent, face of a baby-left-too-long-in-bathwater.

Mama Neeson cooed over Joey, already asleep. Papa Neeson spoke of the snowfall and the roads.

Ellen said very little, other than to thank them for putting her up.

"Our pleasure," Mama Neeson said. "The little ones will love the company."

"You have children?" Ellen winced at her inflection. She didn't *mean* it to sound as if Mama Neeson was too old to have what could be called "little ones."

"Adopted, you could say," Papa Neeson grumbled. "Mama, she loves kids, can't get enough of them, you get the instinct, you see, the sniffs for babies and you got to have them whether your body gives 'em up or not."

Ellen, embarrassed for his wife, shifted uncomfortably in the seat. What a rude man. This was what Frank would be like, under the skin, talking about women and their "sniffs," their "hankerings." Poor Mama Neeson, a houseful of babies and *this man*.

"I have three little ones," Mama Neeson said. "All under nine. How old's yours?"

"Six."

"He's an angel. Papa, ain't he just a little angel sent down from heaven?"

Papa Neeson glanced over to Joey, curled up in a ball against Ellen's side. "Don't say much, does he?"

THE LANDSCAPE WAS white and black. Ellen watched for ice patches in the road, but they went over it all smoothly. Woods rose up suddenly, parting for an empty flat stretch of land. They drove down a fenced road, snow piled all the way to the top of the fence posts. Then, a farmhouse with a barn behind it.

We better not be sleeping in the barn.

Mama Neeson sighed. "Hope they're in bed. Put them to bed hours ago, but you know how they romp..."

"They love to romp," Papa Neeson said.

THE BED WAS LARGE. She and Joey sank into it as soon as the door closed behind them. Ellen was too tired to think, and Joey was still dreaming.

Sleep came quickly and was black and white, full of snowdrifts.

Ellen awoke, thirsty, before dawn.

HALF-ASLEEP, she lifted her head towards the window: the sound of some animal crunching in the snow outside. She looked out—had to open the window because of the frost on the pane.

A hazy purple light brushed across the whiteness of the hills—the sun was somewhere rising beyond the treetops. A large brown bear sniffed along the porch rail. Bears should've frightened her, but this one seemed friendly and stupid, as it lumbered along in the tugging snow, nostrils wiggling.

Sniffing the air; Mama Neeson would be up—four thirty—frying bacon, flipping hotcakes on the griddle, buttering toast. *Country mama.* The little ones would rise from their quilts and trundle beds, ready to go out and milk cows or some such farm thing, and Papa Neeson would get out his shotgun to scare off the bear that came sniffing.

Ellen remembered Papa's phrase: "the sniffs for babies," and it gave her a discomforting thought about the bear.

She lay back on the bed, stroking Joey's fine hair, with this thought in her mind of the bear sniffing for the babies, when she saw a housefly circle above her head; then, another, coming from some corner of the room, joining its mate. Three more arrived.

Finally, she was restless to swat them. She got out of bed and went to her overnight bag for hairspray. This was her favorite method of disposing of houseflies. She shook the can, and then sprayed in the direction of the nine or ten fat black houseflies. They buzzed in curves of infinity. In a minute, they began dropping, one by one, to the rug. Ellen enjoyed taking her boots and slapping each fly into the next life.

Her dry throat and heavy bladder sent her out to the hallway.

❧

FEELING along the wall for the light switch or the door to the bathroom—whichever came first. When she found the switch, she flicked it up, and a single unadorned bulb hummed into dull light.

A little girl stood at the end of the hall, too old for the diaper she wore; her stringy hair falling wildly almost to her feet; her skin bruised in several places—particularly around her mouth, which was swollen on the upper lip.

In her small pudgy fingers was a length of thread.

Ellen was so shocked by this sight that she could not say a word—the girl was only seven or so, and what her appearance indicated about the Neesons...

Papa Neeson was like Frank. Likes to beat people. Likes to beat children. Joey and his black eyes, this girl and her bruised face. I could kill them both.

The little girl's eyes crinkled up as if she were about to cry, wrinkled her forehead and nose, parted her swollen lips.

From the black and white canyon of her mouth a fat green fly crawled the length of her lower lip, and then flew toward the light bulb above Ellen's head.

§

LATER, when the sun was up, and the snow outside her window grew blinding, Ellen knew she must've been half-dreaming, or perhaps it was a trick that the children played —for she'd seen all of them, the two-year-old, the five-year-old, and the girl.

The boys had trooped out from the shadows of the hall. All wearing the filthy diapers, all bruised from beatings or worse. The only difference with the two younger boys was they had not yet torn the thread that had been used to sew their mouths and eyes and ears and nostrils closed.

Such child abuse was beyond imagining. Ellen had seen them only briefly, and afterwards wondered if perhaps she had *seen* wrong. But it was a dream, a very bad one, because the little girl had flicked the light off again. When Ellen reached to turn it back on, they had retreated into the shadows and the feeling of a surreal waking state came upon her. *The Neesons could not possibly be this evil.* With the light on, she saw only houseflies sweeping through the heavy air.

At breakfast, Joey devoured his scrambled eggs like he hadn't eaten in days; Ellen had to admit they tasted better than she'd had before.

"You live close to the earth," Papa Neeson said. "And it gives up its treasures."

Joey said, "Eggs come from chickens."

"Chickens come from eggs," Papa Neeson laughed, "and eggs are the beginning of all life. But we all gather our life from the earth, boy. You city folks don't feel it because you're removed. Out here, well, we get it under our finger-nails, birth, death, and what comes in between."

"You're something of a philosopher," Ellen said, trying to hide her uneasiness. The image of the children still in her head, like a half-remembered dream. She was eager to get on her way, because that dream was beginning to seem more real. She had spent a half hour in the shower trying to talk herself out of having seen the children and what had been done to them: then, ten minutes drying off, positive that she had seen what she'd seen. It was Frank's legacy: he had taught her to doubt what was right before her eyes. She wondered if Papa Neeson performed darker needlework on his babies.

"I'm a realist," Papa Neeson said. His eyes were bright and kind—it shocked her to look into them and think about what he might have done.

Mama Neeson, sinking the last skillet into a washtub next to the stove, turned and said, "Papa just has a talent for making things work, Missus, for putting two and two together. That's how he grows, and that's how he gathers. Why if it weren't for him, where would my children be?"

"Where are they?" Joey asked.

"We have to get back to the train," Ellen said. "They said we'd take off by eleven."

Papa Neeson raised his eyebrows in an aside to his wife.

"I saw some flies at the windows," he said. "They been bad again."

Mama Neeson shrugged her broad shoulders. "They got to let them out at times or they'd be bursting, now, wouldn't they. Must tickle something awful." She wiped her dripping hands on the flower print apron, back and forth like she could never get dry enough. Ellen saw a shining in the old woman's eyes like tears and hurt.

Joey clanked his fork on his plate; Ellen felt a lump in her throat, and imaginary spiders and flies crawling up the back of her neck. Something in the atmosphere had changed, and she didn't want to spend one more minute in this house with these people.

Joey clapped a fly between his hands, catching it mid-air.

"MAMA'S sorry you didn't see the kids," Papa Neeson said, steering over a slick patch on the newly-plowed road.

"But you're not." Ellen said. She was feeling brave. She hated this man like she hated Frank. Maybe she'd report him to some child welfare agency when she got back to the train station. She could see herself killing this man.

"No," Papa Neeson nodded. "I'm not. Mama, she don't understand about other people, but I do."

"Well, I saw them. All three. What you do to them."

Papa Neeson sighed, pulling over and parking at the side of the road. "You don't understand. Don't know if I should waste my breath."

Joey was in the backseat, bundled up in blankets. He yawned, "Why we stopping?"

Ellen directed him to turn around and sit quietly. He was a good boy. "I have a husband who hits children, too."

"I don't hit the kids, lady, and how dare you think I do, why you can just get out of my car right now if that's your attitude."

"I told you, I saw them," she said defiantly.

"You see the threads?"

Ellen could barely stand his smug attitude.

"You see 'em? You know *why* my kids look like that?"

Ellen reached for the door handle. She was going to get out. Fucking country people and their torture masked as discipline. Men, how she hated their power trips. Blood was boiling now; she was capable of anything, like two days ago when she took the baseball bat and slammed it against Frank's chest, hearing ribs cracking. She was not going to let a man hurt her child like that. Never again. The rage was rising up inside her the way it had only done twice in her life before, both times with Frank, both times protecting Joey.

Papa Neeson reached out and grabbed her wrist.

"*Don't hold me like that,*" she snarled.

He let go.

Papa Neeson began crying, pressing his head into the steering wheel. "She just wanted them so bad, I had to go dig 'em up. I love her so much, and I didn't want her to die from hurting, so I just dig 'em up and I figured out what to do and did it."

WHEN HE CALMED, he sat back up, looking straight ahead. "We better get to the junction. Train'll be ready. You got your life moving ahead with it, don't you?"

"Tell me about your children," she said, feeling a slight shiver as she thought of the flies. "What's wrong with them?"

He looked her straight in the eyes, making her flinch because of his intensity.

"Nothing, except they been dead for a long time." He let this sink in. He took a deep breath and looked out at the snowy world. "My wife, she loves 'em like they're her own. I dig 'em up, see, I thought she was gonna die from grief not having none of her own, and I figured it out, you know, about the maggots and the flies, how they make things move if you put enough of 'em inside the bodies."

She wanted him to stop talking. She couldn't stand the pain in his voice.

But he continued.

"I didn't count on 'em lasting this long, but what if they do? What if they *do*, lady? Mama, she loves those babies. We're only humans, lady, and humans need to hold babies, they need to love something other than themselves, don't they? Don't you? You got your boy, you know how much that's worth? Love beyond choosing, ain't it? Love that don't die.

"You know what it's like to hug a child when you never

got to hug one before? So I figured and I figured some more, and I thought about what makes things live, how do we know something's alive, and I figured, when it moves it's alive, and when it don't move, it's dead. So Mama, I had her sew the flies in, but they keep laying eggs and more and more, and the kids, they got the minds of flies, and sometimes they rip out the threads, so sometimes flies get out, but it's a tiny price, ain't it, lady? When you need to love little ones, and you ain't got none, it's a tiny price, a day in hell's all, but then sunshine and children and love, lady, ain't it worth that?"

ELLEN HAD a migraine by the time Papa Neeson dropped them off down at the junction. She barked at Joey. Apologized. Kissed him on the forehead.

She bought Joey an orange soda and made him promise to stand just over by the long bench near the soda machine and not go anywhere.

Ellen went into the restroom to wipe cold water across her face

THE MIRROR IN THE BATHROOM, warped, distorted her features. She thought she looked stunning: brown eyes circled with sleeplessness, the throbbing vein to the left side of her forehead, the dry, cracked lips. She thought of the threads, of the children tugging at them, popping them out to let the flies go. Ran a finger over her lips, imagining Mama Neeson taking her needle and thread, breaking the skin with tiny holes. Ears, nostrils, eyes, mouth, other open-ings, other places where flies could escape.

Flies and life, sewn up into the bodies of dead children, buried by other grieving parents, brought back by the country folks who ran the bed-and-breakfast, and who spoke of children that no one ever saw much of.

And when they did...

Ellen imagined *Mama Neeson kissing the bruised cheek of her little girl, tears in her squinty eyes, tears of joy for having children to love.*

Behind her, someone opened the door.

Stood there.

Waiting for her to turn around.

"Look who I found," Frank said, dragging Joey behind him into the women's room.

TWO WEEKS LATER, she was on the train again with Joey, but it was better weather—snow had melted and the sun was exhaustingly bright.

Frank was dead.

She could think it.

She could remember the feel of the knife in her hands.

FRANK HAD COME at Joey with his own toy dump truck. She had grabbed a kitchen knife—as she'd been planning to do since Frank had hauled them back to Springfield.

She had gone with the knowledge of what she would have to do to keep Frank out of her little boy's life forever.

Then, she had just waited for his temper to flare.

She kept the knife with her, and when she ran in the living room to see Frank slamming the truck against Joey's scalp, she let the boiling blood and rage take her down with them.

The blade went in deep.

She could not stop stabbing her husband.

SHE LIFTED her son in her arms as she stepped off the train, careful on the concrete because there was still some ice.

Joey, wrapped in a blanket, sunglasses on his face, "sleeping," she told the nice lady who had been sitting across from them; Ellen, also wearing sunglasses and too much make-up, a scarf around her head, a heavy wool sweater around her shoulders, exhausted and determined.

Joey's not dead. Not really.

IT HADN'T BEEN hard to track down the Neesons. She had called them before she got on the train, and they were not surprised to hear from her.

"It happens this way," Mama Neeson told her. "Our calling."

Ellen was not sure what to make of that comment, but she was so tired and confused that she let it go.

Later, she might think that something of the Neesons had perhaps rubbed off on her and her son. That, perhaps just *meeting* them might be like inviting something into life that hadn't been considered before.

Something under your fingernails.

SHE CARRIED Joey to the payphone and dropped a coin in; she dialed the number from memory.

"Mr. Neeson?"

"Here already?" he asked.

"I took an early train."

"Mama's still asleep. She was up all night. Worries, you know. Upset for you."

"Well..."

"I'll be down there in a few minutes," he said. "You're sure this is what you want?"

"Love beyond choosing," she reminded him.

A spool of white thread fell from Joey's blanket, bouncing once, twice as it hit the floor, unraveling as it rolled.

People Who Love Life

⁂

Why did he always have to follow her wherever she went and bring her back?

Irene liked to go down to the schoolyard because of the children, the little children. Their faces, *their faces*, their tiny hands, their dresses and shorts and shirts and shoes, so small, so perfect. It bothered her when he volunteered to go, too, because the edge of the schoolyard was her special place, the children were there, and he didn't know anything about children.

Children had that edge; they could *smell* things when they were bad, and they weren't afraid to say it. And when things were truly good, children sensed that, too. Children were the thing.

"Oh, but when *we* were children," the girl had said in the kitchen, and Irene had had to stare at her younger sister long and hard before she realized that she wasn't a girl at all, but a woman in her early forties: Gretchen was still pretty and adolescent, even with her slightly etched face and graying hair.

Irene could not stand her sometimes, although Gretchen on her own was one thing—sweetness and light even though she *knew*, but Gretchen with this man she'd married was quite another. Irene had never really enjoyed his company, although she couldn't ever tell Gretchen how she felt; and so, she was often stuck with him, this William person, even when she went to the schoolyard to watch her children play.

"When *we* were children," Irene replied. "Good lord, I can't even remember, barely."

Gretchen loaded the dishwasher. "I remember like yesterday. Days like today, just like today. Look outside the window, it's just like when we were children and mother was in here cleaning, looking out at us."

But, of course, there were no children out the window now.

Gretchen was the most self-assured person that Irene had ever known, but she lied. Irene knew that about Gretchen: she lied. Gretchen could not possibly remember their childhood accurately, she had no head for memories. She blocked them purposefully, like closing doors on useless rooms. Irene remembered just about everything, but she had lied, also. Irene was not fond of remembering: *days like today, indeed. All days, like today. Unending. I just want to leave. Why won't they just let me leave?*

They had been a family of liars, and had never quite grown out of it, although Irene was tired, today, lying to herself about what she felt and what she wanted. Truly wanted. *I just want to go by myself.*

"You were undoubtedly two of the most spoiled girls in creation, all those toys and the way your mother used to dress you up for Sunday school like little dolls," William had said, and Irene thought:

Why do you live here with us when you're so awful to Gretchen? How you did to her what you did, let alone how I must pay for it, is beyond imagining. But you have no imagination, do you? You think it is the way you see it. In front of your face. The way you see it, with no one else allowed to look.

He was an old man who pretended to be young, but she saw right through that, right to that middle-aged heart with its bloodless beating. He pretended things were all right, that there was good to every purpose.

"We were never really spoiled," Gretchen said, "but there's always been someone to watch out for us."

"Amen to that," William said, clasping his hands together.

He had decided to come with her this day, and so there he was at her right arm, helping her every few steps as if she were a complete cripple.

"I can handle the steps quite well, thank you, William," she said, and knew she sounded testy. Her right leg twisted as she stepped down to the sidewalk. Again, she had lied; stairs were difficult for her, the way her feet went, one moving almost against the other, but once she was on flat ground she was fine. But she was tired of his help.

"All righty, then," he said, and he made it sound like he was trying to be funny.

She could not stand people who spoke like that. People who made fun of everything. People who love life.

If only he'd let her *go* sometimes, instead of following after her like a yappy dog.

"I am not so far gone," she told him, "that I can't walk by myself. You know that, don't you?"

"Oh, Irene, I was trying to be helpful."

"Don't think me ungrateful. You and Gretchen have been kind, since the accident. More than kind. But I don't want kindness, not anymore." She had given up on direct sarcasm, and never thought he would get it, anyway. Why couldn't he just let her go?

"You're almost all healed." He reached over and touched around her face.

Irene gasped.

He was always close to touching her, and *there* of all places, but he had never accomplished more than the slightest graze. She stood still as if he were pulling a stray hair from her forehead.

He touched her scars. His fingers were soft along the place where the skin had bubbled and obscured the vision of her left eye.

Why did his fingers seem so warm, when she knew him to be so cold, so empty? Was he laughing at her, the way he laughed at the whole of creation?

Finally, he removed his hand. "Does it hurt?"

"Not now. Like a headache, sometimes, but the pills take care of that, but please, let's not talk about it, I feel all talked out, and I see it in the mirror every morning, so I don't find it interesting." Would that shut him up? She would like to just have a nice day and watch the children in the schoolyard.

"God loves you, you know, Irene. He really does, and in

His infinite wisdom," and he would've gone on with his smug little litany, too.

But she spat at him, "I don't care for your God, William, and I don't care for you. I was going to spend the day alone, in my own way, and you have to come along with your almighty creator and ruin everything once again."

"I know you don't mean that," he whispered, like a hurt child. "I know you're saying it because of great pain."

"You," she said, "you are my great pain. You and your miracles."

He was walking several steps behind her, and she thought of trying to lose him in the village, but she really must go and see the children when they went out to the playground. She must not miss them.

Perhaps she'd stop in for a cup of coffee, but only for a minute, because the children would be waiting to see her.

Only the children knew how to treat her, how to respect her wishes. They had almost come through for her last time: their tiny hands, so willing, so lovely. It was because children knew things instinctively, they had gut reactions, they were so close to the real pulse of life.

Grownups had lost it all, and certainly men like this William person that Gretchen had married were so out of touch, so *clueless*, that everything was like a car: maintenance and repair, tinkering around with things that were best left to the junkyard. And always the male need for possession.

Well, I do not belong to you.

She limped another quarter mile through the village,

and it was empty. It had been mostly empty when she and Gretchen had been girls, and it was empty when they were in their twenties and thirties, and now it was desolate. She had wanted to leave the village for as long as she could remember, but she'd never had the nerve.

Now she knew of only one route, and damn him, he was going to shadow her.

The sunlight was flat and nothing escaped it: she saw her reflection in the bookstore window. The scars weren't healing at all, they were simply drying. Her mouth looked terrible, and she couldn't bring herself to look at her jaw. Her hair was mostly gone, but the scarf hid that.

The clerk inside the bookstore pretended not to stare at her from behind the counter, but she saw him stealing glances. *I don't mind*, she thought, nodding to him, *let this be a lesson to you. When it's time, it's time.*

William stood behind her. She saw his reflection. "My sister told me once that life was precious," Irene said aloud, knowing he would hear. "And I believed her. But she meant something different than this."

"Life is the greatest gift," he said. He sometimes had a voice like nails on wood, and in the county they said he had a voice like thunder, but he sounded to her most like teeth grinding. Nothing more than teeth, one bone wearing away at another.

She turned to face him. She counted to ten, silently. Her tongue went dry in her mouth. "I am going to have some coffee, and I want to be alone."

She walked on down the sidewalk, trying to stay in the shade.

She passed Fred Smith, whom she hadn't seen since just after the accident when the town meeting was called, and he actually tipped his baseball cap to her, which seemed a rather pleasant gallantry, considering what he'd said about her in the past. *"Way I see it, you belong somewhere between a freak show and a wienie roast,"* Fred had muttered from the *safety of his pickup truck, but she hadn't blamed him because he was right.*

"Well, hey, Miz Hart," he said this time, but he didn't look at her, not directly. Her shoes, but not her face.

She didn't blame him: she was surprised that the young man in the bookstore had tried. *They're all afraid they're going to turn to stone.*

She walked around him into the Five & Dime, but not before she heard Fred say, more stiffly than when he'd greeted her, "Hello, preacher."

And William's absurdly heartfelt reply, "This is the day the Lord has made, Fred, rejoice."

"Yeah, well…" Fred had nothing more to say.

❦

THE LUNCH COUNTER was grease-spattered and vacant.

Ever since the freeway had been built closer to Blowing Rock, the village didn't even have the trucks coming through. *As if the world knew not to come through here. It's a cursed place. Unclean, like in biblical days.*

Jeannie Stamp came out from the washroom and leaned over the counter, nodding when Irene sat on the stool.

"It's dying, all my business is gone, just about," Jeannie said as she poured out the coffee, "Black, you like it? I told that old fart Harry to make sure the county money got thrown our way, but he said wait, and look what's happened now we been waiting long enough, we ain't even on the map. Used to be, ten, twelve people in here by noon, and now, just you and me, Renie."

Jeannie never looked at her directly, either, but Jeannie was always nicer than the rest of the village. Irene had been to school with Jeannie, and had never thought in all her youth that she would ever depend upon her for friendship, but it was the best that was offered these days.

"I'm going to the school," Irene told her, leaning her elbows on the counter, sipping her coffee. It was lukewarm and smelled like dirty socks, but this was the only place to get coffee in town since the trouble when they'd burned down the ice cream shop. It was the older kids, just going crazy and setting fire to things. Even the teenagers knew when something was wrong, when things needed to be torn down. *Maybe the whole village will go. If I can't leave, maybe it will leave me.*

"You think that's a smart move?"

Irene shrugged. "What's smart?"

"School. All those kids I heard about the other day. What happened."

"*Almost* happened, *almost*."

"Well, it could."

"Yes, hon, it could," Irene set the half-empty cup down and could not decide if she should go out in the summer heat again and face Gretchen's husband, or if she should wait another fifteen minutes.

The children would be in the playground soon, and if she didn't see them today, it would be tomorrow, and if it didn't happen today, they might get used to her presence and never do what she knew they wanted to, never be free to be children, *just be children*. Less than twenty children left in the village at all.

"Preacher's talked about the Lord in our lives," Jeannie said. "He says we should be grateful, that God shines His light on us, even here, to the lowliest."

I am so tired of this fundamentalist town, Irene felt a headache coming on, and all her pills were back at the house, so the headache would just have to hammer away at her. *Gretchen and I should've left long ago, back when we had choices, back when we wanted to get out in the world. I should've learned to drive when I was in my twenties. Not wait until I was forty-six and in a stick shift with a sixteen year old. But they would've laughed at me. Luke was the only one who could teach me, the only one I could trust not to tell William, or even Gretchen. They would've laughed, and then he would've wondered why I wanted to leave so badly, and he would've stopped it. He did stop it. And I should never have been pulled from the car. Not back to this godforsaken place.* "If that's true, Jeannie, about God, what about Luke?"

Jeannie looked like a girl who had been scolded. "That's different. Preacher says God helps those He chooses."

"Who chooses? God, or the preacher?"

"Preacher don't have a choice, way I see it. He just got the gift. Always been miracles, always will be. Ain't you happy, being so special and all?"

Irene put two quarters on the counter. "Look me in the eye and ask me that."

"Oh," Jeannie said, "you know I can't do that. You know what happens. You don't want it to happen, do you?"

IRENE WAVED to William as she came back out, into the sunlight.

No one else was on the street, and there he was with his grin, his hopeful grin, like a dog waiting to be kicked. He had that charm, which she found so dull. But in a village like this, he would be king. He would be adored. So he had come here and found Gretchen.

He was the big fish in the small pond.

He was Preacher, and this was his Flock.

Irene had once liked him, a little, but not at all since the accident. She had not even been feeling kindly towards her sister. "I don't understand you," she'd told Gretchen, "why do you even want me here? Isn't it painful?" But Gretchen was so brainwashed by this William person, by his laying on of hands and speaking in tongues, that she was not really the same girl that Irene had grown up with. Gretchen could not see her way out of things, never had been able to; for Gretchen, things were the way they were. Only once had Gretchen asked her about that day, about what happened. And Irene had pretended to have forgotten, as if the accident and the darkness had wiped it away.

"IRENE," William called out, his hands tucked almost sheepishly in his pockets; he was rocking back and forth on his heels, "I was afraid I'd lost you."

He stepped into the street and crossed over to her. He walked like a boy, all bounce and uncertainty.

"I'm going to see the children."

"I'd like to come along."

"Do what you like," she closed her eyes and he touched her elbow with his hand. The bone was broken there, and had not healed where it poked out from her skin. She could move it fine, but she didn't like to be reminded of it.

She wondered how he could touch her the way he did; she sensed his discomfort each time he was close, but now, this day, he seemed more relaxed, as if he were no longer fearful of what had happened to her body. She often wondered: *Do you like what you see? Does it please you to be so close to this monster? Do you love life this much, even when it looks this way?* But she had never been beautiful; Gretchen was always the pretty one, which bothered her until the accident, because afterwards, Irene was happy with Gretchen's beauty. She felt her little sister *should* be the lovely one, the one whose flesh was pleasant and fragrant and satisfying. Irene needed no beauty, she needed nothing.

What she longed for was death, truly, and in death, an escape from this ravaged flesh.

"You're beautiful in God's eyes," he said, his breath like a warm humid wind along her neck.

"You should have left me."

"I couldn't."

"The children, the ones in the ice cream shop. Told me."

"Liars."

"You let him die."

"Those children are liars."

"Your own son."

"God called me to you. To save you."

"But Luke was still *alive*. You could've saved him." She felt exasperated. He was so dense, so stupid. He only saw what he wanted to see. She moaned in frustration, wanting to hit him as hard as she could. "I was dead. Why can't you just let me go?"

❧

THE SCHOOLYARD WAS EMPTY, and she went to sit on a swing. He followed her, but didn't speak again for awhile, so she acted as if he were not there.

This would be a place for miracles.

She saw their faces in the school windows, staring and pointing, some calling. She knew their parents.

Places like this, you know everyone, you had no secrets.

"It could happen again," William said.

She tried to wish him away.

"You should come home with me now," he said.

When she didn't respond, he added, "You want it to happen, don't you?"

❧

IRENE WATCHED the children in the windows: some of them had been at the ice cream shop when the car had smashed into the truck, and the fire had started.

She remembered their faces, fascinated, their screaming, excited voices, as they watched the burning wreck. Her last sight had been of them holding their ice cream cones, and she had felt a peace, even in the pain of death, the numbing cold of fire, a peace from those lovely faces, knowing that the world would pass on without her there, that she would leave them, and they would still eat ice cream, and still talk out of turn, and still grow up into the world without some woman they barely knew by sight named Irene Hart who had stayed her whole dull life in the village.

Her last thought had been, *children.*

It had been a death she enjoyed, and the suffering had

only come when she was pulled from the darkness, and opened her eyes to hear him, this man that Gretchen had married, saying, "And as Christ brought Lazarus from the dead, so I call His servant, Irene Hart, come, come to us, live again in the flesh with us."

IRENE SAT on the swing and began crying. She felt the weight of his hand on her shoulder.

She could not help herself, and in spite of her repulsion at his touch, she asked, "Children are closer to God, aren't they? Closer than us? 'Suffer the little children to come unto me', isn't that the quote?"

"God is close to all of us. All who believe, anyway."

"Oh," she stopped crying and laughed. He came and stood in front of her. She hadn't laughed in ages, and he smiled, probably thinking he was finally seeing the light within her. "Oh, that explains it, *that's it*. It's not God who lifted me up from the burning car, it's something else entirely. It was Luke who God took care of, not me. I get it now, oh, William, you should've told me at the time. It was Luke that God loved, not me."

"Irene, you don't know what you're saying."

"Well, if it's not true, why didn't you save your son? Why did you raise me up?"

William looked her in the eye, and she almost fainted because no one had done that since the accident.

HE WHISPERED SOMETHING, but she knew it before he

whispered it, and she wanted to stop up his mouth before the words had formed, "Because I love you," and she knew he was ashamed and humiliated to have to say it in a schoolyard, in the light of day. "Ever since I saw you, I loved you. I want to be near you. I never want to let you go."

So that was it.

Love.

"You go home now," she said softly.

She turned away from him, swinging to the side, her heels scraping the dirt, happy that he had let that awful feeling out, what he called love, out to evaporate in the shimmering heat of August. It had burned all these years within him, and she had been singed by his fire. She had not known what to call it, and she knew that it was not love, not love at all, but desire.

Had it been only his desire that had brought her back from the dead? *Well*, she thought, *let desire die, then, and let it have no resurrection.*

"I'll see you at supper," he said, and she heard his footsteps on the soft grass as he headed back to the street.

THE SWING SAGGED beneath her weight: *it was made for a child and I am not meant to be here. The children will know, too*, she thought.

The bell rang, and the children poured out onto the playground, and some saw her and some were involved in their games.

Children like golden light on the grassy field, coming slowly, curiously towards her. They called her the names she knew children called, their small, delicate hands, and their wondrous faces, their perfect thoughts.

She had come before, and they had been close to it, but they had not done what they longed to do.

Their hands, their eyes, their instinct so much a part of their flesh.

But today.

Today.

One of the little boys was bold, she thought he must be twelve, and he came up and stared at her fiercely.

"You're ugly," he said. "My daddy said you should be dead. You look dead. You even smell dead."

She looked him in the eye, and did not even flinch.

One of the children behind this boy picked up a small stone and threw it at her, hitting her just above her left eye. Irene smiled, *the children know what to do, they are closer to things, to nature.*

She felt another stone, this one larger, hit the back of her head, and then she was surrounded by beautiful, joyful children.

Irene waited for the darkness as they looked her in the eye and knew what she was.

It was later, when she thought the Kingdom was opening for her that she regained sight, and she welcomed whatever Kingdom there was, whatever light seemed to grow in the dark as the place where she belonged, but it was nothing other than the beam of a flashlight, and the lid of a coffin opening, and a madman above her who had scrambled in the earth to dig up a grave, only to say, "Come to us, live again in the flesh with us!"

265 and Heaven

A NOVELETTE

It began as a routine call about an old drunk out at the trash cans.

Paul was new to the uniform, having only seen a couple of drug busts of the non-violent variety and one DUI.

It was that kind of town. One murder in the past six years, and one cop killed in the line of duty since 1957. He and his little sister had lived there five years, and picked it because it was fairly quiet and calm, a good hospital, good visiting nurses' association, and no one to remember them from nine years before. He had been a security guard back in St. Chappelle right after college, but it had been his dream to be a cop, and now he was, and it was good, most nights.

Most nights, he and his partner just trolled the streets for small-time hookers and signs of domestic violence.

Sometimes they arrived too late at a jumper out on the Pawtuxet Bridge. Sometimes, they watched the jump.

Paul couldn't shake the vision in his mind of the kid who had jumped two weeks back. *Damn lemmings, some of these kids. Just wanting to get out of town so bad they couldn't wait for the bus.*

"Some guy's over in front of the Swan Street apartments knocking over cans and covered with blood," the dispatcher said.

"Christ," Paul muttered. "Swan Street. Why does everything seem to happen over there?"

He glanced at his watch. Nearly midnight.

His partner, Beth, sighed and shook her head when the call came from dispatch.

"I bet I know this guy," she said, "Jesus, I bet it's this old clown."

She turned left at Wilcox, and took two quick rights until they were on Canal Road.

The night fairly steamed with humidity, and the sky threatened more rain.

Paul wiped sweat from the back of his neck.

"He used to be with the circus, a real carny-type." As she spoke, Beth managed to reach across the dash, grab a cigarette from the pack, thrust it between her lips and punch in the lighter while still keeping her eye on the road. "He spends half the year God knows where and then comes back here in the summer. We had to ship him out twice last year."

"What a night," Paul said, barely hiding disgust in his voice.

The flat-topped brick buildings, dim blue windows, dark alleys of downtown passed by as he looked out the window.

The streets were dead.

When Beth pulled the patrol car to the curb, Paul saw him.

A fringe of gray hair around a shiny bald scalp, the checkered shirttail flapping, the saggy brown pants halfway down his butt. The guy stood beneath the streetlamp, his hands over his crotch.

"He jerking off or what?" Beth asked, snorting.

"Poor old bastard," Paul said. "Can we get him to the station?"

"Easy," she said, "you just tell him we're taking him for some free drinks."

As she opened her door, she shouted, "Hey! Fazzo! It's your friend!"

The old man turned, letting go of his crotch. He hadn't been masturbating; but a dark stain grew where he'd touched. He cried out, "Friends? My friends!"

He opened his arms as if to embrace the very darkness beyond the streetlamp.

Paul got out, too, and jogged over to him. "Buddy, what you up to tonight?"

Looking at his uniform, the guy said, "I don't got nothing against cops. Believe you me. Cops are gold in my book."

Paul turned to Beth, whispering, "His breath. Jesus."

The guy said, "I just been having a drink."

"Or two," Beth said. "Look, Fazzo…"

"Fazzo the Fabulous," the guy said. "The greatest magician in the tri-state area."

"We got to take you to another bar."

"You buying?" he asked her.

"Yeah sure. You got a place up here?" Beth nodded towards the flophouse apartments beyond the streetlamp.

Fazzo nodded. "Renting it for thirty five years. Number 265."

Paul shined his flashlight all over Fazzo. "I don't see any blood on him."

"It's the piss," Beth whispered. "Someone reported it as blood. It happens sometimes. Poor old guy."

Beth escorted Fazzo to the car. She turned and nodded towards Paul; he took the signal. He went over to the back staircase. The door was open. He walked inside. The carpeting was damp and stank of mildew.

A junkie sat six steps up, skinny to the bone, leaning against the peeling wallpaper, muttering some junkie incantation.

Paul stepped around him.

The hallway above was narrow, its paint all but stripped off by time. The smell of curry; someone was cooking, and it permeated the hall.

When he got to 265, he knocked. The door was already ajar, and his fist opened it on the first knock.

There was a light somewhere at the back of the apartment.

Paul called out to see if anyone was there. He gagged when he inhaled the fetid air.

All he could see were shadows and shapes, as if the old guy's furniture had been swathed in drop cloths.

He felt along the wall for the light switch. When he found it, he turned on the light. It was a twenty-five watt bulb, which fizzled to life from the center of the living room ceiling. Its light barely illuminated the ceiling itself.

The chairs and couch in the room were covered with old newspapers, some of them damp from urine. The old man hadn't even bothered to make it to the bathroom anymore. There was human excrement behind the couch. Empty whiskey bottles along the floor in front of the television set.

Paul found it hard to ignore the stench of the place.

Beth arrived at that point. "I got him cuffed, not that he needs it. He fell asleep as soon as I sat him down in the car. Jesus!" She covered her mouth and nose. "I thought he'd been living on the street."

Her eyes widened as she took in the other sights.

"Look at this," Paul pointed to the window, shining his flashlight across it.

It was black with dead flies, two or three layers thick.

He continued to the kitchen. "Should I open the fridge, you think?"

"Sure," Beth said. "Looks like Fazzo the Fabulous is going to end up in state hospital for awhile. What the hell?" She picked something up off a shelf and held it up. "Paul, look at this."

In her hands, a wig with long, thin hair. "You think Fazzo steps out on Saturday night in pearls and pumps?"

Paul shook his head, and turned back to the refrigerator. He opened the door, slowly. A blue light within it came on. The refrigerator was stacked three trays high with old meat —clotted steaks, green hamburger, what looked like a roast with a fine coating of mold on it. "Shit," he said, noticing the dead flies encrusted on the shinier cuts of meat. "This guy's lost it. He's not just a drunk. He needs serious help."

Beth walked into the bathroom, and started laughing.

"What's up?" he asked, moving around the boxes in the kitchen. Paul glanced to the open door.

The bathroom light was bright.

"It's clean in here. It's so clean you can eat off it. It must be the one room he never goes in." Beth leaned through the open doorway and gestured for Paul to come around the corner. "This is amazing."

Paul almost tripped over a long-dead plant as he reached her.

§

THE BATHROOM MIRROR WAS SPARKLING, as was the toilet, the pink tiles. Blue and pink guest soap were laid out in fake seashells on either side of the brass spigots of the faucet.

Written in lipstick on the mirror: a phone number.

For a second, he thought he saw something small and green skitter across the shiny tiles and dive behind the shower curtain. A lizard?

Paul went to pull the shower curtain aside, and that's when he found the woman's torso.

§

PAUL WASHED his face six times that night at the station. He wished he hadn't found the torso. It was the sort of image he had only seen in forensics textbooks, never in living color, never that muddy rainbow effect, never all the snakey turns and twists.

He had to put it out of his mind. He didn't want to think about what was left of the woman in the tub.

He had not seen her face, and he was glad. She wasn't entirely human to him without a face.

Her name was Shirley. Fazzo the Fabulous told him. "Shirley Chastain. She was from the Clearwater District. She ran a dry cleaners with her mother. I thought she was a nice sort of girl right up until I cut her. I dug deep in her. She had a gut like a wet velvet curtain, thick, but smooth,

smooth, smooth. She had a funny laugh. A tinkly bell kind of laugh." He had sobered up and was sitting in county jail. Paul stood outside his cell with the county coroner, who took notes as Fazzo spoke. "She had excellent taste in shoes, but no real sense of style. Her skin was like sponge cake."

"You eat her skin?" The coroner asked.

Fazzo laughed. "Hell, no. I mean it *felt* like sponge cake. The way sponge cake used to be, like foam, like perfect foam when you pull it apart." He kneaded the air with his fingers. "I'm not a freakin' cannibal."

Paul asked, "You were a clown or something? Back in your circus days, I mean?"

"No, sir. I wasn't anything like that. I was the world's greatest magician. You know, a great magician — one of the best ever — told me, when I was a kid, he said, 'Fazzo, you're gonna be the biggest, you got what it takes.' Didn't mean shit, but my oh my it sure did feel good to hear it from him."

"I guess you must've been something," Paul said.

Fazzo glanced from the coroner to Paul. "Why you here, kid? You busted me. What are you gawking for?"

"I don't know," Paul said. "You kind of remind me of my dad I guess." It was a joke; Paul glanced at the coroner, and then back at Fazzo. Last time Paul saw his dad, his dad's face was split open from the impact of the crash.

"Shit," the old guy dismissed this with a wave. "I know all about your old man, kid. It's like tattoos on your body. Everybody's story is on their body. Dad and Mom in car wreck, but you were driving. Little sister, too, thrown out of the car. I see it all, kid. You got a secret don't you? That's right, I can see it plain as day. You should never have gone

in 265, cause you're the type it wants. You're here because
you got caught."

"*I* got caught?"

"You went in 265 and you got caught. I pass it to you,
kid. You get the door prize."

"You're some sick puppy," Paul said, turning away.

Fazzo shouted after him, "Don't ever go back there, kid.
You can always get caught and get away. Just like a fish on
the hook. Just don't fight it. That always reels 'em in!" Paul
glanced back at Fazzo. The old man's eyes became slivers.
"It's magic, kid. Real magic. Not the kind on stage or the
kind in storybooks, but the real kind. It costs life sometimes
to make magic. You're already caught, though. Don't go
back there. Next time, it's you." Then Fazzo closed his eyes,
and began humming to himself as if to block out some
other noise.

It sickened Paul further, thinking what a waste of a life.
What a waste of a damned life, not just the dead woman,
but this old clown. Paul said, "Why'd you do it?"

Fazzo stopped his humming. He pointed his finger at
Paul and said, "I was like you, kid. I didn't believe in
anything. That's why it gets you. You believe in something,
it can't get you. You don't believe, and it knows you got an
empty space in your heart just waiting to be filled. You
believe in heaven, kid?"

Paul remained silent.

"It's gonna get you, then, kid. You got to believe in
heaven if you want to get out of 265."

Then, Fazzo told his story. Paul would've left, but Fazzo
had a way of talking that hooked you. Paul leaned against
the wall, thinking he'd take off any minute, but he listened.

"I WAS FAMOUS, kid, sure, back before you were born, and I toured with the Seven Stars of Atlantis Circus, doing some sideshow crap like sword-swallowing and fire-eating before I got the brilliant idea to start bringing up pretty girls to saw in half or make disappear. This was way back when, kid, and there wasn't a lot of entertainment in towns with names like Wolf Creek or Cedar Bend or Silk Hope. The Seven Stars was the best they got, and I turned my act into a showcase.

"I was hot, kid. I blew in like a Nor'easter and blew up like a firecracker. Imagine these hands—these hands—as I directed the greatest magic show in the tri-state area, the illusions, kid, the tricks of the trade, the boxes with trap-doors that opened below the stage, the nights of shooting stars as I exploded one girl-filled cage after another. They turned into white doves flying out across the stunned faces of children and middle-aged women and old men who had lost their dreams but found them inside the tent. Found them in my magic show! It was colossal, stupendous, magnificent!

"I gave them a night of fucking heaven, kid. We turned a dog into a great woolly mammoth, we turned a horse into a unicorn, we turned a heron into a boy and then into a lizard, all within twenty minutes, and then when it was all done, the boy became rabbit and I handed it to some thrilled little girl in the audience to take home for a pet or for supper.

"Once, traveling during a rainy spring, the whole troupe got caught in mud. I used my knowledge of traps and springs to get us all out of there—and was rewarded with

becoming the Master of Ceremonies. It was practically religious, kid, and I was the high priest!

"But the problem was, at least for me, that I believed in
none of it. I could not swallow my own lies. The magic was
a fake. I knew where the animals were hid away to be
sprung up, and the little boy, bounced down into a pile of
sawdust while a snowy egret took his place, or an iguana
popped up wearing a shirt just like the one the boy had on.
The boy could take it, he was good. Best assistant I ever
had. The woman, too, she was great—saw her in half and
she screamed like she was giving birth right on the table—
not a beauty except in the legs. She had legs that went right
on up to her chin.

"When she got hit by the bus in Memphis, everything
changed for me, and I didn't want to do the act again. Joey
wanted to keep going, but I told him we were finished. I
loved that kid. So, we quit the act, and I went to do a little
entertaining in clubs, mostly strip joints. Tell a couple jokes,
do a few tricks with feather fans. Voila! Naked girls appear
from behind my cape! It was not the grandeur of the carni-
val, but it paid the rent, and Joey had a roof over his head
and we both had food in our mouths.

"One month I was a little late on the rent, and we got
thrown out. That's when I came here, and we got the little
place on Swan Street. Well, we didn't get it, it got us.

"But it got you, too, didn't it, kid? It wasn't just you
walking in to 265, it was that you been preparing your
whole life for 265. That other cop, she lives in another
world already, 265 couldn't grab her. But it could grab you,
and it did, huh.

"I knew as soon as I saw you under the streetlamp.

"I recognized you from before.

"You remember before?

"Hey, you want to know why I killed that woman? You really want to know?

"Watch both my hands when I tell you. Remember, I'm a born prestidigitator.

"Here's why: sometimes, you get caught in the doorway.

"Sometimes, when the door comes down, someone doesn't get all the way out.

"You want to find the other half of her body?

"It's in 265.

"Only no one's gonna find it but you, kid.

"You're a member of the club."

PAUL WAS OFF-SHIFT AT 2, and went to grab a beer at the Salty Dog minutes before it closed. Jacko and Ronny got there ahead of him and bought the first round.

"Hell," Paul said. "It was like he sawed her in two."

"He saw her in two? What's that mean?" Jacko asked. He was already drunk.

"No, he sawed her in two. He was a magician. A real loser," Paul shook his head, shivering. "You should've seen it."

Jacko turned to Ronny, winking. "He saw her sawed and we should've seen it."

"Cut it out. It was…unimaginable."

Ronny tipped his glass. "Here's to you, Paulie boy. You got your first glimpse of the real world. It ain't pretty."

Jacko guzzled his beer, coughing when he came up for air. "Yeah, I remember my first torso. Man, it was hacked bad."

"I thought nothing like that happened around here," Paul said. "I thought this was a quiet town."

Jacko laughed, slapping him on the back. "It doesn't happen much, kid. But it always happens once. You got to see hell at least once when you work this job."

Paul took a sip of beer. It tasted sour. He set the mug down. "He called it heaven." But was that really what Fazzo the Fabulous had said? Heaven? Or had he said you had to believe in heaven for 265 to not touch you?

Jacko said, "Christ, forget about it Paulie. Hey, how's that little Marie?"

Paul inhaled the smoke of the bar, like he needed something more inside him than the thought of 265. "She's okay."

❧

WHEN HE GOT home to their little place on Grove, with the front porch light on, he saw her silhouette in the window.

He unlocked the door, noticing that the stone step had gotten scummy from damp and moss.

After he stepped inside, he glanced over to where his sister sat in the semi-dark.

"Hey, Marie," he said.

"I couldn't get the TV to work."

"Sorry, kid," he said, trying not to show exhaustion. "I'll get it fixed tomorrow. You should be asleep."

"I should be," she said.

"How was Mrs. Jackson?"

"Her usual," Marie said.

"How's the pain?"

She didn't answer.

Paul went over and kissed his little sister on the forehead. "I need to go to bed. You should, too."

"I hate what you did to me," she whispered.

She said this more than he cared to remember.

"I hate it, too," he said. Trying not to remember why she could say it in the first place. "You keep your oxygen on all day?"

She may have nodded; he couldn't tell in the dim light.

"I hate what I did to myself," she whispered, but he wasn't sure. She may have said, "I hate what I do to myself." Or, "I hate what I want to do to myself." It was late. He'd had a couple of beers. She had whispered.

The three possibilities of what she said played through his mind every now and then, and in the next few days (staying up late, staring at the ceiling, hearing the hum of the machines that helped keep his beautiful sister alive) he was sure she'd said the last thing.

I hate what I want to do to myself.

THE CLEAN UP crew had been through, photographers got their pictures, the apartment was cordoned off.

Paul stood in the doorway, giving a brief nod to one of the detectives.

He glanced around the apartment; it was trashed.

The bathroom light seeped like pink liquid from under the door.

He didn't go in.

He didn't want to.

He didn't want to think about the torso or the magician or even the lizard he'd seen scuttle into the bathtub.

But it was all he thought about for the next six months.

❦

ON HIS NIGHTS OFF, he'd sit in the living room with Marie and watch television. Marie loved television, and besides her books and magazines, it was the only thing that got her out of herself.

"I saw a great movie last night," she told him.

He glanced over.

The small thin plastic tubing of the oxygen hung from beneath her nostrils, hooked up to the wide machine with blinking lights. The braces on her arms connected to a brace around her torso that nearly made her look robotic.

Still, she looked like Marie under all the metal and wire and tubing.

Pretty. Blond hair cut short. Her eyes bright, occasionally.

Sometimes, he thought, she was happy.

"Yeah?" he said. "Which one?"

"I can't remember the name. It was amazing. A man and woman so in love, but they were divided by time and space. But he wanted her so badly. He sacrificed his life for her. But they had this one…moment. I cried like an idiot."

"You should be watching happy movies," Paul said, somewhat cheerfully.

"Happy or sad doesn't matter," Marie said. "That's where you mix things up too much. Happy and sad are symptoms. It's the thing about movies and books. It's that glimpse of heaven. No one loves anyone like they do in movies and books. No one hurts as wonderfully. I saw this other movie about a woman in a car wreck — just like ours — and she couldn't move from the neck down. Her family spurned her. A friend had to take care of her. She thought of killing herself. Then, the house caught on fire. She had to crawl outside. A little boy helped her. The little boy couldn't talk, and they became friends. But she'd lost everything.."

"I don't like things that make you sad," he said.

"This," Marie nodded to the machines and the walls. "This makes me sad. The stories get me out of this. They get me into heaven. Even if it's only for a few minutes, it's enough. You want to know why people cry at movies even when the movie is happy? I've thought about this a lot. It's because life is never that good. They know that when the screen goes dark, they have to go back to the life off-screen where nothing is as good. People who have cancer in movies have moments of heaven. People who have cancer in real life just have cancer. People in car wrecks in movies and stories get heaven. In real life…"

"So you feel like you're in heaven when you read a story?"

She nodded. "Or see a good movie. Not the whole movie, just a few minutes. But a few minutes of heaven is better than no heaven at all." She closed her eyes for a moment. "You know what I dream of at night?"

"No machines?" he said.

She shook her head. "No. I dream that everything is exactly like it is, only it's absolutely wonderful. Then, I wake up."

"Some dream," he said.

"Paul," she said as if just realizing something important. "I know why people kill themselves. It isn't because they hate anyone. It isn't because they want to escape. It's because they think there's no heaven. Why go on if there's no heaven to get to?"

PAUL WENT to see Fazzo the Fabulous on Death Row. Fazzo had gained some weight in prison, and looked healthier.

"I have to know something," Paul said.

"Yeah, kid?" Fazzo looked at him carefully. "You want to know all about 265, don't you? You been there since I got arrested?"

Paul nodded. Then, as if this were a revelation, he said, "You're sober."

"I have to be in here. No choice. The twelve step program of incarceration…Let me tell you, 265 is a living breathing thing. It's not getting rented out any time soon, either. It waits for the one it marked. You're it, kid. It's waiting for you, and you know it. And there's no use resisting its charms."

"Why did you kill that woman?"

"The forty million dollar question, kid. The forty million dollar question."

"Forget it then."

"Okay, you look like a decent kid. I'll tell you. She was a sweet girl, but she wanted too much heaven. She and me both. Life's job is not to give you too much heaven. But she got a taste for it, just like I did. You get addicted to it. So," Fazzo gestured with his hands in a sawing motion. "She got in but the door came down. I mean, I know I cut into her, using my hands. I know that. Only I wasn't trying to cut into her. I liked her. She was sweet. I was trying to keep it from slamming down so hard on her. They thought I was insane at first, and were going to put me in one of those hospitals. But all the doctors pretty much confirmed that my marbles were around. Only all that boozing I did made me sound nuts."

Fazzo leaned over. "You got someone you love, kid?"

Paul shrugged. "I got my little sister. She's it."

"No other family?"

"I got cousins out of state. Why?"

"No folks?"

Paul shook his head.

"Okay, now it's clear why 265 chose you, kid. You're like me, practically no strings, right? But one beloved in your life. Me, I had Joey."

Paul grimaced.

"Hey!" Fazzo flared up. "It wasn't like that! Joey was a kid whose family threw him out with the garbage. I gave him shelter, and that was it. Wasn't nothing funny about it. Sick thing to think." Then, after a minute he calmed. "I gave Joey what was in 265 and everything was good for awhile. Joey, he had some problems."

"Like what?"

Fazzo shrugged. "We all got problems. Joey, he had leukemia. He was gonna die." Then it was as if a light blinked on in the old man's eyes. "You know about Joey, don't you? It touched you in there, and it let you know about him. Am I right? When it touches you, it lets you know about who's there and who's not, and maybe about who's coming soon. You know about Joey?"

Paul shook his head.

Fazzo seemed disappointed. "Sometimes I think it was all an illusion, like my bag of tricks. In here, all these bricks and bars and grays. Sometimes I forget what it was like to go through the door."

"What happened to Joey?"

"He's still there. I put him there."

"You killed him?"

"Holy shit, kid, you think I'd kill a little boy I loved as if he were my own son? I told you, I put him there, through 265. He's okay there. They treat him decent."

"He's not in the apartment," Paul said, as if trying to grasp something.

"You want me to spell it out for you, kid? 265 is the door to Heaven. You don't have to believe me, and it ain't the Heaven from Jesus Loves Me Yes I Know. It's a better Heaven than that. It's the Heaven to beat all Heavens." Fazzo spat at the glass that separated them. "You come here with questions like a damn reporter and you don't want answers. You want answers you go into that place. You won't like what you find, but it's too late for you. 265 is yours, kid. Go get it. And whoever it is you love, if it's that sister of yours, make sure she gets in it. Make sure she gets Heaven. Maybe that's what it's all about. Maybe for someone to get Heaven, someone else has to get Hell."

"Like that woman?"

Fazzo did not say a word. He closed his eyes and began humming.

Startled, he opened his eyes again and said, "Kid! You got to get home now!"

"What?"

"Now!" Fazzo shouted and smashed his fist against the glass.

The guard standing in the corner behind him rushed up to him, grabbing him by the wrists. "Kid, it's your sister it wants, not you. You got caught, but it's your sister it wants. And there's only one way to get into heaven! Only one way, kid! Go get her now!"

Paul didn't rush home.

He didn't like giving Fazzo the benefit of the doubt. He'd be on shift in another hour, and usually he spent this time by catching a burger and a Coke before going into the station.

He drove the murky streets as the sun lowered behind the stacks of castle-like apartment buildings on Third Street.

It looked as if it would rain in a few minutes.

Trash lay in heaps around the alleys, and he saw the faces of the walking wounded along the stretch of boulevards that were Sunday afternoon empty.

He passed the apartments on Swan Street, doing his best not to glance up to the second floor.

265.

No one would live there, not after a woman's torso was found in the bathtub.

Even squatters would stay away.

Paul drove home. He just wanted to see if she was watching her movies or reading.

He didn't believe Fazzo.

In the living room, the television was on, but without sound.

Soft music played from the bathroom.

Paul knocked on the bathroom door. "Marie?"

After four knocks, he opened it.

The machines were off.

She lay in the tub of red water. On her back. Her face beneath the water's surface like a picture he'd seen once, when they'd both been children, of a mermaid in a lake.

Scratched crudely on the tile with the edge of the scissors she'd used to cut herself free from life, the words:

I don't believe in Heaven.

IT WAS ONLY YEARS LATER, when Paul saw the item in the papers about Fazzo the Fabulous finally getting the chair, after years of living on Death Row, that he thought about 265 again.

He heard, too, that the apartments on Swan Street were being torn down within a week of Fazzo's execution.

Paul had led what he would've called a quiet life. He'd been on the force for fifteen years, and the town had not erupted in anything more than the occasional domestic battle or crack house fire.

He kept Marie's machines in his apartment, and often watched television in the living room feeling as if he were less alone.

But one evening, he went down there, down to Swan Street, down the rows of slums and squats where the city had turned off even the streetlamps.

Standing in front of the old apartments, he glanced at the windows of 265. The boards had come out, and the windows were empty sockets in the face of brick.

He carefully walked up the half-burnt staircase, around

the rubble of bricks and pulpy cardboard, stepping over the fallen boards with the nails sticking straight up.

The apartment no longer had a door. When he went inside, the place had been stripped of all appliance.

The stink of urine and feces permeated the apartment, and he saw the residue of countless squatters who had spent nights within the walls of 265.

Graffiti covered half the wall by the bathroom, all of it spray-painted cuss words, kids' names, lovers' names...

Scrawled in blue across the doorway to the bathroom, the words:

THE SEVEN STARS

The bathroom had been less worked-over. The shower curtain had been torn down, as had the medicine cabinet. But the toilet, cracked and brown, still remained, as did the bathtub and shower nozzle.

Paul closed his eyes, remembering the woman's bloody torso in the tub.

Remembering *Marie in the pink water.*

When he opened his eyes, he said, "All right. You have me. You took Marie. What is it you want?"

He sat on the edge of the tub, waiting for something. He laughed to himself, thinking of how stupid this was, how he was old enough to know better...how Fazzo the Fabulous had butchered some woman up here, and that was all. How Marie had killed herself at their home, and that was all.

There was no Heaven.

He laughed to himself. Reached in his pocket and drew out a pack of cigarettes. Lit one up, and inhaled.

Sometime, just after midnight, he heard the humming

of the flies, and the drip drop of rusty water as it splashed into the tub.

In a moment, he saw the light come up, from the edge of the forest, near the great tree, and two iguanas scuttled across the moss-covered rocks. It came in flashes at first, as if the skin of the world were being stripped away layer by layer, until the white bone of life came through, and then the green of a deep wood. The boy was there, and Paul recognized him without ever having seen his picture.

"You've finally come to join us, then," the boy said. "Marie told me all about you."

"Marie? Is she here?" Paul's tongue dried in his mouth, knowing that this was pure hallucination, but wanting it to be true.

The boy—and it was Joey, Fazzo's friend—nodded, holding his hand out.

The world had turned liquid around him, and for a moment he felt he focused a camera lens in his mind, as the world solidified again.

The great white birds stood like sentries off at some distance. A deer in the wood glanced up at the new intruder. He saw something else, like a veil, through which he could see another person.

Someone watched him from the other side of the gossamer fabric.

Lightning flashed across the green sky. A face emerged in the forest—from the trees and the fern and the birds and the lizards. A face that was neither kind nor cruel.

And then, he saw her — Marie — running to him so fast it took his breath away. She was still twenty, but she had none of the deformities of body, and the machines no longer purred beside her. "Paul! You've come! I knew you would!"

She grabbed his hand, squeezing it. "I've waited forever for you, you should've come earlier."

Joey nodded. "See? I told you he'd come eventually."

Paul grabbed his sister in his arms, pressing as close to her as he could. Tears burst from his eyes, and he felt the warmth of her skin, the smell of her hair, the smell of her—the fragrance of his beautiful, vibrant sister. He no longer cared what illusion had produced this, he did not ever want to let go of her.

But she pulled back, finally. "Paul, you're crying. Don't." She reached up and touched the edge of his cheek.

"I thought I'd never see you again," he said.

"Yes, you did," Marie said. "You believed in 265 all along. They told me you did. They knew you did."

"Who are they?" he asked.

Marie glanced at Joey. "I can't tell you."

"No names," Joey whispered a warning.

The rain splintered through the forest cover like slivers of glass, all around them, and the puddles that formed were small mirror shards reflecting the sky.

Marie grasped Paul's hand.

He could not get over her warmth. "How...how did you get here?"

She put a finger to her lips. "Shh. Isn't it enough that we're here now, together?"

Paul nodded his head.

"It won't last long," Marie said, curiously looking up at the glassy rain as it poured around them.

"The rain?" he asked, feeling that this was better than

any heaven he could imagine. This was the Heaven of all heavens.

"No. Not the rain. I mean about you being here, that's what won't last. Each time is only a glimpse. Like striking a match, it only burns for a short while."

"I don't understand," Paul said.

When Marie looked up at him all he felt was joy. He had never remembered feeling so alive, so much part of the world, so warm with love.

Again, his eyes blurred with tears.

"It's only a glimpse," she whispered. "Each time. When Fazzo was executed, he was the sacrifice. But they need another one. This time, they want the sacrifice to be here, on the threshold. It works longer that way. Just one. Each time. For you to be here."

Her mood changed, as she smiled like a child on her birthday. "Oh, but Paul, it's so wonderful to see you. Next time you come I'll show you the rivers of gold, and the way the trees whisper the secret of immortality. The birds can guide us across the fire mountains. And I have friends here, too, I want you to meet."

"I don't understand," Paul whispered, but the rain began coming down harder, and a glass wall of rain turned shiny and then melted, as he felt her hand grab for him through the glass.

He was sitting in the darkness of the bathroom at 265, a young woman's hand in his, cut off at the wrist because the door had come down too hard, too soon.

❧

For Paul, the hardest one was the first one.

He found her down in Brickton, near the factories. She was not pretty, and looked to him to be at the end of her days from drugs and too many men and too many pimps beating her up. She had burn marks on her arms, and when she got into his car, he thought: I won't be doing anything too awful. Not too awful. It'll be like putting an animal out of its misery.

"You a cop?" she asked.

"No way. I'm just a very desperate guy."

He told her he knew this place, an old apartment, not real pretty, but it was private and it got him off.

When they reached Swan Street, she laughed. "I been in these apartments before. Christ, they look better now than I remember them."

He nodded. "Will you be impressed if I tell you I own them?"

"Really? Wow. You must be loaded."

Paul shrugged. "They went for cheap. The city was going to tear them down. I got that blocked, bought them, fixed them up a bit."

"Looks empty to me."

"I only just started getting them ready for tenants," he said.

They went upstairs.

INSIDE THE APARTMENT, he offered her a drink.

"All right," she said.

"Need to use the bathroom?" he asked, opening the freezer door to pull out the ice tray.

"If you don't mind," she said.

"Go ahead. Take a shower if you feel like it."

"Well, you're buying," the woman said.

When he heard the bathroom door close, Paul took the key from the dresser.

§

STANDING in front of the bathroom door, he waited until he heard the shower turn on.

He checked his watch.

It was two minutes to midnight.

From the shower, she shouted, "Honey? You mind bringing my drink in and scrubbing my back?"

He opened the bathroom door.

Steam poured from under the shower curtain.

Once inside, he turned and locked the door.

He put the key in his breast pocket.

"That you?" she asked.

"Yeah," Paul said. "I'll join you in just a few seconds."

He crouched down.

Beneath the sink, a large wooden box.

Opening it, he lifted the cloth within.

He grabbed the hand-ax that lay there, and then closed the box.

§

PAUL SET the small ax on top of the sink.

He unbuttoned his shirt, and took it off. He hung it on the hook by the door.

Then, he stepped out of his shoes. Undid his belt, and let his trousers fall to the floor.

"Baby?" she asked.

"In a minute," he said. "We'll have some fun."

He pulled off his socks and then his briefs.

Grabbed the hand-ax.

Looked at himself naked in the mirror, ax in fist.

For a second, the glass flashed like lightning, and he saw Marie's face there.

A glimpse.

Then, he pulled back the shower curtain and began opening the door to Heaven.

Fries With That?

A NOVELETTE

When we got interviewed by *People* magazine, Maggy said that I'd always known about my talent, but that isn't true.

She didn't say it to the guy interviewing us, just to me in private. She told him that the gun had felt good and warm in her hand.

"Like a kiss," she said. "Every time I took a shot."

Mags doesn't tell the truth in interviews.

The truth is, I never really knew about my talent much until things started to happen over a long period of time. My gramma didn't even know for sure, at first, at least not till I told her. Now, I wish I had listened to that old woman. She knew how bad it could get.

My mom should've known, too, after that cat. But she didn't catch on too quick, and now, look at the mess. Sure, we could hire good lawyers because of how much both my mom and dad make, and who my dad knows, and we did what we could for Maggy. She's not mad at me or anything, but every now and then she gives me that glare.

But gramma knew, once I told her about the cat and other things. She told me without really telling me about how bad it could get.

Mags said it would've happened anyway, what she did.

❦

I HAVE TO ADMIT, it was fun going on television, and meeting big celebrities like Oprah Winfrey.

They were all nice and really sweet. I thought I looked ugly in that white dress my dad made me wear. He told me that young ladies going on television should look virginal, as if this has ever been a problem for me.

Maggy only wore her usual black, from head to toe. I call it her witch phase, although she thinks she looks thinner like that. She doesn't like me calling her a witch or a bitch, mainly because she's both—she hasn't been to church since confirmation, and the bitch part…well, if you saw her on television, you'd understand.

When she started yelling back at the studio audience, I just about died.

But it figures.

She was up there flailing her arms around and cursing and I know her grandmother just about had a cow watching on the old RCA back at the trailer park.

Maggy doesn't like being called trailer trash either, but that's really what started it all when she and I were showering off after field hockey (which is neither, since we have to play it on what might best be referred to as a gravel pit, and our team has always been lame).

It was before fourth period, and Alison Gall had stolen Maggy's clothes.

ALISON, who is the kind of bitch that no one ever calls bitch, is not exactly the cheerleader type even though she made the squad finally after years of trying. It was her mother pushing her that made her crack the squad, and ever since then she's just been looking for scapegoats for unresolved anger all the time.

So she calls Mags a trailer trash dyke, and Mags throws her against the tiles. And Mags, sounding like some otherworldly monster, says, "I'm gonna kill you someday, Alison, and when I do, you're gonna wish you'd never been born."

Alison picked on a lot of girls, but mainly Mags.

Maggy is a good scapegoat since she doesn't quite fit into Glasgow High (named for a famous writer, like I want to be someday soon).

Maggy is not exactly Glasgow material. She smokes too much, tells everyone but me to fuck off, and sometimes me, and she has what Mr. Herlihy writes on her report card all the time.

"An unusual sense of justice." Mr. Herlihy's easy going, which is why we like him. But Mr. Green always writes, "Margaret has trouble forming bonds with other students due to issues."

Issues.

Such crap.

All of this was read aloud on those talk shows, and then some gooney psychotherapist came out and told Mags what was wrong with her.

Besides which, Maggy and I formed a bond in third grade when she was the kick-ass new girl who talked back to old Mrs. Burley.

And Mr. Green, or anyone for that matter, calling her Margaret when in fact she was christened Maggy Mae after an old song…Nowhere on her birth certificate is the word, "Margaret." And that word would not describe Mags anyway (I can call her Mags. I've earned the right over all these years. You, and others, cannot.)

In third grade, she was just this dark thing. That's all I can tell you. I was of course that whole blond blue eyes ribbon in her hair kind of nice little girl who laughed at boys' jokes as if I knew what the hell they were talking about. But Mags, she was already taller then the tallest kid, long dark hair that obscured most of her face, what I like to call cigarette lips—big pouty pillows right under her nose. Back in those early days, I thought she looked like *not a nice girl*. She looked like trouble and trash, but I got over it fast. I went out to clap the erasers for Mrs. Burley, and there Mags was, behind the dumpster, smoking a Camel.

"WHAT THE FUCK are you staring at?" she asked. I had never before heard a girl use the F word. She had a dark voice. Everything about her back in third grade was dark.

I was too scared to say anything. Truth be told, I peed my panties right there. I thought she was going to eat me or something. She just sucked back that cigarette till there was nothing but ash, and eyed me with those dark eyes.

"I asked you a goddamned question," she said.

"I'm…not staring…I'm really not," I said.

She shook her head in disgust. I saw the rest of her face for the first time when she pulled back her hair a little. She had a tattoo on her left cheek, just next to her earlobe. Just a small star. "Like it?" she asked, when she caught me staring.

"Not really," I said. Back then I had a mouse squeak voice. I was pretty much a little nothing who had pretty handwriting and a yes'm attitude. Just a little pleasing machine. But I did not like dark thoughts or tattoos. Yet.

"I like it," Mags said, letting her hair drop. "You're probably stuck up like every other girl here, ain't you?"

I shook my head. "No. I'm not. Really."

"Here," she said, extending her hand, the next cigarette already lit. "Have a smoke."

"I uh no thanks."

"Have a goddamn smoke," she said. She reached out and grabbed my hand. She thrust the cigarette between my fingers. I stared down at it.

"My mother used to smoke," I squeaked.

"It's good for you."

"No it isn't, the Surgeon General said—"

"You believe that government tool? Smoke," she said.

It was a command.

I delicately put the cigarette between my lips. I thought she was going to kill me if I disobeyed her.

"Inhale, come on, inhale," she commanded.

I sucked back the smoke, and coughed, and sucked, and coughed, and pretty soon I was hooked on the damn things, and I still am. One of life's little pleasures. Come to Marlboro Country. Get the Most Out of Life.

Sure, Mags corrupted me thoroughly. By junior year in high school, she'd taught me all about smoking and drinking and why it was important for a boy to have a big one. It took me awhile to figure out what big ones were, but I was happy Mags had warned me ahead of time.

The vodka helped with that, too.

I hid most of it from my mom and dad, who weren't too cool. They were church going types, and basically so was I.

Unfortunately, I was also heavily into sin as both a concept and an action. After church, I'd sneak off down to the alley behind the Meat Market in town, and me and Mags would smoke and have a few beers and then go out and raise hell. I'm sure God in His Heaven didn't give a rat's ass if we got into trouble now and then.

Sin was not new to my family. My mother once cheated on my father with Dr. Van Graaf, my orthodontist. How do I know? Dad was away on business, and Mom and Dr. Van Graaf were upstairs in bed, that's how I know.

She didn't want me to know; in fact, I was supposed to be staying at Mags' for the night.

Truth was, I was really going to spend the night with Billy Alcott in his backyard tent, along with a bottle of Stoli and a carton of menthols. But Billy was acting like a creep, so I told him I was having my period and he ran like hell.

All boys do, the wimps. His tent sucked, anyway, barely enough room to move your elbows let alone have some teenager on top of you trying to tell you how much he loved you when you knew he didn't give a flyer and had been doing it with Missy Hanscomb three nights before.

But my mother and Billy and Dr. Van Graaf have very little to do with this, my confession.

Yeah, I know, if you saw us on TV or read *People* or maybe that little piece in the *New York Times* or in our local rag, you might know the rest of it. Six kids all lobotomized and hemorrhaging in the middle of Glasgow High School with their signed yearbooks at their feet. Bullets flying. It was something, I'll tell you.

Gramma would've told me, maybe, how to stop it, but she wasn't around by then.

THERE'S ALWAYS MORE to this stuff than meets the eye. *60 Minutes* is doing this thing on us in about a month, and I'm sure it will be more lies. I'm really holding out for Barbara Walters for the interview. Her people haven't contacted me yet. I figure when school starts up in the fall, and things like November Sweeps are going on, she will.

Mags thinks Barbara Walters and her people don't give a flyer about two girls from Minnesota who were suspected of mass murder at the end of their junior year.

But I think based on the coverage we've gotten so far, we're worth the Sweeps Month and maybe even a retro thingy in the spring. I would even say we've put our little town in Minnesota on the map, except there was that movie star who did that back in the seventies before he got eaten up by heroin and a nasty car wreck.

I know that once we get Barbara Walters to interview us —and not just one of her *20/20* interviews, but one of those Specials she does that are so good—the record will be set straight. I'm having trouble convincing Mags to wait till then to tell everything, since we really didn't get a chance on the talk show circuit. Too much yelling and screaming and myth-making. My mother didn't even call them talk shows, she called them Freak Shows of the Very Vapid. I kind of like that. Mom has a way with words.

But Oprah and Jerry Springer weren't like that. They all

have a lot of heart. They were sweet. Mags was hilarious on them. I was just doing my Pretty Little Nothing act, because I didn't want to let the world know the truth yet. I was the Loyal Best Friend. Mom'd totally freak herself if she knew I was writing down what really happened, but Mags is in trouble over this now, and the truth is, she's just protecting me.

All right, Mom has known all along, but she is really good at denying reality. Even when it slaps her in the face. I wish I could do that.

She's known ever since I was about four. She saw what I did to the cat.

Now, first off, I've never liked cats. Please don't hold that against me. I've just never met one that liked me. They all act like little bitches around me, they don't purr, they don't preen, they just growl and slash at my ankles. So it's no surprise to me that I did the *Fries With That?* thing.

That's what Mags calls it.

When we were in fourth grade and I did it to this one kid, Mags said to me, "Fries with that?" She meant it as a double joke.

First, because at all those hamburger fast food places the guy on the speaker says, "Fries with that?" no matter what the fuck you order.

You could order shit on a stick, and he'd say, "Duh, fries with that?"

That's part of it.

The other part is that Fries word. All its meanings.

But wait, back to the cat when I was little.

MOM SAID that the cat was hissing at me, as usual. I was sitting on the kitchen floor.

I just stared at the cat long and hard and suddenly like my eyes rolled back into my head and I turned all pale and started speaking in tongues.

Well, Mom is what Mags called a Super Christian, and even though she knows it probably was not her beloved Holy Ghost talking through me, she always likes to think the best. In fact, I think Mom turned to church-going because of the talent, and gramma had it, as it turns out.

After that, Mom said that cat was not right, and would just walk in circles. Which cracks me up to think of a cat walking in circles all the time. And again, for you cat lovers, it's not that I hate cats, it's that they never like me.

I suppose one day I may meet one who likes me, and then I may take cats on a case-by-case basis. Until then, we really have nothing to do with each other whenever possible.

I told Mags about the cat in eighth grade when I knew for sure she was my absolutely best friend of all friends.

We went from smoking a pack a day to three packs a day each by the time we entered high school. The liquor didn't really kick into high gear till junior year.

We hung out in the girls' room a lot, smoking of course and writing nasty things about girls like Alison Gall and some of the other girls of what we called the Canine Corps. All cheerleaders were a little too kissy face for our tastes, even though they had to go down on the filthy football players.

I really shouldn't have hated Alison so much—that's half my problem. I would obsess on girls and boys I hated, and then I would have no control sometimes. I actually had excellent control, up until the beginning of June when we raised the hell to end all hells, but who knew?

Not me or Mags back when we were scratching our Bic pens into the toilet stall wall. "Alison Sucks Donkeys," I read my exquisite poetry aloud while I scratched.

"No, more sophisticated," Mags said in her smoke-scraped throaty voice.

Then, she lifted her Swiss Army knife and scratched, "ALISON'S DICK IS BIGGER THAN JOEY'S."

"That's so fourth grade," I said, grabbing the cigarette from between Mags' lips and stuffing it in my greedy mouth. I sucked back the smoke and whooshed it out through my nostrils. "Besides which, everybody's dick is bigger than Joey's."

Mags laughed. The stall was tiny, but since we're both pretty skinny, it wasn't too bad. The toilet bowl was almost full of our cigarettes butts.

"What is it she ever did to either of us that makes us hate her so much?" Mags asked. "I almost forget."

"She's just so Alison," I said. Suddenly, Mags thrust her hand over my mouth.

She lipped, *Someone just came in.* The cigarette dropped from her mouth into the toilet, pronto.

The girl's bathroom door swung shut, and we heard little mouse steps over to the sink.

I glanced at Mags, who released her hold on my mouth.

We both knew who it was.

Janine Cunligger—and yeah, it was her real name. I could not make up a name that good even if I tried.

&

JANINE WAS SPOOKY, but not in the same way that Mags is scary. Janine was one of those girls you knew would one day turn psycho on everybody, or else she'd invent the cure for the Common Cold. Maybe she'll end up revolutionizing software or something. She's that kind of girl. Despite the last name Cunligger, she was called Gyro because of her scientific and mathematical bent. Mags nicknamed her this in sixth grade, after Mags got tired of all the boys calling Janine by a not-so-nice revision of her last name. Mags originally called her Gyroscopa, Goddess of Science Nerds, but eventually this became Gyro until Janine herself used it when she introduced herself to new kids.

Janine was also plug ugly, at least as far as any of us knew. Unlike Mags who had the cool hip urban look of dark hair on dark clothes and dark heart, Janine a.k.a. Gyro had a frizz and thick glasses and Pippi Longstocking legs and was flat as a pancake even at sixteen when the rest of us had pretty much Jiffy Popped to our full bra sizes.

And as Mags and I stood silently in the toilet stall, we heard the saddest most mournful sound coming from the sink where Gyro stood letting water run over her hands.

"Jesus," Mags gasped, closing her eyes.

Gyro was sobbing up a storm, and the running water didn't hide it.

I was the first out of the stall. I stood back a ways from Gyro, because she still was a bit spooky in my opinion. I had never really warmed up to her after I'd been held back a year in Chemistry and she had moved on with Honors.

She saw me in the mirror over the sink. Her headband was askew. Her frizz of hair seemed frizzier.

"You okay?" I asked. I felt Mags' hand on my shoulder, as if trying to pull me back.

Gyro leaned over the sink again, pulling her glasses off. "Yeah, fine. Just got some dirt in my eyes."

"You were crying," I said.

"We heard you," Mags added. "What's up?"

Gyro kept pretending until Mags just went up to her and threw her arms around her. "It's okay," Mags said, "We're not gonna hurt you or anything."

Gyro pulled away, shrugging her off. "Yes you are. You're like all the rest of them."

"The hell we are," Mags said.

"That's right," I volunteered weakly. Truth was, I didn't really care to delve into Gyro's problems. She was one of those girls I didn't want to get to know too well because a) we had nothing in common and b) there was nothing I was going to gain by being friends with her. Now my b) choice may seem cold and unfeeling, but I learned years ago that there's no point in making friends if it doesn't help you in some way.

I don't mean namby-pamby help, I mean, if a friendship doesn't take you to a new level, or open up a different world, or feed you in some way, why have it?

All right, maybe I am a bit cold. I got burned by some of those other girls and boys enough to know that you are lucky if you can make one good friend in your lifetime.

Mags was *that* friend.

But Mags has a better soul than I do.

She managed to wrestle her arms around Gyro's shoulders again. Gyro started crying again. I went and hopped up on the edge of the sink. I brought another cig out from the pack, lit it, puffed, and passed it to Gyro.

Gyro didn't hesitate. She snapped it out of my hand and took a long drag on it. I reached into my fanny pack and brought out some Kleenex for her. Then, I drew the flask out. It was rum and Coke, and not a lot of rum so please don't get the idea I was drunk twenty-four hours a day. Mags is the one with the bar in her locker at school, not me.

"So what's the deal?" I asked.

Gyro sucked back another lungful of smoke. On exhaling, she said, "It's Alison Gall."

I looked at Mags.

"We were just talking about her," I said, with glee.

"What's she done to you?" Mags asked. Mags really has the milk of human kindness in her veins. She looks dark and nasty, and she talks like a whore sometimes, but she really is the kind of person who would save a gnat on the ass of a weasel.

And then, Gyro told us. All of it.

It's not really important what she told us. In fact, I think it would hurt her feelings if she knew that I was writing this, and knew that it probably would get published someday since we're so famous now. But let me put it this way: Alison did something to Gyro that was so terrible, something that is the worst thing one girl can do to another girl. I do not make this stuff up.

If you're female, you know what that is.

If you're male, you probably don't have a clue.

But when you're sixteen, and a girl, and another girl does to you what Alison Gall did to Gyro, you would feel on the inside like all the joy in life had been extinguished— no, *stolen* from you by the worst kind of thief. Boys sometimes do this to girls, too, and they're creeps.

But for a girl to do it to another girl is the lowest form of life.

So then and there, the three of us made a pact, Gyro, me and Mags.

We set our plan into motion before Friday, the day of the Prom.

🙠

IT WAS easy enough to lure Alison Gall to the old farm off Route 7.

Not that she was exactly a farm-lovin' girl, but we knew that the guy she really wanted to ball was Quent Appenino, the Italian Stallion quarterback who had transferred from some California school when his folks got divorced.

Quent was built, and had good buns and a great smile. If he weren't such a moron when it came to school, I'd have lusted after him, too.

But he was a big pretty guy and since he'd arrived he'd been going steady with Susie Malloy. Quent was a good boy, too, and didn't cheat, and this drove Alison nuts. So what we did was we told Quent that it was Susie's birthday, and we had this card for her.

We wanted him to be the first to personalize and sign it.

So he takes up like half the card, the doofus, and writes, *You know how much I care for you, baby. You + Me=4-Ever.* Then, pretending I'd forgotten the way out to the farm— which Quent's grandfather owned—I asked him to write down directions on this really thin piece of paper. "I want to drive out with my dad this weekend just for fresh air."

Quent really was a moron. He didn't question this at all.

He just wrote out the directions.

Then, Mags who is a genius at this, carefully traced his note about the directions. Again, trying to imitate his handwriting, which she did remarkably well. She scrawled at the bottom: *Before the Prom, 4 p.m. I want you. Quent.*

"SHE'S GOING TO MELT," I said.

Gyro nodded. "But what do we do when we get her out there?"

"Don't even worry about it. We do what we do," Mags said, passing another cigarette to Gyro.

Gyro had a bad jones for cigs, it turned out. I discovered that we had that in common.

Okay, now here's where it gets hazy.

Not that the Prom coming up was any big deal to us since we weren't seniors. We didn't have steadies, and I'm not big on wearing a big poofy dress with my hair up like Cinderella. Maybe my third grade pre-Mags self would've been into that crap, but I was more of a let's get drunk and break into the arcade kind of girl by junior year. If I wanted a boy sexually, I didn't need all that filler: just give me the guy. The bad influence of my best friend again.

She always said I was the real bad influence, back when we were little.

It was that fourth grade thing, when Jonathan Rice was on the monkey bars and Mags and I were stepping on his hands as he swung around. Jonathan was, I think, a budding masochist, or else he liked to look up my skirt. Back in fourth grade I wore what Mags still calls the Betsy-Wetsy outfits where "You looked like one of those American Girl dolls."

But Jonathan grabbed my ankle. I slipped, landing on my tailbone on the cold metal of the monkey bars, which hurt bad enough, but then I lost my balance and fell down into the gravel.

It was the first time I realized you could actually see stars when you slammed into the earth hard enough. I thought my brain had been knocked to my shins.

Now, maybe Jonathan jogged something in my head a little more than it should've been, or maybe what I did to that cat when I was four just got worse the closer I got to puberty.

Or maybe it was just fate.

That was the first day Mags had ever used the term *Fries With That?* About what I can do. I don't do it often, and in fact, I never planned on doing it.

But I almost fried poor little Jonathan Rice right there on the playground during recess. He came over to me, kneeling down to see if I was okay.

And I just went blank. Like the white dot that's left on the TV. when you turn it off sometimes. I went down this winding tunnel in my head. I figured I must be dying or something.

When I came to, Mags described the whole thing to me.

"Damn, it was scary as all hell," she said. "Jonathan was crying about you, and you start showing the whites of your eyes and frothing at the mouth, and breaking out in rashes all over your face. Then your mouth opens wider than I figured it could go, like a largemouth bass screaming or something, and your tongue starts waggling, and then…"

Mags paused here for effect. Her eyes widened.

"Then…all these words I never heard of come out of your mouth, words that are almost like English but aren't quite, and you're shaking, and I break out in goose bumps all over, and Jonathan starts making choking sounds and then I smell what seems to me to be the smell of toast burning in a toaster, and then it doesn't smell like toast but it smells like when the dentist drills in your mouth at a cavity and how it doesn't hurt because of the Novocain but this weird burning smell comes up…And I look at Jonathan and his face is all red and then the color in his eyes just kind of melts into nothing."

THAT WAS THE DESCRIPTION, but nobody ever blamed me for what happened to Jonathan Rice.

At first, they called it stress blindness, then shock. But Mags and I knew he just got the *Fries With That?* treatment.

She called him Fried Rice.

One day, when Jonathan Rice was in seventh grade, now at a special school for kids, he took a long walk off a short pier.

I've always felt a little guilty about that.

I asked my mother about it then, and she was cagey, but she finally admitted that my gramma had it.

So I go to the nursing home where gramma lays sputtering through her nostrils, god love her, and I tell her what mom told me.

Gramma had these curious eyes back then, pale blue, covered with a translucent milky color. Her skin was as thin as tracing paper, and you could see all these blue veins under the surface. I loved my grandmother, even though she had to wheeze when she breathed. I snuck her cigarettes, too, and played Hearts with her sometimes for hours.

When I tell her about Jonathan Rice, and then the cat,

her eyes fill with tears. Gramma was from Ireland, and she wells up with tears easily, from hearing "I'll Bring You A Daisy A Day," to when she thinks of County Clare and all its green pastures and blue skies. Harp ale does it for her, also.

She reached for my shoulder to steady herself as she rose up on the bed. "You have the evil eye, then," she said, her voice all soft and wispy like cotton candy. "I knew it would show again."

"It's not my eyes," I said. "I speak and other stuff happens, too."

"It's through the eyes," she said. She pointed to the pale blue of her eyes. "Look, you and I have the old blue. Your hair is blond like your daddy's, but you got the old ways in your spirit. They say we're descended from fairies, but we are from the original people of the islands. We have the eyes and we have the talent."

"But I didn't mean to hurt Jonathan." I began crying, still somewhat in my Pretty Little Nothing phase.

"'Evil eye' is what others called it. It's a vision that takes over. It's a reshaper of minds, it's a molder of people's insides." Then, Gramma hugged me close. Her breath was terrible, like a cat's. Her light whiskers scratched my cheek, but her warmth was not to be denied.

I lay there, letting her hold me, the sticky warmth between us, until it grew dark. Before I left, she asked me to learn to focus.

"Through craft," she said. "Talent is nothing but wildness without craft."

"Like witchcraft?" I asked.

"Nothing like that, dearie," Gramma said, her voice going raspy from the long day of cigarette smoking. "The craft of your art. Your art is there, and now you must make it sing."

"I don't know about that."

"But stay away from the dead," she whispered. "It's not meant to be near them."

"Why?"

"Nothing good comes of it when near the dead. Your great-great-grandmother Irene had it, and once, she was at a wake. She thought she heard her dead uncle knocking at his coffin after she'd danced around it a bit."

"Cool" I said.

"Not so cool," Gramma whispered. "Not so cool at all."

She fell asleep soon after, and then a few weeks later, before I could actually ask her how I was to go about perfecting this so-called craft, Gramma died.

The day she died, it felt like someone kicked me in the gut. Death does that to you.

I imagine it didn't feel so wonderful to Gramma, either.

Because I didn't like to think of myself as Evil (I was a God-fearing little Jesus freak back then for the most part, although I was moving closer to my ultimate embrace of hormones and sin as time went on), I dropped the whole Evil Eye phrase. I went with Mags' *Fries With That?* designation.

So, when Mags said to Gyro, the afternoon of the Prom, "Don't worry. We do what we do," I was a little afraid of the *Fries With That?* syndrome coming through.

Mags assured me this was next to impossible. "I mean, it hasn't happened since you were in fourth grade. For all we know, Jonathan Rice just went brain dead right then because of some interior alarm clock."

"Freud said there are no accidents," Gyro cautioned,

although she could not possibly have known about what I accidentally did to Jonathan Rice in fourth grade.

&a.

WE REPEATED a lot of this as we stood over poor Alison Gall, whom we had most heinously trapped at Quent Appenino's grandfather's farm out in the middle of Bumfuck.

Alison wore a cute little yellow pullover that showed her melons to their best advantage and her little tight-ass cheer-leader skirt, knee socks, cute little black shoes, and no underwear to speak of.

Need I mention what a shock she had received when she entered the old barn that had yet another forged love note tacked to its door?

Three furies standing around in the semi-dark of the barn, with rope, duct tape, and gun.

Okay, the gun was a last minute thing.

&a.

GYRO's older brother Lance was a cop wannabe. He was too smart for the local police force, apparently, but still he kept a major stash of Glocks and Smiths & Wessons and big old rifles, none of which Gyro knew much about.

Mags picked out the Glock 17. "I've seen this on TV shows," she said. "At least, I think I've seen this."

"I don't think we need a gun, do we?" I had asked as we stood shivering in Gyro's brother's room, knowing the fearful act we were to perform a few hours down the road.

And then, it was Alison Gall's turn to shiver, which is what I expected when she saw the gun.

Instead, she became the bitch of all bitches.

"What the hell kind of joke is this, you losers?" she asked, and then, looking at the gun, she laughed. "You planning on going to prison for the rest of your lives?"

Mags laughed. She had that great throaty laugh, the kind of laugh that old movie stars have, or old smokers. "Listen, Alison, we're minors, get real. Gyro's dad is a brain surgeon, and Nora's dad is a tax lawyer. Who do you think's going to go to prison?"

"You, trailer trash girl," Alison huffed.

"Shut up," I said.

"Shut up yourself, geek."

"Don't make me bitch slap you," Mags said. She meant business, particularly after the trailer trash comment. "My dad may not be some big professional, but he's been known to spring a few dudes from prison. I doubt reform school is going to take a major army to overcome."

Alison quieted down. She glanced at me, then at Gyro. "Is this a lesbian thing or something?"

I laughed. "You'll wish when it's over."

"No," Gyro said. "We just want you out of the way until after Prom."

"No way!" Alison shouted, and for a moment I felt sorry for the poor thing.

Alison Gall lived for major social events. She never missed a football party, or a dance, or a chance to show off her cheering skills. She was a debutante in the big cotillion up in St. Paul.

For just a second there, I saw the sad little girl beneath

the makeup and the dye job and the "Look How Cute I Am" clothes.

She was just like I was years ago. A Pretty Little Nothing. Trying to make do. Trying to please other people. Dealing with a social structure where girls really had to tread water when the boys around her just got stuff for free.

No wonder she was so nasty to us girls all the time—we were the one group she didn't have to please.

I was about to call the gag off, but this was Gyro's game.

Gyro stepped forward with the rope. After the initial scuffle, we got Alison's hands behind her back.

I only had to hit her once.

By the time the duct tape went over her mouth, Alison's eyes were red from tears. Mascara ran down her cheeks.

"I should shoot you just for being a cheerleader," Mags said, pointing the gun directly at her forehead.

Alison didn't even flinch. I knew why. She was such a Pretty Little Nothing that she thought death was no more terrifying or hurtful than missing the biggest dance of the year. Maybe this was shallow of her, I don't know.

We all want something out of life, don't we? We all want something, and to someone else, it probably sounds stupid and shallow and empty, but to each of us, it's the shining moment that we can always have at the center of our lives.

And Prom was going to be Alison's shining moment.

Here she was a senior, probably going to the local college next year, if at all, and her entire future life depended upon looking back on high school as that peak, that golden moment.

We were taking that away from her.

Mags must've guessed my shift in sympathies. "Don't forget what she did to Gyro," she said.

I shined my flashlight over at Gyro, fury still in her eyes. She carefully wrapped the remainder of her rope around Alison's ankles.

I shut my flashlight off.

I no longer wanted to look at our captive.

And that's when Gyro rose up and took the gun from Mags' hand and aimed it at the side of Alison Gall's head and shot her at point blank range.

SOMETIMES THERE ARE things you do in life and you know when you're doing them that later on you'll hate yourself, or you'll want to go back and erase part of the picture of that moment.

In that millisecond when Gyro fired into Alison's skull, I tried to, at least in my mind, turn the clock back by a minute so I could grab the gun before Gyro could get it.

I know neither Mags nor I had intended to use that gun. It was just a scare tactic. But Gyro, I think, probably had planned Alison's death for at least a week, from at least that moment when she entered the bathroom sobbing, from the moment that we told her that we'd seek a suitable revenge for her humiliation.

Gyro, bullied her entire life, her last name turned into an obscene joke, her hair made fun of, her face, her clothes.

Girls like Alison had done a lot of it.

Maybe even girls like me.

And she rolled all of that into one moment with a gun in a barn and a cheerleader who had pissed her off.

THE SILENCE AFTERWARDS was like a roar of locusts in my head.

I thought I heard light bulbs sparking and popping all around us. I thought it was the Fourth of July, from the crashes and booms inside my head.

Alison lay on her side, half her scalp blown off. Part of her face was on the dirt, as if the bullet had unmasked her.

Mags was the first to speak. "Oh, Christ, Gyro."

"Yeah," Gyro nodded, tossing the gun down. "I know. I shouldn't have. But I had to before it went the other way."

"Went the other way?" I asked.

But I knew what she meant.

If you didn't put a bullet in the head of the one who tormented you, you put the bullet in your own head.

It was always either-or when it came to vengeance.

"All right, now, we're fucked," Mags said. "Now we're really fucked." She slapped the side of her face. "Christ, my heart is beating like it's gonna jump out from my chest."

"Funny," Gyro said, almost kindly. "I've never felt this calm. You?"

"I have no idea what I'm feeling," I said.

"As long as she doesn't get the *Fries With That?* feeling, we're fine," Mags managed to joke.

❦

LONG AFTER THE Prom was over, we sat in that dark barn with the corpse, passing cigarettes around until our packs were empty.

"Gyro," I said, offering her my flask. "You may go to jail for this. Wait, not 'may', 'will'."

Mags waved the last of her cigarette, tracing a red line in the air. "We're accomplices. Or accessories."

"Accessories," Gyro gasped after taking a long swig of my special brew. "But I'm the killer."

"You think she was going to change later?" I asked.

"Huh?"

"Well, I mean, this wasn't her prom dress. I wonder what she was going to wear to the dance."

Gyro gave me a look like I was crazy.

I shrugged. "The one thing I can say for Alison is she had some nice dresses."

"People loved her," Mags whispered, reverentially. "I don't know why, but boys and parents and local business people, and little kids all loved her. Alison Gall, the bitch." Then she laughed. "I can't believe we're sitting here with a cheerleader's body drinking bad rum and Coke from a cheap flask on Prom Night."

"It does lead one to suspect we're insane," I said, drunkenly.

The flask was dry by the next go round.

"Almost insane. If we were insane, we'd probably play with her or something," Gyro said.

"Yuck," I said.

"That is disgusting." Mags shivered. "One thing, though. We need a plan of action now."

Instead, we went swimming.

OUT BACK WAS that duck pond, empty of ducks at two a.m., and Mags was the first of us to shed her clothes. She grabbed the old rope swing, and swung out over the middle of the pond before dropping.

The splash was huge. Mags bobbed up laughing. Gyro told me she wasn't in the mood, but I convinced her we should go in because of how filthy and stinky we'd all gotten since she'd shot Alison Gall in the head.

Soon, all three of us were in the pond, splashing and laughing and trying to forget the millisecond of bad judgment when we decided to set any of this in motion in the first place.

In the moonlight, Gyro came up from the water, and both Mags and I gasped.

"What is it? What's wrong?" Gyro asked.

I looked at Mags and then glanced back at Gyro. With her frizz brought down by the water, and her glasses off, and naked so we could see her breasts—

"You are the most beautiful girl in school," I said.

"No kidding. Look at you," Mags asked. "Why hide so much under the frizzy hair and crappy clothes?"

Gyro covered her breasts with her hands. "You're making fun of me."

"No," I said. "I swear, Gyro—"

"Janine," Mags corrected me. "No girl who looks like this could be Gyroscopa. Jesus, Janine, you look a movie star. And you've got those champagne glass breasts."

"And not the fluted kind," I joked.

"You're embarrassing me," Gyro said. "Seriously. Call me Gyro, I don't like being called Janine."

"I can't anymore," Mags said. "No way. Christ, Janine. You're a murderess and a beauty. Surprises galore."

"You may prove popular in prison," I said. It was meant

as a joke, but suddenly they both went silent for too many seconds.

"Please," Gyro began sobbing. She swam over to the muddy shore.

❦

THERE WAS NOTHING TO DO, or at least, we didn't figure out what the hell we were going to do yet. We sure as shit couldn't go home.

We couldn't just leave Alison's body there in the barn.

We toyed with the idea of pinning the murder on Quent Appenino, because the notes would be in his handwriting.

And he *was* stupid.

But that story would probably have flaws we couldn't figure out.

We thought about saying some strange man did it, but what if some innocent guy matching the description got the chair over this or something?

We still had shreds and scraps of conscience, after all.

Then, 'round about five thirty, just as the first pink rays of June sunlight appeared, Mags slapped me on the shoulder.

"You!" she cried out.

"What the—"

"*Fries With That!*" Mags began dancing around in a circle, her blouse still not buttoned up so her breasts kind of swung out like ripe pears about to fall.

"What's that mean?" Gyro asked.

I shrugged.

Mags clapped her hands together and stood still. "It's her thing. It's like an ability. It's like a magic thingy."

"No it isn't. It's like the evil eye."

"No negative thoughts today," Mags announced boldly. "Now, Nora, you can fry people's brains, right?"

I shrugged again. "Animals, people. Only done it twice that I know of."

"What?" Gyro asked, her beauty still apparent in the early light.

"Okay," Mags said. She paced in a circle around me like some mad professor. "Okay. So! You know how this ability of yours works?"

"Nope," I said. "It's inherited. It's like having a bunion as far as I'm concerned."

"Wait — you can inherit bunions?" Mags asked.

"Like a recessive gene," Gyro volunteered, still with a confused look on her face.

"Exactly, and it's there. It's inside you. It's sleeping, but," Mags stopped pacing and stood almost nose-to-nose with me. Her breath was sour.

Her voice dropped to a whisper. "Ever tried it on a dead girl?"

Gyro probably whined about not understanding us or something, and Mags probably went on with her ravings, but actually the idea burst within me as Mags said that one sentence.

Ever tried it on a dead girl?

Yeah, my gramma's words came back to me then. "*Stay away from the dead.*"

Then I remembered what she'd told me about my great-grandmother. How something had been knocking from inside her uncle's coffin...

BIRDS BEGAN SINGING before the light was fully up that morning.

We were worried about when the farm folk would come out to their barn, even though there were no animals to be seen in it, only the basics of farm machinery.

So, we took Alison up, using Mags' sweatshirt to jam her face against her skull. Any little bloody bits, we covered up with straw and dirt. We took her back to her car, and put her in the trunk.

It was a cute little Toyota with leather seats. Alison had been so spoiled in her lifetime. But honestly, if you're going to die young, might as well have had the best of everything.

So Mags and Gyro drove Alison's car and I drove my mother's Buick back to my house.

MY HOUSE WAS THE BIGGEST, and my room was the furthest from the front door and the closest to two side doors. We would not be noticed by my parents at all, given that it was Saturday morning, which meant Country Club B.S. for both of them.

They laid Alison on my bed, keeping her bloodied head on Mags' sweatshirt.

Gyro looked at me gravely. "I don't know if I can believe all the stuff she told me in the car, but if you can do anything, it might help."

I looked at Mags. My best friend in the whole world. Better than best. Best of the best. She seemed small and vulnerable now. The way I felt on the inside.

I looked down at poor Alison.

"It's not working," I said after a few minutes.

"How does it work?" Gyro asked.

"I need to get mad at her."

"Stimulus, response," Gyro nodded. "And between stimulus and response there's a pause. In the pause, we decide what the response will be."

"Huh?" Mags asked.

Gyro nodded again to herself. I could practically see the little wheels turning.

Hesitating only a moment, she walked over to me, leaned close, and whispered something in my ear.

The explosion from inside my head seemed to knock me back against the wall. The room began spinning, and I swear—I swear—I saw a fire burst across the wallpaper, ripping and devouring the flower print, until the walls were charred—

And I was there with Alison's corpse, Alison's bloodied corpse, but poison spewed from inside me, and then my vision blackened.

⚓

WHEN I AWOKE, I was on the floor, fever in my head, and Mags kneeling beside me.

"What the fuck did she whisper?" she asked.

I looked at Mags, wondering for a moment where I was and what was going on.

Gyro stood beside the bed, looking down.

"What made you so mad at Alison again?" Mags asked, and then turned to Gyro. "What'd you say to her?"

My mind returned from blankness. "She said...she said..."

I could barely recall the words that Gyro had whispered to me.

"Please...help...oh god," Alison's voice came like a scratched up old cat from the thing on the bed.

How long we all stood in the room, waiting for what was to come, I'm not sure. My memory is spotty on this.

But Alison, her face still sliding off, eventually sat up, and all of us saw what my *Fries With That?* had brought back from the dead:

A bitch that looked like hell.

I DON'T NEED to go into a lot of the rest.

I'm waiting for the Barbara Walters interview. I want to give an exclusive.

Suffice it to say that we had one week left of school, and Alison Gall was alive again.

No need to go into the surgery that Gyro did using some medical equipment we grabbed from her father's office, or the fact that Alison was there inside her body but not on the surface yet, the way most of us are. Alison was down deep. Somehow I had rewired some circuits in her, while others had been permanently damaged.

She barely said more than squat anymore.

We made up a story for her mother about how we rescued her at the Prom, how she'd fallen down some stairs drunk after coming in with some boy from out of town.

Her now ex-boyfriend believed this, as did most everyone else. Thus the stitches, thus her slowness, thus the fact that while she still performed routine tasks, like getting up in the morning, showering, eating, dressing for school, even cheerleader practice,

Alison Gall was, for all intents and purposes, not all there. I wouldn't exactly use the kind of words you might use for somebody who comes back from the dead and might actually still be somewhat brain dead and might shuffle along, hiding the rotting of their corpse...because Alison kind of was like that, but kind of not, and I don't like name-calling anymore.

Not since it happened.

She was hideous to see, too. Her face, with the tiny threads, her hair a bit lopsided. From the neck down she was still gorgeous, but the meaner boys started calling her a two-bagger hump, "in case the bag falls off her head, you wear one yourself."

Now and then, in the last days of school that year, I would sit across from her, and a little shriek like a seagull makes would come from deep down in her throat.

❧

MAGS AND GYRO and I didn't talk much, but nodded to each other in the halls every now and then. I smoked in the girl's bathroom sometimes, hoping Mags would come in, but she never did.

Then on the last day of school, Alison Gall — moving in a fumbly daze down the hallway — turned to her ex-boyfriend Joey...and I saw it coming.

I don't know why I didn't think of it before, but I should've.

We all should've wondered what would happen if Alison came back.

What she might be able to do if her brain got *Fries With That?* from death to life.

I saw her pupils go up under her eyelids. I watched in fascination as a strange rash spread across her face. She opened her mouth wider than a scream.

And I knew.

I felt it.

She had it now, too. Whatever I had endowed her with, it had opened up something in her, too. Maybe we all have it within us, and only some of us have it at the surface.

She had *Fries With That?*

Shit, I thought. *It's contagious. Shit. Just like gramma said to me. "Stay away from the dead."*

And now, she did it to Joey. His body began twitching, and the blue of his eyes melted across his face like punctured egg yolks.

Like lightning, it passed around the hall, five other kids, some innocent of past association with Alison, some not so innocent. All shaking and shivering, foaming at the mouths, their eyes rolling up in their heads.

It was contagious. I had passed it on. I was the Typhoid Mary of *Fries with That?*

Five kids, and Mags came down the hall and watched it, too. Others came out, but ran when they saw the jolts and smelled the burning.

Mags turns to me, shaking her head. Not at me, I guess,

but at our bad decision. At our bad cover up of Gyro's killing of Alison and us as accomplices in murder.

There was a lot of love in her gaze as she looked at me.

It was either-or, I could tell.

Either it ended right there, or it goes on, and who knows how many brains would fry because I have this little talent inherited from my gramma's side, a little talent that no doctor has figured out yet though god knows they probed and poked inside my head enough these past couple months.

I know what she's going to do, and I'm wondering why she still has it on her.

Why she carries it.

And that's when Mags pulled out the Glock from the inside pocket on her black denim jacket and started firing at all the kids who were fizzling into the Fryer that Alison is beaming at them.

I guess she just didn't want to take it anymore.

Later on, when Mags was taken in, I went to visit her.

❧

"DON'T TELL THEM WHAT HAPPENED," she whispered. "I'll be out in a couple of years anyway. I'm a teenager. How much can they do?"

"But it's not your fault," I said.

"Look," Mags said. "I'm from the trailers. You and Gyro are Country Club Acres girls. Like Alison. You wouldn't survive what I'm going through right now."

Then, the tears welled in her eyes. "You are my best friend. It's no big deal for me to be here."

We both had a good cry that afternoon.

I felt the same way I did when my gramma had been alive. That kind of warmth for her. There were times when I wanted to hug Mags tight and never let her go. I could watch her face, the way her eyes sink into it, the way her dark hair hangs like a canopy over and around it, I could watch her face for hours. She has this perfect way of being. Even when she's going through hell.

Then I asked her why she had done it. I mean, I knew *why*, really.

I knew that we had started something that wouldn't stop on its own.

But Mags surprised me.

She said, "Because I have wanted to shoot those kids since the third grade when I first met any of them. Fried brains or no."

Mags is probably the boldest person I know.

Bold as they come.

But her boldness is losing its edge. I think jail did that to her.

LATER, all the talk shows started, and then Mags was let off because Alison had recovered from her wounds.

You can't kill the dead twice, I guess.

Alison was living on some machines and spilled a fake story about someone other than Mags doing the shooting. Even though it was an obvious lie I was happy to know that Alison had regained her speech a bit more; and I was thrilled that Mags was no longer the prime suspect.

Then, of course, we all found out that Alison somehow escaped the hospital, pulling out all her wires.

THERE'S a rumor that she wrote something in blood on the hospital wall, about coming after each of us, me, Mags and Gyro, but I'm not going to sit around getting scared over this.

Life is too short.

Alison's probably doing some zombie strip show up in Duluth or something by now.

Gyro has stayed out of the limelight, but occasionally she calls after midnight. Crying, whispering, full of fear of things that might happen.

She's afraid of Alison, but I think Alison probably did what she should've done before we even had decided to abduct her.

Got the hell out of town.

Dead or alive, it's all any of us wants to do.

OF COURSE, *that's* the true story.

Mags is covering for Gyro when she tells it her way.

Her way has me as an insaniac and Gyro as an innocent and Alison Gall as the bitch goddess.

Mags says the truth is that she and I went nuts one day in school. That she had stolen Gyro's brother's gun. That I laughed while she fired the shots at Alison and the others.

Sometimes, she tells me on the phone that she doesn't really believe the truth anymore.

She told me, "It couldn't happen the way we saw it. It just couldn't. It had to be us, Nora. You and me. Maybe we just got too fucked up in life to know what was really happening around us. I don't know. I'm not smart enough."

Mags lost her courage sometime after all the TV shows and newspapers and *People* magazine. She's still my best friend, and I admire the hell out of her, I really do.

But I wish she'd face the truth.

Yeah, there's more, like what Alison did to humiliate Gyro. And what Gyro whispered in my ear to make me so mad I could focus my *Fries With That?* on poor dead Alison.

I mean, even thinking it again makes me mad enough to spit, but I'm saving it for when Barbara Walters' people call me.

The Machinery of Night

❦

H e thinks:

Our thoughts make us solid.

And daylight. Daylight affects our vision so we believe in solids, in mass, in the religion of material and weight.

But when the night washes over us like a flood, it draws back the veil. Pagans knew this; Buddhists knew this; maybe even some Christians know it, which is why they fear the devil and all his works so much.

The devil is night. The devil is low definition. The devil is where one ends another begins and all of it a great stream. The devil is darkness. It's a mechanism for seeing without seeing.

Starlight reveals how fluid we are. How there is no beginning and end. Christ said I am the Alpha and the Omega, but the darkness says there is no beginning and end, there is only world without end, world without definition, world without boundary. How to erase the lines between the boundaries is the thing.

Then he stops thinking. Light, somewhere, light spitting out of the hole in the sky.

The night recedes again, the world hardens. Walls arise, windows, doors, beds, restraints.

"WHO DID THIS?"

"The ones who come in the night."

"Stop that. Who did this? Tell me right now. I mean now. Come on. One of you did this."

"I told you. It doesn't surprise me you don't believe us. You don't believe in much, do you?"

Human feces spread like a post-modern landscape across the green wall.

The words: *I FORGIVE YOU SON* in curlicue shit paint.

Layton glanced at the three of them, knowing that not one man among them would confess. All it meant was more work for him. More cleaning, more scrubbing, all the things he hated about his job.

Meanwhile, the world spun — outside the window, he could see the river as it ran beside the spindly trees, the flooding having subsided three days earlier; the sun through morning mist; the gray doves like a child's paper airplanes floating on the breeze, finally landing on the outer wall, beyond the razor-wired fence.

He wanted to be out there.

He wanted to quit his job that day, but he was still waiting for things to happen — he waited for the other offer from a better hospital, or even a nice administrative position at the cancer society.

Anywhere but here, this place where no one ever seemed

to get better, where the depressed remained bleary-eyed, their blood nearly all Thorazine and Prozac at this point; or the criminals, the ones who had done terrible things out there in the world and now were with him, with Layton Conner, behind these walls; and who, after all, were any of them? It was said that even one of the nurses had ended up in a bed down on Ward Six, her mind scrambled because she let them in, she let the patients' world engulf her own until she didn't know there was an Outside.

Look outside when they get to you.

Just for a second.

You need to do this to keep yourself safe.

When they are getting inside you, look out the nearest window for a second, look at your shoes, look at anything that will take your mind away from them for a moment so they won't own you.

He wished he'd had a cigarette on his break. He felt the addiction kicking in, and even with the patch on his arm, it wasn't enough drug to keep him sane in this environment.

He glanced from the window to the three men — Nix, Hopper, and Dreiling, each with his secret history, secret insanity, secret darkness.

He looked beyond the three patients to the far wall where one of them had taken their excrement and had written the words.

Dreiling, who had prettier hair than any of the others in the ward, shook his locks out and grinned. "It's music," he said, and the interminable humming began; Nix clapped his hands in the air, catching imaginary flies, or perhaps keeping time with Dreiling's annoying tune.

Hopper, who was rather nice in Layton's opinion, gave

an 'aw, shucks,' look, shook his head, and whispered something to himself.

"You can't do this anymore," Layton said, easing away from his own frustration. "It's not going to help when Dr. Glover comes in and sees this."

At the mention of the psych director's name, all three shivered slightly as if a ghost had kissed them on the neck right at that moment.

Layton felt a little powerful invoking the name of the dreaded man.

Nix's face broke out in sweaty beads, and he put his hand up to his throat. "I...I can't swallow..."

"Of course you can, now, Nix, come on, take a deep breath," Layton stepped forward, pulling Nix's hand away. "Let go. You can swallow just fine."

"I can't," Nix said somewhat despondently, but in fact, he could. "I hate Dr. Glover. And Dr. Harper. And you nurses."

"Do you ever think she'll stop?" Hopper asked later while Layton guided him back to his own room for the daily dose of meds.

"What's that?"

"She dreams all of it, her and the baby, and the old man, all of them." Hopper whispered, a secret, and Layton nodded as if he knew what the hell the tattooed man was babbling about, and then he gave him the little pink drink from the little white cups, and eventually, Hopper fell asleep on the cot while Layton fastened the restraints to his arms.

"THIS IS NOT EVERYTHING I'm about," Layton said to the

girl in the bar later, a mug moving swiftly to his lips. He had bored her with his day.

She was cute. She laughed at his jokes; she smiled at the stories of Nix, Hopper, Dr. Glover, Shea, Shaw, and Rogers and the Night Nurse.

It was getting on towards evening, and he had stopped in for a quick drink or two before heading back to his place on Chrome Street. The day had been long, with two major eruptions (as Hansen called them) between inmates.

First — in the showers — what had begun as a fist fight between two very violent individuals escalated to a riot with a dozen patients.

Then, as Layton finished up his shift, he'd heard the screams from Room 47.

He ran down the hall to intervene with Daisy, the Flower girl, when she didn't want to get her sponge bath.

Daisy was sweet, and Layton hated seeing her get hurt, particularly from the techs and nurses on the floor, all of whom seemed to loathe the woman for no apparent reason.

Once he'd calmed her down, she'd gone to her bath fairly easily; he watched while they held her and then he had taken the sponge himself, frothy with soap, and had spread it across her neck and arms and along her back before the female nurse took over.

He felt bad for poor Daisy, but still, she had made him stay an extra two hours — for which he got no pay.

And now, the bar, the beer, and the pretty girl who could not be more than twenty-two; even so she worked hard to exude girlishness.

Her skirt too short, her laugh too tinkly, her eyes much too shadowed. "But the insane, that's who you work with?"

He shrugged. "That's one way of looking at them.

They're ordinary people who have had something go wrong. Sometimes, what went wrong is small and nearly unimportant, but it's enough to make them want to attempt suicide. Sometimes, it's a big wrong, and a few of them have murdered or harmed others. Sad thing is, bottom line, they're there to be protected from themselves more than anything."

"Crazy people," she shook her head. "I can't imagine. My mother went crazy during the storms…"

"They were bad," he grinned, noticing that something seemed to be ripening about her right there, in the bar, at nine o'clock in the evening, fertility swept her hair and lifted her breasts and reddened her lips like a Nile goddess. He wanted her. He wanted to touch her.

"When the river flooded, we had to go to my grandfather's place in the hills, and we almost didn't get my mother out in time," she laughed, shaking her head.

He bought her a beer, she sipped it, and he had another one, and it seemed as if he'd just ordered another one when he was in the dark with her, in a small bed, and he was almost inhaling her skin and kissing down and up the smoothness of her.

Even when they made love, he looked beyond her, out the arched window of the bedroom in her mother's house, at the moon casting nets of light across the river, sparkling on its rumbling surface; across from them, up the third hill, the asylum waited to snatch his days.

He smoked three cigarettes afterward, and fell asleep in the crook of her arm.

"I can't offer you coffee," she said. *Angela.* That was her name. Or was it something else?

Out the window: night.

He smiled, almost afraid he would forget her name.

"Mom would throw a fit if she knew you were here. Got to be quiet."

"How old *are* you?"

"Nineteen," she said.

Shit, he thought.

"You?" she asked.

"Twenty-eight."

"When you were ten," she said.

"Back when you were still a baby."

"When you were ten," she repeated, "you found your father crawling on all fours and braying like a mule."

At first it didn't register, and then the memory returned.

"How did you know that?" he gasped.

"You told me last night. Remember? You wept."

"I wept?"

She kissed his cheek as he buttoned his shirt. "I thought it was sweet. It's why you became a nurse. Remember? Your father attacked you. You had to somehow take care of it all. I can only imagine."

Layton laughed, hugging her. "My god, what was in that beer?"

"Shh," she said, covering his lips with her hand. "I have to get her breakfast and then get ready for class. You need to go."

"What time is it?" He glanced at the clock on the table. It was nearly six; not quite light out. "Damn it."

"A LOT CAN HAPPEN in twenty minutes," Sheila said, her starched blouse looking like white armor covering her starched soul. "In twenty minutes I could've been home in bed already."

"Sorry. I'll come in early tomorrow." Layton took up one of the pens from the cup, and signed his name on the yellow paper next to her hand.

"Well, I'm exhausted," Sheila said. Her eyes would not meet his — typical — and she signed off on her papers, her shift done, passing him the clipboard. "Jones and Marshall are on today, and at nine, Harper comes in to do meds. Glover is over at State for three days. You need to do better on sharps check; I found this."

She drew something from her pocket. Passed it to him.

He glanced at the thing in his hand — a safety pin.

Her voice was gravel and rain. "Nix had it. Don't know how he got it. Said something about some people giving it to him. He's been known to kill with things like that."

"I can imagine," Layton said, trying to keep it light.

Sheila was senior staff and stupid, a terrible combination. She had Doc Ellis's ear, and that meant she could make sure his review bit the dust, no raise, and no promotion to an easier ward.

He grinned. "Thanks for covering for me. Twenty minutes is too much. Had a car issue."

"Oh," Sheila said, her voice now all sleet. "That's twice in six weeks. Better get it into the shop."

After she left — making sure to check his keys for him like he was a baby — he started on the basic rounds with one of the psych techs.

Sharps check, whites check, laundry baskets rolled out as more staffers arrived, coffee in the vending room, twice-told jokes about the boy who grew trees on his back, complaints from Shaw and Rogers about their treatment, a backed up toilet, followed by basic bed check — Rance had the sniffles, and Layton quickly checked his temp only to find a high fever and then, oh shit, the day was screwed.

Harper arrived and began a mini-quarantine to make sure it wasn't anything worse than the flu — six ended up in Rance's room, all with fevers, all beginning to moan about the demons who were scratching at them or their skin falling off, or any number of odd complaints.

Diarrhea on the floor, dripping, spitting, and Layton going between them with juice and toast, just hoping for once they'd all get the plague and die.

When he finally got to Nix's room, he unstrapped him. "I thought Shaw would've done this by now, damn it," Layton said, muttering to himself, but Nix laughed.

"That's the first time you've ever said anything that made sense, Mr. Conner," Nix said, "and now, if you don't mind, a little privacy?"

Layton nodded and turned his back. He watched the wall, and tried to ignore the pissing sounds coming from the toilet in the corner.

"All done," Nix said.

"Glad to see no writing on the wall today," Layton said, turning.

Nix had a face that was a genetic mix of wise child and prematurely old troll — Layton had never noticed 'til now that Nix had a scar on his chin, or that he was beginning to go bald. His blond hair receded from a point on his crown.

How old was he?

Layton thought he was forty, but he might've been mid-thirties. It was on his chart, but who looked at the charts anymore? Administrative bullshit.

"She finally stopped," Nix said, getting fidgety. His face became stormy — his brows twitched, his lips curled, his skin began wrinkling with nervous spasms.

Needs his meds. "You sleep okay?"

"Not really," Nix giggled, his fingers beginning their familiar snapping.

Where the fuck is Rogers and the med cart?

"Couldn't sleep — "

"At all?" Layton asked.

"The baby kept me up, so I had to wander." Nix said, and then went to the sink and began washing up. He shook like a drunk. Where the hell was the med cart? Layton watched him in the steel mirror. "I went out and had a drink or two and then made friends."

"Oh did you," Layton nodded. He glanced at the open door.

The squeaking whine of the med cart wheels echoed along the green corridor. Somewhere a fly buzzed. Out the window?

He glanced outside, through the bars and glass, past the pavement, the fences, to the river and the valley. God, he wished he could be anywhere but in this room.

Layton went and sat down on the mattress. It was clean, unlike other patients' rooms.

"Another night on the town?"

Nix turned slowly, his face shiny with water. "Yeah. I met someone and we spent the night together."

"Well," Layton grinned. "Not a total loss then."

Stretched his arms out, and hopped up again.

Nix was an easy patient for the most part; violent when

he was on the outside, but inside he was pretty much a kitten. Nix never went for the eyes. He spoke sensibly except when he ventured into some delusional chatter.

Layton went to the sink and grabbed a towel for the patient.

Taking the towel, wiping his hands slowly, Nix said, "Not a total loss at all. But then...that baby was still wailing. She hadn't changed him, that's why. She doesn't know how important it is. See, the thing is, she can understand all this movement, this jumble of molecules, but he's just a baby, his mind hasn't quite sorted it out. She thinks because he's a baby he's better at it. I had to change him myself."

"Is that how you got the safety pin?"

"The *what*?" Covering his face in the white towel, Nix's features came through the cloth. Layton shivered slightly.

Something about the towel on the face reminded him of his father's madness. Form without expression. The open mouth without sound.

"Nurse Allen found it, this little pin," Layton grabbed the towel back, rolling it into a ball. "She took it from you. Last night."

"Oh, that," Nix swept a hand in the air. "That night nurse is no good. She's a brick. She finds that and she thinks I'm just plotting to stab her in the neck twenty times with it or plunge it into her heart and extract it. She's crazy."

Layton wanted to add:

It's what you did to two women on the Outside, Nix. Why wouldn't she think you'd use it on her, too?

❧

LAYTON MET Angela again the following Saturday, they

got a little drunk again, ended up down on the muddy bank of the river, found a dry rock, kissed, almost began to make love, but she said she just wasn't in the right mood.

"It's my mother," she said. "She's been giving me hell lately."

"I keep forgetting you're nineteen."

"I turned twenty."

"When?"

"Thursday."

"Happy Birthday."

"I don't care about birthdays or age. Or anything. It's all this proof. It means nothing. If I told you I was twenty seven, you wouldn't really know the difference. It's just revolutions of the earth. Years go by. Gravity pulls. We all buy into it."

Angela reached into her breast pocket and withdrew a pack of cigarettes. She offered him one — he snapped it up — and then sucked one up between her lips, lit it, puffed, and sighed. "All learning is about trapping. Keeps you trapped inside this...vehicle...we call a body. We learn that we're flesh and bone, but somewhere it's all particles. Somehow the particles convince us we're solid. I took molecular biology last semester and barely understood a word, but the way I see it, we're all just convincing ourselves that anything we are or see is solid, but it's not. It's confetti. Bits and pieces and then it's all like this river. Look at the river — silt and fish and water and amoebas and all kinds of things, and we call it river, but it's all one thing, and who's really to say that the fish actually moves or if it becomes water and in the next second is fish again only because it was water?"

"Well," he said, nibbling on her ear, "college and beer are doing you a lot of good I see."

"It's hard to swallow some of the bullshit."

"Yeah, tell me about it. It's like being raised Catholic."

"You? Catholic?"

He laughed. "Yeah, you know all that belief shit. Even science is full of its little beliefs, and half the problem is buying into them or not. Just like you said."

"Well," she shrugged, "I believe in a lot of what you'd probably call 'belief shit'."

"I gave up believing in anything I can't see when my father died," he said.

He wanted to laugh and make a joke of this, but he couldn't.

She opened her mouth to speak, but smoke came out.

SHE STUBBED the cigarette out on the rock.

"My mother is basically dying," Angela began, almost inaudibly.

She said it again a bit louder.

Layton had nothing to add. He wanted to say something wise and kind, but no words came to mind.

"She's dying, and I'm just getting started on life. She's a nightmare at times. I've wished her dead with each surgery. For her own sake. I've wished her gone. Can't imagine having a daughter like me."

She brightened for a second. "Change the subject, quick. I don't want to think about it."

"I had a boring week," he said. "You don't want to hear about it. I'm sorry about…"

"I really mean it. Change the subject. Poor baby. Boredom is worse than dying. Change the subject. Your work, your boyhood, your religious awakening, anything."

"In my job, boredom is good."

"Well, then." She lit another cigarette. "Tell me how it was boring."

"No attacks, no riots, no bizarre rituals involving stray cats, no eyes getting popped out."

"Something to celebrate."

"Along with your birthday."

"Now I feel like it," she said, leaning into him, and he felt her ripen again, as if she wanted him to open her, to be part of her.

The cigarette went into the mud, his hands found their way beneath her blouse, her hands encircled his back.

Nature took over — he found himself making love to her on the rock, in the torn fingernail of light along the banks of the flooded river.

They dozed afterward for just a few minutes; then she said something; he opened his eyes but was still in a half-dream.

"You see? You're in it, too. You think you're outside but you're really in," she said.

When he asked her what she meant by that, she acted as if he'd dreamt the words she'd just said.

❧

IT WAS TWO A.M. when he walked her home, and kissed her on the forehead.

She looked surprised. "That's it? Fatherly kiss on the old noggin?"

"You took all my passion." He chuckled.

"Ah," she nodded. "Well, I best get some sleep. I have a Physics exam Monday, bright and early."

"Physics? Ouch," Layton grinned. "My worst subject."

"I kind of like it. We have a bizarre professor who talks about string theory and molecular shake-ups and why we can't just go through chairs and things."

"Okay," Layton nodded. "You lost me. I'm just a nurse."

"Don't play dumb," she swatted him playfully. "Hey, wait, before you go, you need to give me something."

"Oh I think I did already."

"Not that, you cad," she said. "Something to show you care."

He reached into his pockets.

"Christ, I've got nothing. No mementos at all. Wait," he brought up a half-roll of *Lifesavers*. "There you go. To save your life with."

He pressed it into her hand, and she giggled and told him that until they met again she would treasure each and every tropical fruit flavor.

❧

"WHERE DID YOU GET THOSE?" Layton asked.

It was a few weeks later and Angela had not been answering his calls and no one answered her door, and now he was at work feeling the worst heartache of his life — and Nix the Needle had a half-roll of tropical fruit *Lifesavers* in his hand.

"You going to take those off me?" Nix asked, tugging at the restraints that held his hands to the bed. "Don't I even have a right to candy?"

"Give it to me," Layton said, plucking the roll from the man's hands. "Where did you get —"

Nix looked up into his eyes, soulfully, and whispered in a soft voice, "She's dying, and I'm just getting started on life. She's a nightmare at times. I've wished her dead with each surgery. For her own sake. I've wished her gone. Can't imagine having a daughter like me. Change the subject, quick. I don't want to think about it."

"I'M AFRAID FOR YOU," Dr. Glover said.

Mid-afternoon, Layton would be off-shift soon. "I'm afraid in a way that I was afraid for Molly Sternberg."

"Please. Molly had a history of —"

"All of us have histories," Glover said. "None of us is immune to this. You work with mentally unstable people — sociopaths as well — and you become enmeshed. You begin to experience a similar dissociation from reality that they also experience. It is not that unusual. It is somewhat expected."

Glover scratched at the side of his head. "Don't worry, Conner, I'm not going to put you away. You haven't identified yourself as insane. But it wouldn't surprise me that you might just need a little distance. When was your last vacation?"

"Three months ago."

"Perhaps this is just one of those things," Glover added.

"Those things? You're a psychiatrist," Layton nodded his head slightly hoping that the doctor would laugh it off.

"Because I'm trained in a way of handling medical issues doesn't mean I have all the answers. Sometimes the unexplainable occurs. Sometimes it's a delusion. Sometimes it happens. I've been here long enough to realize that there's more to the world than has been catalogued in the medical texts. Now, what did Nicholas say?"

"He said exactly what this woman said the previous weekend."

"Precisely?"

"As precisely as I could recall it."

"You could recall it?"

"Christ," Layton said. He stood up. "I'd like a few days off."

"Speak to your supervisor; as far as I'm concerned, take any amount of time you want off. Your job is secure." Glover glanced over to his bookshelf. "You know, Conner, you've been here a few years. You know your ward inside and out. You've seen a lot. You've handled a lot. On the one hand, this could be your mind playing tricks on you."

Glover reached beneath his glasses and rubbed two fingers along the bridge of his nose. He shut his eyes for a moment. "On the *other* hand, sometimes there are things that come through the patients. I'm not even sure what I mean by that."

He took his glasses off. "Without my glasses, you are blurred." He put them back on. "Now I see you clearly. Does that mean that when I see you blurred that you are in fact blurred and that my vision is perfect but your image is in flux?"

"Sir?"

"All I'm saying is, we can't know everything. Assuming that Nicholas Holland said what you heard, perhaps he did know what this woman said to you. Perhaps he made it up and by some strange coincidence, for the first time in his own history, he said the exact words to disturb you. But I've learned in twenty-eight years as a psychiatrist handling the more extreme cases of human insanity, that —" Glover leaned toward him. "We know nothing of the human mind. We are still in the Dark Ages of psychiatry. We are fumbling. Do you know what Nicholas said to me when he first entered this place? He told me that when the night came, the mechanisms changed, and that while I was eating supper the night before with my wife, he had already seen to it that the pie in the kitchen had fallen to the floor."

Layton, caught up for a moment, asked, "Did it?"

Glover drew back, laughing. "No, of course not. And we hadn't *had* any dessert. It was a complete fabrication. But how was I to know? I didn't even mention it to my wife. I thought it was just a rambling delusion on his part.

"But a year or so later, I attended a dinner party at a colleague's home. Some of the doctors were telling tales out of school. The usual — patients who sat up in the middle of operations, the near-malpractice suits that managed to get cleaned up in some hilarious way, the patients who hallucinated bizarre images — and so I had my glass of wine and told the story about Nicholas claiming to break into the house. I had them rolling mainly because I recalled all the details he added — how he sipped milk from the fridge, how he peed in the sink. And then I mentioned the pie claim, I said, 'and he then told me that he dropped a pie on the kitchen floor just so I wouldn't eat it.'

"And Layton? I saw it in my wife's face, out of the corner of my eye, even then I saw that she had gone white as if something dreadful had come over her. She said nothing at dinner, but on the way home she told me that she had bought a pie at the A&P and warmed it in the oven for a bit before letting it cool on the cutting board by the sink. 'And,' I asked, 'did it fall on the floor?' She told me it had not, but that someone had broken the crust, a man, she thought, because the handprint was big. Handprint? Yes, she said. It scared her because it was nearly perfect, almost as if someone had baked his hand into the crust. She threw it out, not wanting to even think about it. So, you see, perhaps Nicholas knew something. Perhaps he didn't. How could he? I am a man of some education and knowledge of science, Layton, but I have no basic explanation for this — or for you. Except to say: take a few days off and let this go."

AND THEN, on his day off, Layton saw Angela again. It was just after nine at night, and the rain began.

Layton was going to have a late dinner at the *Hong Kong Moon* restaurant when he noticed her walking out of the convenience store with a small bag of groceries.

When he caught up to her at her car, she didn't look happy to see him at all.

He wanted to ask about the Lifesavers, but it seemed trivial and stupid now.

"Oh, hi," she said. "I'm sorry I haven't been around. My mother died. There was a lot to take care of."

"God, I'm sorry."

She got in the little car.

He stood there, the blur of rain on the car window obscuring her features. He felt the shiver that always came at the end of new love.

And then, she began laughing.

For just a second — was it the rain? His tears? —he thought that it all shimmered.

Not just her, but the rain and the glass and the metal of the car.

※

IT TOOK Layton twenty minutes to get up the hill, flash his badge at the guards, nod to the night nurse who seemed surprised to see him, and make his way down the ward.

He found Nix sitting up on his mattress, his hair soaked. Nix glanced up, then back down to his own upturned palms.

"My nerves are all tingly," Nix said.

"Tell me everything," Layton said.

Nix didn't look up from his hands. Then he licked his lips like a hungry child. "You don't know this for sure, Conner, what you're thinking. Whatever it is you're thinking."

"Do you know who Angela is?"

Nix grinned. "I have known many angels."

"*Angela*. She's the one who gave you the Lifesavers."

"I have saved several lives," Nix said.

Layton rushed over and grabbed him by the shoulders, lifting him to his feet.

They stared eye to eye; sweat ran down Nix's face. "What the hell *is* it you do? What is it about the baby crying and the woman and the things that you babble about?"

Nix's grin faded. "It's the machinery. It's how it works. It's how we work. It's how the world changes in the dark, Conner. It's how when light particles are lessened, it's not just about seeing, it's about how in absolute darkness it can change. We can change."

Layton pushed him back down on the bed. "Half an hour ago you were a woman in a car."

"Was I?" Nix asked, almost slyly. "Was I? Well, then, Nurse Conner, you have already begun your journey. Do you remember being inside her, this Angela? How you pushed in, how she opened, how she made those little noises that made you push to greater and greater heights, how she turned twenty on a particular week and how she told you all about her dying mother and how you fell in love and how she broke your heart one night in the rain? Do you remember playing with her body, or asking her to do something that you find in your heart of hearts to be repulsive and lowly but which brings you great pleasure? Do you remember when she told you all her secrets, even the one about her uncle, or the time you both laughed at once over something you seemed to think of at the same time, as if you had so much in common, Nurse Conner, that this might just be the girl for you, this might just be Miss Right and you just might be the luckiest man in the world? And then you told her that awful secret, the dark secret, the one you thought you could trust her with, the one about your father's madness, about how it pushed you to the edge and how one night you…"

Later, when two psych techs pulled him off Nix, Layton could not remember raising his fists, let alone bringing them down nearly forty times over Nix's head, nor could he remember through the trial that even after he'd begun to break the skin of Nix's face, long after the patient was dead, particles of bone from the patient's jaw and nose had splintered and some had gone, needle-like, into the palm of Layton's hand.

⁊⧫

NEARLY A YEAR LATER, Layton tried to sit up in bed, but the restraints held him fast.

He wanted to shout for the night nurse, but whom could he trust?

He knew them all, he knew they thought he was one of the many criminally insane, but he knew the staff well, and he didn't understand why they should restrain him when he had only tried to kill himself once, and had botched the job anyway.

It was the whisper of night coming up under the barred window, the last light of day was nearly vanished, and he still felt drowsy from the last med administered at two.

The nights were the worst, because of the people who moved through the dark, who came and went and he watched in horror as they did what had to be done.

Even Nix, even he came through, his face sometimes a bloody tangle, a forest of twisted flesh and bone, sometimes it was just his face, beads of sweat on his forehead, that trollish look, that milky complexion.

The machinery hummed and if he could just believe strongly enough, he could slip through the restraints and join them, he could go and be anywhere and anyone, but it never seemed to happen.

Some of the other patients came and went; the walls rippled like a flooding river; the air itself became vivid with the movement of nearly invisible molecules as they went like clouds of mosquitoes, forming and splitting apart again.

Layton, in restraints, tried to pray.

His heartbeat raced as he watched a swollen bubble of glass move along the window.

"It's belief," he whispered. "Belief makes it move. It's absolute belief," but it wasn't coming for him, the molecules weren't changing, the mechanism of darkness was not clicking into place.

"Please let me go. Please," he begged, and then, as happened nightly, his voice became louder, sobs and screams.

One of the nurses came by with another med.

As she wiped the sweat from his forehead, he told her how they left nightly, how when the sun went down the machinery of night made it happen and their molecules swirled and how even the two men he had killed in his life, his father and Nix, sometimes came to him and made him do terrible things in the dark.

"And the woman who spoke to the courts? Her name was Angela, but she's really one of the men I killed, only you can't ever really kill anyone, you can't, it's just a rearrangement of molecules and at night they can change again or if they want they can stay as they were that night for a whole day and they can even come to your trial and talk about you and things you told them and how you seemed to be going slowly mad only you never ever went mad, if anything it's complete sanity, it's the kind of sanity that's like the sun at noon all bright and sharp and please don't turn off the light, that's all I ask, when you leave and I get sleepy from the pills, please leave the lights on," his voice softened, and the nurse nodded.

WHEN HE AWOKE LATER — when the meds were begin-ning to wear off — the room was dark and he felt the brush of a thousand particles that whispered with the voice of his father.

The Wolf

❦

The man and the boy had been tracking the wolf since sunrise, but by the time the moon came up they made camp along the ridge.

"Put your rifle over there," the man told the boy, pointing to a pile of rocks covered with fern. "Always put your rifle as far from you and the fire as possible. Accidents happen when they're too close. We don't sleep with them. The wolf won't attack us. It's sheep he's after, not you. Not me."

The boy at first questioned this, because he liked to have his rifle close to him when he hunted. After a few minutes of consideration, the boy decided that the rancher had hired the man to lead, and he would let him. The boy also had done something he wished he hadn't that afternoon, by shooting at what he thought might be the wolf, but turned out to be a silver fox.

By the fire, after supper, they sat across from each other. "We might have had him at the bluffs," the man said. "He's smarter than us, I think."

"I didn't mean to shoot at it," the boy said.

"It doesn't matter."

"I thought I saw him."

"Foxes can look like wolves, sometimes. Coyotes, too."

"It was a stupid mistake."

"I don't care. You're young."

"I'm the best hunter for a hundred miles."

"I can tell."

"Mister, maybe they pay you money to hunt wolves, but when I hunt, it's for the love of the sport," the boy said. "I can take anything out fast. Once I target it, it's mine and that's the end of it."

"I'm not here to argue with you, son."

"I'm not your son."

They went silent again. After he had relieved himself in the woods, the man checked their rifles, and then felt for the small gun beneath his jacket. The man returned to the fire and saw that the boy still sat there.

"We need to get up before first light," he said.

"How many wolves you kill?" the boy asked.

"What?"

The boy glared at him in the firelight. "How many?"

"Twenty. Maybe more."

"That's not a lot."

"No," the man said. "It's not."

"When I'm your age, I bet I'll have more than twenty pelts."

"I don't keep souvenirs like scalps," the man said. "You need to sleep closer to the fire. Take your coat and anything in your pack. Cover yourself good. In a few hours, it'll be colder than you can imagine."

"I hunt a lot," the boy said. "I know how cold it gets up here."

The man did not sleep much. Just before dawn, he rose and rekindled the fire and drew an old rusty skillet from his pack. He made breakfast with the meager supplies he'd brought.

The boy awoke to the smells, and after a mug of coffee began laughing.

"You look like crap," the boy said.

They wandered off the main trails that morning.

THE MAN SAW evidence of the wolf's passing through a route between narrow rocks. There was blood of fresh kill and the rotting smell of a dead animal in the air as they moved further along through the pines. He motioned for the boy to remain still. The man went up along moss-covered rock, through underbrush, and finally came to a cliff's edge overlooking the valley. He glanced out over it to see the distant lake and the dots that were the ranches below. He saw three whitetail deer in a clearing among the trees just above the rocks where he stood.

He sensed the wolf, yet did not see him.

The boy followed him up the trail. When the boy drew close to him, the man whispered, "He knows we're following him. This is a problem now. Yesterday, he didn't know."

The boy remained silent until they had made camp for the night.

"It ain't my fault."

"No one's blaming you."

"You are. You think I scared him off. When I shot my rifle."

The man continued to peel an apple as he leaned back against his pack. "You can't look for blame all the time."

"It was one mistake," the boy said. "I won three hunting trophies before I was fifteen."

The man glanced at him, nodding.

"I bet they paid you a lot of money to do this," the boy said after a minute. "I bet it's a racket you got. You set wolves free down in the valley. Then, eventually, they hire you."

The man laughed at first, but then saw that the boy meant every word. "There would be easier ways to make a living."

"I just can't figure why they'd hire a stranger when we got a lot of hunters in the valley," the boy said. "That's all I meant."

"What did you do makes you special to that town?" the man asked.

The boy wouldn't tell him. He shook his head and said, "I just hunt. That's all. I can hunt and trap and shoot. I win a lot of trophies at the fairground. I can shoot just about anything. Could since I was a boy. First kill was a rabbit when I was ten."

"Jack rabbit?"

"Peter Cottontail," the boy said.

The man said, "What's the last thing you killed?"

The boy didn't answer.

The man said, "First thing I ever killed was a wolf. I was younger than you. You kill a wolf, you start to understand it."

After that, there wasn't much talk around the fire, and

the man chuckled to himself when he rolled over to sleep. They had to sleep close beside each other for warmth. The boy's breathing kept him awake for another two hours.

The next day, they went off toward Needle Heights, the bony points of the mountain that crossed into the mountain range leading up north.

The boy asked him what he smelled in the air, and what signs of the wolf he followed, for the boy could not track as well as the man and knew it.

At twilight, the man told him, "I learned from the old mountain men, when I was a boy. There are ways to track wolves. Different from tracking other animals. There was a mountain man, half-Cherokee, half-Scot. He was an old man, and he took me out to hunt wolves back in the days when we all hunted wolves. He told me that a wolf that got a taste for sheep would draw other wolves down to the ranches. You have to kill them before they can get back up to their pack. Usually, it's the young males. You see it with them first. Old wolves, they know not to go in the valleys, to the ranches. The young ones just see sheep and want them. We tracked this wolf for nine days, and when we finally cornered him, he didn't seem like a wolf anymore. He seemed like a man. I felt as if I knew him, just like I know you. I saw his eyes and I could almost tell what he was thinking. He wanted what you might want. Yes, you. What a lot of men want. He wanted a bite of it. A piece of it. He had wiles and instinct. He knew that if he found a pen full of sheep he might eat better than if he spent his time chasing deer or rabbit."

"Wolves are like rabid dogs," the boy said.

"You just never met one yet," the man said. "They're smart. When they feel threatened, they attack. When you hunt a wolf, you don't let him know he's being hunted until you absolutely have to do it. You wait. You have patience.

You let him think you're just part of the scenery. Just another wolf, maybe. This wolf.

He's just looking for the sheep and then a place to hide. When he finds the prize sheep, that's the one he wants. He doesn't want the sickly or the scrawny. He wants the best."

"It's funny we kill 'em, then," the boy said. "'Cause that's the way some people are. Some people I could name. Where I live."

"Wolves know each other," the man said. "When I had that wolf cornered, when I was younger than you, that wolf looked at me and knew I was a wolf, too. He'd met his match. Only I wasn't a wolf until that day. I didn't want to take a bite of anything until that day. You think you're a wolf, son?"

"A wolf? No."

"Some people are sheep. Maybe most people. And a few people in a thousand may be the vigilant dog that guards the sheep. Now and then, there's even a shepherd. But whenever a group of sheep are together, a wolf always comes 'round. You can count on it. That's why I get work. I'm an expert at wolf killing. They know it in towns in this region. Somebody talks to somebody, and they call me in and pay my fee," the man said. "And I track the wolf. I don't make errors. I don't let the wolf know he's being tracked. I usually work alone. I make sure the wolf I kill is the wolf that's causing distress for people. I don't just kill wolves because I can. I find the right wolf and I do my business."

"I think all of them should just be killed. Every wolf.

They all eventually will come down to the sheep. That's what I think," the boy said.

"That would be wrong," the man said, looking the boy in the eye. "What if a man killed another man? Should all men be killed because that one man did wrong? Of course not."

"We're talking wolves, not men."

"Some men are wolves," the man said.

WHEN THEY HAD CROSSED into the deep forest, the man thought for sure the wolf was near. He motioned for the boy to remain silent and at the ready. The man pointed toward the ramble up ahead, overgrown with dead vines.

He gave the signal for the boy to step ahead of him.

The boy raised his rifle up. He stepped slowly between the rocks and trees.

Breaking the silence, the man said, "I was wrong. It's not him."

The boy glanced back at him. His face gleamed bright red with sweat. "How do you know?"

"It's a bitch," the man said. "Heavy with cubs. I don't hunt like that."

The boy moved forward. The man raised his rifle and shot it into the air above the boy's head.

Birds flew out from the underbrush, and the boy turned around in anger.

AT CAMP THAT NIGHT, the boy said, "You did that to scare me."

The man nodded. "We are after one wolf only. We don't shoot any others."

"How do you know she wasn't the wolf?"

"I know the wolf is male. I know its size. I know the color of its coat. And I know its track. This was not the wolf."

"I say kill them all," the boy said.

"You're not a hunter if that's how you feel," the man said. "You may win a hundred trophies, son, but a hunter does not wish to kill them all."

"I hate wolves," the boy said. "I'm tired. I want to go home. The food is awful. Your coffee's awful. I want to be in my bed. At home."

"I know you do," the man said. "You shouldn't have come with me. But here you are. Make the best of it. We'll have him soon." After a moment, the man asked, "Why did you come?"

"I owe it to him. The rancher."

"What do you owe him?"

"I made a mistake once, on his ranch. With him. I need to make it right."

"Mistakes can be forgiven," the man said. "But it's not good to make them."

The boy's lip turned up into a snarl. "That was a mistake. What you did today. Shooting like that. Warning the wolf. He was probably nearby."

"Everyone makes mistakes."

"I bet when they hired you…"

"They?" the man asked.

"The people in town. The ranchers. I bet when they

hired you they thought you'd have this done fast. They sent me to learn from you, I bet. Learn. What I learned so far is you worry about wolves too much."

"I wasn't hired by people. I was hired by a person."

The boy thought about this for a moment, and seemed to chew on it. "The rancher was good to me once, but that changed. Maybe it was the wolf attacking his stock. Maybe it was something else."

"You see him as a rancher. I know him as a man who lost his only daughter."

The boy went silent for several minutes. The man watched him.

Then, the boy said, "Not my fault, either."

"I believe you," the man said.

"I didn't do that to her," the boy said.

"I believe you," the man said. "But he hired me to track this wolf. You came along because he wanted you to know what it meant to track a wolf. That's all."

"She was a good girl," the boy said. "We would've been married if…it doesn't matter. It was an accident."

"I know nothing about her or you," the man said. "I just know I was hired to track the wolf. You are the local boy who has all the hunting trophies. So you came with me."

"I wanted to help him. Her father. To make up for it," the boy said.

"If it was an accident," the man said, "then there was nothing to make up for."

The man glanced over at the rifles, placed beyond the fire, in a ditch between rocks and a rotting log.

The boy began to get up as if he, too, thought about the rifles.

The man drew out the gun tucked under his coat, and pointed it at the boy. "Stay where you are, son," he said.

"You're not tracking the wolf," the boy said.

The man stood up and moved closer to the boy. He whispered to the boy that he should not be afraid.

The boy looked as if he might turn and run at any minute, but the man's whispers were calming. The man spoke about how everything would be all right.

"I didn't kill her," the boy said. "Her father is crazy. I didn't kill her. She decided to do what she did. I had no part of it. I was hunting with my uncles. She thought I had abandoned her. I would've married her. I would've come back. If I had known. I would have. She was good. She was a wonderful girl. I knew I wanted a girl like that. Any man would. You would've if you had known her. She was like an angel to people. I saw it the minute I laid eyes on her. She was one of the good ones. Not all people are good, are they? But she was. She was a good one."

The man aimed the gun to the side of the boy's head.

"Most people are sheep," the man said. "A few are the dogs that guard the sheep. Now and then there is a shepherd, but they are rare. But there are always wolves. A wolf wants to find the best of the sheep and devour it. That is all a wolf wants to do when it finds sheep. That is all it can do."

AFTER THE MAN bound the boy's hands and legs, he went to get his rifle. He stood several feet back from the boy, estimating where best to make the killing shot.

The Wicked

Poor little Charlie, the man grinned.

His hands were shaking as he stood there at the edge of the field. All those boys, and Charlie there, standing with his fat little glove on his hand, his scrawny legs poking out from his balloon shorts, his baseball cap askew, his blond hair thrusting out from his cap like straw.

Poor little Charlie. His mother was a lazy drunk. She drove a Buick with the windows blacked out so no one could watch her drink while she stopped at the light.

His father was a workaholic who spent idle hours with the factory girls down at the road houses out on the parkway.

They took a two week vacation together as a family every year, usually to the Caribbean, hiring a local girl to take care of the boy.

All the neighbors knew this, apparently, and felt sad for the boy.

"Always alone," the busybody down the block from them had told the man four weeks before.

Local gossip, told just in passing, in the local market when Charlie walked down the aisles looking for some candles.

"His mother collects candles," the busybody had said. "Poor little Charlie. You know, even on their holidays, his parents have practically nothing to do with him. No wonder he's the way he is."

Charlie was all alone most of the time.

The man had watched Charlie more than just at the house, but also when the boy walked from the bus stop, on Linden Avenue, all the way over to the small yellow house on Backus Street.

The boy dragged his feet sometimes when he walked.

Charlie kept his eyes down, and his hands over his books, which he hugged to his chest like treasured possessions.

The man would sit in his car, and slowly follow the boy as he rounded the corner.

He would see the aura around the boy that begged to be taken.

Once, the man had gotten quite daring, and walked into the empty lot behind Charlie's house.

He'd crouched down at the back fence—an old wooden fence ready to fall down in a slight wind. The nervousness was delightful. If a neighbor caught him, or a passing patrol car, it might be the end for him.

He crouched there for an hour before Charlie came down the steps of his house. Charlie shuffled his feet as he went to the little dirt and gravel area. It was almost a pit, beneath the dying crabapple tree where Charlie liked to play.

The man had carved a small opening in the worn fence with his Swiss Army knife.

Just to watch Charlie play.

All afternoon, Charlie had played by himself. He sat down in the filthy pit, arranging stones in a circle around himself. The flies that always seemed to be seeking him out rose and fell like dust around each of his movements. Then he lit a match, and waved it around. He lit four small candles, no doubt filched from his mother's kitchen without permission.

That was the marvelous things about little boys. They could get up to such innocent mischief.

He watched Charlie for a long time that afternoon as he sat in the pit and watched the candles as they burned. Charlie had held his hands over the flames a bit, and then closed his eyes and hummed even more.

Charlie was a typical victim boy. His imagination took him away from the squalor of his existence.

The man liked that about him. Knew that what he needed to do to Charlie was good for the boy. It wasn't as if Charlie would even care about the pain.

And the money he'd get from bringing the boy in, and taking the photographs: it was good compensation, but not the same as the sensation Charlie would give him.

Murder was, after all, more a feeling than an action.

ON ANOTHER NIGHT, while he drove around the neighborhood to get a feel for it, the man saw Charlie up in his bedroom window.

The boy stood, without his shirt on, at the open

window. He held his hands straight out into the night. He was humming again, and the man had laughed.

Oh, poor little Charlie. Poor little Charlie who had no friends, whose parents were negligent and terrible, and who only had himself and his sad imagination to comfort him.

Now, Saturday morning, eleven a.m., with the Little League game winding down, it was nearly time.

The man glanced at his watch.

Only ten minutes or so to go.

They were in the last inning of play, and Charlie's team was losing miserably.

Not that Charlie seemed to mind. He stood in the outfield, apparently humming to himself.

The man tried to keep from grinning. He remembered the other little boys, how they begged for death.

Charlie would beg, too.

The man felt the warm sweat along the back of his neck.

Someone, coming up behind him, said, "You're Charlie's dad?"

The man turned.

It was one of the fathers.

The fathers all had the same faces, and he knew why. They had abandoned sensation years ago. They had gotten fat and bald and were terribly nice. They had a glaze of niceness all about them as if they'd been too long in the freezer of nice.

This one wore a black polo shirt and khaki shorts. All the hair that should've been on the top of his head was at the back of his neck. One day when this father got older and wealthier, that hair would crawl up again. He was one of those nonsexual fathers, with the wife who refused, with the pasty morals of one who would not find the thrill elsewhere. He had sad dog eyes. "Put me out of my misery" eyes.

The man nodded. "Yeah. I'm so proud of him."

"I'm Hank Wilson. Billy's dad. That Charlie, he's a… quiet boy," the father said.

The father offered him a cup of coffee, which he accepted so as not to seem out of place. "All the fathers hang out after the game. You should come sit with us."

"Oh, no, really. I like it here. Where I am." Could the father see through him? It didn't seem likely.

"My kid told me that Charlie's real smart." The father said this as a form of compensation for that other thing that hung in the air. *Charlie is not a good Little Leaguer. Charlie's a weakling.* "He told me he did some amazing things with that science project of his."

"Oh?" the man said. "He never brags at home. I had no idea." Sip of coffee. A brief flash of grin. A gentle nod. All to fit in.

The father laughed. "Well, Charlie's probably as modest as he is smart. Billy told me that he made this piece of paper turn into fire and then into a rock. He said even the teacher was amazed. But Charlie told them it was all scientific."

"He's strange," the man said, and then wished he hadn't. Then, he made a joke of it. "I mean, it's strange, considering how unscientific his mother and I are."

"That's just it. That's just it. I met your wife when she dropped by three weeks back, and she said almost the same thing." The father was searching his face for something. For what? He couldn't figure out.

At first, the man thought that the father was looking for some crack in the mask he was presenting. Then, he knew. The father simply wanted to make sure they saw eye-to-eye.

The crack of the bat — a fly ball — made them both look back at the game.

"Well," the man said. "Charlie is brilliant, isn't he. Young and smart. Not much of an athlete, though."

"Kids can't be good at everything." The father sipped his coffee.

The man sipped his coffee, too. A brief silence.

The man was about to say something so that the father would move away. Maybe say that he had a headache. Maybe that he needed to get something from his car.

Then, the father said, "Your wife told me about the cat."

The man nodded. He was going to go along with this.

"I hope you don't mind my bringing it up. But since I'm a psychologist..."

"Really?" the man said. Could the psychologist see his nervousness? No. He was too good at hiding it.

"Yes. So when I spoke to your wife..."

"Oh, now I remember," the man nodded. "Yes. Yes. She told me she spoke to you...about it."

"Oh, good. I didn't want to be breaking a confidence. But most of the other kids know about it anyway. I just didn't want to cause problems at home."

"No," the man grinned, wishing he were anywhere but standing at the outer edge of the park, talking to Billy Wilson's father. "No secrets between us. We try and keep up with what's going on with Charlie. That cat..."

"Well, it scared the other kids. I'm sure you talked to Mrs. Reilly yourself."

The man tried to place the name. Mrs. Reilly. The owner of the cat? Mrs. Reilly, the school teacher? Mrs. Reilly, the mother of one of the other boys? He sipped the last of the coffee. He peered into the coffee residue at the bottom of the cup.

"I've been meaning to," he said.

"Well, I guess since it's summer, it can wait. Frankly, I'm surprised about how she reacted herself. It seemed rather unprofessional."

"Women," the man said, hoping the father had a sense of humor.

The father gave him an odd look.

He can see through me.

He knows what I'm thinking.

But the father chuckled. "I wouldn't say that. She's a good teacher, too. But I guess she just reached the boiling point with the cat. It was a neighbor's?"

The man nodded.

"Well, I'm just happy to hear your wife got him some help. A counselor over in the city, I guess."

The man nodded.

"I don't mean to get into it here, but it does explain a bit why the other kids are a bit...shy...of being around Charlie." When the father said this, the man glanced out at the playing field.

Charlie stood off by himself, his face turned up to the sun. His baseball cap had fallen off, and his blond straw hair seemed longer than usual.

He shut his eyes. He whispered something as if he were wishing to be somewhere else. The man knew about this, because he'd seen other little boys do it when they wanted to be somewhere else.

They held their heads back, closed their eyes, and whispered.

Or prayed.

But now the man noticed the other boys. They played the game, paying little attention to Charlie.

As he watched the boys move around, trying to catch a fly ball or running to change position, he noticed something that he'd missed before, in every single game.

Yet it had been there.

It had happened since late spring when the Little League started up.

It wasn't that they just didn't like Charlie, or that they made fun of him.

In all the months he'd spent watching Charlie, picking him out, he'd never seen the other kids interact in any way at all with the boy.

On the field, it was as if there were an invisible barrier around Charlie, a horseshoe shaped magnetic field that the other boys moved around, without ever getting close to Charlie.

Without ever coming within a certain number of feet of him.

&

THE FATHER TAPPED HIS SHOULDER. "I'm sure it was a one time thing. I'm sure it's not one of those worst-case scenarios where he'll be scarred for life."

The man kept his eyes on the boys as they played the game around Charlie. "I never noticed."

"Huh?"

"I never noticed how the other boys were shy around him. I thought it was the other way around."

"I guess it was…before. But something changed last year. Your wife said it was on your vacation to the islands.

The Caribbean. She said…" The father patted him on the shoulder. "Oh, she just said something about how you two hired that babysitter. That native woman. To watch him. And how she taught him all kinds of crazy things."

He didn't like men's hands on him. It made him squirm. He took a step forward to be out of patting reach.

"My wife didn't tell me. Oh, wait. Yes, that island woman. I can't recall her name," the man said. He kept his eyes on Charlie who nodded his head side to side. "My wife doesn't always tell me everything about this kind of problem. And of course, Charlie doesn't."

"We dads are always the last to know," the father said. "Well, when Charlie killed the cat," and the man was glad he hadn't turned back to face the father, because this revelation nearly made him choke, and his eyes widened, "your wife told me that it was an accident. I buy that. I really do. Accidents happen. It's not good to leave little kids with animals. And hell, Billy killed a bird with his slingshot once and we were none too happy about that. But kids do these things, right? But for Charlie to cut out its heart and bring it into school. Well, you know the rest. Mrs. Reilly got ferocious and ended up slapping him too hard."

"Oh, right," the man said, as if he were recollecting. "The bruise."

"I'm sure the school district'll fire her over it eventually. But Billy told me Charlie did this thing after she slapped him. And he made the lights go off in the classroom."

"Made the lights go off?"

But the father kept talking, "And then made them flicker on and off. And Mrs. Reilly started screaming, and Charlie started saying something over and over. Some kind of nursery rhyme. And Billy said Judy Goffman tried to get out, but the door wouldn't open. And then Charlie made Mrs. Reilly eat the cat's heart right in front of the other kids." The father was silent for a moment. "Your wife didn't tell you?"

The man shrugged. "Our marriage has its ups and downs. You know. She protects Charlie a lot. Too much."

"Sure," the father said.

The man could detect that edge in the father's voice, as if maybe he suspected something wasn't quite right.

"Well, then Charlie, well, I know boys, and I understand these things, he apparently shows the other boys something. Only Billy won't tell me what it is. I'm sure it's nothing much. Maybe that dead cat, huh? Billy said something about not being able to tell, or else he'd get killed."

"What happened to the teacher?" The man tried to hide his nervousness. It was no longer pleasurable. It felt like insects stinging him.

"I told you, the school district will probably fire her. You can't hit kids. Not these days. Well, they'll wait until she's better."

"Better?"

"She was in an unfortunate accident early in the summer. But when she's better…"

"What is it he showed the other kids?"

"That's the big question."

The man was getting a headache.

The boys shouted from the field.

The father said, "Oh, gosh, the game's over. Give me a call if you need some help."

The father handed him his business card.

The man curled it up in a small paper ball and dropped

it on the ground once the father had returned to the group of other fathers.

Charlie stayed in the outfield, raising his hands up to the sky as if he had won or lost the game all by himself.

When the field was clear, Charlie walked by himself, dragging his feet as he went, heading to Green Street.

The man picked up his backpack. He reached inside it, digging around the soup cans and rope for the stun gun.

When Charlie neared, he said, "Hi Charlie."

Charlie glanced up. "Hi. Who're you?"

"Your mom sent me."

Charlie screwed up his face slightly. He squinted. "She did? My mom?"

The man nodded.

When they got to his car, the man told him about what was in the trunk of the car.

He always did this with boys. It was the simplest thing.

With girls, you had to show them something. Usually something pretty. Girls were harder because they usually wouldn't come near the car.

With boys, it was easy.

"Real firecrackers?" Charlie asked, his eyes brightening.

"Yeah, Roman candles, black cats, all kinds of things." He thrust the key into the trunk, twisting it.

The trunk popped open.

"Aren't they against the law?" Charlie's voice was like

innocence with just a spark of corruption. Boys were like that.

"Not around Fourth of July time," the man said.

"Fourth of July happened already." Charlie peered into the dark trunk. There was a blanket, two small pillows, and rope.

"Where are they?" he asked.

"Under the blanket."

As Charlie reached for the blanket, the man brought the stun gun down and pressed it against the small of the boy's back.

THE MAN GLANCED ABOUT as the crackling sound went off.

The suburban streets seemed empty and painted with sunshine.

He only had a minute or less.

THE FATHERS and sons were off in the lot on the far side of the park celebrating both victory and defeat as the man dumped Charlie into the trunk.

From his backpack, he withdrew the duct tape. He measured off a bit of it, and taped it over Charlie's mouth. Then he brought out a length of rope from the backpack and tied the boy's arms behind his back. Then his legs. Then he put the pillows under the boy's head.

Shut the trunk.

The sweat on his forehead was thick.

He stared at the trunk.

"Damn it," he whispered.

IN HIS MIND, he tried to remember what he'd done with the car keys. *Unlocked the trunk. Stunned the boy. Dumped the boy in. Reached for the duct tape*

Set the keys on the blanket.

"Damn it to hell," he whispered.

He glanced down the block. A teenager rode his bike slowly by. A flock of sparrows flew overhead, chattering as they vanished into an oak tree's branches, thick with summer green.

He brought out his Swiss Army knife and jimmied the lock.

The blade broke off.

The father who had spoken to him, drove slowly alongside him in his Cadillac. He lowered his window. "Where's Charlie?"

The man shrugged. "He wanted to walk home. You know kids."

"Got problems?"

The man laughed, but it was a fake jittery laugh. *Don't give yourself away.* "I locked them in the trunk. My keys. Stupid me."

"Want me to call a locksmith?"

The man waved him away. "No, but thanks! I have an extra set at home. I'll just walk over and get it myself. Probably catch up with my kid."

"Sounds good," the father said, and then drove off.

ᥡ

"DAMN IT ALL TO HELL," the man muttered.

He went and sat in the front seat of the car. He glanced about, looking for some instrument, something, anything that might jimmy the trunk open.

He looked at himself in the rearview mirror. Looked like hell. He looked like a junkie dying for his fix, unable to get it.

His fix was in the trunk.

A patrol car drove up alongside him, stopping. It was that kind of neighborhood. Patrol cars were always around. He'd noticed that. It had been an acceptable risk, but now it was unacceptable.

Completely unacceptable.

He picked this place to scope out a kid because it was just this kind of neighborhood that was easiest to hit. It seemed safe.

In the world, there was no "safe."

A cop, big and burly, strutting as if he owned the block and everything in it, got out of the car, and tapped on his window.

ᥡ

THE MAN ROLLED the car window down.

The cop leaned in. "Hank Wilson told me you were having some car trouble."

"Hank Wilson?"

"Billy's dad," the cop said. "You're Charlie's dad, right? I've known little Charlie since he started school. Wild kid." The cop flashed a funny look. The guy talked a mile a minute. "I've known him since he was five and almost ran in front of my car. Almost gave me a heart attack."

"Thanks. Everything's fine. I just locked my keys in the trunk."

"Can't you just pop it open from inside?" the cop asked, peering through the window.

"Wish I could. Nothing works right in this old pile of junk," the man said.

"You sure?"

The man offered up a blank stare. "Don't you think I would've done that already?"

The cop shrugged. "Trying to help. Well, jeez, Charlie's dad. What must that be like?"

The man felt sweat break out on the back of his neck. "Yeah, he's a handful."

"That time we caught him with that baby. Remember that? I know he didn't know what he was doing. Kids never think about death like it really is. I got worried we were gonna have a pan of baby soup on our hands, know what I mean? Just a joke. Glad he didn't really hurt that baby. There'da been hell to pay. Hey, I can help you with that," the cop said.

He went back to his car, and returned with a long thin bar. "Come on, I'll show you how to use it."

The man got out of the car and leaned against the door. He wasn't sure if his heart was still beating. He heard a clanging noise in the back of his head.

"Here, it's easy, done this a million times," the cop said.

THE MAN WALKED to the back of the car.

The cop took the long slender metal bar and pressed it into the lock. "This isn't going to be wonderful for your lock, but I assume you were going to have to get a locksmith anyway?"

"No, really," the man said, touching the cop's arm. "I have an extra set of keys at home."

"Oh," the cop said, retracting the instrument. "Okay. You want me to give you a ride?"

The man glanced at the trunk. Charlie would be awake by now.

"It's a nice day. I don't mind the walk," the man said.

"You sure? I don't mind," the cop said.

"I need the exercise."

The cop nodded. "Don't we all. Well, good to meet you, Mister..."

The man tried to remember Charlie's last name.

Charlie Jones.

Charlie Howard.

Charlie Randel.

Charlie...

"Carter. Mike Carter."

"Mike Carter," the cop said thoughtfully.

The man wondered if the cop knew Charlie's father's first name.

"I knew a Mike Carter back in high school. You never went to..."

"I grew up in the South," the man said.

"Oh," the cop grinned. "Well, good to meet you, sir. That Charlie of yours is something. I know he's a big joker, but man I've had to rescue more kids and dogs from his clutches. He'll grow up to be something, he sure will."

THE COP WAITED by the car, writing something up in his log book, which frightened the man a bit, but it was too late. It's not like he could go back and erase this day, this day that had begun so perfectly.

All the man needed to do was walk around the corner to the drugstore, buy a screwdriver and do some major damage to the trunk of his car. Then, tie it shut, and drive back to his place.

He would take Charlie down into the cellar, where no one ever heard the screams, and then he could go to work on him and set up the cameras to take the pictures.

The man walked down Green Street, remembering that there was a convenience store just a block or two over.

The heat of the day was getting to him, and he wished he had planned for such possible mistakes with an extra set of keys, but he had been too eager.

That was always his problem.

He was too eager to get on with it. He had always been overly cautious before, but he'd been younger then, and now, he was getting sloppy.

He had thought Charlie was such a perfect target, and everything had seemed as if it pointed to this day, but maybe he was wrong.

Still, he got an adrenaline high, knowing that Charlie was in that trunk and that he had passed himself off as the boy's father—the ultimate thrill—knowing that a cop had almost opened that trunk.

HE FOUND a small screwdriver down the second aisle of the convenience store, and slipped it into his back pocket.

Part of the thrill was shoplifting. It aroused him a bit too, watching the young woman at the counter who watched him. She knew he was up to something, but she had missed that second—no, that millisecond—when he'd stolen the screwdriver.

It took him ten minutes to get back to the park, and at first he thought he was on the wrong street.

Then, he saw the police car.

৯৯

THE COP DROVE up beside him at the sidewalk. "Sorry, Mike. I called your wife."

"My…wife," the man said.

"Yeah I figured I'd save you the trip home, but she said she didn't have any extra sets of keys."

"My wife said that?" the man asked. He felt something clutch at his throat.

The cop nodded. "She told me to tow it. She told me you had about twenty outstanding parking tickets and two speeding tickets and your license was suspended." The cop shrugged. "I had to follow up. Dispatch hasn't confirmed, but your wife swore up and down on a stack of Bibles. She sounded a little funny, too, so maybe you better get home."

"My *wife*," the man repeated again as if he could not believe any of it.

"Look, I'm sorry. But you're lucky the Sheriff hasn't sent someone out to arrest you yet." The cop paused, while the man took all this in. "One other thing, Mike. You got one nasty old lady."

"My wife lied," the man said, stunned.

"Well, maybe she did, but I can't take that chance. If you don't have tickets, I'll go down personally with you and get that car. But until our computers come back up at Dispatch, I'm going to assume for the good of my job that she may be telling the truth. Seems to me, Mike, I remember someone down at the office mentioning those tickets when I had to go talk to Charlie about how not to hurt little babies. Seems to me."

"Yes, now I remember. Yes, the tickets." The man felt his mouth go dry. "Where was it towed?"

"Impounded, Mike. You can't get it back today. On Monday, go down and pay your fines and it's all yours."

The man watched the police car as it slowly drove on down the road.

The cop glanced in his side view mirror and looked back.

ALL RIGHT. *All right. Enough.*

He could get it. There's a way to get it. To get the boy. To get in the trunk and get the boy out of the trunk and then get the boy somewhere else. The boy would have to be killed right away. The fun was out of it now. The fun was definitely out the door.

But it could be fixed. It could be fixed and then it would be all right.

THE MAN HAD NO FRIENDS. He had business associates,

but they never liked to be called in times of trouble. He had his parents, but they didn't really like to hear from him either. He was very much a loner. He walked across the park and sat in the bleachers as the afternoon wore on, wondering how he would get to the car, and ultimately, to Charlie.

When it came to him, it was like a pinprick at the back of his skull.

He would just leave Charlie there.

The old car would be in the lot for at least a month before anyone would decide to do anything about it.

In a month, he'd be in some other country.

He could create a new identity. Sure, they might find the other kids buried beneath the house, but that would be all right. He would already be someone else, somewhere else.

It seemed like a plan.

The more he went over it, the better it sounded.

It was either that or suicide, and he hated the thought of not being on earth anymore. He wasn't even sure that it would serve anything to kill himself. And Mexico was nice. He heard good things about Puerto Vallarta. Even Costa Rica was supposed to be lovely. He could just get a house on the edge of a beach and be free.

He had lots of money.

Then he remembered.

The money was in the cellar of his house.

His house was fifteen miles away.

He glanced at his backpack, sitting beneath the tree where he'd left it that afternoon.

He kept almost everything he needed with him, except the cash.

One could not be too careful.

IT WAS NEARLY seven at night, still fairly light out, when he began the walk home. By one a.m., he arrived at the small house at the end of the cul-de-sac. The lights were off, but the front window seemed to reflect some yellow light from inside.

The man was usually very good about turning lights off when they were unused, but he was getting sloppy, he knew. As he stepped up to the door, he remembered that he had no key.

Of course you have no key, you fool. You locked it in the trunk with poor little Charlie.

He thought it again, Poor Little Charlie.

The boy had been doomed from the start of his life. The misfit of that little boring suburb and those boring people. He was off in his own world half the time anyway. The trunk would not be a big change for him.

Poor Charlie.

Humming his tunes, whispering his prayers, cutting the hearts out of dead cats.

That last bit was a strange sort of thing. Even as a child himself, the man had never cut hearts out of anything he'd killed.

It was too intricate.

Too *primitive.*

He preferred the torture and the pictures, but not hearts. Nothing so…so…*visceral.*

Poor crazy little misfit Charlie.

The man took the screwdriver and jammed it against

the door. The old wood crackled and gave, and after a few moments, the door flew open.

He went inside, flicking on the overhead lights.

§⦚

THE PLACE WAS empty of all things.

He hated cluttered homes. He liked sparse. He liked clearings, not thickets.

There, on the bare living room floor, a little boy sat in a circle of small stones and candles. Red and white chalk markings of foreign symbols were all over the floor.

A ram's skull in the center of the circle, at the boy's feet.

Circling in and around the flames, houseflies, as if they'd been trapped by the dozens in the house all day.

Charlie had his hands up in the air, his legs crossed in front of him, his shirt off. He wore only his shorts. His skin was covered with painted symbols. Paint covered his face, one half, blood red, the other, bone white.

Charlie looked up at him.

"You left me to die."

The man grasped the wall to steady himself. "How did you…"

"You put me in that trunk and left me to die. By the power of the Loa, and Chango, my guardian, I send to you all that you were gonna do to me."

The overhead light began flickering on and off.

Charlie grinned. His voice changed, as if he'd swallowed something distasteful. "We're going to spend the night here, just you and me. That's what you want, huh?"

"How?" was all the man could say, and as he stood there, some gut level instinct told him to run.

When he turned, the door slammed shut right in front of his face. He tried the knob. The door was locked.

"Poor man," Charlie said. "Poor little misfit man."

The man turned around to face the boy.

I'll kill him. I'll kill the little creep.

Charlie's lips moved but made no sound. The candle flames rose up like spears, and a smell of sulfur permeated the room.

A growling, as of some panther, came from back near the dining room, but the man could not see for all the smoke and fire.

Then all the lights went out.

The man grew faint, unable to breathe, and felt his knees buckling under him just as he lost consciousness.

WHEN THE MAN AWOKE, he found breathing difficult.

The tape over his mouth prevented him from screaming, but he tried anyway.

He guessed where he was. He smelled gasoline and oil and the way trunks of cars smelled. He didn't know how the little boy had done it.

Something else was in the dark place with him. He sensed it there.

It began to growl after the second day.

Or was it a hum?

That was it.

A little boy humming.

After two months, a nice family bought the old rundown car at an auction the town had twice a year.

One of their neighbors, a little boy named Charlie Carter dropped by and gave them an extra set of keys that he swore he found in the park down the street.

The new owner of the car didn't believe the little boy, but Charlie convinced him to go out and try it on the trunk, which — up until that morning — had remained unopened.

Ice Palace

※❦※

I once helped murder a boy when I was nineteen. Only we didn't think of ourselves as boys back then.

It was in college, at a university in the mountains of Virginia, when the snow had piled up and the parties were in full swing.

I lived with my brothers—we weren't blood relations except through the college fraternity system.

It was February, and certain aspects of fraternity hazing were not yet complete. It was always in the harshest part of the season that the sadistic rituals took place on campus, from paddling to raiding to a particularly cruel torture called Ice Palace.

I was just buttoning up my shirt, about to start shaving, when Nate Wick, known as the Wicked Wick or the Flaccid Wick, grabbed me by the collar and slammed me against the wall; the whole world shook and I cussed him out something fierce; his face was all scrunched up like he was about to cry. He had hair growing from his ears even at twenty-one, and fat cheeks like a cherub gone to seed. I socked him in the jaw, 'cause he could be crazy sometimes, even if he *was* my fraternity brother. He took the blow pretty good, and my fist ached like a son of a bitch, and he dropped on my bed, right on the wet towel, so it made a smack kind of sound, and if he hadn't been naked I'd have grabbed *him* by *his* collar and heave-hoed him right onto the balcony, where it was twenty below and iced smooth.

"Damn it, Wick," I said, "you drive me, you know that? You drive me, Christ."

"Drive you what? Nuts?"

"You just drive me, that's all," I said, finally catching my breath.

Nate said, slyly, "I know what you want, Underdog. I know what you want." I felt my face going red. Something disturbed me about his comment.

"What the jizz you shittin'?" Stan, ever the poet, said from the doorway to my room. Stan was naked, too, which was pretty much how the guys went around on a Saturday morning in February when the nearest open road to the girls' college was ten miles away.

It was funny, being as generally modest as I was, how I'd got used to all this flaunted nakedness in the ice-cold mornings. Myself, I never got out of the showers except with a big blue towel around my waist, and never left my room except with a shirt and khakis on.

Nate began laughing, and I figured given his jugface that I hadn't even caused him a moment's pain; but I was still mad 'cause I hated being surprised like that.

Everything in that frat house was a surprise attack, especially on Big Weekends.

Nate was on edge on account of his girl might not be

making it down for Fancy Dress, so there was a chance he might be the dateless wonder.

Nate said, "Look, Underdog, we got the pledges coming over for Ice Palace, and you look like a queer from Lynchburg."

"If that's what you think, jerk-off, then you better not lie naked on my bed too long with that come-hither look on your face," I said.

I went back to shaving in the bowl I'd put beneath the mirror in my room for privacy; it saved me from running to the communal and much-pissed-upon bathroom every time I needed to shave or wash.

Stan said, "Fuck the fuck it very."

It was a line he said often, sober or drunk, and I couldn't figure it out for the life of me. He had patches of hair up and down his body, armpits to knees, like he had some ape pattern baldness problem. "I can't wait for tonight, girls, I'm gonna get me some fine pussy, *fine* pussy."

"Underdog," Nate addressed me in his usual manner, "the Hose Queen's coming down tonight. You want to get laid?"

"No thanks, and get out of here, willya?"

This particular winter semester, in my second year, Nate, who was my big brother in the House, wanted me to learn how to be a man as only Nate knew how.

It wasn't enough that I was flunking Physics for Poets because of the midweek grain parties, nor that I had no interest in cow punching or whore hopping.

Nate was a wild man and rich redneck from Alabama, and his life was something to marvel at. He had learned the ropes of human sexuality at twelve from his babysitter; at seventeen, he'd saved an entire boatload of immigrants off the coast of Bermuda — losing three toes in the process.

He *knew* life, how to live it, which paths to go down, when and where to get a hard-on and what to do about it — and with whom. The bizarre part was, he was an honors student, his old man ran one of the growing tobacco companies, and he never, *ever* had a hangover.

Somebody stuck a condom in the scrambled eggs that morning, a typical frat joke, so I passed on breakfast and headed up to the Hill to do some studying on campus.

I didn't have a date for the Fancy Dress Ball that night, even though I'd bought two tickets well in advance thinking this girl I knew from high school, Colleen, might want to go, or maybe I'd meet someone else last minute. But Colleen was not to be wooed down to what she called the "last bastion of the old South."

I called three girls I knew "down the road," but each had had a date since October. One of them was kind enough to say she could set me up with this really homely girl who majored in Chemistry. I passed, and figured I'd get some studying done for once, and let them all go to hell. I was determined to spend the day studying, not scrounging for dates or hazing freshmen.

But Nate was not one to give up easily in his quest to keep me from doing anything productive. He hunted me down on campus, shut my American history book for me, sat on the edge of my desk, and said, "You missed Ice Palace."

"Big deal. Jesus H., quit following me around like some kind of retriever."

"Jonno told a good one. Got us laughing right off. Bug Boy practically froze to death, we had to let him off after about half an hour, just 'cause we were getting bored watching his lips turn purple. Only one part left."

I groaned. "Yeah, yeah, the crowning of the King. It's like being with Nazis in kindergarten."

"Hey, it takes a special kind of guy to be King of the Palace." Nate Wick had a snarly way of talking that was both seductive and distancing, as if he were an untamed dog waiting for the right master. "Ice Palace is almost as good as fish dunking."

"I hate the whole thing. Ice Palace could make one of them sick."

"You liked it well enough last year."

"Well, I was drunk last year. I liked lots of things then."

"Well, piss on you, Underdog. Sometimes I wish the old you would come back, the one that would stay out all night and really howl." But his mood changed again. "We're gonna kidnap Lewis," he said, like he was planning out the day in his head. He grinned so bright I thought the sun had come out from the gray sky outside the window.

"When?"

"This afternoon. Few hours."

"Shit," I said. "Jesus, of all days. He's your King? Christ, Wick, that poor son of a bitch won't last three hours in the cold. He's got bronchial asthma, he'll come down with something." The truth was, I was protective of Stewart Lewis, who didn't even have the hapless luck to be a brain, for he was skinny and homely and not too bright; if he hadn't been a legacy, he would've gotten blackballed by sixty percent of the House. But his old man was a major brother back in his day, so the frat had no choice, because it was in the charter to take legacies no matter what. I had known Stewart Lewis back at St. Sebastian's, the Episcopal school

I'd gone to before college. Lewis was always a weenie, always sick, always a mama's boy, always something not so good.

Nate dismissed Lewis with a snap, and then a slap on the desk. "He's a Spam, don't worry about him. We're gonna take him to Crawford's Dump, stick him in the snow, pay Donkeyman to watch him, tie him up, nothing bad. We won't leave him there all night, you fiend. Just a couple of hours, and then I'll go get him in time for Fancy Dress. I doubt he's got a date, though. He's such a Spam. Maybe we'll write on him. The usual. Scare the kid a little. Just a shit speck. He'll get to wear his Jockeys, whatta you want? Whatta you want?"

"You always sound homo to me when you talk about it," I said, hoping to get him angry. I was only a sophomore, but I'd hated hazing so much from the year before—I'd been too blotto to protest much—that I felt very protective of the poor freshmen pledges who went along with any idiotic torture that seniors like Nate devised.

"Maybe I am homo, Underdog. Wanta suck it to find out?" Here he whipped out his thing, which was not the most unusual sight between frat brothers, and was, perhaps, a big reason why we were all so homophobic. Then he put it back in his trousers, zipped up, and said, "You gonna go tonight?"

"Why? You want to buy my ticket?"

"Just wondering. I'm not always as insensitive as I seem, buttface."

It started to snow again, and the wind picked up outside, whistling around the old brick and columns along the colonnade; feather flakes seesawed beyond the beveled glass of the windows. It was an ancient campus, from the

1700s, all columns and Greek Parthenon-types and mountain vistas, and I wished I was somewhere, anywhere, else.

"Look," Nate said, "Helen's coming up from Hollins. She likes you. She said she wants to see you." Helen was his girl friend, a pretty girl who, for some reason, idolized Nate, possibly because she was more unbalanced than she seemed —there was a hint of this in her Sylvia Plath-like scribblings. I thought she was too good for him.

"That's nice," I said. "Look, Nate, I don't want Lewis to go to Ice Palace. He'll get sick. If Dean Trask hears about it, we could get shut down. Think about that. I mean, a half hour of Ice Palace is one thing, but three or four hours, and it's snowing…it's not that funny."

Nate laughed, drumming his fists into the desk. I'd seen him pummel a stray dog like that once, just because the dog was in his way.

That was how he used his fists most of the time.

He said, "I think it's a goddamn laugh riot."

I avoided the frat house until six, when hunger got the best of me. I was wary of most of my brothers, because I wasn't good at taking any kind of teasing, and that seemed to be their primary business in college.

When I entered the foyer, I smelled the steaks—it was a special night, Fancy Dress Ball and all that, and so our cook was doing it up good, steak and asparagus and biscuits and potatoes and fruit and apple pie.

Most of the brothers had taken their dates out to dinner, but the poorer among us sat at the long tables, not yet dressed in black tie, with dates astride hard-backed chairs. Plain girls, too, for the most part, until, upstairs, in a guarded bathroom, they would make up and spray, Vaseline their teeth for smiles and for other, more urgent desires, later; spruced with expensive, oversize gowns, transforming from ordinary faces and bodies to creatures of unconscionable beauty, perhaps gaudy in the garish light of the upstairs bathroom, but almost mythic, the Woman in All Her Glorious Aspects, in the dimmed, squinting light over at the student center, where the dance would take place.

Nate called out, "Underdog!"

He was at the last table, with Helen at his side. She looked up briefly, and then down at her plate again — a flash of curiosity about me, about what I'd been up to since summer.

She was skinny—looked like she had starved herself for this one night—and she'd greased her hair back around her ears with some sort of conditioner.

I went over and took a chair, grabbed some slop, and lopped it on my plate. "Helen," I said.

"Hey, Charlie," she said sweetly, her accent growing more Southern with each year she spent in Virginia. She did not look up from her plate; it was obvious she hadn't eaten.

Nate lip-farted. "Call him Underdog. Humble but lovable."

I smiled at Nate. "Things go okay with Lewis?"

Nate winked. "Fine, fine."

"He around?"

"Yeah. I don't know. I guess he was upset."

I wasn't sure whether to believe Nate or not, but Helen must've detected my doubt. She said, "He said he was going to a movie. He was very upset. Y'all are so dang insensitive. It's what I hate, absolutely hate, about y'all being in a fraternity and all."

"Helen's on the rag," Nate half-whispered, loud enough for all six tables to hear.

I looked to Helen, and reached my hand across to touch hers because I felt so bad for her at that moment, stuck with Nate,

Nate who bragged about doing her on his water bed, about muff-diving her in the backseat of her father's Continental, taking her every which way but loose up in the carillon tower of chapel when she didn't want it but loved it anyway.

I didn't know Helen well, but I wanted to touch her more than anything.

Helen glanced up at me, her eyes dry.

Nate was clanking his fork on the side of his plate. He was always jealous when it came to Helen, and he must've seen the way she looked at me.

"Why don't you just fuck her?" he asked, shoving himself away from the table, his chair falling backward.

He was drunk; so that was it. He stomped across the room, and went upstairs.

Helen said, "I hate him."

"Nah," I said, "he's a jerk sometimes. But he has his good side."

Helen laughed. "No, he doesn't. I don't know why I'm even here."

She shut her eyes, her face taut, hands clenched in fists. "Because I'm a good girl. Because I do what I'm told."

She said it like it was taking her medicine, an antidote to some other, more profound venom. "I'm not really a very good girl. Will you go with me tonight? I don't want to go with him. I'd rather die, frankly. He brings out the worst in me."

THERE ARE certain humiliations we will withstand when we are young, if it means that we can become part of something bigger than just ourselves, by ourselves. This notion upheld all the tortures of hazing.

Ice Palace was a peculiar ritual, in which a tunnel at least the length of a man's body was dug out in the snow. The pledges had to dig it, for they were virtual slaves to the upperclassmen. Then, one at a time, the pledges were stripped down to their underwear. Each was then hosed down with water, and sent into the tunnel, which was now deemed the Ice Palace. The pledge had to sit back in the freezing ice and tell a joke until every upperclassman present laughed.

When I endured Ice Palace, I got them cracking up within ten minutes; but I was good with jokes. There had even been something of a respite from the outer world when I had crawled into that ice cave, shivering for sure, but also experiencing a strange pleasure, as if I were protected in a way I didn't quite understand. Some pledges could not tell a joke to save their lives, however, and so it could be a painful, if not simply a chilling, experience. This was one of the least pleasant aspects of hazing. The other rituals (egg yolk passing from mouth to mouth, or fish dunking in a toilet) were disgusting, but essentially harmless. Even paddling was child's play, with the only casualty being a sore butt for a few days.

But Ice Palace...

I thought of Stewart Lewis, with his taped-up glasses on his beaky nose, his small peapod eyes, that squirmy way he had of moving as if he had worms or something, and of the humiliation of the whole ritual, particularly of being chosen to be the King of Ice Palace, as he had been. King of

Ice Palace: the honor at the shit end of life's stick, the pledge chosen basically because he was commonly known as the Spam, the Nerd, the Loser, the Meat. There was always one pledge that fit this bill—almost as if, each year, the brothers decided to admit someone they could torture, someone who was so desperate to be accepted that he would take it.

The King's hands and feet were roped together, and he was to be sealed up in Ice Palace until someone came to get him out. Cold water was hosed over the entire tunnel in order to truly give it a thick layer of ice. Then, after a set period of time, the Brother High Alpha, which in our case was Nate, would break open the door to Ice Palace.

The King would come forth from his white chamber, freezing and cursing, yet somehow stronger, and more part of the group than he could ever be through ordinary means. If the chosen one tried to get out early, there was Donkeyman, the local wino.

He was as scary as any nightmare, his face elongated, his ears out and pointy like a mule's, only three teeth in his head, and barely a nose at all, just two flared nostrils exhaling frosty clouds of carbon dioxide. The freshmen weren't familiar enough with the university to have seen Donkeyman yet, for Donkeyman was a creature of alleyways and Dumpsters.

He was perfectly harmless, but he looked like a demon lover of donkeys.

Ice Palace was a fraternity secret and, by all accounts, illegal, at least as far as the college went. If it had been known that it was an ongoing ritual, the entire fraternity system, which was then enjoying a rebirth in popularity, would have been shut down.

There was a story that back in the late fifties a boy had died in Ice Palace.

"THAT'S THE BOY," Helen whispered in my ear. We were slow dancing, off the dance floor. She had abandoned Nate to his drunken fury earlier in the evening. Because I owned my own tux, she grabbed me and we'd gone to the Student Center and the Fancy Dress Ball before I could protest much.

I felt a little guilty for snaking my big brother's date, but she was pretty, and he was acting like an asshole, anyway.

I glanced up from her shoulder, for I had been watching the bone there, beneath the skin, so delicate, so feminine. Smelling her, too, like jasmine with the snow just on the other side of the walls, and here, there were flowers and sandalwood. "Huh?" I asked.

"That boy," she said, dreamily, "the one they put in the snow."

We stopped dancing, and I turned around to look at Stewart Lewis. "I didn't know he was going to be—" I said, but then, there was no Stewart.

Just Stan the Man, who came over and slapped me on the back. "Fuck the fuck it very," he said, his breath stinking of whiskey. "So, Underdoggie, you got Nate's squeeze, bravo, good job, didn't deserve her, the Flaccid Wick didn't, my god, this wine tastes like cow jism." His eyes barely registered either of us; his date, Marlene, stood off to the side, avoiding just about everyone.

"Stan wasn't Ice Palace King," I told Helen. "Is that who you saw in Ice Palace?"

"I didn't see him." Helen turned away from me, waving to a friend. "Nate told me it was him. Isn't that Stewart?" and then, to Stan, "Aren't you Stewart Lewis?"

"The Spamster?" Stan guffawed. "Lawdy, no, Miss Scarlett, I don't know nothing about birthin' no babies."

"He's too drunk to make sense," I said. "Nate told you?"

Helen shrugged. "I thought this guy was Stewart. You boys all look alike with your khakis and down jackets. Are you sure you're not Stewart?"

Stan grinned, but wobbled back to Marlene, who apparently scolded him for something.

"Jesus, I wonder if he ever let Lewis out," I said. "Look, Helen, you wait here, I'll be back in a while."

"Charlie," Helen said, not even startled. "Charlie."

"What?" I snapped, and then blurted, "My god. My god. It'll kill Lewis. It'll kill him."

I left her there, and ran through the make-out room just beyond the dance floor, out through the French doors, down the icy steps, almost slipping on the concrete pavement. The town was a small one, almost a town in miniature, and I didn't own a car. It would be a ten minute jog down Stonewall Drive to get to the House, and to Nate, if he was still there.

The night was a furious one. The wind picked up, and the temperature dropped at least twenty degrees.

I was a decent runner then, but I'd had two beers, and this, with the wind, seemed to slow all motion down by half. I felt like an hour had passed before I arrived at the back entrance to the frat house.

The lights were off in the kitchen; I flicked them up. The place was a mess, like a child's giant toy box overturned, but this was usual. What was unusual were the marks on the wall, as if someone had tried finger painting with bacon grease—which there was plenty of around, for it was stored and used in another hazing ritual.

"Nate! Wick! Where the fuck are you?" I took the stairs two at a time, and came to his room on the second floor.

He lay in bed, with the light on. He was wearing his tux. He opened his eyes. "Underdog."

"Where's Lewis?"

"Lewis? Who the fuck cares? That human spittoon. You stole my girl, Underdog. You stole my girl." He rolled over, away from me, facing the wall. "You stole my girl. But fuck it. Like Stan says, fuck the fuck it very."

I couldn't believe that even Nate would leave Lewis in Ice Palace for the eight hours he would've been in it by now. I almost laughed at myself for worrying. I caught my breath, my hands on my knees, bent over slightly. I looked at the poster of the naked girl with the snake that Nate had on his wall. She was some movie actress, I don't remember who, but her belly seemed to meet the boa constrictor in an almost motherly caress. "Whew, Nate. Whoa, boy. You almost had me going. You know, you miserable—you know I ran all the way down here from Fancy Dress, just to...just to—"

"He's still in it." He didn't turn to face me, but his voice was smug. "And I'm the only one who knows where he is."

"You're joking."

"I'm joking, but the joke's on Lewis. Or should I say, you can now find Spam in the freezer section of your local supermarket."

I went over and grabbed him by the back of his collar and hauled him off the bed. When he turned to face me, I slapped his face four times. "Where is he?"

Calmly, Nate said, "What the hell do you care?" There were tears in his eyes. "What the hell do you care? It might as well be me in there, for all any of you care. Why don't you like me, Underdog? Why?" His tears were both a shock and a revelation to me: He was only a nine-year-old in a twenty-one-year-old's body, the jugface was a mask, the rough talk, a cover, the attitude, a sham.

And I said what I felt, although I regretted it within the hour.

I said, "Because you're not even human."

WE TOOK HIS CAR, but I drove.

"You said you were doing Ice Palace at Crawford's Dump," I said, "so we'll go there first. You better hope to god Lewis had the sense to break out of there."

"I don't know," he said, a singsong to his voice. "I gave Donkeyman some Chivas to do double duty. I told him to hit Spam on the head with the shovel if he tried to get out. We hosed it down pretty good. Twenty below. Nice thick ice. Ice you could skate on. Ice Palazzo." Nate was still crying, bawling like a baby, and singing; he had cracked; he was drunk; he kept trying to grab the wheel while I was driving.

Crawford's Dump was the old graveyard just outside town, but there were few markers, and even fewer showed through the heavy snow. I skidded the Volkswagen to a stop on the slick shoulder of the potholed, salt-strewn road, and left the headlights on. We tromped in our tuxes through the Styrofoam crunch of snow, and each time Nate tried to pull away I socked him in the shoulder and cussed him out. The

snow and a clouded moon provided a soft light, making the
dumping ground of the dead romantic, beautiful, sublime.
Even Nate, when I spat my fury at him, looked beautiful,
too, with the tears streaming, and his eyes always on me.
The dump descended into a small valley, where the entire
cemetery spread out all around us.

"Where?"

Nate shrugged. His tears ceased. The wind, too, died,
but we heard it howling around us, up the hill. Trucks out
on the interstate blew their horns, one to another, and even
the music from the Fancy Dress Ball, playing "The Swing,"
could be made out.

"Where, Nate? Tell me."

"Wherever Donkeyman is. You stole my girl,
Underdog."

"Look, asshole, Lewis is going to die. You hear me? You
will have murdered a human being. Don't you get it? You
tell me where that stupid Ice Palace is, or I will kill you with
my bare hands."

Nate blinked twice. "Suck my dick."

I got a good clear shot at his jaw, my second in one day,
and then a knee in the groin before he swung back; he only
clipped me, but I was off balance, and fell into the snow.

I thought for a second—just a second—I felt a gentle
tugging.

There, in the snow.

Like a soft mitten, pulling me down.

Nate jumped on top of me, spitting all over my face as
he spoke. "You are my best friend, Underdog, you are my
best friend in the world. Who the fuck cares about Lewis?
Are you in love with him or something? Are you? Is that all
you want? Lewis? Why are you doing this to me?" He began

boxing my ears with snow, until I felt them go numb; I tried to heave him off me, but Nate was heavy; I felt that gentle tugging again. Soft. Like kittens on my back.

And then, something I had always known would happen, did happen. I just had never had a clue as to the form it would take.

Nate Wick kissed me on the lips as warmly and sweetly as any lover ever had.

SOMETHING CLICKED FOR ME THEN, and for the longest minute in the world, I shut my eyes and just felt the warmth of those lips, and the even tempo of my own breathing through my nostrils.

I was somewhere else, and the cold of the snow was almost burning now, like a bed of warm coals against my tuxedo. His hands remained around my ears, and the sound of distant music, and trucks, too—their own music—voices up on the hillside, passersby to whom we were invisible. The whiteness of snow, the indigo sky, all there, but without me seeing or hearing.

His lips were rough and chapped, and I felt my own lips opening like a purse that had been kept too long shut; his upper lip grazed my teeth. His breath was a caustic brewery, but I held each one for as long as I could. I hated this boy, this man, so much; I hated him, and yet tied like this, together, unnaturally if we were to believe those who ran the world, we were perverse brothers, children playing. The blood rushed to my face, an unbearable burning sensation. I opened my eyes; his remained closed. I kissed a corner of his lips, and then the other.

He made a deep noise, a churning machine somewhere within his gut, or igniting along his spine, as he rose and fell again, softly, like the tugging I felt in the rabbit-fur snow beneath my back. The knob of desire, or prick, or dick, or wang, whatever we had called it through all the shared moments of college life, pressed from his pants against mine. I shivered as much from embarrassment as from lust; but there was no one around, you see, no one within miles. I remembered him in the showers, soaping his underarms like he was scrubbing a saddle, tender and quick and then sandpapering at the last; the tumescence he had, which I noticed only peripherally. I hated him. I hated him.

He pressed the side of his face against mine, and it was like holding someone for the first time, this boy, this innocent, angry, drunken boy. I wrapped my arms around him. "I love you," he whispered, and even though I smelled the alcohol, I sighed.

He said, "Lewis was nothing. He was nothing."

And then my mind came back to me, through this physical revelation, through this lightning-swift understanding of all I had done before in my life, as well as much of what Nate himself had done.

Lewis.

Stewart Lewis. The freshman that Nate Wick had chosen as King of Ice Palace.

"You fucked Lewis," I said. "You fucked him and then you buried him. Get the fuck off me!" I shoved hard, and he rolled back.

"No," he said, rather meekly, not breaking eye contact with me. "I didn't. He wouldn't let me. He...he didn't want me."

I would've liked to have died right there, my secret self that I had worked so hard to hide buried forever in snow, but I was worried about Lewis. The kiss had made me forget him, briefly, but the reality of who and what Nate Wick was came back to me, a sour taste in the back of my throat. "Get up, get up."

I stood, kicking him in the side.

He gazed forlornly up at the moon, which had swept off its clouds. The lover's moon, I thought, the horny poking male moon, the prick of light, the howling desire of man's madness.

I felt dirty, and picked up fresh snow and rubbed it on my face, my lips, to get that awful taste of *him* off me.

"It's so white," Nate said, packing a snowball, which he threw at me as I wandered the valley.

AT LAST, I saw a solitary figure, a minute man standing guard: the illustrious Donkeyman, his shovel stuck firmly into a heap of snow. He was the whitest man I had ever seen, and even at night, he seemed to glow in the dark.

His chin stretched downward like putty, the ears demonic; blubbery lips, nostrils drippy with snot. He grinned, and brayed some greeting—the bottle of Chivas Regal lay empty beside him, along with several piss stains at his feet.

"Preppy boy, how you doin'?" he asked congenially, waving the flashlight that he held tight in his gloved left hand.

He wore a deerstalker hat and an oversized tan duster around his shoulders — one that a frat brother had no doubt loaned him for the night. "King a Ice Palace in there. I done my job. You got another bottle?"

I took the shovel up and asked, "Where?"

"I said, you got another bottle? Done my job. Icy Palace, nobody goes in, nobody goes out."

I threatened him with the shovel, until he pointed out the mound, not three feet away. I tapped it with the edge of the shovel. Hard as a rock. The ice of its outer layer gleamed, for Donkeyman shone his flashlight upon it.

"Lewis?" I shouted. "Lewis!"

I listened, but heard only the giggling of Donkeyman as he lit a cigarette and puckered his lips at the first puff.

"King a Icy Palace ain't been talkin' since about six, seven. Done a good damn job. Best. You boys know it, too." He spat in the snow.

I took the shovel up, down, up, down. The blade struck the outer edge of the Ice Palace. It was like breaking rocks in two.

The ice finally creaked and cracked where I struck down.

⚓

I LOOKED through the opening I had dug. Nate was already there at my side, perhaps sobering up a bit, because he seemed nervous and worried. Donkeyman patted me on the back now and again in my labor, cheering me on. We were some crew.

"Lewis? Stewart!" I shouted into the tunnel.

Silence.

"I only had him make it maybe six feet in," Nate said, with some regret.

I grabbed Donkeyman's flashlight, and shone it into Ice Palace. The tunnel in the ice and snow did go about six feet or so, but then there seemed to be a twist. Handprints in the ice, too, along the shiny white and silver walls. There were the ropes. "He got out," I said, almost relieved. "He got out."

"He got out," Nate said, solemnly.

"Thank god, thank you god for saving Lewis's life." I stood, leaning against the shovel.

Donkeyman said, "He got out?"

"Underdog," Nate said.

"Thank god, you better thank god, Wick, because if he had died in there…well, you are one lucky SOB."

Nate looked stunned. "He didn't get out, Charlie." Finally, for the first time in his life, calling me by my real name.

"What do you mean?"

"I mean what I said. He didn't get out."

"He must've. See for yourself." I showed him the tunnel, and swirled the flashlight around to show the shape of the curve, to the left, barely visible. "He got loose and dug around that way. The lucky bastard must've gone for about six more feet or something, and then tunneled up."

"He didn't get out," Nate repeated. He shoved me aside, and crawled into Ice Palace.

I watched him shimmy through the thin tunnel, blocking my light.

"Nate, get out of there," I called after him.

I heard his words echo through Ice Palace: "I'm telling you, he didn't get out. I put him here, Charlie, I put him here, so I should know."

"What's he mean by that?" I asked Donkeyman, as if he would have a coherent answer.

Donkeyman scratched his scalp beneath his cap and said, "Don't know. The boy already got Icy Palaced."

I crawled in a ways, shining the flashlight first up ahead, and then to the frozen walls. I saw Lewis's hand prints, as if he'd pressed against the snow to try and push his way out. He must've realized that this end of the tunnel would be iced over from the water that Nate would toss over it.

So Lewis—you smart dog—you figured on digging some more, I thought, *you miserable lucky nerd!* Nate turned left, at the twist in the tunnel.

I noticed a certain indentation in the inner wall.

A word?

I held the flashlight at an angle to make them out.

RESUR

Then, a hint of red. A bit of fingernail. Lewis had cut his fingers in the stiff snow. He had stopped writing.

"Nate?" I called, but there was no answer, so I shuffled on my hands and knees, my back low but still pressing the ceiling, to catch up with him.

I turned the corner to the left, and stopped, for something was different.

I shone the flashlight all around.

I couldn't see Nate at all, anywhere; the tunnel seemed to descend at the turn, rather than do the logical thing, which was to move forward and up. If Lewis were to escape, surely he would've tried to push *up*?

"Nate?" I cried through what now seemed an eternal tunnel of ice. "Nate!"

My voice echoed.

There were other hand prints there, in the ice, none of

them the same. All were smeared, and some seemed impossibly thin; in one indentation, I saw what might've been a silken patch of the thinnest skin. I began to back up, to get out of the tunnel. As I reversed as far as I could, I turned a bit, shining the flashlight back toward the entrance.

It was once again sealed.

"Donkeyman!" I shouted. "Donkeyman!"

I thought I heard him laughing, but perhaps it was not on the outside, but within this chamber, this tapeworm that had no end. This chamber of ice. I slammed my fist into the ceiling, but succeeded only in skinning my knuckles. Somehow, Donkeyman had sealed us in there again. I moved forward, the only place to go, past the hieroglyphs of hands and the sides of smooth bony faces, a thread of skin here, a spray of torn hair under my knees. The tunnel descended and then widened, so I could move about a bit more; there was less air here, and what there was of it began to stink like sewage.

And then something grabbed me by the wrist, and shook the flashlight out of my hand. It rolled to the side, shining its light against the wall, casting gray-white-yellow shadow.

I was in a room with others.

Nate whispered, "I killed him, Charlie. I killed Lewis."

I was too numb to be shocked by what seemed inevitable, for I'd had a feeling from the beginning of the day that Nate would kill Stewart Lewis.

Nate leaned over and kissed me gently on the cheek, then my right ear. Something moved in front of us. "I love you, Charlie. I'm scared. I mean, I'm really scared. I never been this scared." His face shuddered, and I drew away from his caress.

I leaned forward, picking up the flashlight, and shot its beam directly in front of us.

"Oh god," Nate said.

It was Stewart Lewis, hunched in a wider chamber, his white Oxford shirt torn and bloody, with red and black slices through the skin of his chest. His khakis were muddy and soaked.

I had never seen him without his glasses, but he seemed handsomer, with his hair slicked back, and a pale cast to his face. Around him, others, young men all, young and decayed, slashes along their arms, or blue flesh as if their blood were frozen, half-naked, tendons dangling from some, others as beautiful as if they were alive, and in some respects I knew they were, and in some respects they had not lived in a very long time.

Nate said, "King of Ice Palace."

Lewis grinned, naughtily, and leaned into us, until his lips were practically an inch from my face. "Pleasures beyond life, Charlie, beyond the snow. The warmth of life, the sun within the flesh."

Lewis turned his face toward Nate, who clung to my sleeve. "One of you," he said, his voice the same hopeless soprano of an undeveloped choirboy, but the face, full of fierce authority, his lips drawn back, his eyes ice ice ice. "One of you," he said, "is mine."

Nate let go of my arm, recoiling from me, and said, "Him. Charlie. You can fuck him. You can do whatever you want to him."

"Oh, Nate," Lewis said, "you wanted me, in the woods, you held the knife to my throat because you wanted me."

"I'm not like that," Nate said, pressing himself back against the wall. "He is. Charlie's like that. It was because you wanted me to do it. That was all. I have a girl friend. *Charlie*, tell him about Helen. *Tell him.*

"You miserable—" I said, pushing at him. And then I turned to Stewart Lewis. "Lewis, what happened, what... what...are you?"

"King of Ice Palace, Charlie, just the way Nate wanted me. Frozen, consenting, helpless. Nate, give me your tongue, give me your wet sweet tongue, give me the fire of your breath, give me the secret you." Lewis leaned into Nate, and I moved to the side, but could not get too far from them. Lewis and Nate had locked mouths, and I heard a gurgling, but not of terror or pain. It turned into a tender moan, like a kitten searching for its mother's milk. I watched in the white chamber as color returned to Nate's pale face, for this love was being passed between them, this frozen and glorious and fearful love.

All the young and dead men in the chamber watched as Nate pushed himself against the wall as if trying to break out of there. His hand traced a line along the shiny wall, gripping, becoming a clench of delight as Lewis leaned forward into him. Stewart Lewis was only newly resurrected, but it made me think how beautiful physical love could be, between two people, a doorway between two separate entities, that submission on both parts, that surrender to the warmth and the gasps of physical contact.

I knew then why men enjoyed watching the sexual act almost as much as participating in it:

Because it is a celebration of the perverse, no matter the context—the thrusting buttocks, the muscular legs tight and kicking as if in combat, the slobbering mouth, the exquisite beauty of lost consciousness.

That can happen to me, yes, and that, too, you think

when you watch one enter the other, one clasp his hands around the other's shuddering flesh.

I loved Nate Wick, and I loved Stewart Lewis, and I loved the boys who had died, for the ritual of the ice had been known since before I came into the world.

All of them, crowned for a season through years of winter, Kings of Ice Palace.

&.

LEAVING ICE PALACE, while difficult, is not impossible, for the King is not a tyrant, neither is his court a prison. Nate never followed me out to the other side when the morning broke, but I think he was safer in there. I did not run from that place, but departed after having left my own hand prints along its white walls.

I helped murder a boy once, or perhaps he had just become a man that night and did not want to return to the warming climates. He was my brother, although he was no blood relation. I do not believe that he is, in any real sense, dead, although his family has given up on him, as has his girl friend, Helen.

Ice Palace: I do not wish to live there, not yet, although I venture into its white, secret chamber often on dark winter nights.

It is a secret chamber, Ice Palace.

But, even so, it is never as cold or as lonely as my days in the world above.

Why My Doll is Evil

A POEM

S he came from Japan
  In 1963
 My father, on business, saw her in a shop window
 With her fan and her obi
 And her curious smile
 She stood on a chest of drawers

I COULD NOT SLEEP some nights
  Looking at that placid face,
  So shiny and white in the nightlight's halo.
  She beckons and repels with her gently curved hand.
  Her lips move at night,
  But she has no voice.

THINGS HAPPEN in houses
  Where families live.

     . . .

SHE WATCHED,
    And I watched her watch.
    She smiled as it happened,
    Held her fan close,
    But her gaze told me nothing.
    I watched her lips move,
    But she remained silent
    While it happened.

Now, in the attic,
    She rests,
    For she knows more than she can say.
    Her black hair is ragged,
    Her obi torn,
    Her perfect feet, tucked into wooden sandals,
    Arthritic at her age.
    But she smiles,
    Holds her fan just so,
    Without voice,
    Reminds me of things that happened
    In families,
    While she stood
    Watch.

The Five

The wall was up against the carport, and Naomi, who was just beginning the gangly phase, stretched out across it like she was trying to climb up the side of the house to the roof.

She heard the sound first.

She knew about the cat, the wild one that lived out in the Wash. Somehow, it had survived the pack of coyotes that roamed there, and she had thought she saw it come near the house a few times before. But there was no mistaking the mewling sounds of kittens, and so she presented the problem to her father.

"They'll die in there."

"No," he said. "The mother cat knows what she's doing. She's got the kittens there so the coyotes won't get them. When they're old enough, she'll bring them out. They're animals, Nomy, they go by instinct and nature. The mother cat knows best. The wall's sturdy enough, too. Walls are good, safe places from predators."

"What's a predator?"

"Anything that's a threat. Anything that might eat a cat."

"Like a coyote?"

"Exactly."

"Where's the father cat?"

"At work."

He showed Naomi where the weak part of the wall was, and how to press her ear up against it with a glass. Her eyes went wide and squinty, alternately, and she accidentally dropped the glass, which broke.

"You'll have to clean that up," he said.

Naomi — barefoot — stepped carefully around the chips of glass as she went to fetch the broom.

She took a few swipes at the broken glass and leaned against the wall again.

Her father was, by this time, just starting up the lawn mower in the side yard. She wanted to ask him more about the cat, but he was preoccupied, and since (she'd been warned) this was one of his few days off for the summer, she decided not to bother him.

She went indoors and told her mother about the cat and the kittens and her mother was more concerned. Her mother was much more sentimental about animals than her father, and went outside with her immediately to examine the wall.

"There's the hole near the drainpipe. I don't know how she did it, but she squeezed in there. Good for her. She protected her children." Naomi's mother pointed up to beneath the eaves, where the pipe only partially covered a hole that her father had put into the wall accidentally when he was repairing the roof.

"I've seen her before," Naomi said. "The mother cat. She

watches gophers over in the field. She's very tough looking. My father says she's doing it because of instinct."

Her mother looked from Naomi over to her husband, mowing. "It's his day off and he mows. We see him at breakfast and before bed, and on his day off he mows."

"It's his instinct," Naomi said. The air was smoky with lawn mower exhaust and fresh-cut grass; motes of dust and dandelion fluff sprayed across the yellow day.

SHE THOUGHT about the kittens all afternoon, and wondered how many there were.

"I think several," her mother told her. "Maybe five."

"Why don't people have babies all at once like that?"

Her mother laughed, "Some do. They're crazy. Trust me, when you're ready to have children, you won't want several at once."

"I can't wait to have babies," Naomi said. "When I have babies, I'll protect them just like the Mom cat."

"You're much too young to think that."

"You had me when you were eighteen."

"So, you have nine more years to go and you need to pick up a husband along the way."

Her father, who had been listening to all this even while he read the paper, said, "I don't think it's right to encourage her, Jean."

Her mother glanced at her father, and then back at Naomi.

The living room was all done in blues, and Naomi sometimes felt it was a vast sea, and she was floating on a cushion, and her parents were miles away, underwater.

Her father, his voice bubbling and indistinct, said something about something or other that they'd told her before about something to do with something, but Naomi had known when to block him out, when to put him beneath the waves.

❧

NAOMI CLIMBED the drainpipe just after dinner, with a flashlight held in her mouth making her feel like she would throw up any second.

She grasped one edge of roof, and cut her fingers on the sharp metal of the pipe, and lodged her left foot in the space between the pipe and the wall. She directed the flashlight down the hole, and saw a pair of fierce red eyes, and movement.

Nothing more than that.

The eyes scared her a bit, and she tried to pull her foot free so she could shimmy down, but her foot was caught.

The mother cat moved up into the hole until its face was right near hers. Naomi heard a low growl, which didn't sound like a cat at all. She dropped the flashlight, and felt a claw swipe across her face.

She managed to get her foot free, and dropped five feet to the ground, landing on her rear. She felt a sharp pain in her legs.

Her mother came outside at the noise, and ran to get her.

"*Naomi*," her mother gasped. "What in god's name are you doing?"

She rushed to Naomi, lifting her up.

"My leg." It hurt so much she didn't want to move at

all, but her mother carried her into the light of the carport. She was trailing blood. It didn't spurt out like she thought it might, but just came in drips and drabs like the rain when it was spitting.

"It's glass," her mother said. She removed it; Naomi didn't have time to cry out. Tears were seeping from her eyes. The pain in her leg, just along the calf, was burning.

Her father had heard the shouting, and he came out, too. He was in white boxer shorts and a faded gray T-shirt. He said, "what's going on here?"

"She cut herself," her mother said.

"I told her to sweep up the glass," he said, and then turned to her, and more softly said, "didn't I tell you to clean up the broken glass, Nomy?"

Naomi could barely see him for her tears. She looked from one to the other, and then back, but it was all a blur.

"We've got to take her to the emergency room."

Her father said, "yeah, and who's coming up with the three hundred bucks?"

"Insurance."

"Canceled."

Her mother said nothing.

"We can sew it up here, can't we?"

Her mother seemed about to say something. Almost a sound came out of her mouth. Then, after a moment, she said, "I guess I could. Jesus, Dan. What if this were worse?"

"It's just a cut. It's only glass. You know how to put in stitches."

Her mother asked her, "sweetie, is that all right with you?"

"If it's what my father wants," she said.

Her father said, "she always calls me that. Isn't that strange? 'My father'. Why is she like this?"

Her mother ignored him. She felt the warmth of her mother's hand on her damp cheek. "It's okay to cry when things hurt."

"She never looks me in the eye, either. You ever notice that? You're Mommy, but I get 'my father'. Christ." Her father said something else, but even the sounds were starting to blur because Naomi thought she heard the kittens mewling in the wall, just the other side, and they were getting louder and louder.

Even later, when her mother took out her sewing kit and told her it wouldn't hurt as much as it looked like, even then, she thought she heard them.

THE STITCHES CAME out a week later, and although there was a broad white scar, it wasn't so bad. She could still jump rope, although she felt a gentle tugging. She hadn't been outside much; she'd got a fever, which, according to her mother, was from an infection in her leg. But all she'd had to do was lie around and watch old *I Love Lucy* shows, and eat Saltines and guzzle cola. Not the worst thing, she figured. As soon as she was able, she went out to check on the kittens.

She had a can of tuna with her; she knew cats loved it, and her mother would never miss it. She set up the step ladder, and climbed up.

But the hole was no longer there.

It had been sealed up. White plaster was spread across it.

She asked her mother about it.

"They got old enough to leave," her mother said, "and so the Mom cat took them back out to the field to hunt mice."

"What about the coyotes?"

"Wild cats are usually smarter than coyotes. Really, honey. They're fine."

❧

ALTHOUGH SHE WASN'T EVER SUPPOSED to go into the field that adjoined her father's property, Naomi untangled her way through the blackberry and boysenberry vines, and went anyway.

The grass in the field was high and yellow; foxtails shot out at her and embedded themselves in her socks. She picked them out carefully. There was an old rusted out tractor in the middle of the field, and she found several small stiff balloons near it, and a pipe made completely of brass.

She kept searching through the grass. Something moved along the mound where the grass grew thickest.

A great tree, dead from lightning, stood guardian of this spot. A peregrine falcon sat at its highest point.

She looked up and down, and all around, which was something she'd once heard about.

The grass quivered. The falcon flew off across the field and glided above the orange groves.

She saw two ears rise slowly above the grass.

A coyote crouched four feet away from her. Its yellow-brown head came into view. It was beautiful.

She stood still for several seconds.

She had never seen a coyote this close.

And then, the animal turned and ran off down the field, towards the Wash.

Naomi had been holding her breath the whole time, not realizing it.

The sun was up and boiling, and she looked back across to her house. It seemed too far away. She sat down in the grass for a minute, feeling the leftover heat of fever break across her forehead. She cupped her hands together like she was praying, and rested her head against them. She whispered into the dry earth, "Don't let anything hurt the kittens."

When she awoke, the sun was all the way across the sky. Ants crawled across her hands; some were in her hair. She had to brush them out. She felt like she'd been sleeping for years, it had been that peaceful. Her mother was calling to her from the back yard. She stood, brushed dirt and insects from her, and ran in the direction of the familiar voice. She jumped around the thorny vines, but her leg started to hurt again, so she ended up limping her way up the driveway. She went along the side of the carport to get to the back gate, when something leapt out in front of her.

It was the mother cat. Snarling.

Naomi froze.

The mother cat watched her.

Naomi looked around for the kittens but saw none.

And then she heard them.

She followed the sound.

Pressed her ear against the carport wall.

She heard them.

Inside the wall.

The five.

WHEN HER FATHER got home from work, he went in and sat in front of the television to watch the ten o'clock news. Naomi was supposed to be getting ready for bed, but she had been pressing herself up against the wall in the living room, because she thought she heard something moving behind it.

She wandered into the den, following the sounds.

Her father glanced over, then back to the television.

The noise in the wall seemed to stop at the entrance to the den.

Naomi leaned against the door. "You didn't take the kittens out, did you?"

He looked at her. His eyes seemed to be sunken into the shriveled skin around them; his eyeglasses magnified them until she felt he was staring right through her.

"Nomy?" he asked.

"You left them in the wall."

He grinned. "Don't be silly. I took them out. All five. Set them down. The mother carried them into the vines. Don't be silly."

"I heard them. I saw the big cat. She was angry."

"Don't be silly," he said, more firmly. He took his glasses off.

She realized that she was alone in the room with him, and she didn't like it. She never liked being alone with him. Not inside the house.

She ran down the hall to her mother's room. Her mother lay in bed, reading a book. She set it down.

Naomi climbed up on the bed. "Mommy, I have a question."

Her mother patted a space beside her. Naomi scooted closer. She lay down, resting her head on her mother's arm.

"It's about the kittens in the wall."

Naomi looked up at the ceiling, which was all white, and thought she saw clouds moving across it, almost forming a face.

"What I want to know," she said, "is, did the cat take the kittens out before he covered the hole?"

Her mother said, "why?"

"I heard the kittens earlier."

"Before dinner?"

Naomi nodded. The cloud face in the ceiling melted away.

"You didn't tell me you heard them."

"I was really angry. I thought you lied to me."

"I wouldn't lie to you."

"I asked my father, and he said I was being silly."

"Well, it's not silly if you thought you heard them. But you must've imagined it. I saw them leave. With the Mom cat."

"I saw her, too. She looked angry. She looked like she was mad at me for letting her babies get put in the wall like that."

"Oh," her mother said, stroking her fine, dark hair, "cats don't think things like that. She was probably just asking for milk. Maybe she's getting tamer. Maybe one day she and all the kittens, grown up, will come back because you were so nice to them."

"I was sure I heard them."

"Maybe you wanted to hear them."

Naomi was fairly confused, but had never known her mother to lie.

Her mother said, "you got sunburned today."

"I saw a coyote in the field."

"You went in the field?"

"I was looking for the kittens."

"Oh, you. Don't tell your father."

෫෪

IN THE MORNING, she returned to the carport wall. She pressed a drinking glass to it, and then applied her ear.

Nothing.

No sound.

She tapped on the wall with her fingers.

No sound.

And then...*something.*

Almost nothing.

Almost a whine.

And then, as if a dam had burst, the screaming, shrieking of small kittens, and the sound of frantic clawing.

She almost dropped the glass, but remembering her leg, she caught it in time. *I wouldn't lie to you,* she heard her mother say, a memory.

I wouldn't lie to you.

She put the glass up to the wall.

Nothing.

Silence.

Sound of her own heart, beating rapidly.

෫෪

THAT NIGHT, she lay in bed, unable to sleep. In the daylight, she would be all right, but at night she had to stay up because of things in the dark. She thought she had forgotten how to breathe; then realized, she was still inhaling and exhaling.

About one in the morning, her door opened.

Someone stood there, so she had to close her eyes.

She counted her breaths, and hoped it wouldn't be him.

She felt the kiss on her forehead.

That, and the touching her on the outside of the blanket, was all he ever did, the nighttime father, but it was enough to make her wish she were dead and wonder where her mother was to protect her.

But as she lay there, she heard them again.

The kittens.

Mewling sweetly, for tuna or milk.

They had traveled to find her, through the small spaces within the walls, to find her and tell her they were all right.

She fell asleep before the door opened again, listening to them, wondering if they were happy, if they were catching the mice that she knew occasionally crawled into other holes and vents and cracks. The five were still there, her kittens, her kittens, and she knew it would turn out fine now.

"What's wrong with her?"

"Well, Dan, if we'd taken her to the hospital instead of letting the infection go like that…"

"And somebody would've accused us of child abuse. That's all that ever happens anymore. And it's not some infection, Jean. Look at her. Why is she doing that?"

"I think she's sick. Her fever's back."

"What's gotten into her?"

Naomi heard them, but paid no attention, because the kittens were getting louder. They were three months old now, and they sounded more like cats. They played there, behind the diamond shaped wallpaper in the kitchen, just behind the toaster. One had caught a mouse or something, and they were playing with it—she could hear the frightened squeaks. She pressed the palms of her hands against the wallpaper, trying to open up the wall, but no matter how much she pressed, nothing gave.

Her father said, "she shouldn't be crawling around like that. She looks like an animal."

"Sweetie," her mother said, stroking her hair. "don't You think you need to get back in bed?"

She glanced up at her mother, "I love them," she said, unable to control an enormous smile, "I love them so much, Mommy."

Her mother wasn't look at her. She said, "I'm taking her to a doctor right now."

"HELLO, NAOMI." The doctor was bald and sweet looking, like a grandfather.

"Hello," she replied.

"That leg's healing okay. Looks like whoever stitched it, did it right."

"Mommy did it. She used to be a nurse."

"I know. She used to work with me. Did you know that?"

No reply.

"What seems to be the problem?" he asked. He put the

stethoscope against her chest. She breathed in and out. Then, a funny looking thermometer, which he called a "gun," went in her ear. Lights in her eyes. A tongue depressor slipped to the back of her throat almost gagging her.

"I don't know," she said, finally.

"Your Mommy's really worried."

"I don't know why."

"She says you listen to the walls."

Naomi shook her head. "Not the walls. The five."

"Five what?"

"Kittens. Each of them know me. I love them so much."

"How did the kittens get there?"

She looked at him, unsure if she should trust him. "I can't tell you."

"All right, then."

He gave her a shot in the arm, which she didn't feel at all. She thought that was strange, so she told him.

"Not at all?"

"I didn't even feel it."

He put his hand under his chin. Then he reached to her arm and pinched.

"Did you feel that?"

She shook her head.

Then, he went over to a counter on the other side of the room. He returned with a plastic bottle. He took the lid off and held it under her nose. "Smell this."

She sniffed.

"Sniff again," he said.

She sniffed hard.

"What does it smell like?"

"I dunno. Water, maybe?"

He was trying to smile at her response, she could tell, but couldn't quite do it. "Is there anything you want to tell me?" he asked.

"About what?"

"Anything. Your Mommy or Daddy. How you feel about things."

She thought a minute, "nope."

And that was it, he took her out to the waiting area where her mother was sitting. Then, she was asked to sit and wait while her mother had a checkup, too.

On the way home, in the car, her mother was in a mood. "Are you playing games?"

Shook her head.

"Well, I think you are. Are you trying to destroy this family? Because if you are, young lady, if you are..." Her mother's hands were shaking so hard, she had to pull the car over to the side of the road.

Naomi began to say something, but she saw that her mother wasn't listening, so she shut her mouth.

And as her mother started lecturing her, Naomi realized that she could barely hear a word her mother said.

THE NIGHTS WERE PEACEFUL. She could press her ear against the wall, and hear them, playing and hunting and crawling around one another. She kept trying to think up good names for them, but each time she came up with something, she forgot which was which.

Then, when the bedroom door opened—which didn't happen very often anymore—she listened to the cats (for they had grown in size), and sometimes, if she closed her eyes really tight, she could almost imagine what they looked like. All gray tabbies like their mother, of course, but one with a little bit of white in a star pattern on its chest, and two of them had green eyes, while the rest had blue.

One had gotten very fat from all the mice and roaches it had devoured over the past weeks, and another seemed all skin and bones; and yet, not deprived at all.

&.

ONE DAY, a woman in a suit came by.

She had some manila files in her hand. Naomi's mother and father were very tense.

The woman asked several questions, mainly to her parents, but Naomi was listening for the sound of the five.

"Naomi?" her father said. "Answer the lady, please."

Naomi looked up; her father's voice had gotten really small, like it was caught in a jar somewhere and couldn't get out. She looked at the lady, and then to her mother. Her mother's forehead held beads of sweat.

"Yes, ma'am." She looked back to the lady.

"How are you feeling, dear?"

Naomi said, "fine."

"You were sick for awhile."

Naomi nodded. "I'm better now. It was the flu."

"Have you had a good summer vacation?"

Naomi cocked her head to the side; she squinted her eyes. "Can you hear them?"

The lady said, "who?"

"All of them. They just caught something. Maybe a mouse. Maybe a sparrow got in. I thought I heard one. Do you think that's possible?"

❧

AFTER THE LADY LEFT, her father exploded with rage. "I am so sick and tired of you running our lives like this!"

Who was he talking to? Naomi heard the runt of the litter tearing at the bird's wings, feathers flying. The five could be brutal, sometimes.

They stalked their prey like lions, and brought a bird or mouse down quickly, but then played with it until the small creature died of fear more than anything.

Something beautiful about taking something so small and playing with it.

"There are no fucking cats in the fucking walls," her father's voice intruded.

He came over to her; lifted her up from under her arms. "I am going to tell you what happened to those kittens, right now," he said.

Her mother said, "Jesus, Dan, you're going to hurt her like that," but the voices rushed beneath some invisible glass, caught, silent.

Her father began screaming something—she knew by the movements of his mouth—but all she heard was the one she was calling Scamp tussle over the sparrow's head.

Yowler tore at the beak with her claws, but lost most of the skull, which Scamp took down in one gulp.

Hugo ignored them—he was not one to join in when food was being torn apart—he preferred to lick the bones clean later, after the carcass was stripped.

"I'm going to show you once and for all," her father's voice came back, and she was being dragged out the backdoor, around to the carport wall.

He dropped her to the ground, and went around the wall, into the carport.

She heard Fiona whisper something to Zelda about some centipedes that she had trapped in a spider web behind the wall at the back of the refrigerator.

Her father came back around the corner with a large hammer.

"You just watch what you see," he said, and slammed the hammer into the wall, down where the kittens had once been born.

Back and forth, he worked the hammer, chips of wall flew up, and beneath them, chicken wire, and there, in a small mound, surrounded with bits of cloth and newspaper were small dried things.

"See?" her father said, poking at them with his hammer. From one, a dozen wriggling gray-white maggots emerged.

"Do you fucking see them?" He shouted, his voice receding again.

She looked at them, all stiff and bony and withered like apricots.

Her heart was beating fast. She felt something wet came up her throat. Lights flickered.

Were they the bodies of the mice that the five had caught, in storage for future meals?

And then she thought she was going to faint. She saw pinpricks of darkness play along the edge of her vision, and then an eclipse came over the sun.

The world faded; her father faded; and she reached her hand into the new hole in the wall, and pressed her head through, too.

Her whole body seemed to move forward, and she saw pipes and wires and dust as she went.

"I CAN HEAR HER," her mother said, "I think she made a noise."

Her father said nothing.

After a minute: "For three days, she does her weird, unintelligible sounds, and now she snarls her upper lip and you think she's on the road to recovery."

"She said something. Honey? Are you trying to say something?"

But Naomi didn't care to speak with them at the moment.

She held Hugo in her lap, stroking him carefully, carefully, because he didn't like his fur ruffled. Scamp was playing with the ball of thread; the others slept, piled together.

"Look at her," her father said.

"Sweetie?" her mother said, beyond the wall. "Are you trying to talk? Is there something you want to say?"

"You think holding her is going to help?" her father said. "You think she's ever going to get better if you coddle her like that? All that rocking back and forth. She knows what she's doing. She's not stupid."

Zelda rolled on her back and stretched out, a great yawn escaping her jaws. Her whiskers brushed against Naomi's ankle. It tickled.

"Sweetie?" her mother asked.

"She's just doing this," her father said. "It's all for attention. And look at you, giving it to her. She's just doing this to hurt us."

"No, look at her lips. She's trying to say something. Look, Dan. My god, she's trying to talk. Oh, sweetie,

Nomy, baby, tell Mommy what's wrong. Are you okay? Baby?"

On the other side of the wall, Naomi pressed her face into the dust-covered fur and listened to the purring, the gentle and steady hum beneath the skin that was like a lullaby. It was warm there, with the five, with the walls around them.

Her father said, "my god, she's starting in again."

"Shut up, Dan. Let her."

"I can't stand this. How can you sit there and cradle her and not scream out loud when she does this?"

"Maybe I care about her," her mother said.

Naomi mewled and rocked and mewled and rocked, safe from predators, safe in the wall.

She watched as one of the cats sat up, her hackles rising, hunting some creature that had the misfortune of entering this most secret and wonderful domain.

The Dark Game

A NOVELLA

I saw a painting in a gallery once that depicted a man's hands, bound together.

Its title: "Victory is Freedom of Mind and Body."

I believe that is true. I would go further and say that victory is freedom of mind *from* body.

Separation from the thing that imprisons us.

Flight.

Perhaps freedom from life itself.

That is victory.

Life is brutal.

It's like this whip and these ropes. It hurts. It scars. But we must take it.

We must find some pleasure and solace within this terrible lashing.

You want to hear it all? You want me to tell you how it went, in the prison camp? Why I like the ropes?

You want to play the game with me?

First let me tell you this:

Youth is something you put in a drawer somewhere.

You lose the thought of it behind socks and letters and medals and old passport photos and keys that no longer fit locks.

You wear it when you're of the right age, and you do things that you ought not to, and then as you gain perspective with age, you put it away, and you close the drawer.

And you lock it.

Then, you live the life you've built toward, and no one needs to see what's in that drawer.

A secret is something to be hidden.

If is hidden well enough, it never becomes a fact. It is just something that is not there when you go to look for it. It is the thing missing, but the thing that is not missed.

That's how I feel.

That is why I don't revisit those times, often.

The camp.

Or the motel room.

Or the smokehouse.

But since you have me here, like this, I'll tell you.

Maybe you'll leave after that. Maybe you won't want to stay here once you know about me.

§.

BEFORE THE WAR, I was in a motel room with a girl I met outside the base.

For fun she tied me up and when she did it, I went someplace else in my head. My hands tied, my feet bound. I remember she smelled like orange blossoms, and she enjoyed tightening the thin ropes around my hands.

But my mind was just gone – drifting upward into darkness, into another place. Back to Burnley Island, I guess, and that's where I've always ended up – *my memories, my family, my home.*

I was just not there anymore. The game had taken me over.

It had become automatic for me.

It was second nature.

In the war, things got worse for me.

The game got worse.

But it wasn't so bad when I was a kid.

EARLY MEMORY:

Winter.

Bitter cold.

Wind whistling around me, boxing my ears, as I trudged through three feet of snow to get out to the smoke-house. I was ten, perhaps. Heavy with a burden.

It was the dog I'd had since he was a foundling of two or three years old, and I was too young to remember bringing him home from a walk in the woods.

He was dying now, of some undiagnosed malady. In those days, you didn't take the dog to the vet when it was its time.

You took him someplace and you shot him.

And this freezing February day, that was what I was to do.

My father marched behind me. I could not bring myself to turn and look over my shoulder to see how he kept pace. I was weeping, and it would be the first and last time I would weep for years.

I held my dog – a small mutt, no bigger than my arms

could carry – and he looked up at me as if he understood that something not wonderful was to come.

At the smokehouse I stopped and prayed. I wished that God would intervene, just this once.

I would trade, I promised God, my life for this dog's. I would do anything God wanted me to do if he would just take a minute and breathe new life into my dog's body. I would build a chapel.

No, I would build a *cathedral*.

The snow bit at my cheeks and nose.

❧

MY DOG, whose name was Mac, whimpered and groaned.

"Go on, son," my father said.

He called me "son" more than he ever used "Gordie" or "Gordon."

Sometimes I thought he wasn't sure of my name. That I was just another son to him. Another child to deal with before I became a man.

I reached up, and opened the door to the smokehouse. I barely kept my balance, for the dog had grown too heavy for me.

My father lit the lantern inside the building – the smokehouse was old-fashioned, and my mother felt it was a fire hazard, but my father insisted on using it.

A yellow flickering light filled the small room.

After I set Mac down on some straw, I kissed him on the muzzle and kept my prayers going – my deals with God to change this, somehow.

Then, my father handed me the pistol and told me to get it over with quickly.

"Misery is terrible. That animal is in misery. When you brought him home, you promised to take care of him. That is a commitment. This is a way to take care of him, so he won't be in any more pain. You can stop his pain. He won't get better, son. He won't."

"I can't," I said.

"You have to. You promised. You promised me. And you promised that dog when you brought him home. He has had a good life here. But now he's sick. And he needs to be taken care of."

I looked at my dog's face and saw the terribleness of all existence in his eyes. In his shivering form.

And that is when I learned about how life doesn't matter at all.

Not one bit.

It is a misery. A wretchedness foisted on us by a God who turns His back on all.

We live on a planet of ice, and the only thing we human beings can do is endure it and try to make sure that we don't add to the misery too much.

HERE IS MY LIFE:

I was born on Burnley Island, in a house called Hawthorn, and I grew up in a family called Raglan that had a history on that island.

We were shepherding people, I'm told, originally. We came with Welsh and Scots and English in our blood, and we were dark and swarthy, as I am, a perfect descendant of the Raglan clan.

My father was a brute, and I don't say that lightly. He

was a man more likely to lash with a belt or a switch than to scold with words. He was quick to judge, and hot tempered, and I suppose I joined the army to get away from him more than anything else.

I went off to see the world and fight the good fight, and found myself one dawn in the heat of a jungle, in the boredom of a company that was lost, our communications screwed beyond all measure, and I had a "fuck all" attitude toward the war and the jungle.

I was nineteen, and the last place I wanted to be was in that miasma of heat, humidity and the stink of swamp.

And then, before much time had passed, the enemy got us.

No need to go into specifics.

It was ugly.

There were a dozen of us originally, but by the time I regained consciousness, tied like a pig to a stick, there were only eight or so – counting me and my buddy, Gup (short for Guppy, which was a kinder name than his original nickname, which was Shrimp), Davy, who seemed too young to be a soldier, a man I had no liking for (named Larry Pastor), and Stoddard.

I knew what to do if captured – name, rank, serial number, and nothing else.

The truth was, I was scared spitless and we'd all heard the stories of the POWs and how no Geneva Convention was going to stop our enemy from torturing us and then dropping us in some mosquito breeding ground, dead, when it was all over.

None of us was commander.

We were just soldiers, and we had no valuable information at all, and no reason for a negotiation with our commanders.

BUT HOPE IS the last thing to go, and so we had it.

I had it, and Gup had it, although Stoddard had already told me that he knew he'd die in the jungle and he didn't give a damn because his girl was already pregnant by some other guy and his folks had disowned him for some reason he wouldn't say, and what the hell was the point?

That was his attitude, and even though I felt we lived on Ice Planet and life was a hurdle into chaos, I still hoped.

For the best. For life. For good to come out of bad.

I WOKE UP LATER ON, pain running through my arms and legs like they'd had nails driven into them. I crouched in a dark hole in the ground that smelled like feces and had just a grate at the top so I could see a little of the sky.

Luckily, I still had a pack of gum on me – I kept it in this small pouch at the back inside of my skivvies that my mother had sewn for me to hide money.

Instead, I hid Wrigley's gum there.

I took a sliver of a piece and began chewing it just to feel as if I were still an American and that things mattered even if I was in a hole in the ground.

I WAS a little boy when my mother taught me the game,

only it wasn't really a game the way she told me about it. It was a way to get calm and to try and get through pain. I guess I was probably four when she taught me it.

She said my grandmother had taught her, and that her grandfather knew about it, too.

It was like make believe, but when I had scarlet fever as a kid, I really needed something to help me get through it. I was sure I was going to die, even though I didn't know what death was at four.

But scarlet fever gave me an inkling.

I WAS FEVERISH AND DELUSIONAL, and I remember being wrapped in blankets and taken in the car to Dr. Winding over in Palmerston, and lying naked on his ice cold metal table while his nurse drew out the longest needle I had ever seen in my life and they told me it wouldn't hurt, but I screamed and screamed and my mother and father had to hold me down while that needle went into my butt.

Even though I still had fever, it wasn't quite so bad. But my butt stung, and, wrapped in blankets on the way home, I was in my mother's arms, a baby again. She whispered to me to try the game, that's what she called it.

I named it the Dark Game later on. When it got to me.

At home, in my room, she sat beside my bed and told me to close my eyes despite my moans and groans, and she told me to take her hand. But I couldn't close my eyes. I kept opening them.

Finally she took a handkerchief and put it over my eyes like a blindfold. She began the rhyme. I said it along with her in a singsong kind of voice.

After a bit, she and I were somewhere else, in the woods, in darkness, and I could not feel the pain or the fever at all.

She told me that it was a way the mind worked that was like magic, that it got you out of yourself and out of where you were.

⁊❦

WHEN I BEGAN to teach my friends how to do it as a kid, she pulled me aside and told me that I should keep it to myself.

"Why?" I asked.

"Because it can be bad, too. It's important to stay in the world. To not delve into that too much. If you need God, there's church. If you need friends, don't go off into your head too much."

But I didn't understand what she meant then, and I'm not sure I do now.

Or maybe I do and I just don't want to look at it.

"It's a daylight game," she said. "Between you and me. It's a Raglan game. It's just to make things easier when they're rough."

I played it, all by myself, my eyes closed, that wintry day in the smokehouse when I shot my dog, too.

I played it in that hole in the middle of the jungle without a hope in hell of getting out of there alive.

⁊❦

THE FIRST DAY AND NIGHT, They watched me.

'They' being the enemy.

I don't want to call them what we called them back
then. It was racist. It was nasty. It was a nasty place to be. I
hated their guts.

They were Enemy.

They were *They*.

We were *Us*.

My boys – that's how I thought of Gup and Stoddard
and Davy – screamed at night. I heard them clearly. I'm
pretty sure Stoddard died right away.

That's what I heard, anyway.

I could picture him working hard to piss off the Enemy,
even if his nuts were being nailed to the wall. Gup might
hang in there. Davy, I worried most about. He was practically just a kid.

I began to discover my darkness in my dirty pit of a
bedroom. I began to feel my environment.

I guess I was about twenty feet down. Some kind of
well.

Maybe it had been dug up for water.

Or prisoners. I don't know. It was deep but not wide.

❧

I HAD JUST enough room to sit with my knees nearly
touching my chest. It was dirt and rock, and they lowered
water down after midnight, just a cup on a string. Half the
water had dropped out of the cup by the time it
reached me.

Not even a cup, I discovered. A turtle shell. Drank out
of it because I was damn thirsty, and I soon discovered that
if I didn't drink out of it fast, they yanked it back up.

They.

Sons of bitches.

I stared up through the grate, trying to see the stars or at least something that meant the hole was not just an o in the earth that had no beginning and no end.

❧

MEMORY:

Back to Texas, back to the night I got tied up, back when I was barely more than a kid and out on an adventure.

The girl who tied me up was named Genie, and she could be had in that sunbaked Texas town for less than twenty bucks.

I was too young to be sure what I could do with a girl like that – I had left my sheltered island a virgin of eighteen, and knew that I would have six months or so before getting my orders overseas into the heart of the war.

I didn't want to die a virgin; and I doubt there has been a virgin in existence that wanted to die in that state, untouched by another.

So, when my buddies and me went out to the local rat bar called *The Swinging Star*, playing pool and chugging too many beers, I let down my guard a bit when one of my friends, named Harry Hoakes, slapped me on the back and whispered in my ear with his sour mash breath that he and a couple of the guys were going down to Red Town, a part of the desert where the whores were cheap and fast and you could buy a few for a good deal less than a week's pay.

I look back with shame, of course, upon this youthful episode in my life.

I do not proudly admit that my first experience with a

woman was at the hands of a seasoned pro of twenty-six, but it is what it is – or, it was what it was. I was drunk, stupid, pretty sure I was going to die in some distant jungle, so I went with my *compadres* out in a truck that some townie drove – no doubt the pimp for the Red Town girls.

We unloaded outside yet another bar, and went in, and there they were, like glittery fool's gold, or broken glass mistaken for diamonds on a moonlit highway.

Harry Hoakes looked like a movie star and was from L.A. and had this air of magic around him, no matter what he did.

He died in the war, within a year. I heard he stepped on a mine and it just ripped him up.

But that night, he was completely on and alive like lightning – all around you and illuminating the dark.

This landscape was alien to me – slovenly, lazily pretty girls who looked the way whores are supposed to, not quite unhappy yet with their situation, not quite sure of how they landed in that desert canyon, not quite hardened to the way their lives would surely go.

When you're eighteen and in the army, whores don't seem sad or needy or even lesser.

They seem like angels who don't ask for the reasons of your interest. They know you want them, and they're perfectly fine with that.

Harry Hoakes introduced me to the girls like they were his sisters. The one who sidled up to me was Genie.

"I'm like that old movie star, Gene Tierney. From *Laura*. You ever see *Laura*? It's a beautiful movie. I'm gonna be a movie star someday. I *am*."

She was a big brunette with big teeth, from the Midwest, she said, a farm girl who wanted adventure, and intended to wind up in Hollywood in a couple of months – some producer had discovered her already and she was just waiting to hear from him, she told me all of it so fast it made me laugh.

Then, she asked me what I wanted to do.

ॐ

WE GOT a bottle of Jack Daniels and went back to the motel and plunked down the few bucks for a two-hour stay.

After that, she brought out those ropes from some little overnight bag she lugged around with her.

She told me that since I was a virgin, she wanted to make sure I didn't do any of the work.

That's what she called it, and I guess it was her work.

But when the ropes went on, I went off somewhere.

I was no longer in a rundown motel with a big toothed girl, but back on Burnley Island.

ॐ

IT WAS WINTER (as my memories of that New England island often are in a hot, dry, desert place) and my father tied me up to the post that sat at the center of the smokehouse.

He told me I had been bad to do what I had done, and that he had to teach me a lesson.

I was, perhaps, fourteen, my shirt had been torn off my back, and I felt the sting of his cat – a cat-o-nine-tails that he kept to discourage my brothers and me from doing the bad things we often did.

But in my Dark Game memory, I didn't feel pain from

the stings – I felt myself glowing, becoming a powerful creature beneath the lashes.

I felt as if I were commanding my father to whip me, to
torment me with the bad things I'd been doing. I felt as if I
were a god, and he were merely my servant.

And soon, in the Dark Game, it was my father with his
shirt torn, tied to the post, and I had the whip, and I was
lashing at him and telling him that he was a bad, bad man.

When I opened my eyes, the game done, I found that I
was tied to that bed in the motel in Texas. Outside, the
sound of trucks going by.

IN A CORNER OF THE ROOM, the a woman lay, a crumpled
rag doll, her face bloodied.

HARRY HOAKES CAME A-KNOCKING at the motel room
door. I was tied up in Room 13, which made it lucky, I
guess.

He was drunk from his own bottle of Jack Daniels, and
he nearly busted down the door to get to me.

INSIDE, he looked at me, tied up and naked on the dirty
bed, and then at Genie, her big teeth all but knocked out,
lying in a corner, her eyes wide.

He stared at me, then at her.

"I passed out," I said.

"Jesus H." He scratched his head, dropping his nearly empty bottle. His fly was open from his time with his girl. He was too drunk to process everything. "What the hell?"

"I don't know. I passed out. We didn't even do anything."

"Must've been her pimp," he said.

"She's got a pimp?"

"What, you think she's a nice girl from Iowa?"

"Maybe she's not dead," I said.

"If she's not dead, then she's the greatest actress in the world. Because she's dead like I ever saw dead."

"She thought she was going to be like Gene Tierney."

"Who?"

"That pretty actress with the overbite. In *Laura*. You ever see *Laura*?"

He looked at me kind of funny, and then shook his head. "We are up the legendary creek, my friend. You got a dead whore in your room, and you're...well, naked as a jaybird tied up." Then, he let out a laugh. "Christ, you could not have made this up if you wanted to."

"Help me out of these ropes," I said. "Houdini I ain't."

IN THE HOLE, in the prison, the enemy would sometimes stand over the grate and spit.

They did this a lot, and now and then, they'd take a leak down on me. I'd hear *them* laughing up above.

This might've been happened over a few days or a few weeks. I barely saw the sun in that time, because the grate got covered by a board during the day. They didn't want me to get that Vitamin D from the few rays of the sun, I guess. It was like living in a cave, and time seemed to evaporate.

I lived in endless night.

They'd get me out of there sometimes, too. Usually when it was dark.

They'd send a rope down, and I was to bind my hands to it and they'd pull me up.

Why did I go?

They fed me during those times. Fed me much better than if I stayed in the hole and ignored the rope.

They brought me up and gave me fish or frog or some kind of large maggot cooked with thick flat leaves around it that didn't taste half-bad to a starving guy.

They pretended to be friendly, and the one who spoke English, who I called Harry Hoax after my friend from Texas, because he sounded a little like the real Harry Hoakes, he made light jokes with me about my situation that actually were pretty funny.

So my new friend Hoax took me aside into the mud-brown cell where I'd get the sumptuous feast, and he told me that he was my only friend.

"Your men already betrayed you," Hoax said. "They have told the commander everything. The position of other companies. The plans of the General."

I looked at him, grinning. "I bet they have. Good for them."

"Yes," Hoax said. "It is good. How are you feeling? I see sores on your shoulder."

"I'm fine."

"You seem in good spirits. Are you praying to your god?"

"God has more important things to worry about than me."

"I bet you are thirsty."

"Somewhat."

"Good. We have some pure water for you. And even a small cup of wine. Specially for you."

"To what do I owe this sudden bout of hospitality?"

"We are not primitive people. We may live and fight among the trees and swamps, but we have a sense of culture. You are important to us. We want you happy and healthy."

"That's why you put me in a hole in the ground."

"War is evil. I know that. We know that."

"Am I talking to 'I' or 'We'?"

He laughed.

"Very good. Here," he said, glancing at the doorway.

A young attractive woman entered, a wooden tray in her hands. On the tray, a small porcelain cup, and beside it some palm leaves. Atop the leaves, more of the fried grub I'd had before, and then what looked like a rabbit's leg, also cooked.

After setting this down in front of me, she left and returned moments later with a jug of water.

"You see? We treat you well," Hoax said. "All we ask is that you tell us a few things. They are minor, unimportant questions, really."

"I thought my friends told all. I certainly don't know more than they do," I said.

Suddenly, I heard a wail from one of the other cells.

I tried to place the voice as one of my team, but I could not. I wasn't even sure it was human.

Hoax closed his eyes for a moment as if he didn't enjoy

the sound, either. Then, he nodded to the girl with the jug. She rose and poured water into the cup.

I brought the cup to my lips and drank too fast. She refilled the cup; while I sat there with Hoax, she made sure I always had water.

"There is a small bit of opium in the water," he said, softly. "You have pain, and it will help with it."

"You're drugging me?"

He sighed. "I feel bad for the state you're in. It is just a distillation of the poppy. Not enough to make you crave it. Just enough to ease any physical torment you might be feeling."

After a moment, I nodded. "That's kind of you."

"You are different from the others," he said. "You are not like other Americans, Gordon. You have a deeper quality. We do not want to hurt you. We want to bring you into realignment with truth."

"Ah," I said, feeling a bit blurred around the edges. I assumed this was the opium.

Hoax began the routine questioning that had been done before, and I gave him the standard answer, which was no answer at all.

At the end of this, my meal finished, he sighed.

He told me that he wished me no harm but that the war would end with their victory and our defeat and that all my pain would be for nothing.

"Perhaps," I told him. "Or perhaps not."

Two interrogators came in. I recognized in their eyes the sadism I'd seen before. These were pleasure torturers.

I would be their toy for the night.

Hoax left the cell looking a little sad.

The interrogators bound my hands and ankles, and began to play a game that I believe is called, in torturing circles, the Thousand Scratches.

But it didn't matter what they did to my body.

I closed my eyes, and I could begin the rhyme I'd learned as a child:

Oranges and lemons say the bells of St. Clement's.

And then, my mind eroded into darkness: I returned to the smokehouse, tied to the post, with my father's cat-o-nine-tails snapping hard at my scarred shoulders.

MY FATHER and I had good moments, too.

He took me hunting and fishing. We spent idle summer Sundays out on a skiff that he'd borrowed from a friend down in the harbor, and he told me of his abiding love for the sea.

He took me on his occasional deep sea fishing voyages, and he brought me closer to him when my sister Nora drowned off the island, coming home from the mainland on a small boat when a storm hit.

My father pulled me aside and wept with me, the closest he'd ever come to showing genuine softness and true compassion.

If I felt something other than love for him, it was no doubt honor.

I hated him for the whippings, but I knew that some demon drove him to it. I was willing to take it for the building of my character.

PERHAPS THESE DAYS, people might call the police if a boy were being whipped by his father. But in those times, not long ago, it was considered nobody's business outside of the family's own concern.

My father's demons were many, but he seemed to have an overzealous Christian sense of the Devil and of Angels and of saving his children from the Burning Fires of Hell.

He'd shout at me, while he whipped, that this hurt him more than it hurt me, and that angels and Jesus wept as the lash ripped against my skin but that if I were to go to heaven, I must repent of my sinful ways, of the bad things I had done, and I must turn to Jesus and to God's grace and His iron will.

I was, he told me, of the Devil.

OH, the bad things I'd done, they were truly bad, I suppose.

I smoked a bit, and I drank sometimes when I was far too young to drink liquor.

Once, I tried to set fire to the smokehouse, but only managed to burn most of the field nearby and many of the small thorny trees.

He had also caught me in the woods, in a way that a boy doesn't want to be caught, and that was part of my sin.

I deserved the whippings, and took them, playing the game to get through them, and then would spend a feverish night with my grandmother's salve all over my back to help speed the healing.

I honored and respected my father, even then, and I also thought of ways I might kill him someday.

But I never did.

⚜

ONCE I AWOKE from the game, after the interrogators – my impersonal demons – had left their scratches all over my too-thin body.

They returned me to my pit, to my dark filthy bed.

Sometime later – days, perhaps – I was brought out again.

This time, Hoax was not happy with me. It seemed that my comrades had not said as much as they'd wanted. It seemed that none of us was behaving.

This time, I was to have a night of theater, he told me.

"Might I have a bit of that opium water?" I asked. I might've begged. I liked the stuff and I wanted to make my time in this Hell as pleasant as possible.

"Perhaps after," he said, rather sadly.

I was brought into a cell lit by the wavering flame of a candle.

In a corner, my buddy Davy, *sweet little Davy.*

His eyes, swollen from beatings.

His jaw cracked.

A festering wound on his scrawny arm.

Ropes again. This time, on his wrists and ankles.

Four men held the ends of the rope.

"This is a play we call the Tug of War," Hoax told me.

Then, he began asking me questions.

Tears came to my eyes, but I had nothing to tell them.

❦

THE FOUR MEN tugged at the ropes and I heard Davy's bones pop, one by one, as they pulled, and his jaw dropped open, slack, but he was still alive.

Until one of the men pulled what seemed to be the forearm right out of Davy's skin.

Oh, but the game kicked in again, you see, at that point, and I missed most of the evening's entertainment by flying off to Burnley Island, by going somewhere I would be punished for my sins, but they were *my* sins alone and it was *my* punishment and no one else's.

❦

WHEN I CAME out of the game, I was missing a finger and had no memory of it being taken or of the burning metal that had cauterized it to keep it from bleeding.

Hoax, however, told me the next time I was hauled up that I was a man of iron.

"You didn't make a sound. You seemed…"

"To be someplace else," I said.

He nodded. "Where did you go? The one you call Axeman was using a dull small scissor to cut off your finger. Why didn't you flinch?"

"Magic," I told him. "What's on the menu for tonight?"

"Menu?"

"Bugs? Rats? Frogs?"

"Oh," he said, smiling. "Supper. Well, tonight, we have a special treat. Tongue."

"Cow?"

"Pig. But it's very good. Wild pig makes a wonderful dish."

When I was finished with supper – and it truly was sumptuous compared to my previous ones – they brought another from my company, the scrappy little guy we called Gup.

As WITH THE previous show with Davy, he had obviously been beaten, and perhaps his left leg was broken, also, for he hobbled in and nearly collapsed when the interrogators let go of his arms.

"Your friend cannot speak," Hoax whispered in my ear, like a mosquito circling. "He has, unfortunately, just this afternoon, lost his tongue under the Axeman's blade."

Now, Hoax didn't say that the tongue I had just eaten was my buddy's.

He didn't have to.

Maybe it was, and maybe it wasn't.

But he obviously wanted to give me that message, no matter what the truth of it might be.

I DIDN'T EAT for a few days more, but finally, pulled out of the hole again, I gobbled down the food they brought me – a stew made from strips of meat and leaves that tasted terrible but completely satisfied the gnawing in my gut.

Again, Gup was brought out, this time missing both hands, cauterized and bandaged at the wrist.

"His hands fell like leaves from a dying tree," Hoax told me.

"Very poetic," I said, trying to keep my mind from thinking about Gup and the Axeman too much, and forcing myself to keep out of drifting into the Dark Game.

To remain in the moment.

"Have you ever tasted human flesh?" Hoax asked.

I looked at poor Gup's face.

I wished him to die right there. I prayed to God. I prayed to the Devil. I prayed to the Queen of Heaven, Mary, the Mother of God, *Blessed is the Fruit of her Womb, Jesus.*

I prayed that his spirit would be pulled from his body before another night passed.

This entertainment of Hoax's went on for several nights, but each time I refused to answer his questions.

❖

I WILL ADMIT with nothing but shame that I began to crave the meals brought to me, and I convinced myself – no doubt for survival's sake – that this was *not* the body of Gup that I slowly consumed, sliced from him day after day and cooked up with spices and aromatic flowers to make dishes that I began to love.

This was simply meat that had been taken from the body of pigs and rats and snakes and lizards and frogs and fish and other creatures of this Enemy's country.

This, a steamy bowl before me, did not hold Gup's foot, sliced into slivers, swimming in fragrant soup.

This was *not* a bit of flayed skin from Gup's buttocks,

wrapped within an elephant ear palm leaf that had been buttered and baked into a moist but crunchy crust.

Yet, nightly, Gup was there, before me.

Soon an eye was gone, then his nose, his ears, toes and left foot, his lips sliced off, until I saw him no longer as a man at all, as a friend, as a former buddy, as one of the team.

I saw him as the supplier of my life.

IN A DREAM, in the hole, I had a vision of the great snake of life, devouring its own tail.

Life eats life, the image of the snake seemed to tell me. Life devours itself. You are part of this, and so is Gup. The snake is the whip in my father's hand. The whip is in my hand and reaches from my bloodied back to whip my father's hand. The torturer and the tortured are each playing a part and cannot be without the other.

I awoke from this dream and knew then that life was neither beautiful nor perfect nor magical.

Life was simply the gutter of heaven, the place where offal and waste stagnated, encircled with pestilence.

I BEGAN to love my suppers with Hoax.

Even when the Axeman came to me, a razor in his hand, and my mind shooting off to the game, I began to enjoy my contact with these cosmic barbarians and I looked forward to whatever they had in store.

I had forgotten my army, my country, and my friends.

There was only my hole and my cell, and my smoke-house back on my beloved home island.

It was the whole universe, and I could not tell whether it was heaven or hell.

Then, coming from the Dark Game out into the cell again, it was pain in my crotch that had me screaming, yet I felt distant from the scream.

I felt I could measure the scream and how it flew along the cell walls, bouncing up and down and back again.

They took another one of my fingers, but worse, one of my nuts was felled that night.

The Axeman had done it with his little razor.

I hadn't answered the questions and they had taken my left ball after slicing off my next finger down from my already-torn-off pinkie.

When I came around, I was in the cell, screaming, and one of my guys – Larry Pastor – sat across from me, watching me, his face trembling as if with an impending storm of sobs.

I had become the new entertainment for someone else now.

I was the star of the show.

§

THE NEXT NIGHT, I had the best supper yet, with Larry staring at me from across the room, his face a grimace.

What was I eating? My finger? My testicle? Or simply some special sliced rat over a bed of eel-leaves?

"It's all right," I told him. "It tastes good. It really does."

§

I WASN'T sure what I ate most nights, but the strangest thing of all was that I had begun gaining weight.

I still drank a bit of the opium water – Hoax would bring in barely a thimbleful. I guess he wanted to keep me pliable yet sober enough when necessary.

I attributed my gain in bulk to a combination of the fatty meat they fed me, as well as sitting in a hole in the ground for days on end.

Hoax commented on my healthy look and I could see it in Larry Pastor's eyes – while he got thinner and thinner, no doubt refusing to eat any meat offered him, I was beginning to pack on the pounds.

Truth was, I felt better.

I felt as if my mind had adjusted to the hole and the cell.

I began to realize that, contrary to what Hoax might've thought, I never even felt I was going to escape. I just refused to tell Hoax or his beloved Axeman any military plans or secrets because I knew that once I told, I was as good as dead.

The meals would stop.

They'd leave me in the hole and either forget about me completely, or fill it in with dirt and rocks.

I began to see my imprisonment as a kind of luxury hotel – a fancy five-star place.

I began living in my head a lot, believing that I went on adventures when I was in the hole. I used the Dark Game to get out – I began to see the world again.

I WAS IN PARIS, briefly, for a moonlit walk along the Seine

with a beautiful girl who reminded me of a teacher I'd once had a crush on.

I ate a delicious breakfast on the Champs-Élysées, buttered almond croissant and a demitasse of espresso while watching traffic as it headed toward the Arc de Triomphe.

Another voyage out, I sat upon a striped blanket along the beach of some tropical island, surrounded by bare breasted beauties. I feasted on juicy mango and velvet coconut milk, feeling warm breezes as the shadows of palm trees cast thin lines along the pumice-strewn sand.

In the cell, I'd go to Burnley Island, to a moment in the past; but in the hole, I'd be somewhere magnificent, off on some adventure that was like a wish fulfillment of my boyhood.

Perhaps this saved me.

Perhaps it damned me.

IN MY RARE moments of lucidity, I'd try to stay grounded by chewing on a small bit of the Wrigley's gum – the little I had left. A tiny infinitesimal piece. It reminded me of who I was, where I was, why I was there.

I began to talk to Hoax, without even knowing that I might be giving away secrets.

I TOLD him all kinds of things. Not military secrets. Just about my life.

About my nocturnal adventures.

Hoax became my best friend, and I suppose months passed.

Other soldiers were captured. Sometimes I saw their faces, and now and then I recognized them.

But they were part of the *Show* now. I watched the Show, or they watched me in their version of the Show.

But Hoax didn't let the Axeman cut from me again.

≈

My performances for the horror of the new recruits tended to be drawn from the contortionist's trade. My limbs were pummeled and pulled and twisted.

I felt none of it, off in my game.

I was valuable. I began telling things here and there. Nothing important, of course, but I'd become quite a good storyteller as I gained weight from my substantial meals.

My tales of wonder and awe for my host, the polite Mr. Hoax, were about life outside of the jungle, and he loved these adventures into other worlds. He had studied the works of Shakespeare, so now and then we'd talk about *Macbeth* or about *Othello*, and I told him about *Moby Dick* and how my island was somewhat like Nantucket and had been part of the whaling trade.

He loved American movies, too, so we talked about them at some length, and he offered up critiques that were quite well-thought-out about how Americans approached movies as opposed to other cultures. He also enjoyed discussing famous wars, and warriors of the ancient world.

≈

THESE CONVERSATIONS often went on during the torture of another countryman of mine, usually roughly my age, once handsome, once with dreams and a sense of goodness of the world, all of them still having some meat on their bones.

I watched a man weep as the Axeman sliced off both of his ears, and then held them high for me as if ready to toss them to a trained seal.

I am ashamed to admit that, deluded and not really as sane as I should've been, I clapped for this performance because I thought it was some kind of special effects magic.

The Axeman was good at his job.

I had no idea what Hoax had in store for me, but soon enough, he brought me into a lower level of Hell with him.

HERE's the thing about the Dark Game:

By itself, it's simply a mind trick. It's a way to open doors inside you and to escape. Pain. Hurt. Sorrow.

That's all it is.

But in that prison camp, with the techniques they taught purely by trying them on me, I learned how to add another level to the game.

How to make it go deeper.

And when it did, something truly magnificent came of it.

"BRAINWASHING."

It sounds like some medical experiment.

But it's really simple.

You just put the subject in a position of separation from every sensory detail.

And then you go to work on him.

I had been prepared for it, in my training.

But I guess you're never really prepared for this kind of thing, not after months in a hole in the ground, not after watching your friends get their noses and eyes and ears and hands cut off in front of you.

Not after they feed you what might be your left ball.

HOAX HAD ME BOUND UP, hands in front of me, but tied to another rope that went to my ankles.

They positioned me, standing, in the middle of a cell.

Plugged a fan into the wall. I guessed this was to help block out any noise beyond the cell wall.

Then, each wall was covered with a dark cloth to block out even the cracks of light that might come in.

Additionally, Hoax tied a blindfold around my eyes.

Plunged into absolute darkness, I felt Hoax touch my hands.

"You are going to be here for several hours," he said. "You are not going to touch the wall. Or sit down. Or fall. Should you fall, you will be strung up so that you are dangling from the ceiling with a stick thrust between your arms to keep you balanced.

"So, do not fall, that is my advice, my friend. You are to keep silent. If you cannot keep silent, our mutual friend Axeman will cut out your tongue and sew your lips together. Understood?

"This is for your betterment. We find that you are truly a patriot to the world, to freedom, and to honor. We want you to realign yourself with nature and man's true calling, instead of with this monster you have served in America. You have been deluded by your country, and we intend to help you recover. You are special to us, and to me, Gordon. You are worth realigning. I consider you my friend."

These were the last words I heard for many hours, during which my bones ached, my bowels let loose without my being able to control them.

After awhile, I felt as if I were floating.

The sound of the fan – a buzzing like a thousand black flies – seemed to take over my mind, as if it were what my brain generated: the noise of a cosmic buzzing.

Somewhere beneath it, after awhile, I heard Hoax's voice again, only I could not make out what he was saying.

I was fairly certain, however, that he existed inside my head, washing my brains the way he might wash his hands with a feminine delicacy, planting ideas and truths known only to the Enemy, trying to make me over into one of his house servants.

I went into the Dark Game. I heard Hoax clearly inside the game itself. I understood how this brainwashing could serve the Dark Game – and how it could help me survive.

GETTING into your brain isn't the problem with brainwashing. Anyone with a good mental crowbar can unlock that mush of gray matter.

It's making your mind separate from your body so

completely that your body becomes a servant to someone else's mind.

That is the goal of brainwashing.

They are not cleansing the brain. They are turning it off, and switching on another brain, imprinting another set of memories and values and thoughts so that your past is no longer there.

It is wiped out, but not so completely – you think you are the same person. But someone else has invaded you.

The Other. The one who has turned off one switch has juiced you from another one.

And you are that person's mind now. You are that person's imagination.

That is what I learned. That is how I began to understand that the Dark Game was not just for one to go off on flights of fancy. To protect you from some pain of life.

It could be changed, using this brainwashing.

IT COULD BECOME a way to turn a switch in another – to implant your own mind into another's mind, so that he no longer had his own perception but might, at least briefly, have yours.

I knew there was a way I could use this on Hoax.

On the Axeman.

I KNEW that there was a way I could put the Dark Game into them so that I might escape.

THEY TOLD me later that I stood there for twenty hours.

They told me later that I had been realigned.

But I had not been.

The Dark Game had saved me. It had protected me. It had kept me from letting their words and thoughts press into my gray matter.

When they brought me out into the sunlight – for the first time in many months – they rejoiced and called me *Comrade* and *Friend* and *Healed One*.

But, on the inside, I had already begun planning how I would destroy them, set their camp on fire, and sow the ashes with salt so that those demons might never rise again.

BUT I'VE GOT to pull you back to that night when I was young and in a bad part of some Texas town.

Remember?

Me, tied to the bed, the dead whore on the floor and the real Harry Hoakes, my buddy, my pal, untying me, his breath all whiskey and perfume absorbed from his girl for the night.

"She thought she was going to be like Gene Tierney," I said, and then, "Jesus, I'm going to end up in jail for this."

"Or you'll be in the jungle. In the goddamned war. Which do you want?"

"I choose the goddamned war."

Harry grinned, slightly, despite everything. "You didn't do it. You were tied up. I'm a witness to that."

I got up and got dressed as fast as I could, tripping over my trousers as I yanked them up.

"You let her tie you up?" He laughed.

I shot him a glance that shut him up.

"What are we going to do?" He said.

"We ain't gonna get caught, that's for damn sure," I said.

Next thing I remember, we're dragging that body out to Harry's car, and we plop her in the trunk.

I looked at her once, in that fizzling little light of the trunk, before we shut it down on her.

Her face.

She was somewhere else.

That's what Death is, I thought. It's going into the Dark Game for good.

I had no feeling for her. She was no longer there.

But the drive out to the mesa, thirty miles away from Red Town, the whole way I kept wondering how she had been murdered, and why I woke up from the Dark Game with the strange feeling of pleasure in my loins as if I had truly lost my virginity that night.

But that remains a Mystery with a capital M.

Part of me has felt all these years that I had untied myself, had beaten her to death, and then had somehow wrapped myself up in the ropes again.

Houdini, after all.

WE BURIED her in a desolate spot, so deep that the coyotes and scavengers wouldn't be able to dig her up.

I heard, years later, that Red Town eventually flourished

and became more than a saloon and whorehouse railroad stop. It expanded out into the mesa.

I think that at some point a shopping mall was built near that grave of the girl who thought she looked like Gene Tierney and kept a rope in her overnight bag.

HARRY SAID TO ME, at four that morning, driving back to base, "No matter what happens, we can't ever say we met her. Or were even there. The other girls won't tell. They don't like cops. But you and I have to be clear on this. We were never there."

"Where?" I asked, and then Harry muttered, "Jesus," and I knew our friendship was over that morning.

When I heard he died later, in the war, I felt bad for him. I missed him, too. We had done our time together, and that's a bond that remains even after death.

I wonder if he ever got over the sight that had greeted him when he stepped out of the ordinary world of red light night and into that motel room of me tied up and a dead woman on the floor.

But now, he's in the Dark Game.

SUDDENLY, like an overnight celebrity, I became revered among the Enemy in our camp.

No longer made to sleep in the hole, I had a straw mattress beneath me, and I ate regular food with some of the lower officers.

More of my own countrymen arrived at the camp. I

observed them as they trooped in, proud and wounded. Some of them spat at the ground as they marched by me.

❧

THE CAMP SPREAD across a flat wetland area with long planks laid across muddy ground, rising to low hills where most of the buildings sat, and behind which on a kind of plateau, dotted with the holding wells for prisoners.

The commander's headquarters sat at the highest point of one of the hills, and I got to calling it Mount Olympus. The pits and holes where the Americans were kept, I called Tartarus.

I taught Hoax about the various levels of Hell, and he and I cooked up a scheme to begin a new set of torments for my countrymen.

❧

WE WOULD TAKE *Dante's Inferno*, which was easy enough to find even with the supposed anti-European sentiment of the Enemy and from it create elaborate Rings of Hell for the prisoners.

Next, I talked about the cannibal torture. I suggested a whole new way to do this.

Why even use the Axeman? For despite his pleasure in the art of cutting flesh and bone from a live victim, wouldn't there be a more effective Host of such theatrics?

Why not *me*, their countryman?

What would be more horrifying than a well-fed compatriot slicing off the lips of his fellow American in front of the remnants of a once-proud platoon?

A USO show from Hell, I called it. We'll make it a grand show, a hot ticket in the hot jungle. A feast for the eyes and ears. We'd entertain Hoax's soldiers, as well as mesmerize my American friends.

It took Hoax several days to see this as the grandiose and intriguing idea that it might be.

But then he smiled and nodded. "Yes, my friend Gordon, this might be quite a wonderful and acceptable entertainment."

The USO Show from Hell would begin.

❧

We'd have beautiful girls dancing for the boys.

Then, we'd have the main event. I'd do a comedy routine, I told Hoax.

I'd strip them of their dignity. I'd cut off bits and pieces of the happiest, sweetest guy they knew, the youngest of their friends, the ones they thought of as mascots and baby brothers.

Right before their eyes.

"They'll tell you what you want to know," I said. "They'll divulge their mother and father's addresses if you want, once we do this."

Hoax, not suspicious in the least, was thrilled.

Yet, he still didn't completely trust me, for he felt the Axeman should be there to do the slicing.

I wasn't to be handed knives or razors. I was still a prisoner, albeit a *Friend of Our Country*, as they proclaimed loudly, nightly, into the pits and holes of Tartarus, making sure that every single captured American soldier knew my name and where I'd been born and what I'd done for my newly adopted fatherland.

Once everything was set, the prisoners began building the stadium.

§&

I OVERSAW ITS CONSTRUCTION, and they worked tirelessly and swiftly, for I told them that it was a monument to their Dead.

That it was their Memorial and that they must take pride in it.

I spent some nights with them, talking of how we were going to be well-treated by our captors, and that they must trust me, despite appearances.

They didn't trust me at all, I could tell, but they had the resignation of those who wait for freedom to come from outside their sphere. The helicopter raids from the sky, perhaps, they hoped. The end of the war itself was not too much to wish for in their current state.

They had lost all will to escape. They were broken, yet capable men.

They did as I told them to do.

I also spent nights with them, playing the Dark Game.

I needed their minds. I need to bring them into a state of calm and of service.

I needed for them to hear only *my* voice among all the voices of their prison.

The bleachers went up, the theater backdrop created.

§&

WITHIN TWO WEEKS, it was, by the standards of the jungle, a beautiful imitation of an amphitheater, and could seat forty or fifty men.

The night of what I called *The Most Magnificent Show in the Universe*, finally arrived.

A banner announcing this, painted from human blood, hung from the wall.

❧

THE CELEBRITIES of our Damnation were there: the Commander, with his long face and inscrutable gaze; my friend Hoax, a chubby, round-faced fellow who whispered in the Commander's ear, no doubt about the show to come; the Enemy soldiers, dressed as if for an evening at the theater.

No doubt the women with some of them were not wives, but girlfriends who lived in the nearby Enemy Town, just beyond our Doom City.

The girls had fine red or blue dresses on, as if they would go to a celebration after the show. The men were dressed in full military garb. Cocktails were served, a rarity at this outpost, but the liquor had been distilled from a local flower, and left behind a scent in the air like jasmine.

The atmosphere fairly crackled with the electric moment to come.

I felt as if we were going to stage a great Broadway show. Or a spectacular Fourth of July fireworks demonstration.

It would be, I was certain, the inauguration of some wonderful event that might be remembered and talked about for years to come.

Was I nervous? Of course. How could I pull off such a

scheme? What if I were found out? What if something went wrong? If one thing had gone wrong, one tiny thing, all of it would fall like dominoes and it would make stepping on a mine seem like a walk in the park.

THE USUAL EXCITEMENT of opening night spread, even among my countrymen. They were brought in, roped at the hands, shackled at the legs, shuffling to their seats, although I kept a contingent backstage, those American actors in the drama to unfold.

Footlights consisted of small fatty candles laid in a semicircle around the stage floor.

The backdrop, an enormous canvas that had once been an officer's tent covering but was now painted with scenes of the Enemy's Great Leader, stepping on all symbols of the USA. There was a ragged Statue of Liberty crumbling, there Uncle Sam, blinded and toothless his top hat a wreck, and there along the edges was our president being corn-holed by one of our great generals.

Just seeing the backdrop made the Enemy guard cheer and raise their glasses.

What they didn't know, of course, was that I had made sure that a quite a bit of the opium water that I had grown to know well was stirred into their drinks.

I led them in their national anthem. They stood and sang bravely and happily, they drank – all, including the girls – I could tell from their expressions that they had begun to go into a blurred state – the strong alcohol and the poppy milk made themselves known.

As THE CROWD QUIETED, and the lights came up, I announced from my perch at the edge of the stage:

"We are gathered here for a momentous occasion! This is the inauguration of a great moment of historical significance!

"We are all the proud and the brave who have learned so much from our new masters, our friends and who wish to teach us the error of our ways and the true path of life! Here, on this very stage, you will see the wonders of transformation!

"You will see the magic of the ancients! The famous tricks of the fakirs of India! The secrets of the alchemists of old Europe! The mystical wonders of the sorcerers of ancient Mesopotamia!"

I spouted all the bullshit I could, and Hoax stood up and translated every word for the Enemy. They laughed, and brawled while some of my countrymen portrayed the President and our military leaders. They tripped, simulating intercourse with each other, acting like buffoons and idiots, all at my command.

The laughter from the stadium was enormous, even from Americans, whom I had brought into a state of the Dark Game just for this evening.

Hoax probably laughed the hardest, and once, when I glanced up at him, I saw the Enemy Commander slap him on the shoulder and whisper some approval in his ear that made Hoax beam.

The dancing girls came out next – they writhed and gyrated for the men. I had given them unhealthy doses of the local drink, and they began touching each other and taking off their clothes until they were nearly naked. This got the Enemy to cheer further, and the girls threw garments up to them.

My own countrymen sat quietly, as I had commanded for them to do in the Dark Game.

I could see that their eyes were glazed over, and they awaited my word.

Finally, to the delight of all, I announced the evening's entertainments.

"Tonight, good gentlemen and ladies, for your pleasure, the Axeman and I will carve up several Americans before your eyes. They will devour one another, as that is the way of our kind, and you will see how corrupt in our very beings we truly are. But first, I ask for volunteers from among you. For I want you to participate greatly tonight. Do I have any takers?"

The Enemy ranks roared approval, and many leapt from their seats to volunteer. But I wanted a special man to come forward. I wanted an important man.

"Commander!" I called out.

"Yes!" cried my countrymen, "Commander!"

Hoax laughed, clapping his hands, turning to his leader. "Commander!" he said.

§

THE COMMANDER SHOOK his head violently, laughing the entire time.

While he resisted coming forward, I brought the few remaining men from my own company out on the stage. They were further along in the Dark Game than the other prisoners.

Each was blindfolded, and they held each other's hands. I had spent four nights with the three of them to make sure that their minds were switched into another realm, so that my voice and my mind was their only guide.

"Commander!" I cried out again, and even the Axeman, coming up beside me, raised his glinting blade as it caught the last of the sunlight and called the Commander by full name.

§

FINALLY, goaded, blurred from drink, the Commander came down from the bleachers.

I raised a hand and called out a word of cheer, and all the Americans began clapping for him, and soon the guards clapped as well, whistling, as their beloved leader stepped up on stage.

"We have a magic show tonight!" I shouted to the noisy audience. "But we must have silence, now! Absolute silence!"

Within a minute or two, those in the bleachers quieted.

I glanced up at Hoax who smiled and nodded as if watching his prize protégé.

§

I THOUGHT of my friend Harry, blown to bits by a landmine. I thought of little Davy, tortured in front of me, tortured until his last breath left him.

I crouched down at the edge of the stage and blew out more than half the candles.

The sun had begun its descent and a gradually-creeping darkness seeped in like a dreadful mist.

Only six or so candles remained flickering, providing scant illumination to our stage. It was an effect I'd worked on – the backdrop now seemed ominous and evil – the Commander's face on the backdrop seemed to have gone in shades into a diseased, corrupt form rather than the healthy look that backdrop had when sunlight was upon it.

The crowd quieted even further, although I heard murmurs among the Enemy that set my teeth on edge.

They had begun to feel uneasy.

THE COMMANDER STEPPED up next to me, and patted me on the shoulder.

He announced to the crowd that I was a shining example of the realignment procedure that had been developed in the Great City.

I told the Axeman that it was time to begin the carving of the Americans.

He brought the blade up to the ear of one of my boys.

I STOPPED HIM, and announced, "Why an ear? Can you make a good purse from it, ladies?"

A tittering came from the women in the bleachers as if this were the cutest of jokes.

"I think not! Why not flay him alive? Right now? But even better, see how his friends," I pointed to the other two men, "don't know what's to come? Their ears are stuffed with wax. Their eyes are covered! Why not have them skin their friend for the delight of the Commander?"

Cheers went up, as I had expected.

In the dark, of course, it was the Americans who began the cheer, but in a stadium, cheers and claps become contagious. People want to be enthused about a show, and so the Enemy began crying out for more.

Then, when they quieted, I asked the Axeman for his blade.

Now, this was the point when my nerves nearly destroyed what I was about to do.

What if?

I felt sweat break out along my back. If he didn't pass me that weapon, none of this would work. If the drinks and the crowd didn't work on him, if he suspected anything...

THE AXEMAN GAVE me a strange look, but his commander, the Supreme Leader of the camp, nodded to him, and shouted in their language.

The pressure of an audience watching did exactly what I wanted it to do – the Commander was caught up in the magic of the theatrical moment. He wanted the show to go on as planned.

Reluctantly, the Axeman passed me the blade.

It was heavy, and its edge was sharp.

"YOU WILL NOW SEE," I announced, "one of the Corrupt

Americans be skinned before you, and before your Commander, by his own compatriots!"

The audience went silent as I passed the blade to one of my blindfolded men.

Quickly, however, I took it back, and whispered to the three men whose ears were not, in fact, blocked, "Now. To your left."

I turned with the blade, and stabbed the Axeman in the groin, and then cut my way up into his belly and sternum –

As the audience began to gasp –

The three men, blindfolded, grabbed the Commander and tore at him as if they were wild dogs.

ᛒ

IN THEIR HEADS, they were wolves, in fact, and they believed that they were tearing at a stag in the hunt.

The commander screeched, but the men were strong, and in the darkness of the stadium, the Enemy rose, panicking, but it was too late.

They had drunk the opium and liquor, and my countrymen had already risen up with gnashing teeth and a strength that they had never known they'd had in their bodies.

I wanted to see Hoax one last time, to see the look on his face when he knew that this had not gone his way. That he had misplaced any trust he had in me.

But I couldn't find his face in the confusion.

I heard what sounded like wolves tearing at bleating sheep in the dark.

ᛒ

THE BEAUTY of the escape of my men – men from various platoons who now thought of me as their hero – was that none could remember the show at all.

By dawn, not all the prisoners had survived. Many had died in the fight.

But those who lived, blood on their faces and blotching their clothes, awoke without memory of the past year.

They didn't know the atrocity committed against them, neither did they know of their own savagery, which had killed the Enemy in the camp.

By dawn, I commanded the men, still under the influence of the Dark Game, to set fire to the last of Hell.

AN OLD MEMORY: I was sixteen, and my father lay dying in his bed.

My mother, who had to take up work now, needed me home to help nurse him while he was in pain.

I sat each day with him, and one morning, when I brought his breakfast, which he barely touched, he told me, "You're an evil son-of-a-bitch, Gordie. You show the world how good you are, but I know who you are on the inside. I've seen it since you were a baby. You have the Devil in you, and you spend your time hiding it."

I sat with him, patiently, nodding so that I might not appear to be the bad child.

Then, when he was through talking about my evil and how I was going to Hell, I offered him a glass of water.

He drank it, greedily, and passed the glass back to me.

"I still love you, dad," I said.

"I know you do," he said.

In the afternoon, he died, peacefully, in his sleep.

I missed him terribly.

His lifeless body, in that bed, made me remember the day he had me shoot my dog and had taught me about how sometimes, Death could be a friend.

THERE. I've told you it all.

I've told you about the war, and the young woman, and my father.

My youth, pulled from the drawer, so you can look at it and judge me.

I should be tied up.

Bound.

Whipped.

It is the only way for me to go out of this body, the freedom of my mind to wander.

It intensifies the Dark Game for me.

I don't want to remember anymore.

I want to close the drawer now.

I want to lock up the past.

I give to you, my wife, Mia, the key.

O, Rare and Most Exquisite

O, Rare and Most Exquisite

"WHAT IS HUMAN LOVE?"

I have heard my mother ask this when she was sick or when she was weary from the wood-rotted dams of marriage and children.

It's a question that haunts my every waking hour.

I, myself, never experienced love. I once learned about it secondhand.

When I was seventeen, I worked in a retirement home in its cafeteria. After early shifts, I sometimes went up to the third floor.

THIS WAS THE NURSING FACILITY, and I suppose I went there to feel needed; all the elderly patients begged for attention, often someone to just sit with them, hold their hand, watch the sun as it stretched down across the far-off trees heavy with summer green.

I don't know why I was so taken with the older people, but I felt more comfortable around them than I often did around my peers.

One day, an old man was shouting from his bed, "O, rare and most exquisite. O, God, O God, O, rare and most exquisite creation! Why hast thou forsaken me?"

His voice was strong and echoed down the slick corridor; his neighbors, in adjacent beds, cried out for relief from his moans and groans. Since the orderlies ignored all this, routinely, I went to his room to find out what the trouble was about.

He was a ruffian.

Bastards always lived the longest, it was a rule of thumb on the nursing floor.

This man was a prince among bastards.

Something about the lizard leather of his skin, and the grease of his hair, and the way his forehead dug into his eyebrows as if he were trying to close his translucent blue eyes by forcing the thick skin down over them. He had no kindness in him; but I sat down on the edge of his bed, patted his hand, which shook, and asked him what the matter was.

"Love," he said. "All my life, I pursued nothing but love. And look where it's gotten me."

He was a rasping old crow, the kind my brother used to shoot at in trees.

"Did you have lunch yet?" I asked. The patients could become irritable if they hadn't eaten.

"I will not eat this raw sewage you call food."

"You can have roast beef, if you want. And pie."

"I will not eat."

He closed his eyes. I figured he was about to go to sleep so I began to get up off the bed.

"Bring me the box under the bed," he whispered.

I did as he asked.

I drew out a cheap strongbox that could be bought in a dime store. When I set it beside him, he reached under the blankets to retrieve a small key.

"Open it for me." He passed the key over to me.

I put the key in the hole, turned it and brought the lid up.

The box was filled with sand.

"Reach in," he said.

I stuck my hands down deep and felt what seemed to be a stick or perhaps a quill. I took it out.

It was a dried flower with only a few petals remaining.

"Do you know about love?" he asked me.

I grinned. "Sure."

"You're too young," he said, shaking his head.

He took the dried flower from my hand and brought it up to his nose. Dust from the petals fell across his upper lip.

"You think love is about kindness and dedication and caring. But it is not. It is about tearing flesh with hot pincers."

I wondered if he was sane; many of the patients were not.

"This is the most rare flower that has ever existed," he said. "It is more than sixty years old. It is the most valuable thing I own. I am going to die soon, boy. Smell it. Smell it."

He pressed the withered blossom into the palm of my

hand, and cupped his shaking fingers under mine. "Smell it."

I lifted it up to my nose.

For just a second, I imagined the scent of a distant sea, and island breezes of blossoming fruit trees and perfumes. Then, nothing but the rubbing alcohol and urine of the nursing floor.

"I will give this to you," he said. "to keep, if you promise to take care of it."

Without thinking, I said, "It's dead."

He shook his head, a rage flaring behind his eyes, a life in him I wouldn't have expected. "You don't know about love," he grabbed my arm, and his grip was hard as stone, "and you'll live just like I did, boy, unless you listen good, and life will give you its own whipping so that one day you'll end up in this bed smelling like this and crying out to the god of death just for escape from this idiot skin so that the pain of memory will stop."

To calm him, because now I knew he was crazy, I said, "Okay. Tell me."

"Love," he said, "is the darkest gift. It takes all that you are, and it destroys you."

And he told me about the flower of his youth.

HIS NAME WAS GUS, and he was a gardener at a house that overlooked the Hudson River.

The year was 1925, and his employer was an invalid in his fifties, with a young wife. The wife's name was Jo, and she was from a poor family, but she had made a good marriage, for the house and grounds occupied a hundred acres. As head gardener, Gus had a staff of six beneath him. Jo would come out in the mornings, bringing coffee to the workers. She was from a family of laborers, so she understood their needs, and she encouraged their familiarity. Her husband barely noticed her, and if he did, he wouldn't approve of her mixing with the staff.

One morning she came down to Gus where he stood in the maze of roses, with the dew barely settled upon them, and she kissed him lightly on the cheek. He wasn't sure how to take this. She was wearing her robe, as she always did when she brought the coffee out to the men, although it revealed nothing of her figure. She was the most beautiful woman he had ever seen, with thick dark hair, worn long and out of fashion, a throwback to the long Victorian tresses of his mother's generation. She had almond-shaped eyes, and skin like olives soaked in brandy.

He had never seen a woman this exotic in his hometown of Wappingers Falls.

She smelled of oil and rosewater, and she did not greet him, ever, without something sweet on her lips, so that her breath was a pleasure to feel against his skin. She drew back from him, and with her heavy accent, said, "Gus, my handsome boy of flowers, what will you find for me today?"

Gus had had girls before, since he was fourteen, but they had been lust pursuits, for none of the girls of the Falls, or of Poughkeepsie, or even the college girl he had touched in Connecticut, stirred in him what he felt with Jo. He called her, to his men, "my Jo," for he felt that, if things were different, she would not be with this wealthy man with his palsied body, but with him. Gus and Jo—he wrote it on the oak tree down near the river, he carved it into a stone he had placed in the center of the rose garden.

When she kissed him on the cheek, he waited a minute, then grabbed her in his arms, for he could no longer contain himself, and they made love there, in the morning, before the sun was far up in the sky.

He knew that she loved him, so he went that day to find her the most beautiful flower that could be had. It was a passion of hers, to have the most beautiful things, for she had lived most of her life with only the ugly and the dull. He wished he were wealthy so that he might fly to China, or to the south of France, or to the stars, to bring back the rarest of blooms. But, having four bits on him, he took the train into New York City, and eventually came to a neighborhood that sold nothing but flowers, stall upon stall. But it was midsummer, and all the flowers available were the same that he could grow along the river.

As he was about to leave, not knowing how he could return to his Jo without something very special, a woman near one of the stalls said, "You don't like these, do you?"

Gus turned, and there was a woman of about twenty-two. Very plain, although pretty in the way that he thought all women basically pretty. She was small and pale, and she wore no makeup, but her eyes were large and lovely. "I've been watching you," she said.

"You have?"

"Yes. Do you think that's rude? To watch someone?"

"It depends."

"I think it's rude. But then," she said, smiling like a mischievous child, "I've never been ashamed of my own behavior, only the behavior of others. I'm ashamed of yours. Here I've watched you for fifteen minutes, and you barely took your eyes off the flowers. How rude do you think that is? Very. You like flowers, don't you?"

"I'm a gardener. I take care of them."

"Lovely," she said wistfully. "Imagine a life of caring for beautiful things. Imagine when you're very old, and look back on it. What lovely memories you'll have."

Although she seemed forthright, the way he knew city people were, there was something fitful in the way she spoke, almost hesitant somewhere in the flow of words, as if all this snappy talk was a cover for extreme shyness. And yet, he knew, city women were rarely shy.

He had not come all the way to the city to flirt with shop girls. "I'm looking for something out of the ordinary."

She offered a curious smile, tilting her head back. She was a shade beautiful in the thin shaft of daylight that pressed between the stalls. She was no Jo, but she would make some young man fall in love with her, he knew that much. Some city boy who worked in the local grocer's, or ran a bakery. Or, perhaps, even a junior bondsman. She would eventually live in one of the boxcar apartments in Brooklyn, and be the most wonderful and ordinary bride. She would have four children, and grow old without fear. Not like Jo, who was destined for romance and passion and tragedy and great redemption, not Italian Jo of olive skin and rose water. The woman said, "I know a place where you can find very unusual flowers."

"I want a beauty," he said.

"For a lady?"

Because Gus knew how women could be, and because he detected that he might get further along with this girl if he feigned interest in her, he lied. "No. Just for me. I appreciate beautiful flowers."

He felt bad then, a little, because now he knew that he was leading her on, but she seemed to know where the interesting flowers were, and all he could think of was Jo and how she loved flowers. Gus was considered handsome in his day, and women often showed him special attention, so he was used to handling them, charming them. "I need a beauty," he repeated.

"I'm not saying beautiful," she cautioned him, and began walking between the stalls, through an alley, leading him, "but unusual. Sometimes unusual is better than beautiful."

⚜

SHE WORE A KIND OF APRON, he noticed, the long kind that covered her dress, and he wondered if she was the local butcher's daughter, or if she was a cook.

The alley was steamy; there was some sort of kitchen down one end of it, a laundry, too. He heard someone shouting somewhere in a foreign language.

The woman came to an open pit, with a thin metal staircase leading down to a room, and she hiked her apron up a bit, and held her hand out for him to steady her as she descended.

"My balance isn't too good," she told him. "I have a heart problem—nothing serious—but it makes me light-headed sometimes on stairs."

"There're flowers down there?" he asked as he went down the steps slowly.

"It's one of my father's storage rooms. He has a flower shop on Seventh Avenue, but there's an icehouse above us, and we get shavings for free. They stay colder down here," she said, and turned a light up just as he had reached the last step. "There's another room three doors down, beneath the laundry. We keep some there, too."

The room was all of redbrick, and it was chilly, like winter. "We're right underneath the storage part of the icehouse."

As the feeble light grew strong, he saw that they were surrounded by flowers, some of them brilliant vermillion sprays, others deep purples and blacks, still more of pile upon pile of dappled yellows on reds on greens.

"These are all fresh cut," she said, "you can have any you want. My father grows them underneath the laundry, and when he cuts them, we keep them on ice until we ship them. Here," she said, reaching into a bowl that seemed to be carved out of ice. She brought up tiny red and blue blossoms, like snowballs, but in miniature. She brought them up to his face, and the aroma was incredible; it reminded him of Jo's skin when he pressed his face against her breasts and tasted the brightness of morning.

The woman kissed him, and he responded, but it was not like his kiss with Jo. This woman seemed colder, and he knew he was kissing her just because he wanted the blossoms. He remembered the cold kiss all the way to the big house, as he carried the gift to his beloved.

Jo was shocked by the tiny, perfect flowers.

He'd left them for her in a crystal bowl of water on the dining room table so that she would see them first when she came to have breakfast. He heard her cry out, sweetly, and then she came to the kitchen window to search the back garden for him. She tried to open it, but it had rained the night before and all that morning, so it was stuck. She rushed around to the back door, ran barefoot into the garden and grabbed his hand.

"Sweetest, precious, blessed," she gasped. "Where did you find them? Their smell—so lovely."

He had saved one small blossom in his hand. He crushed it against her neck, softly. He kissed her as if he owned her, and he told her how much he loved her.

She drew back from him then, and he saw something change in her eyes.

"No," she said.

⁂

WHEN THOSE FLOWERS DIED, he ventured back into the city, down the alley, but the entrance to the pit was closed.

He rapped on the metal doors several times, but there was no response. He went around to the entrance to the icehouse and asked the manager there about the flowers, but he seemed to not know much about it other than the fact that the storage room was closed for the day.

Gus was desperate, had brought his month's pay in order to buy armloads of the flowers, but instead, ended up in an Irish bar on Horace Street drinking away most of it. Jo didn't love him, he knew that now. How could he be such a fool, anyway? Jo could never leave her husband, never in a thousand years.

Oh, but for another moment in her arms, another moment of that sweet mystery of her breath against his neck!

He stayed in the city overnight, sleeping in a flophouse, and was up early, and this time went to directly to the laundry. The man who ran it took him to the back room, where the steam thickened. Gus heard the sounds of machines being pushed and pressed and clanked and rapped, as a dozen or more people worked in the hot fog of the shop.

The owner took him farther back, until they came to a stairway.

"Down," the man said, nodding, and then disappeared into the fog.

Gus descended the steps, never sure when he would touch bottom, for the steam was still heavy. Once in the depths, he noticed a sickly yellow light a ways off. He went towards it, brushing against what he assumed were flowers growing in their pots.

Then someone touched his arm.

"Gus." It was the woman from the week before. "It's me. Moira."

"I didn't know your name," he told her. "I didn't know how to find you."

"How long did the flowers last?"

"Six days."

"How sad," she said, and leaned against him. He kissed her, but the way he would kiss his sister, because he didn't really want to lead her on.

The mist from the laundry enveloped the outline of her face, causing her skin to shine a yellow-white like candles in luminaria, revealing years that he had not anticipated—he had thought she might be a girl in her early twenties, but in this steam she appeared older, ashes shining under her skin.

"I loved the flowers."

"What else do you love, Gus?"

He didn't answer. He pulled away from her, and felt the edges of thick-lipped petals.

She said, "We keep the exotics here. There's an orchid from the Fiji Islands—it's not properly an orchid, but it has the look of one. It's tiny, but very rare. In its natural state, it's a parasite on fruit trees, but here, it's the most beautiful thing in the world."

"I never paid you for the last one."

"Gus," she said, and reached up to cup the side of his face in the palm of her hand, "whatever is mine, is yours."

She retreated into the mist, and in a few moments laid in the palm of his hand a flower so small that he could barely see it. She set another of its kind into a jewelry box and said, "This is more precious than any jewel I know of. But if I give it to you, I want you to tell me one thing."

He waited to hear her request.

"I want you to tell me—no, promise me—you will take care of this better than those last ones. This should live, if cared for, for over a month. You do love flowers, don't you?"

"Yes," he said, and, because he wanted this tiny flower so much for his Jo, he brought Moira close to him and pressed his lips against hers, and kissed around her glowing face, tasting the steam from the laundry. He wanted it so badly, he knew this flower would somehow win his Jo. Somehow, she would manage to leave her husband, and they would run away together, maybe even to the Fiji Islands to live off mango and to braid beautiful Jo's hair with the island parasite flowers.

Yet there was something about Moira that he liked, too. She wasn't Jo, but she was different from any woman he knew. When he drew his face back from hers, her face was radiant and shining, and not the middle-aged woman he had thought just a minute before. She was a young girl, after all, barely out of her teens, with all the enthusiasm of fresh, new life. He wondered what his life would be like with a girl like this, what living in the city with her would feel like, what it would be like to live surrounded by the frozen and burning flowers.

There were tears in Moira's eyes when she left him, and he sensed that she knew why he wanted the beautiful flowers.

And still, she gave him the rare and exquisite ruby blossom.

The tiny flower died fourteen days after.

GUS COULD NOT RETURN to the city for more than six weeks.

A drought held the valley in its grip and he had to take special pains to make sure that the gardens didn't die. Jo didn't come and see him, but he knew that it was for the best. She was married, he was merely the gardener, and no matter how many gorgeous flowers he brought to her, she would never be his. He thought of Moira, and her sweetness and mystery; her generosity was something he had never experienced before in a woman, for the ones he had known were often selfish and arrogant in their beauty. He also knew that the old man must suspect his overfamiliarity with Jo, and so his days would be numbered in the Hudson River house.

One afternoon he took off again for the city, but it took several hours, as there was an automobile stuck on the tracks just before coming into Grand Central Station. He got there in the evening, and went to the laundry, but both it and the icehouse were closed for the day.

He remembered that Moira had mentioned her father's shop, and so he went into the flower district and scoured each one, asking after her. Finally, he came to the shop on Seventh Avenue and there she was, sitting behind a counter arranging iris in a crystal vase.

She turned to see him, and in the light of early evening she was the simple girl he had seen the first day they had met.

How the mist and the ice could change her features, but in the daylight world, she was who she was!

"Gus," she said, "I thought you weren't coming back. Ever."

"I had to," he said, not able to help his grin, or the sweat of fear that evaporated along his forehead, fear that he would not find her. It was like in the moving pictures, when the lover and his beloved were reunited at the end. He ran around the counter and grabbed her up in his arms.

"Oh, Moira, Moira," he buried his face in her neck, and she was laughing freely, happily.

She closed the shop and pulled down the shade.

"Gus, I want you to know, I love you. I know you might not love me, but I love you."

Here he was, a gardener, and she, a flower shop girl. How could a more perfect pair be created, one for the other?

"There's something I want to give you," she said.

"You've given me—" he began, but she didn't let him finish.

"Something I want to give you," she began unbuttoning the top of her blouse.

When she was completely naked, he saw what was different about her. "I could never give my heart freely … knowing I was … different … like this …"

He stepped back, away from her.

"Who did this to you?" he asked, his voice trembling.

She looked at him with those wide, perfect eyes, and said, "I was born this way."

The threads.

There, in the whiteness of her thighs.

He was horrified, and fascinated, for he had never seen this before.

Her genitals had been sewn together, you see, with some thread that was strong, yet silken and impossibly slender, like a spider's web. She brought his hand there, to the center of her being, and she asked him to be careful with her. "As careful as you are with the flowers."

"It's monstrous," he said, trying to hide the revulsion in his voice, trying to draw back his fingers.

"Break the threads," she said, "and I will show you the most beautiful flower that has ever been created."

"I can't." He shivered.

Tears welled in her eyes. "I love you with all my being," she said, "and I want to give you this … this … even if it means …" Her voice trailed off.

He found himself plucking at the threads, then pulling at them, until finally he got down on his hands and knees and placed his mouth there, and bit into the threads to open her.

There must have been some pain, but she only cried out once, then was silent.

The skin beneath his fingers curled, blossoming, and there was a smell, no, a scent, like a spice wind across a tropical shore. Her pelvis opened, prolapsed like a flower blooming suddenly, in one night, and her skin folded backward on itself, with streaks of red and yellow and white bursting forth from the wound, from the pollen that spread golden, and the wonderful colors that radiated from between her thighs, until there was nothing but flower.

He cupped his hands around it. It was the most exotic flower he had ever seen, in his hands, it was the beauty that had been inside her, and she had allowed him to open her, to hold this rare flower in his hands.

Gus wondered if he had gone insane, or if this indeed was the most precious of all flowers, this gift of love, this sacrifice that she had made for him.

He concealed the bloom in a hatbox and carried it back to the estate with him.

In the morning, he entered the great house without knocking, and his heart pounded as loud as his footsteps as he crossed the grand foyer. He called to the mistress of the house boldly.

"Jo!" he shouted, "Jo! Look what I have brought you!"

He didn't care if the old man heard him, he didn't care if he would be without a job, none of it mattered, for he had found the greatest gift for his Jo, the woman who would not now deny him. He knew he loved her now, his Jo, he knew what love was now, what the sacrifice of love meant.

She was already dressed for riding, and she blushed when she saw him. "You shouldn't come in like this. You have no right."

He opened the hatbox and retrieved the flower.

"This is for you," he said, and she ran to him, taking it up in her hands, smelling it, wiping its petals across her lips.

"It's beautiful," she said, smiling, clasping his hand, and just as quickly letting go. "Darling," she called out, turning to the staircase, "darling, look at the lovely flower our Gus has brought us, look," and like a young girl in love, she ran up the stairs, with the flower, to the bedroom where the old man coughed and wheezed.

Gus stood there, in the hall, feeling as if his heart had stopped.

*

"IT WAS THREE DAYS LATER," he told me as I sat on the edge of the nursing room bed, "that the flower died, and Jo put it out with the garbage. But I retrieved it, what was left of it, so that I would always remember that love. What love was. What terror it is."

The old man began weeping, like a baby.

"It's all right," I said, "it's just a bad dream. Just like a bad dream."

"But it happened, boy," he said, and he passed me the flower. "I want you to keep this. I'm going to die someday soon. Maybe within a month, who knows?"

"I couldn't," I said, shaking my head. "It's yours."

"No," he said, grinning madly. "It never was mine. Have you ever been with a woman, boy?"

I shook my head.

"How old are you?"

"Seventeen. Just last month."

"Ah, seventeen. A special time. What do you think human love is, boy?"

I shrugged. "Caring. Between people. I guess."

"Oh, no," a smile blossomed across his face. "It's not caring, boy, it's not caring. It's opening up your skin to someone else, and opening theirs, too. Everything I told you is true, boy. I want you to take this dried flower—"

I held it in my hand. For a moment I believed his story and I found myself feeling sad, too. I thought of her, of Moira, giving herself up like that. "She loved you."

"Her? She never loved me," he said. "Never."

"How can you say that? You just told me—"

His voice deepened. He sounded as evil as I have ever heard a man sound.

"Jo never loved me."

"Not Jo," I said as I looked at the dried flower. "Moira."

He plucked it from my fingers and held the last of its petals in his open palm.

"You thought that was Moira? Oh, no, boy, I buried her beneath the garden. This is Jo. She eventually left her husband for me. And then, when I had her...O, Lord, when I had her, boy, I tore her apart, I made her bloom, and I left her to dry in sand the way she had dried my heart." He laughed, clinging more tightly to my arm so that I could not get away.

"Her flower was not as pretty as Moira's. Moira. Lovely Moira." He sniffed the air, as if he could still smell the fragrance of the opening flower. "I made Jo bloom, boy, and then I stepped on her flower, and I kept it in darkness and dust. Now, boy, that's what love is."

He laughed even while he crushed the dried blossom with his free hand, turning it to dust.

"O, rare and most exquisite!" He shouted after me as I pulled away from him and backed out of that madman's room.

"O, why," he laughed, "why hast thou forsaken me?"

The Little Mermaid

The beach house was large, and an entire glass wall looked out upon the flat brown sand below the hill, to the brief line of pavement for the boat landing, down where the pelicans and gulls cracked their clams and oysters and crabs.

Alice didn't see the birds or the beach much. That first year she kept the curtains drawn shut. Sometimes she opened them, standing at the window, smoking a cigarette.

The ocean was a haze most of the winter, but that was fine by her. She wasn't an ocean person. She could not even swim, and she never waded. She considered herself more of an isolationist, and that is precisely what the beach house offered.

She drank a lot of her father's stored wine (a wood bin had been converted into a wine cellar), and left the house only twice a week to go see a therapist in Nag's Head.

Molly came down for a visit that lasted approximately six hours before the mother-daughter anger got out of hand; Molly still didn't understand the divorce, and being a mother now herself, and perhaps (Alice surmised) in a bad marriage, Molly was young enough to still believe in staying together for the sake of family.

Alice read a lot of books, particularly long fat ones that took her mind off life and her miserableness at it. When she thought of it, she practiced her own brand of yoga based on having watched a morning television show once. When the hangovers from the red wine became unbearable, she slacked off drinking and became a coffee addict. This prompted her to frenetic activity in the winter; she began jogging on the beach, finally unable to avoid the outdoors and health (which she kept in check by smoking and drinking coffee sometimes into the wee hours), and thus she met the old man who collected shells.

He was, at first, barely a face to her, for while her jogging was slow enough to distinguish features on the few beachcombers who came down her way, she had stopped looking anyone in the face. She noticed his hands, actually, and the cracked, worm-holed shells he held in them. His hands were tanned and rough. Then, another day, she noticed his knees: rather knobby, with fat blue veins down the sides of them. Finally, she met him the day she sprained her ankle at a place where the sand sank. She sat on a large piece of driftwood—moving the red kelp to the side—and rubbed her ankle. He walked right up to her. "You okay?"

She nodded. She still could not bring herself to look at his face. She looked at his feet: he was barefoot, as was she, with a particularly nasty looking ingrown toenail on his big toe.

"If you run, you should wear shoes," he said. "The sand tugs at your heel. It's very bad for your arches. It's made for crabs and seaweed, not people, this beach is."

"I'll take that into consideration next time," she said testily. She rubbed her foot.

"Here," he said, dropping to his knees. She could no longer avoid his face. He was probably in his late sixties; old enough to be her father by a hair. He had brown eyes and thin lips. He must've been handsome, but it had turned to sand, his skin had, and his nose, the shiny red of a lifelong drinker.

He took her foot in his hands and rubbed.

"Please," she said, pulling her foot back. It hurt when she did it.

"I'm a doctor," he said. "Retired now, but I know something about feet. We'll just massage it a little."

"Well," she said noncommittally. No one was around to watch, and it did feel good. He pressed his thumbs into the soft flesh at her ankle; the sensation burned at first, but then, as he continued, it felt warm and pleasant. She had had a headache; it melted.

He watched her. "You need to keep off this for a few days. I can wrap it for you, if you like."

Because she was financially broke from countless therapy sessions and the divorce itself and would not be able to afford any medical expense if her foot's condition worsened, she agreed to this. She leaned against his shoulder, and he guided her back to her house.

In the master bathroom, he heated torn rags of old towels in the sink with hot water. Then he squeezed them, and tied them around her ankle and foot. "The heat," he said, "it helps. They say it's ice that helps, but not for this. It'll swell up from the heat, but it needs to."

Alice, who knew nothing of medicine, nodded as if she did.

"Sometimes we need fluids to collect. They carry away the bad stuff."

She almost laughed. "Sorry, sorry," she said, "it's just that it sounded so undoctorly."

He grinned. He was a warm man, she decided. Not like her ex. This old man, he was a good country doctor who cared. He was a house call kind of doctor. He said, "I try my best. I find that all that medical jargon gets in the way of patient care. Sometimes nature knows best."

"I couldn't agree more."

He continued to massage her foot through the warm wet rags.

"You collect shells?" she asked, not wanting him to stop.

"I'm rather aimless these days. Since my wife died."

"I'm sorry."

"Oh, we had quite a life together. Life, while it lasts, has its own secrets."

Alice didn't quite understand him, but she really didn't want to get into the dead wife as a topic of conversation any more than she wanted to start prattling on about her husband.

"So I walk the beaches like I'm waiting for a ship to come in or something. Like an old salt. Do you believe in mermaids?" His eyes glistened a bit, as if he practiced this question and its anticipated response.

"No."

"I used to, when I was a boy." He grinned dopily. "Do you know that when a man becomes old, he begins to remember what he believed in as a child and it all comes back to him?"

Something sweet in his voice; that boy that was him

thousands of years before, that little boy, was still there in his eyes. She smiled. He rubbed.

"I believed that out in that ocean was a lovely mermaid. She and I knew each other, and when I was four, I would go down to the beach early in the morning, before anyone else was up, and stand on the edge of the land and sing mermaid songs to her. I imagined her fins and her tail, how if she were on land I would carry her to a safe place, and how she would tell me all the secrets of the sea. And I, in turn would tell her how much I loved her, how much I wanted to be with her," he said.

Alice began weeping upon hearing this. She could not control it, and it was not just about the pathetic little four-year-old who sang to the nonexistent mermaids; it was about everything she'd wished for as a child, all within her grasp, gone now, like sand, like seawater, the way memory always left her bereft and longing for innocence. He slid his hands from her feet and placed them on either side of her face. They were comfortingly cold.

"A beautiful woman should never cry," he said.

"I'm sorry."

"No, don't say that either. Your tears are like the mermaids'."

She opened her eyes to him and felt that lustful heat of first love again, just as if he were not old and she were not middle-aged.

He caressed her, and they fell across the bed, her ankle's throbbing becoming a distant and occasional pinching. They kissed, weeping, both of them, and then he kissed her every arch and turn and curve.

Afterward, she fell asleep.

When she awoke, the pain was excruciating. The room,

shrouded in darkness. The curtains were still drawn shut. She gasped; a light came on.

Her doctor-lover stood over her.

The pain was in her foot. She wasn't thinking clearly because of the pain.

She reached down to touch her foot, anticipating a throbbing ankle.

But her hand, sliding down her leg, ended at a stump.

She touched the air where her foot should've been.

He said, "I had to operate, Alice." He knew her name now, even though she didn't know his.

His words seemed meaningless, until on the third try to find her foot where it should've been, she suddenly understood.

Her screaming might've been heard had the night surf not boomed, had the winter not brought with it a tree-bending wind.

The operation was not completed for six days; it was a blur to Alice, for he kept her drunk and on painkillers.

☙

WHEN SHE AWOKE, clear-headed, she felt nothing but a constant stinging all up and down her spine, as if her skin had been scraped and she'd been rolled in salt.

There was dried blood on the sheets. Several hypodermic needles lay carelessly beside her. Fish scales, too, spread out in a vermillion and blue desert, piled high, as if every fish in the ocean had been skinned and thrown about. The smell was intolerable: oily and fishy. And the flies! Everywhere, the blue and green flies.

She tried to sit up, but her back hurt too much. She

fought this, but then parts of her body, including her arms, felt paralyzed. She wondered what drugs he'd been administering to her—strangely, she felt euphoric, and fought this feeling.

She lay back down, closed her eyes, willing this dream to depart.

She awoke again when he came back into the room.

"ONE LAST THING," he said, holding the serrated knife up to her throat.

The blade had been warmed with the fire on the gas stove. She felt no pain as he took the knife and scored several slits just below her chin.

Afterward, she could not even speak or scream, but could only open her mouth and emit a bleating noise.

He lifted her up into his arms, kissing her nipples as if they were sacred, and carried her out to the beach. "I will take you out to your city, my love, and set you free," he said as he laid her down in the bottom of a small boat. She could only stare at him. She felt resigned to death, which would be better than the results of the torture he had put her through.

Out to sea, he rolled her over the edge of the boat.

At first she wanted to drown, but something within her fought against it. She managed to grasp hold of some rocks out beyond the breakwater. She held on to them for over an hour as the freezing salt water smashed against the back of her head.

She grasped at the edge of a rock; it cut at her hands, but she held on.

If I just hang on for another minute, she thought. Just another ten seconds and I'll be fine. God will rescue me. Or someone will see me. Will see what he's done to me, this madman. I haven't lived all my life to come to this. I know something will happen. Something will pull me out of this.

The waves crashed around her, like glass shattering against her face.

Please, God, someone, help me.

All she could taste was the stinging salt. Something animal within her was clinging to all that she knew of life now, not her marriage or her family or her career, but this serrated rock and this icy sea.

From the shore she heard him, even at the distance. His boat already docked. The old man stood there, singing.

Alice held on to the rock for as long as she could.

Then she let go.

§

THE OLD MAN stayed on the shore for hours, his voice faltering only when dark arrived. He had a great and lovely baritone, and he sang of all the secrets of the sea.

A couple, walking along the beach that evening, held each other more tightly. His song sparked within them a memory of love and regret, and such beautiful and heartrending longing.

They watched from a distance as the old man raised his hands up, his songs batting against the wind, against the crash of the surf, against all that life had to offer.

The Rendering Man

"We're gonna die someday," Thalia said, "all of us. Mama and Daddy, and then you and then me. I wonder if anyone's gonna care enough to think about Thalia Inez Canty, or if I'll just be dust under their feet."

She stood in the doorway, still holding the ladle that dripped with potato chowder.

Her brother was raking dried grass over the manure in the yard. "What the heck kind of thing's that supposed to mean?"

"Something died last night." Thalia sniffed the air. "I can smell it. Out in the sty. Smelt it all night long, whatever it is. Always me that's first to smell the dead. 'Member the cat, the one by the thresher? I know when things's dead. I can smell something new that's dead, just like that. Made me think of how everything ends."

"We'll check your stink out later. All you need to think about right now is getting your little bottom back inside that house to stir the soup so's we'll have something decent come suppertime." Her brother returned to his work, and she to hers. She hoped that one day she would have a real job and be able to get away from this corner of low sky and dead land.

The year was 1934, and there weren't too many jobs in Moncure County, when Thalia Canty was eleven, so her father went off to Dowery, eighty miles to the northeast, to work in an accountant's office, and her mother kept the books at the Bowend Motel on Fourth Street, night shift. Daddy was home on weekends, and Mama slept through the day, got up at noon, was out the door by four, and back in bed come three a.m. It was up to Thalia's brother, Lucius, to run the house, and make sure the two of them fed the pigs and chickens, and kept the doors bolted so the winds— they'd come up suddenly in March—didn't pull them off their hinges. There was school, too, but it seemed a tiny part of the day, at least to Thalia, for the work of the house seemed to slow the hours down until the gray Oklahoma sky was like an hourglass that never emptied of sand. Lucius was a hard worker, and since he was fifteen, he did most of the heavy moving, but she was always with him, cleaning, tossing feed to the chickens, picking persimmons from the neighbor's yard (out back by the stable where no one could see) to bake in a pie. And it was on the occasion of going to check on the old sow that Thalia and her brother eventually came face-to-face with the Rendering Man.

The pig was dead, and already drawing flies. Evening was coming on strong and windy, a southern wind which meant the smell of the animal would come right in through the cracks in the walls. Lucius said, "She been dead a good long time. Look at her snout."

"Toldja I smelled her last night." Thalia peeked around him, scrunched back, wanting to hide in his lengthening shadow. The snout had been torn at— blood caked around the mouth. "Musta been them yaller dogs," she said, imitating her father's strong southern accent, "cain't even leave her alone when she's dead."

The pig was enormous, and although Lucius thrust planks beneath her to try and move her a ways, she wouldn't budge. "Won't be taking her to the butcher, I reckon," he said.

Thalia smirked. "Worthless yaller dogs."

"Didn't like bacon, anyways."

"Me, too. Or ham."

"Or sausage with biscuits and grease."

"Chitlins. Hated chitlins. Hated knuckles. Couldn't chaw a knuckle to save my life."

"Ribs. Made me sick, thought a ribs all drownin' in molasses and chili, drippin' over the barbecue pit," Lucius said, and then drew his hat down, practically making the sign of the cross on his chest. "Oh, Lord, what I wouldn't give for some of her."

Thalia whispered, "Just a piece of skin fried up in the skillet."

"All hairy and crisp, greasy and smelly."

"Yes." Thalia sighed. "Praise the Lord, yes. Like to melt in my mouth right now. I'd even eat her all rotten like that. Maybe not."

The old sow lay there, flies making halos around her face.

Thalia felt the familiar hunger come on; it wasn't that they didn't have food regularly, it was that they rarely ate the meat they raised—they'd sold the cows off, and the pigs were always for the butcher and the local price so that they could afford other things. Usually they had beans and rice or eggs and griddle cakes. The only meat they ever seemed to eat was chicken, and Thalia could smell chicken in her dreams sometimes, and didn't think she'd ever get the sour taste out of her throat.

She wanted to eat that pig. Cut it up, hocks, head, ribs, all of it. She would've liked to take a chaw on the knuckle.

"She ain't worth a nickel now," Thalia said, then, brightening, "You sure we can't eat her?"

Lucius shook his head. "For all we know, she's been out here six, seven hours. Look at those flies. Already laid eggs in her ears. Even the dogs didn't go much into her—look, see? They left off. Somethin' was wrong." He shuffled over to his sister and dropped his arm around her shoulder. She pressed her head into the warmth of his side. Sometimes he was like a mama and daddy, both, to her.

"She was old. I guess. Even pigs die when they get old." Thalia didn't want to believe that Death, which had come for Granny three years before, could possibly want a pig unless it had been properly slaughtered and divvied up.

"Maybe it died natural. Or maybe," and her brother looked down the road to the Leavon place. There was a wind that came down from the sloping hillside sometimes, and coughed dust across the road between their place and the old widow's. "Could be she was poisoned."

Thalia glanced down to the old gray house with its flag in front, still out from Armistice Day, year before last. A witch lived in that house, they called her the Grass Widow because she entertained men like she was running a roadhouse; she lived alone, though, with her eighteen cats as company. Thalia knew that the Grass Widow had wanted to buy the old sow for the past two years, but her parents had refused because she wasn't offering enough money and the

Cantys were raising her to be the biggest, most expensive hog in the county. And now, what was the purpose? The sow was fly-ridden and rotting. Worthless. Didn't matter if the Grass Widow killed it or not. It recalled for her a saying her daddy often said in moments like this:

"How the mighty are fallen." Even among the kingdom of pigs.

Lucius pulled her closer to him and leaned down a bit to whisper in her ear. "I ain't sayin' anything, Thay, but the Widow wanted that sow and she knew Daddy wasn't never gonna sell it to her. I heard she hexed the Horleichs' cows so they dried up."

"Ain't no witches," Thalia said, disturbed by her brother's suspicions. "Just fairy tales, that's what Mama says."

"And the Bible says there is. And since the Bible's the only book ever written with truth in it, you better believe there's witches, and they're just like her, mean and vengeful and working hexes on anything they covet." Lucius put his hand across his sister's shoulder and hugged her in close to him again. He kissed her gently on her forehead, right above her small red birthmark. "Don't you be scared of her, though, Thay, we're God-fearin' people, and she can't hurt us 'less we shut out our lights under bushels."

Thalia knew her brother well enough to know he never lied. So the old Grass Widow was a witch. She looked at her brother, then back to the pig. "We gonna bury her?"

"The sow? Naw, too much work. Let's get it in the wheelbarrow and take it around near the coops. Stinks so bad, nobody's gonna notice a dead pig, and then when Mama gets home in the mornin', I'll take the truck. We can drive the sow out to the Renderin' Man." This seemed a good plan, because Thalia knew that the Rendering Man could give them something in exchange for the carcass—if not money, then some other service or work. The Rendering Man had come by some time back for the old horse, Dinah, sick on her feet and worthless. He took Dinah into his factory, and gave Thalia's father three dollars and two smoked hams. She was aware that the Rendering Man had a great love for animals, both dead and alive, for he paid money for them regardless. He was a tall, thin man with a potbelly, and a grin like walrus's, two teeth thrusting down on either side of his lip. He always had red cheeks, like Santa Claus, and told her he knew magic. She had asked him (when she was younger), "What kind of magic?"

He had said, "The kind where you give me something, and I turn it into something else." Then he showed her his wallet. She felt it. He'd said, "It used to be a snake." She drew her hand back; looked at the wallet; at the Rendering Man; at the wallet; at her hand. She'd been only six or seven then, but she knew that the Rendering Man was someone powerful.

If anyone could help with the dead sow, he could.

The next morning was cool and the sky was fretted with strips of clouds. Thalia had to tear off her apron as she raced from the house to climb up beside Lucius in the truck. "I didn't know you's gonna take off so quick," she panted, slamming the truck door shut beside her. "I barely got the dishes done."

"Got to get the old sow to the Rendering Man, or we may as well just open a bottleneck fly circus out back." Thalia glanced in the back; the sow lay there peacefully, so different from its brutal, nasty dumb animal life when it would attack anything that came in its pen. It was much nicer dead. "What's it, anyways?" she asked.

"Thay, honey?"

"Renderin'."

"Oh," Lucius laughed, turning down the Post Road, "it's taking animals and things and turning them into something else."

"Witchcraft's like that"

"Naw, not like that. This is natural. You take the pig, say, and you put it in a big pot of boiling water, and the bones, see, they go over here, and the skin goes over there, and then, over there's the fat. Why you think they call a football a pigskin?"

Thalia's eyes widened. "Oh my goodness."

"And hog bristle brushes—they get those from renderin'. And what else? Maybe the fat can be used for greasing something, maybe…"

"Goodness' sakes," Thalia said, imitating her mother's voice. "I had no idea. And he pays good money for this, does he?"

"Any money on a dead sow's been eaten by maggots's good money, Thay."

It struck her, what happened to the old horse. "He kill Dinah, too? Dinah got turned into fat and bones and skin and guts even whilst she was alive? Somebody use her fat to grease up their wheels?"

Lucius said nothing; he whistled faintly.

She felt tears threatening to bust out of her eyes. She held them back. She had loved that old horse, had seen it as a friend. Her father had lied to her about what happened to Dinah; he had said that she just went to retire in greener pastures out behind the Rendering Man's place.

She took a swallow of air. "I wished somebody'd told me, so I coulda said a proper goodbye."

"My strong, brave little sister," Lucius said, and brought the truck to an abrupt stop. "Here we are." Then he turned to her, cupping her chin in his hand the way her father did whenever she needed talking to. "Death ain't bad for those that die, remember, it's only bad for the rest of us. We got to suffer and carry on. The Dead, they get to be at peace in the arms of the Lord. Don't ever cry for the Dead, Thay, better let them cry for us." He brought his hand back down to his side. "See, the Rendering Man's just sort of a part of Nature. He takes all God's creatures and makes sure their suffering is over, but makes them useful, even so."

"I don't care about the sow," she said. "Rendering Man can do what he likes with it. I just wish we coulda et it." She tried to hide her tears, sniffed them back; it wasn't just her horse Dinah, or the sow, but something about her own flesh that bothered her, as if she and the sow could be in the same spot one day, rendered, and she didn't like that idea.

The Rendering Man's place was made of stone, and was like a fruit crate turned upside down—flat on top, with slits for windows. There were two big smokestacks rising up from behind it like insect feelers; yellow-black smoke rose up from one of them, discoloring the sky and making a stink in the general vicinity. Somebody's old mule was tied to a skinny tree in the front yard. Soon to be rendered, Thalia thought. Poor thing. She got out of the truck and walked around to pet it. The mule was old; its face was almost white, and made her think of her granny, all white of hair and skin at the end of her life.

The Rendering Man had a wife with yellow hair like summer wheat; she stood in the front doorway with a large apron that had once been white, now filthy, covering her enormous German thighs tight as skin across a drum.

"*Guten Tag,*" the lady said, and she came out and scooped Thalia into her arms like she was a tin angel, smothered her scalp with kisses. "*Ach, mein Liebchen.* You are grown so tall. Last I saw you, you was barely over with the cradle."

Just guessing as to what might be smeared on the woman's apron made Thalia slip through her arms again so that no dead animal bits would touch her. "Hello, ma'am," she said in her most formal voice.

The lady looked at her brother. "Herr Lucius, you are very grown. How is your *Mutter?*"

"Just fine, ma'am," Lucius said, "we got the old sow in the back." He rapped on the side of the truck. "Just went last night. No good eating. Thought you might be interested."

"*Ach, da,* yes, of naturally we are," she said, "come in, come in, children, Father is still at the table *mit* breakfast. You will have some ham? Fresh milk and butter, too. Little Thalia, you are so thin, we must put some fat on those bones," and the Rendering Man's wife led them down the narrow hall to the kitchen. The kitchen table was small, which made its crowded plates seem all the more enormous: fried eggs on one, on another long fat sausages tied with ribbon at the end, then there were dishes of bread and jam and butter. Thalia's eyes were about to burst just taking it all in—slices of fat-laced ham, jewels of sweets in a brightly painted plate, and two pitchers, one full of thick milk, and the other, orange juice.

The Rendering Man sat in a chair, a napkin tucked into his collar. He had a scar on the left side of his face, as if an animal had scratched him deeply there. Grease had dripped down his chin and along his neck. He had his usual grin and sparkle to his eyes. "Well, my young friends. You've brought me something, have you?"

His wife put her hand over her left breast as if she was about to faint, her eyes rolling to the back of her head. "*Ach,* a great pig, *Schatze.* They will want more than just the usual payment for that one."

Thalia asked, "Can I have a piece of ham, please?" The Rendering Man patted the place beside him. "Sit with me, both of you, yes, Eva, bring another chair. We will talk business over a good meal, won't we, Lucius? And you, sweet little bird, you must try my wife's elegant pastries. She learned how to make them in her home country, they are so light and delicate, like the sundried skin of a dove, but I scare you, my little bird, it is not a dove, it is bread and sugar and butter!"

After she'd eaten her fill, ignoring the conversation between her brother and the Rendering Man, Thalia asked, "How come you pay good money for dead animals, Mister?"

He drank from a large mug of coffee, wiped his lips, glanced at her brother, then at her. "Even dead, we are worth something, little bird."

"I know that. Lucius told me about the fat and bones and whiskers. But folks'd dump those animals for free. Why you pay money for them?"

The Rendering Man looked at his wife, and they both laughed. "Maybe I'm a terrible businessman," he said, shaking his head. "But," he calmed, "you see, my pet, I can sell these things for more money than I pay. I am not the only man capable of rendering. There is competition in this world. If I pay you two dollars today for your dead pig, and

send you home with sweets, you will bring me more business later on, am I right?"

"I s'pose."

"So, by paying you, I keep you coming to me. And I get
more skins and fat and bones to sell to places that make
soap and dog food and other things. I would be lying if I
didn't tell you that I make more money off your pig than
you do. But it is a service, little bird."

"I see." Thalia nodded, finishing off the last of the
bacon. "It seems like a terrible thing to do."

"Thay, now, apologize for that." Lucius reached over and
pinched her shoulder.

She shrugged him off.

The Rendering Man said, 'it is most terrible. But this is
part of how we all must live our lives. Someone must do the
rendering. If not, everything would go to waste and we
would have dead pigs rotting with flies on the side of the
road, and the smell."

"But you're like a buzzard or something."

The man held his index finger up and shook it like a
teacher about to give a lesson. "If I saw myself as a buzzard or
jackal I could not look in the mirror. But others have said this
to my face, little bird, and it never hurts to hear it. I see myself
as a man who takes the weak and weary and useless empty
shells of our animal brethren and breathes new life into them,
makes them go on in some other fashion. I see it as a noble
profession. It is only a pity that we do not render ourselves,
for what a tragedy it is to be buried and left for useless, for
worm fodder, when we could be brushing a beautiful woman's
hair, or adorning her purse, or even, perhaps, providing shade
from the glare of a lamp so that she might read her book and

not harm her eyes. It is a way to soften the blow of death, you see, for it brings forth new life. And one other thing, sweet," he brought his face closer to hers until she could smell his breath of sausage and ham, "we each have a purpose in life, and our destiny is to seek it out, whatever the cost, and make ourselves one with it. It is like brown eyes or blond hair or short and tall, it is there in us, and will come out no matter how much we try to hide it. I did not choose this life; it chose me. I think you understand, little bird, yes. You and I know."

Thalia thought about what he'd said all the way home. She tried not to imagine the old sow being tossed in a vat and stirred up in the boiling water until it started to separate into its different parts. Lucius scolded her for trying to take the Rendering Man to task, but she ignored him. She felt like a whole new world had been opened to her, a way of seeing things that she had not thought of before, and when she stepped out of the truck, at her home, she heard the crunch of the grass beneath her feet differently, the chirping of crickets, too, a lovely song, and a flock of starlings shot from the side of the barn just as she tramped across the muddy expanse that led to the chicken coops— the starlings were her sign from the world that there was no end to life, for they flew in a pattern, which seemed to her to approximate the scar on the left-hand side of the Rendering Man's face.

It was like destiny.

She climbed up on the fence post and looked down the road. A dust wind was blowing across to the Grass Widow's house, and she heard the cats, all of them, yowling as if in heat, and she wondered if that old witch had really poisoned the pig.

THALIA WAS ALMOST TWENTY-NINE, and on a train in Europe, when she thought she recognized the man sitting across from her. She was now calling herself just Lia, and had not lived in Oklahoma since she left for New York in 1939 to work as a secretary—she'd taught herself shorthand and typing at the motel where her mother had worked. Then, during the war, Lucius died fighting in France, and her mother and father, whom she'd never developed much of a relationship with, called her back to the old farm. Instead, she took up with a rich and spoiled playboy who had managed to get out of serving in the military because of flatfeet, and went to live with him at his house overlooking the Hudson River. She went through a period of grief for the loss of her brother, after which she married the playboy in question. Then, whether out of guilt or general self-destruction, her husband managed to get involved in the war, ended up in a labor camp, and had died there not two weeks before liberation. She had inherited quite a bit of money after an initial fight with one of her husband's illegitimate children. It was 1952, and she wanted to see Germany now, to see what had happened, and where her husband of just a few months had died; she had been to Paris already to see the hotel where her brother supposedly breathed his last, suffering at the hands of the Nazis but dying a patriot, unwilling to divulge top secret information. She was fascinated by the whole thing: the war, Paris, labor camps, and Nazis.

She had grown lovely over the years; she was tall, as her father and brother had been, but had her mother's eyes, and had learned, somewhere between Oklahoma and New York, to project great beauty without having inherited much.

The man across from her, on the train, had a scar on the left-hand side of his face.

It sparked a series of memories for her, like lightning flashing behind her eyes. The stone house on the Post Road, the smokestacks, the mule in the front yard, an enormous breakfast that still made her feel fat and well-fed whenever she thought of it.

It was the Rendering Man from home.

On this train. Traveling through Germany from France. Now, what are the chances, she wondered, of that happening? Particularly after what happened when she was eleven.

Not possible, she thought.

He's a phantom. I'm hallucinating. Granny hallucinated that she saw her son Toby back from the First World War walking toward her even without his legs.

She closed her eyes; opened them. He was still there. Something so ordinary about him that she knew he was actually sitting there and not just an image conjured from her inner psyche.

He spoke first. "I know you, don't I?"

She pretended, out of politeness, that he must not be talking to her. There was a large German woman sitting beside her, with a little boy on the other side. The German woman nodded politely to her but didn't acknowledge the man across from them. Her little boy had a card trick that he was trying to show his mother, but she paid no attention.

"Miss? Excuse me?" he said.

Then it struck her: He spoke English perfectly, and yet he looked very German.

He grinned when she glanced back at him. "See? I knew

I knew you, when I saw you in the station. I said to myself, you have met that girl somewhere before. Where are you from, if I may ask?"

"New York," she lied, curious as to whether this really could possibly be the Rendering Man. How could it? He would have to be, what? Sixty? This man didn't seem that old, although he was not young by any stretch. "I'm a reporter."

He wagged his finger at her, like a father scolding his child. "You are not a reporter, miss, I think I am not saying you are a liar, I am only saying that that is not true. Where is your notebook? Even a pencil? You are American, and your accent is New York, but I detect a southern influence. Yes, I think so. I hope you don't mind my little game. I enjoy guessing about people and their origins." She felt uncomfortable, but nodded. "I enjoy games, too, to pass the time."

She glanced at the German woman who was bringing out a picnic for her son. Bread and soup, but no meat. There was not a lot of meat to go around even six years after the war.

The man said, "You are a woman of fortune, I think. Lovely jewelry, and your dress is quite expensive, at least here in Europe. And I heard you talking with the conductor—your French is not so good, I think, and your German is worse. You drew out a brand of cigarettes from a gold case, both very expensive. So you are on the Grand Tour of Europe, and like all Americans with time on their hands, you want to see the Monster Germany, the Fallen."

"Very perceptive," she said. She brought her cigarette case out and offered him one of its contents.

He shook his head. "I think these are bad for the skin and the breathing, don't you?"

She shrugged. "It all goes someday."

He grinned. "Yes, it does. The sooner we accept that, the better for the world. And I know your name now, my dear, my little bird, you are the little Thalia Canty from Moncure County, Oklahoma."

She shivered, took a smoke, coughed, stubbed the cigarette out. She had white gloves on her hands; she looked at them. She remembered the German wife's apron, smeared with dark brown stains. She didn't look up for a few minutes.

"I would say this is some coincidence, little bird," the Rendering Man said, "but it is not, not really. The real coincidence happened in the Alsace, when you got off the train for lunch. I was speaking with a butcher who is a friend of mine, and I saw you go into the cafe. I wouldn't have recognized you at all, for I have not seen you since you were a child, but you made a lasting impression on me that morning we had breakfast together. I saw it in you, growing, just as it had grown in me. Once that happens, it is like a halo around you. It's still there; perhaps someone might say it is a play of light, the aurora borealis of the flesh, but I can recognize it. I followed you back to the train, got my ticket, and found where you were seated. But still I wasn't positive it was you, until just a moment ago. It was the way you looked at my face. The scar. It was a souvenir from a large cat that gouged me quite deeply. No ordinary cat, of course, but a tiger, sick, from the circus. The tiger haunts me to this day, by way of the scar. Do you believe in haunting? Ah, I think not, you are no doubt a good Disciple of Christ and do not believe that a circus cat could haunt a man. Yet I see it sometimes in my dreams, its eyes, and teeth, and the paw reaching up to drag at my flesh. I wake my wife up at night, just so she will stay up with me and make sure there is no tiger there. I know it is dead, but I have learned in life that sometimes these angels, as I call them (yes, dear, even the tiger is an angel, for it had some message for me), do not stay dead too long. Perhaps I am your angel, little bird; you must admit it is strange to meet someone from just around the bend on the other side of the world."

She looked at him again but tried not to see him in focus, because she felt the pressing need to avoid this man at all costs. "I'm sorry, sir. You do have me pegged, but I can't for the life of me place you."

He smiled, his cheeks red. He wore a dark navy coat, and beneath it, a gray shirt. When he spoke again, it was as if he had paid no attention to her denial. "My wife, Eva, she is in Cologne, where we live, and where I should be going now. We came to Germany in 1935, because Eva's parents were ill and because, well, you must remember the unfortunate circumstance. I was only too glad to leave Oklahoma, since I didn't seem to get along with too many people there, and Germany seemed to be a place I could settle into. I found odd jobs, as well as established a successful rendering business again. And then, well ..." He spread his hands out as if it were enough to excuse what happened to Germany. "But I knew you and I would meet again, little bird, it was there on your face. Your fascination and repulsion—is that not what magnets do to each other, pull and push? Yet they are meant to be together. Destiny. You see, I saw your brother before he died, and I told him what was to come."

She dropped all pretense now. 'What kind of game are you playing?"

"No game, Thalia Canty."

"Lia Fallon. Thalia Canty died in Oklahoma in the thirties."

"Names change through the years, even faces, but you are the little bird."

"And you are the Rendering Man."

He gasped with pleasure. "Yes, that would be how you know me. Tell me, did you run because of what you did?"

She didn't answer. "What about Lucius?"

The Rendering Man looked out the dark window as a town flew by. Rain sprinkled across the glass. "First, you must tell me."

"All right. I forgave myself for that a long time ago. I was only eleven, and you were partly responsible."

"Did I use the knife?"

She squinted her eyes. Wished she were not sitting there. "I didn't know what I was doing, not really."

"Seventeen cats must've put up quite a howl."

"I told you. I didn't know what I was really doing."

"Yes, you did. How long after before you ran?"

"I ran away four times before I turned seventeen. Only made it as far as St. Louis most of the time."

"That's a long way from home for a little girl."

"I had an aunt there. She let me stay a month at a time. She understood."

"But not your mama and daddy," he said with some contempt in his voice. "A woman's murdered, we all called her the Grass Widow. Remember? Those Okies all thought she was a witch. She was sad and lonely. Then all she was was dead. She and her cats, chopped up and boiled."

"Rendered," she said.

"Rendered. So they come for me, and thank God I was able to get my wife out of the house safely before the whole town burned it down."

"How was I to know they'd come after you?"

He was silent, but glaring.

"I didn't mean for you to get in trouble."

"Do you know what they did to me?" he asked.

She nodded.

He continued, "I still have a limp. That's my way of joking; they broke no bones. Bruises and cuts, my hearing was not good until 1937, and I lost the good vision in my right eye—it's just shadows and light on that side. Pain in memory brings few spasms to the flesh. It is the past. Little bird, but you think I am only angry at you. All those years, you are terrified you will run into me, so when you can, you get out for good. I was sure that little town was going to make another Bruno Hauptmann out of me. Killing a sad widow and her pets and boiling them for bones and fat. But even so, I was not upset with you, not too much. Not really. Because I knew you had it in you, I saw it that day, that we were cut from the same cloth, only you had not had the angel cross your path and tell you of your calling. It is not evil or dark, my sweet, it is the one calling that gives meaning to our short, idiotic lives; we are the gardeners of the infinite, you and I."

"Tell me about my brother," she pleaded softly. The German woman next to her seemed to sense the strangeness of the conversation, and took her son by the hand and led him out of the cabin.

"He did not die bravely," the Rendering Man said, "if that's what you're after. He was hit in the leg, and when I found him, he had been in a hotel with some French girl, and was a scandal for bleeding on the sheets. I was called in by my commander, and went about my business."

"You worked with the French?"

He shook his head. "I told you, I continued my successful rendering business in Germany, and expanded to a factory just outside of Paris in '43. Usually the men were dead, but sometimes, as was the case with your brother, little bird, I had to stop their hearts. Your brother did not recognize me, and I only recognized him when I saw his identification. As he died, do you know what he told me? He told me that he was paying for the sins that his sister had committed in her lifetime. He cried like a little baby. It was most embarrassing. To think, I once paid him two dollars and a good sausage for a dead pig."

Lia stood up. "You are dreadful," she said. "You are the most dreadful human being who has ever existed upon the face of the earth."

"I am, if you insist. But I am your tiger, your angel," the Rendering Man said. He reached deep into the pocket of his coat and withdrew something small. He handed it to her.

She didn't want to take it, but grabbed it anyway.

"It is his. He would've wanted you to have it."

She thought, at first, it was a joke, because the small leather coin purse didn't seem to be the kind of thing Lucius would have.

When she realized what it was, she left the cabin and walked down the slender hall, all the way to the end of the train. She wanted to throw herself off, but instead stood and shivered in the cold wet rain of Germany, and did not return to the cabin again.

She could not get over the feeling that the part of the coin purse that drew shut resembled wrinkled human lips.

"HE'S HERE," the old woman said.

She heard the squeaking wheels of the orderly's cart down the corridor.

"He's here. I know he's here. Oh, dear God, he's here."

"Will you shut up, lady?" the old man in the wheelchair said.

An orderly came by and moved the man's chair on down the hall.

The old woman could not sit up well in bed. She looked at the green ceiling. The window was open. She felt a breeze. It was spring. It always seemed to be spring. A newspaper lay across her stomach. She lifted it up. Had she just been reading it? Where were her glasses?

Oh, there. She put them on. Looked at the newspaper. It was *The New York Times.* The date of the paper was March 24, 1994.

She called out for help, and soon an orderly (the handsome one with the bright smile) was there, like a genie summoned from a lamp.

"I thought I saw a man in this room," she said.

"Mrs. Ehrlich, nobody's in here."

"I want you to check that closet. I think he's there."

The orderly stepped over to the closet. He opened the door, and moved some of the clothes around. He turned to smile at her.

"I'm sure I saw him there. Waiting. Crouching," she said. "But he may have slipped beneath the bed." Again, a check beneath the bed. The orderly sat down in the chair beside the bed. "He's not here."

"How old am I? I'm not very old, really, I'm not losing my wits yet, am I? Dear God in heaven, am I?"

"No, Mrs. Ehrlich. You're seventy-one going on eleven."

"Why'd you say that?"

"What?"

"Going on eleven. Why eleven? Is there a conspiracy here?"

"No, ma'am."

"You know him, don't you? You know him and you're just not saying."

"Are you missing Mr. Ehrlich again?"

"Mr. Ehrlich, Mr. Vanik, Mr. Fallon, one husband after another, young man, nobody can miss them because nobody can remember them. Are you sure I haven't had an unannounced visitor?"

The orderly shook his head.

She closed her eyes, and when she opened them, the orderly was gone. It had grown dark. Where is my mind? She thought. Where has it gone? Why am I here at seventy-one when all my friends are still out in the world living; why, my granny was eighty-eight before senility befell her, how dare life play with me so unfairly.

She reached for her glass of water and took a sip.

Still, she thought she sensed his presence in the room with her, and could not sleep the rest of the night. Before dawn, she became convinced that the Rendering Man was somewhere nearby lurking; she tried to dress, but the illness had taken over her arms to such a great extent that she could not even get her bra on.

She sat up, half-naked, on her bed, the light from the hallway like a spotlight for the throbbing in her skull.

"I have led a wicked life," Thalia whispered to the morning. She found the strength at five-thirty to get her dressing gown around her shoulders and to walk down the hall, sure that she would see him at every step.

The door to Minnie Cheever's door was open, which was odd, and she stepped into it.

"Minnie?"

Her friend, nearly ninety-three, was not in her bed. Thalia looked around, and finally found Minnie lying on the floor near the bathroom. Thalia checked her friend's pulse; she was alive, but barely. Thalia's limbs hurt, but she used Minnie's wheelchair to get Minnie down the hallway, onto the elevator, and down to the basement, where the endless kitchen began.

They found her there, two cooks and one orderly, like that, caught at last.

Thalia Canty, chopping Minnie Cheever up into small pieces and dropping each piece into one of several large pots, boiling with water, on the stove.

She turned when she heard their footsteps, and smiled. "I knew you were here. We're like destiny, you and me, Mister Rendering Man, but you'll never have me, will you?" She held her arms out for them to see. "I scraped off all the fat and skin I could, Mister Rendering Man, you can have all these others, but you ain't never gonna get my hide and fat and bones to keep useful in this damned world. You hear me? You ain't never gonna render Thalia, and this I swear!"

She tried to laugh, but it sounded like a saw scraping metal. The joke was on the Rendering Man, after all, for she would never, ever render herself up to him.

It took two men to hold her down. In a short time, her heart gave out.

When her body was taken to the morgue, it was discovered that she'd been scraping herself raw, to within an eighth of an inch of her internal organs.

❧

A YOUNG WOMAN, a candy striper named Nancy, going through Thalia's closet to help clean it out, discovered the dried skins beneath a pile of filthy clothing.

The skins, from Thalia's own body, sewn together, crudely representing a man. Thalia had drawn eyes and lips and a nose on the face — and a scar.

Those who found Thalia Canty, as well as the candy striper who fainted at the sight of the skin, later thought they saw her sometimes, in their bedrooms, or in traffic, or just over their shoulders, clutching her rendering knife.

She would live in their hearts forever.

An angel.

A tiger.

The Fruit of Her Womb

I woke up one morning, after a nightmare, and turned to my wife.

"I feel like there's no hope left in the world," I said.

I felt all my entire long life seep through in that one sentence.

Her voice was calm, and she held me.

"Old man," she said, her sweet mocking. "You need to get your joy back."

After several such mornings, she and I had to make some decisions.

We had some savings, and the leftovers of my inheritance. I felt it was time to retire to the country.

When I tallied our savings, I told Jackie it was time for the move while we were still fairly young and able, and she went along with it because she always adapted herself to whatever was available.

The truth was, I had lost my love for life, and I needed a plot of earth. I just didn't know where or when I would need to be buried in it.

I wanted a small town, with woods, with groves, with jays bickering at the window and the sound of locusts in the summer evening—and then, when I turned seventy or so, I wanted to die.

These were my projections, and having been an actuary, I knew that given my height, weight, and predilection for tobacco, that death by stroke might come in the next decade.

And we found all the birds and gardens and quiet in Groveton, not two hours out of Los Angeles, and more, we found a house and I found a reason to wake up in the morning.

The house was beautiful on the outside, a mess within. It had a name: *Tierraroja*, because one of the owners (there had been nine) was named Redlander and decided to Spanish it up a bit in keeping with the looks of the place.

An adobe, built in the forties, it had been a featured spread in *Sunset*, The Magazine of Western Living, in 1947, as "typifying the California blend of Spanish and Midwestern influences." Its rooms were few, considering its length: three small bedrooms, a modest living room and kitchen, but enormous corridors connecting each chamber around a courtyard full of bird of paradise, trumpet-flower vine, and bougainvillea.

Beyond the adobe wall out back, criss-crossed thatches of blackberry vines, dried and mangled by incompetent gardeners, providing natural nests for foxes and opossums. All this opened onto a vast field, empty except for a few rows of orange trees, the last of its grove—ownership unknown, the field separated the property from a neighbor who lived a good four acres away.

We loved it, and the price was reasonable, as we'd just

moved out of a place in the city that was smaller and more expensive.

Jackie had a carpenter redo the kitchen cabinets the same day escrow closed. I asked the realtor about the empty field, and he reassured me that the owner, who was a very private person, had no wish to sell the vacant lot. We would have the kind of house we had dreamed of, where I could relax in my relatively early retirement (at sixty), and where Jackie could put in the art studio she'd dreamed of since she'd been twenty.

It was on the third day of our occupation of the place that we found the urn. It was ugly, misshapen from too much tossing about, a bit of faux Victoriana, dull green nymphs against a dark green background. Jackie found it at the back of the linen closet, behind some old Christmas wrapping papers that had been left behind, presumably by a previous resident. The urn was topped with a lid that looked as if it were an ashtray put to a new use, and sealed with wax.

My wife shook it. "Something inside."

"Here," I said, and she passed it to me. I gave it a couple of good shakes. "Rocks," I said. I sniff everything before I let it get too close to me; this is an odd habit at best, annoying at worst, and applies to clothes, my wife, the dog, and especially socks—a habit acquired in childhood from observing my father doing the same, and feeling a certain pride in a heightened nasal sense as if it were an inherited trait. So I put the urn to my nose. "Stinks. Like cat vomit." I looked at the pictures. Not just nymphs, but three nymphs dancing with ribbons between them. On closer inspection, I saw that the nymphs had rather nasty expressions on their faces. In one's hand was a spindle of thread, another held the thread out, and the last held a pair of scissors. "It's the Fates in some young aspect," I told my wife, remembering from my sketchy education in the Mediterranean myth pool. "See, this one spins the thread of life, this one measures it out, and this one cuts it. Or something like that."

Jackie didn't bother looking. She smiled and said, sarcastically, "You're such a classicist."

"It's pretty ugly," I said. I was ready to take it out to the trash barrel, but Jackie signaled for me to pass it to her.

"I want to keep it," she said, "I can use it for holding paintbrushes or something." Jackie was one of those people who hated to waste things; she would turn every old coffee can into something like a pencil holder or a planter, and once even tried to make broken glasses into some unusual sculpture.

My wife turned the garage into her studio. The garage door opened on both sides, so that while she painted, she could have an open air environment; the fumes would come up at me, in the bedroom, where I stayed up nights reading, waiting for her to come to bed. But she loved her studio, loved the painting, the fumes, the oils, the ability to look out into the night and find her inspiration. I played with my computer some nights, called some buddies now and again from the old job, and read every book I could on the history of the small California town to which we had come to enjoy the good life. I was even going to have a servant, of sorts: a gardener, named Stu, highly recommended by our realtor, to tend the courtyard and to keep the blackberry bushes, ever encroaching, in check, and to bring in ripe plums in August from the two small trees in the back. I was happy about this arrangement, because I knew nothing about dirt and digging and weeding, beyond the basics. And I didn't intend to spend my retirement doing something that I seemed incapable of. Stu and I got on, barely—he was not a man of many words, and, although only ten years or so younger than I, we seemed to have no common ground to even begin a conversation. He liked his plants and bushes, and I liked my books and solitude.

Within weeks of being settled, I knew I had nothing to do with my time. I found myself going into town on small, useless errands, to get paper clips, or to see if I could find *The New York Times* at some newsstand within a fifteen mile radius. The town, while not worth describing, was less planned than it was spontaneous; it had been a citrus boomtown before the Second World War, and after, it was a town for people to find cute places in, but to not do much else. From the freeway, it looked like stucco and smog, but from within, it was pretty, quaint, quiet, and even charming on a cool October afternoon. The library captivated my interests, since I had been a history teacher and was an avid reader. It was full of documents about the town and its architecture, fairly unique to southern California, because most of its buildings were a hundred years old rather than built since 1966.

I found our house, Tierraroja, had at least one story about it. This I learned, briefly, at first, from a local newspaper account from 1952. It seemed the Redlander family had left suddenly, and the house was empty; no one could discover the mystery of their whereabouts. When I went to the librarian, a man named Ed Laughlin, he asked me why I was so interested in the house.

"I live there," I said.

He smiled. "Yeah, right."

"No, really. My wife and I moved in the middle of September."

He chuckled. "Who's your realtor?"

I told him the name.

Again he laughed. "Should've known. She's been trying to unload that place for two years."

"Are there ghosts?" I asked, hoping that there might be just for something different.

He shook his head. "Nothing that unbelievable. Just that old Joe Redlander chopped up his wife and kids one night. Nobody knew it until about a year after they were gone. The new owners found body parts all over the place, hidden in secret places. They found Joe eventually up in Mojave, but he claimed he didn't do it. He'd found them like that, he said, but the police weren't buying because first off he ran and second off his prints were all over the ax. Heard he blew his brains out up in Atascadero or someplace like it."

I PARKED in front of my wife's studio; the doors were open, letting in the last of October sun, almost a light blue sunlight, through her canvases and jars, making her brown-gray hair seem almost cool and icy. I went up to her, kissed her, and looked at the painting she was doing. It was from memory, of the pond that had been behind her mother's house back in Connecticut. She had just put the light on the water; and it wasn't New England light, but sprays of California light. I waved to Stu, our gardener, who was trimming back what had in midsummer been a blossoming trumpet vine, but which was becoming, as winter approached, a tangle of gray sticks.

"He's so dedicated," Jackie said, "I think I'm going to ask him to sit for a portrait. His face—it has those wonderful crags in it. He's just about our age, but he looks younger, and then, those lines. And the way he holds the flowers sometimes." She shook her head in subtle awe, and I wondered if my wife was in the throes of a schoolgirl crush on our gardener.

"We had some murders in our house," I told her, figuring it was the best way to make her think of something other than Stu.

She grinned, shaking her head at me as if I'd been a bad boy. "Good God, you'd think you'd have better things to do than make up stories just to frighten me."

"No, really. I was down at the library. The guy who named our house killed his family. You're not afraid, are you?"

She gave me what I had come, through the years, to call her Look Of False Brain Damage. Then she set the large flat board she used as a palette down on the cement floor, and began dipping her brushes in turpentine.

"Well, I'm finished for the day," she said. "You making dinner, or me?"

I shrugged. "I guess I can. Spaghetti or chicken?"

"Spaghetti's fine," she said, and then, bending over, picked something up. It was the urn. "I still can't get this lid off. I've been prying and prying. Think my Mister Strongman can do it?"

She passed it to me. I made a brave attempt, but could not get the old ashtray off the urn.

"You tried melting the wax?"

She shook her head. "Not yet. You're so smart and strong," mocking me, "I'm sure you can get it open for me."

I gave the urn a good shake, and heard that thing inside it again. Hard. Like a large rock. "You know," I said, "this guy Redlander chopped his wife and kids up—there were three—and then put their body parts in weird places in the house. Maybe they didn't find all of them. Maybe one of them's in here. Maybe it's the missing hand of little Katy Redlander."

Jackie made a face. "Don't you dare try and scare me."

"Maybe," I said, "it's Mrs. Redlander's left breast, all hardened around the mummified nipple."

I didn't bother trying to open the urn until after dinner. Jackie went into the living room to watch TV, and I stayed in the kitchen. I turned on the gas stove and put the edge of the urn's top near it. Wax began dripping down into the flame, making blue hisses. When the wax seemed to be loosening enough, I pulled on the ashtray, and it made a sucking sound. Then I twisted it, and it came off. I wondered if, in fact, little Katy Redlander's missing hand might not be inside the urn. I sniffed at it, and it smelled of tobacco. I held the urn up and tipped it, and out dropped a smoking pipe.

I picked it up off the floor, setting the urn on the edge of the counter. I sniffed the pipe. Smelled like cherry tobacco. A very uninteresting find, although the pipe was quite beautifully carved in rich red wood, a satyr's face. A satyr, I thought, to chase the nymphs of fate on the outside of the urn. Carved clumsily, as if by a child, into the base of the satyr's bearded chin, were the initials "J. R."

Joe Redlander.

"So that's why it's covered with an ashtray," my wife said

when I showed her. "Somebody was trying to quit smoking."

"So he seals his pipe up and hides it."

"Or has someone else hide it for him."

"Joe Redlander," I said.

"Who?"

"The guy—you know, the guy I told you about."

"Oh, right. The Lizzie Borden of Groveton, California."

I paced about the room, holding the pipe in one hand, the urn in the other. Jackie kept shooing me around so she could watch TV in peace, but I kept crossing in front of her. "His wife wants him to quit smoking the pipe. But he wants it. So she seals it up and hides it. He begs her for it. He begs the kids, maybe even bribes them, to show him where Mommy put it. But the kids know better, or else they don't have a clue. And then, when it gets to be too much, he gets the ax he's chopped up all the wood with that afternoon, and he says, 'Dolores.'"

Jackie interrupted. "Dolores?"

"Whatever," I said. "Joe says, 'Nancy, if you don't tell me where my pipe is, I'm taking you and the kids out.' And she thinks he's joking, so she laughs, and he," and here I mimed whacking my invisible wife with the pipe.

As if she had a moment of supreme victory, Jackie said, "Ah, just like you and your pistachio ice cream?"

"I never chopped you up for that, did I?"

"You would've liked to. You were going to become a blimp the way you ate it. I did you a favor by throwing it out. The way you whined for days after that, you'd think I took away your soul."

I made a *Three Stooges* eye-poking gesture at her and an appropriate noise. "Okay, anyway, so then he goes to the kids, and they're screaming, so he does them, too. And to think, if he'd only looked behind the old wrapping paper…"

"The paper was old," Jackie said, "but I don't think it was from the fifties. And that pipe could've belonged to anybody. Jesus, Jim, you need a hobby."

"Look at the initials," I said to prove my case, passing the pipe over to her.

She looked at the pipe, its carved face, and then squinted at the satyr's beard.

"J. R.," I said, "Joe Redlander. The man who killed his family."

"Your initials, too, Mister Smartypants. Could be James Richter," she reminded me, "maybe the pipe's meant for you."

Later, I put some tobacco in the pipe (for I was an inveterate smoker) and lit up, as if this would give me some inspiration.

❧

I FOUND THE OLD CRIME, and the pipe and urn, occupying my thoughts after that. The wrapping paper wasn't from the fifties, I discovered, but a kind that was sold by Girl Rangers in the mid-seventies. So, I figured, someone else had found the urn, too, and had hidden it. Maybe someone else knew of its secret. I went to the linen closet and looked back at the cubbyhole where the urn had been secreted; I reached back to it and found that by pushing one of the shelves aside, there was another hiding area. I moved the towels around and brought the shelf out. I leaned forward and reached back into this newfound hole, and came up with only a wadded scrap of notebook paper. It was wrapped in a spider web, which I dusted off, and then unfolded the paper. It was yellowed, and the kind that had large gaps between the thin red lines—the kind of paper children use before they've become adept at rocker curves and the like. In scraggly block letters in ink, it had several figures written across it. It actually looked like a pictographic language, until I realized that it was not some ancient tongue recorded, but the doodlings of perhaps a six-year-old. At the bottom, an initial: "K." I folded it neatly and put it in my pocket. I would ignore it, perhaps throw it out. I didn't even tell Jackie about finding it, because I didn't want her to know the extent to which I was fascinated by the story of the Redlander family.

I went back and read the obituaries of the old local newspaper, *The Groveton Daily*. For 1952, March 17, it listed Virginia Redlander and her children, Eric, eleven, May Lynne, nine, and Katherine, seven. So there was a Katy Redlander after all, I thought, how clairvoyant of me to have guessed it, considering I couldn't predict weather or my own wife's mood with anything greater than five percent accuracy. So little Katy had written what looked like a highly stylized hieroglyphics and had put it back in her secret place, not far from the urn.

"Or maybe you're just bored to death," Jackie said when I finally showed her the wrinkled piece of paper that had occupied my mind for three nights in a row.

We were in bed, and she was feeling amorous, while I was being indifferent to sex. "These diagrams," I said, pointing to the one that looked as if it had an eye in the middle of it, with some kind of strange animal (a unicorn?) in its iris, "you think a second-grader really did this?"

"My exact question to you," my wife said, turning over finally. "I think, Jim, maybe you need to go back into teaching at least part-time or as a substitute, because you're driving yourself and me crazy with all this weirdness."

I hadn't even noticed how weird I had become in the past few nights. I looked around my side of the king-size bed, and there were books on Egyptology, and runes, and Greek mythology. I had checked out half the local library's classical section, because those diagrams of Katy's resembled a mix of mythic images, and I wondered if there were some key to it all.

But I was being weird. So I leaned into my wife, kissing her neck. "I love you," I said.

"I was sure you were enamored of Katy Redlander's ghost."

"I'll throw those things out tomorrow," I whispered, and she turned her face so I could kiss her, and we made love that night, but it was not like it had been when I'd felt more vital. I knew, at my age, I was still fairly young, but I did not believe it, and as my wife and I held each other, afterward, I wondered why it was not as interesting as when I was twenty, or thirty, or even forty, why sex and even food were pleasures that were losing their taste for me; and I wondered why life had to slip like that, why, I thought, looking out the window at the few deciduous trees in the yard, their leaves having turned the pale yellow of California autumn, why can't we be like leaves, more beautiful when we are closer to the ends of our lives?

I thought I saw something there, as I looked at the trees, something dark against the floodlights, not quite human, trotting away from the window as if it had just watched us.

IN THE MORNING I went to check the window, as if I would see footprints, but there were none. Jackie skipped her painting that day, and was going to drive into Los Angeles to visit with a friend, so I took to wandering. The empty field that bordered us beckoned me with its orange trees, for they held small but juicy yellow-green fruit, and I decided it was high time to pick an orange right from the tree. The grass in the field was just turning green again because of a recent rain, and I waded through it, mindful of snakes and fire ants. When I approached the fat orange trees, I glanced back at my house: It seemed tiny, like a house on the edge of a toy train track. The trees were powerfully aromatic, for some tiny white blossoms still clung to the branches; most of the oranges were wrinkled and inedible, but there were a few, at the highest branches, that were plump and only just mature. I got a stick and knocked on the uppermost branches until I managed to bat one down. It rolled into the rich earth that was dark and grassless between the several trees, and I went to retrieve it.

There, on the ground, someone had drawn, with a stick, one of the same diagrams I had seen on Katy's paper.

The eye with the unicorn.

I looked around the other trees, and by each of them, another drawing or diagram. A sketch of a dog? Or a pig? And then several lines with forked endings—snakes?

But something else, too, there, in the dirt, beneath one of the orange trees: an animal, torn up beyond recognition, the size of a small dog.

Dressed as if for a celebration with dozens of tiny

orange blossoms stitched with a gay red thread through its mouth and around its eyes, and sutured along its guts.

IT WAS A PIG, as best I could determine, because in spite of its mutilations, its corkscrew tail was intact, and rather than stink of slaughter, it smelled fragrant with orange and just the scent of mint and sweet pepper—both of which grew wild in any direction across the field.

Children, I thought, and then: Katy Redlander.

The conflicting thought: but she's dead.

Then: a playmate.

Some friend of hers from 1952, who giggled over arcane rituals they'd found in—a book? *The Golden Bough?* Or Jasper's *The Birth of Mythology!*

Some friend who grew up—would be, what? Forty-nine or so now? And still believed in ritual sacrifice in a sacred grove?

I had read reports of Satanic cults in surrounding towns, and of fringe fundamentalist groups that held snakes and drank poison—how far from that was this?

I left the animal there and went to spend the rest of the day in the library. I looked up pigs in both the Frazer and Jasper texts. In Frazer, pigs were associated with the Eleusinian Mysteries, the rites of Demeter, and the loss of Persephone for half the year—a resurrection cult. But it was in Jasper's *Birth of Mythology* that I struck gold. In the fifth chapter, on mystery cults, Jasper writes:

"What 20th century man fails to realize about these so-called 'cults' is that these rites brought the god or goddess closer to man, so that man, in his ignorance, would be inducted into the mystery of creation. The virgin would be buried with the other offerings for a moon, during which time the participants would dance and sing themselves into a frenzy, and fast, and often commit heinous acts as a way of unleashing the chaos of the human and divine soul, intermingled—all in the name of keeping the world spinning the correct way, of keeping it all in balance. Thus, when the virgin was buried alive, it was not an act of cruelty, but of unbound love for the child and for the very breath of life, for the virgin represented the eternal daughter, who died, was buried, and then resurrected into the arms of the Great Mother after a time in Hell. This is not so different from the rites of crucifixion, and burial of Christ, after all? And in this act, the young woman who was sacrificed mated with the God, and returned to impart wisdom to the other participants in the Mysteries…"

Beneath this were the diagrams I had found in the wadded paper.

On the following page, a color plate showing the urn, of which mine was an obvious replica, of what I had thought were the Three Fates, dancing.

The caption beneath it read: "The furies in disguise, dancing to lure youths into their circle, so that they might torment them into eternity."

I remembered a quote from somewhere: "Those whom the gods would punish, they first make mad." And the story of Orestes, who had brought tragedy and dishonor down upon his House, tormented by the Furies in their most horrible aspect.

Joe Redlander with an ax in his hand, holding down little Katy's neck while he went chop-chop-chop.

I could picture the house in disarray, the walls splattered

with red, the boy trying to crawl away even while his father slammed the ax into his skull; and the mother, dead, cradling her other daughter, as if both were sleeping on the small rug in the hallway.

I closed my eyes, almost weeping; when I opened them, I was still in the armchair of the reference room of the library. Ed Laughlin, the librarian I'd spoken with before, stood near me. He wore a pale suit that hid most of his paunch; his hair was slick and white, drawn back from the bald spot on top of his head. He squinted to read the cover of the book I had in my hands.

"You feeling okay?" he asked, then, before I could answer, he said, "Ah, the ancient world. Fascinating. Coincidentally, I hope you noticed who donated most of our reference works on mythology, particularly fertility cults."

He gestured for the book, and I handed it to him. He flipped it closed, then opened it to the inside cover. He passed it back to me.

I was not surprised.

The bookplate read: "From the Library of Joseph and Virginia Redlander."

"He kills his family and then donates books?" I asked.

Ed didn't smile. "Believe it or not, Joe was a smart man, well-read, quiet, but strong. Admired, here in town, too. When a man cracks, you never know where the light's gonna show through. I guess with Joe it just showed through a bit strong."

"Did you know them well?"

He shook his head. "Barely. I was involved in the library here, but also the County museum over in Berdoo. Joe was always nice. Careful with books, too. That's about how well

I knew him. A hello-goodbye-nice weather kind of thing. It bothers you too, though, huh?"

I assumed he meant living in the house, knowing about the murders. "Not too much. I find it more fascinating than frightening."

"Well, always got to be some mystery in life, anyway, stirs the blood up a little, but it seems strange to me she never showed."

I asked, "Who?"

"The oldest one. Kim. She was sweet and pretty. Fifteen. Some say she ran about a year before the killings—she may have had a boyfriend here, met on the sly because her folks were real strict about that kind of thing. Maybe she ran off with him. Maybe she did the killings, gossip was. But I don't think so—she was fifteen and sweet and small, like a little bird. Me, I think she got killed, too, only Joe, he did it somewhere else. I hope I'm wrong; I hope that pretty little girl is all grown up and living across the world and putting it all behind her best she can."

❧

MY WIFE WAS SITTING at her canvas, painting, and I arrived swearing, as I went through the area packed with art supplies that surrounded her. "Damn it all," I said, "this is the only garage in creation without garage things."

"Damn right," she responded, "now take your damn language and get the hell out of here." All of this in a calm, carefully modulated voice.

I gave a false laugh and slapped the inside wall with my hand. "Now, where in hell would a shovel be when I need one?"

Jackie pointed with her paintbrush to the courtyard. "He'd know, Mister Brainiac." She looked more beautiful now, with the late afternoon light on her hair, her face seeming unlined, like she always had, to me, and it amazed me, that moment, how love did that between two people: how it takes you out of time, and makes you virtually untouchable.

I turned in the direction of her pointing—it was to Stu, our gardener, kneeling beside the bird of paradise, trimming back the dying stems that thrust from between the enormous, stiff leaves. I went out into the yard. "You have a shovel I can borrow?"

He didn't hear me at first.

He was humming. When he noticed my shadow, he turned toward me.

He'd begun to look older than his age. Not on the surface of his skin (except in laugh and smile lines), but in something I'd seen mainly in cities: a hard life. Not difficult, for all lives are difficult to varying degrees and some people suffer with more relish than others; but hard, as if the lessons learned were not pleasant ones. I had always thought the gardening life would be a fairly serene one.

"I need a shovel," I repeated.

"No problem," he said, and stood. He led me out to his truck and reached in the back of it, withdrawing a hoe and a shovel. "I assume," he said, "You're planting."

"Just digging," I said.

He nodded, handed me the shovel, and set the hoe back down.

"You've done a good job around here," I said.

He almost smiled with pride, but another kind of pride

seemed to hold him back. "It's my life," he said simply, then returned to work.

I watched him go, his overalls muddy, the muscles in his back and shoulders so pronounced that he seemed to ripple like something dropped into still water. Then I turned. I didn't know if I was going to bury a dead animal, or to dig something up, something that had been in the ground for four decades. I used the shovel to press my way through the blackberry bush fence that had become thin with autumn, and headed into the field.

The stink of the dead pig came back to me, along with the scent of its orange blossom garlands. There was a wind from downfield, and it brought with it these, and other smells: of car exhaust, of pies baking, of rotting oranges and other fruit ripening. It almost made bearable the task I was about. When I got to the brief clutch of orange trees, I saw the flies had devoured much of the dead animal, but, oddly, the local coyotes had left it alone.

Behind me, a man's voice: "You planning on burying it?"

I turned; it was Stu, the gardener. He shrugged. "Decided to follow you out here. Figured you could use some help."

He reached up to a branch of one of the trees and plucked off a small blossom. He brought it to his nose, inhaled, and then to his lips. It seemed to me that he kissed the blossom before letting it fall.

"Do you know anything about this?" I asked, indicating the pig. "Local kids?"

Stu shook his head. He had kind but weary eyes, as if he'd been on the longest journey and had seen much, but now wanted only sleep. "You won't be burying the pig, will you, Mr. Richter?"

"No," I said.

"What the hell," he said. "I know you know about it."

"What's that?"

"I hear her sometimes," he said, "when I touch the leaves."

"Who?"

He looked dead at me, almost angrily. "I don't have nothing to hide. I didn't put her there." He pointed to the ground beneath the dead pig.

"The dead girl."

He whispered, "Not dead." His eyes seemed to grow smaller, lids pressing down hard, like pressing grapes for wine, tears. "I don't believe it."

"You were her friend," I said.

"I love her. I always will love her." Stu wiped at his eyes. "Look around. This field used to be nothing. Dirt. Nothing would grow. No orange trees. And your house, dead all around, a desert. But she's done this." He spread his arms out wide, as if measuring the distance of the earth.

"Did you do it?" I asked, even though I didn't want to.

"I killed the pig, if that's what you're asking. It's an offering."

"To whom? To Kim Redlander?" I glanced at the ground, wondering how deep she had been buried; buried alive for a mystery more ancient than what was written down in a book.

"To the goddess," he said.

We went out into the field, as two farmers might after a long day of work, and spoke of the past.

He said, "I have faith in this. I have faith. It wasn't

strong at first. He told me he and her mother went all crazy and it was their festival time or something, and what he did to the other kid — and to Kim — was because she didn't come up that spring. He went wild, Joe did. I read all the books, later, and I came to a kind of understanding. I spoke to Joe before he killed himself. He lost his faith, you know? He didn't believe anymore. But I had nothing but faith. I know she's there. Look." He showed me the palm of his dirt-smeared hand. "She's in the earth, I can see her, there."

Joe Redlander and his family buried their daughter alive, I thought.

For the Mother of Creation, buried her in the earth, Persephone going to the underworld to be with her sworn consort, and they must have expected her to return in the spring. A family of religious nuts, and one teenage boy, hopelessly in love with a girl.

In love forever.

"It never happened," Stu said, "that's what her dad told me. They waited in the spring, and she didn't return. But I knew she was still here. I know she'll come back, one fine spring day. Till then, gardening seems to bring me closer to her."

"She's dead, Stu. I know you weren't responsible. But she's dead. It's been over forty years." I was shivering a little, because I sensed the truth in his story.

He looked across the land, back to the orange trees. "She's in everything here, everything. You may not believe, but I do. I've known things. I've seen things. She's down there, fifteen, beautiful, her hands touching the roots of the trees. She's going to come up one day. I absolutely know it."

As we both stood there, I knew that I was going to have to fire Stu, because there was something unbalanced in his story, in his fervor. I didn't think I could bear to look out the windows and see him gardening, thinking of love and loss as he tended flowers.

I knew I would lose sleep for many nights to come, looking out at that field, wondering.

THEN, one night the following April, someone set fire to the field, and in spite of the best efforts of the local firemen, my wife and I awoke the next morning and found we were living next door to a blackened wasteland. I got my morning coffee and went to the edge of the field, near the road. The orange trees were standing, but had been turned to crouching embers. I walked across dirt, stepping around the bits of twig that continued to give off breaths of fugitive smoke.

Where the girl had been buried: a deep gouge in the earth.

I watched the field after that but saw nothing special. In a month new grass was growing, and by summer, only through the dark bald patches could anyone tell that there'd been a fire at all.

And today, while my wife painted a picture of the courtyard, I went into the garage and found an old tool, a scythe. I took it up and went out into the field to mow. This action was not taken because of some fear or knowledge, for the Mystery remained—I didn't know if some animal had been digging at the hole where Kim Redlander was offered to the world, or if Stu himself had dug her up days before, moving rotting bones to another resting place. I didn't go to the field with any knowledge. I went singing into the field, cutting the hair of the earth, propelled by an urge that seemed older than any other.

Some have called this instinct the Mystery, but the simpler term is Stu's:

Faith.

I swiped the scythe across the fruit of her womb, then gave thanks and praise to the Mother all that day, for I could feel Her now, walking among her children; I spilled my own blood in the moistened dirt for Her.

My wife called to me, waving from the yard, and I turned, holding fast to the bloodied scythe, while I heard a young girl whisper in my ear that faith demands sacrifice.

Life was precious, for that moment, full of meaning, and wonder.

I walked wearily but gladly across the field, and when I reached my wife, her face brightened.

"You've found it," she said.

"What's that?"

"Your joy," and she seemed truly happy for me.

"I have."

I thought of Joe Redlander, and Stu, and Kim, the believers who brought me to this place.

The scythe seemed to shine like a crescent moon in my hand as I brought it across my wife's neck.

The Night Before Alec Got Married

You can never be too sure or too stupid, but you *can* be too horny—Alec Delbanco, he was smart, but men are never very smart in that one area, and it got him right where you don't want to be got, not if you're twenty-four and on the run because something's after you, only it doesn't have a name and maybe it doesn't even have a face but you can see it sometimes in their faces looking out at you like it's some kind of tourist on a world cruise and you're one of the Wonders of the World to It.

You call it an *It* because you don't know if It's been noticed by anyone else, and you can't really talk about It, because if you did, maybe that's when It would get you.

It got Alec that night, and he didn't even have to say one word about it. Boy, was he smart, he was practically Phi-Fucking-Beta Kappa from Stanford, and then the job with Kelleher-Darden with an eighty-thousand-a-year salary for a twenty-two-year-old asshole you used to get drunk with—well, everybody figured Alec had just grabbed the golden ring and had not let go.

And handsome! He'd been a stud since the age of twelve, if you remembered far back enough when every girl you'd ever had a crush on seemed to only want to get near you so they could get within breathing distance of your friend.

Still, Alec Delbanco never forgot a friend, and you got some fringe benefits from knowing him all those years, beautiful girls who wouldn't normally give you the time of day all around you—you couldn't touch them, of course, not in the light of day, not with them in the room, that is, but, oh! when the lights were out and you were alone in bed with your hand and a little imagination—you had them all every which way but loose!

You loved Alec, though, really loved him.

Like a brother, I mean, because you'd practically grown up with him since you could remember. He was better than a brother, too, because your own brothers were kind of missing something in the compassion department.

I wouldn't *fuck* a guy, no way, but if I *had* to fuck a guy —I mean, like the Nazis had me in this torture rack and told me I'd have to fuck a guy or get it cut off, well, I couldn't fuck just anyone—it would have to be Alec, and not just 'cause he was pretty, but because I have feelings for him—but not like you think.

Once, in the showers after gym, he was leaning around to get his towel and I swear to God this is true, I thought he was a girl. From the back, he's all lean and muscular. I thought he looked like, you know, one of those Olympic women swimmers, taut and strong but kind of attractive, too.

So, yeah, if pressed into it, I guess you could say I'd do him.

But this isn't about me or what I would do if the Fourth Reich came along—and it just might if you read the papers —it's about Alec and the night before he got married. His girl, Luce, was out with a whole gaggle down at the marina getting toasted on margaritas and opening cute little presents, while you and me were over on Sunset trying to find just the right pro to come in and do a little dance over Alec's face when he least suspected it. I didn't like Luce too much—she was always kind of a bitch to me, almost like she thought I wanted Alec more than she did. I've got to be honest here, I would've preferred Alec to marry a hooker and at least be happy rather than wed Lucille C. St. Gerard, a fifth generation Californian from Sacramento who debuted at every second-rate cotillion north of Bakersfield.

So we cruise Sunset, all the way from, say, La Cienega up to Raleigh Heights, and it's getting close to nine—you'd think every working girl in the world would be out by that time—Saturday night, party night, but we only see a bunch of tired old dogs pounding the pavement. You and me, we're doing St. Pauli Girl, but keeping the bottles low so the cops don't notice, when I see what I think is just about the most beautiful piece of work this side of the Pacific and I slam on the brakes and cross a lane to park.

"Look at her, holy mother of fuck, look at her," I say, and barely remember to put on the parking brake. I leap out of the Mustang—it's a convertible—and practically dive right over to her. She's got everything, and packed tight: a nice rack of tits, thin waist, and child-bearing hips.

"Hey, little boy," she says, "you want some sugar in your coffee tonight?"

I've never picked up a whore, so I feel real tongue-tied.

"You want a date?" She's got teeth all the way down her

throat, it seems, big white flashy teeth with a couple of gold caps in the way back. She's practically steaming there like an oyster out of the fish market, and I start to feel like a twelve-year-old of rage hormones and dripping wick.

"Listen," I say, "I got this friend. Alec."

She looks at you in the car. "That him? He's cute."

"No, no, that's not him. We're throwing a bachelor party tonight. We need a stripper."

"I can do that. I can do all of you boys."

"Well, more than a stripper," I say.

She shrugs. "I can do that, too."

"We want you to get him alone and, you know…" I say.

She smiles. "A dance and a fuck? It'll cost you."

"Not just a dance and not just a fuck, okay? We want the Dance of Seven Veils, like Salome did, we want you to really get him to want you, and then it's got to be more than fireworks, more than an explosion, it's got to be the Big O."

"The Big O?"

"You know, the Orgasm at the End of the Universe. The Big One. The kind that guys dream about in their sleep, the kind that most of us never get."

She looks at me sideways, like maybe I'm some kind of creep with diarrhea of the mouth. "You just talking? You don't really want the Big O, nothin' like that, do you?"

I shake my head. "Every trick you got. Think you can do it?"

She has a look in her eyes like she's thinking, but cagily —she has a few secrets, I guess, and she guards them. Her eyes are muddy brown, and when she looks back at me, they look like tiny little pebbles, hard and round.

"Baby," she says, "I think I can do anything. You pay, I'm gonna make sure it happens." She glances down the street. There's a big fat guy wearing a Hawaiian shirt. "My manager," she says. "You need to talk with him, I think. I ain't too good at the business side of things."

Because I don't want to talk to him, I get you to do it, and the whole thing's arranged, even though it's going to cost us four hundred bucks, plus whatever she makes in her dance and if it goes over two hours, another four hundred. Two hundred *in advance*, so I pay the pimp and we give him the address, tell him to be there at eleven and then we head on back to the party.

Now, this is the part where I'm really stupid, I guess, but you can't have a stripper come to the party without giving somebody an address.

But I guess this pimp looks at the money and figures there's more where that came from—so he must've gotten this idea—and I'm only assuming.

You and me, we look like nice preppie kind of guys, shit, we practically have ties on from work, and I'm wearing five hundred dollar Italian shoes.

So he decides that when he takes his girl over, he better pack something, because you never know how much cash you can get out of rich, scared, drunk guys at a bachelor party. I don't know a thing about guns, but this pimp probably had the automatic kind, and I figure that's how you got two of your fingers shot off before midnight.

But I'm getting ahead of myself—it's easy to do when you're spilling your guts and you can't always remember the sequence of events; especially if you're trying to second-guess everyone around you. The thing with your fingers, it didn't happen until about eleven fifty-five, and the thing with Luce, that happened just before ten, after we'd gotten back, hoisted a few more St. Pauli Girls and watched Long Jean Silver and her amazing stump-screwing of another woman in one of the six videos you rented from that scuzzy video store down in Long Beach. But something happened before even that, and that was when we stopped for more beer at 7-Eleven and I bought a bunch of multicolored rubbers, all fancy, and then pricked them full of holes and you and I laughed our heads off thinking about Alec and Luce on their honeymoon, thinking they were doing some family planning by wearing the rubbers. I don't think I've ever laughed so hard.

So I stuff the rubbers in my jacket pocket. As I'm pulling out of the *7-Eleven*, a car almost hits the Mustang, then swerves and crashes into a wall; the front half is all crushed, but the driver seems okay.

"Should we call for help?" you ask, and I say, "Oh, right, like the cops are gonna love the beer in the car and all." So we pass this woman in the car, and she looks at us for a second, and I got to tell you, I will never, as long as I live, forget that look. Women are like this swamp or something, all dark and mysterious, but still you got to explore 'em, it's a guy thing. You know, I always say that if you were to put some fur around a garbage disposal, we'd all still take turns at it, even if it was turned on. But women, they have this power, that woman in the car, it was like she'd cursed us, you and me both. But we drive on, get to the house, ring the doorbell like twenty times before you remember you've got a key, and we get up to the party just in time to

hear one of Ben Winter's dumb blonde jokes. Billy Bucknell
had been throwing up since about eight o'clock, and the
bastard is still drinking. MoJo keeps stuffing his fat face
with Cheetos, every now and then burping or farting; three
guys I don't know are there, too, not that into the flicks,
more into the poker game and cigars; Alec's little brother
Pasco is sneaking peeks at the TV screen, but pretending to
be more into a bowl of pretzels. And Alec—where the hell is
he? Back in the can, ralphing his guts out—he's not too
good at mixing the finer liquors with the baser variety, but
our motto through college had always been that if you boot
then you can keep on drinking. Alec was going to become a
severe alcoholic, by the look of things, because within ten
minutes of coming out of the bathroom, he's already mixing
Zombies with Todd Ramey ("from Wisconsin," he kept
telling everybody who gave a fuck).

So Alec is battered and sloshed from the twin bombs of
imminent marriage and bad booze, but he still has the
classic smile and his dark hair still parts perfectly to one
floppy side.

"Hey, you," he flags me down with an overflowing
plastic cup, "get it over here, man," he says, putting his arm
out for a big hug. "Dude, you should've seen the mud
getting flung at dinner, her sister's a major twat."

When I get close to him, his breath is like unto a toilet
bowl; I pull back a little to let a breeze from the ocean
beyond the open window protect me. You keep looking at
your watch; you're nervous, I guess, about the whore. I say.
"So, Alec, I saw Pasco. Getting tall these days, that boy is."

This brings a tear to Alec's eye. "My baby brother.
Gettin' older. Already he's climbed into more panties than
me. HEY!" shouting across the room, "PASQUALE!"

His brother glances over, shakes his head, maybe even rolls his eyes, and looks away.

"He's pissed 'cause he's taking her side in this." Alec makes some obscure but definitely obscene gesture toward his brother.

"Whose side?"

"Luce's. She and that sister—Jesus, is all I can say. Just Jesus. Hey, you wanna get stoned? C'mon, please? Wanna get stoned?"

I shake my head, but I can tell that you want to get stoned 'cause you're all shivering, and I'm afraid you're about to blow it and tell him this whore's coming from the city, the kind with a pimp. But you don't blow it; you go over to get another drink, and I think that's a good idea. "What's up with Luce?"

"Ah, that bitch. Thinks she owns me. God, this is a good party, all my friends." Alec begins crying; he was always verging on the sentimental, ever since I'd first met him. It was some Italian thing, I guess (he always said it was), about not needing to keep a tight rein on emotions, all the stuff. I kind of liked him for it, because I've never been a good one with the tears and open with anger. So, anyway, he tells me all about this thing with Luce, how she heard some story from her sister about Alec Delbanco and this girl at a party from about a week back and suddenly she's claiming that he's doing everything that walks the earth. "She has this trust thing, it's something I don't understand," he says. "I mean, I trust her, hell, I'd trust her even if she was jawing some guy right in the backseat while I was driving, why the hell doesn't she trust me? It's not like I was unfaithful to her or anything, I was just, well, pursuing a little."

"Women." I shake my head, amazed that yet another woman failed to understand a man so completely. "And it's not like you were even married."

We both crack up at this, drunk as we are. "She even called me an asshole," he says, and we laugh some more.

"Of course," I say, coming down from the laughing high. "It's true. I mean, we're all assholes. Basically. All men are assholes."

"Basically," he concurs, and we crack up again.

As if this were the greatest cue in the world, the French doors open—we're at your folks' house at Redondo, with the cliff and the balcony and the moon-swept Pacific just out there—out there—and it's the door to the balcony, so whoever it is has to have climbed up the trellis or something to get to the second floor, and who do you think's standing there with a tight green dress and a big old ribbon tied around her waist looking like Malibu Barbie on a date, but Luce, more Nautilized and Jazzercised than when I'd last seen her, and she just keeps coming like a barracuda right toward Alec and spits in his face.

He's still laughing from the joke, too, so now he's all shiny and laughing and hiccuping like he might start throwing up again.

Luce looks at me. "When he sobers up, tell him there won't be a wedding, tell him I know all about it, and tell him he can go to hell."

Then she turns and sort of flounces out of the room, down the hall stairs, presumably to go out the front door now.

"What," Alec says, shaking his head, "she fly up here on her broom?"

"Must've," I say, "so, wedding's off?"

"Jesus, if I listened to her, the wedding would've been off for the past six months. Trust me, man, she's gonna be there tomorrow, it's costing her dad too much and her ego way too much—she'd rather wait and get divorced later on, I know her, I know my Luce." And it was true about Luce —she'd rather worry about divorce in a couple of years than NOT GETTING MARRIED. She attached a lot of status to Alec—his family was rich, he was rich, and they were going to live in Palos Fucking Verde Estates and have a house big enough for the two of them and any lovers that snuck in the back door.

But with love, who knows? Could be once that ring was on his finger, he'd be the most faithful little lapdog the world has ever known. Could be she would be, too, and then they'd sink into the marriage trap where sex is an outmoded idea, and lust gets swept between the rug and the floor.

But not the night of his Bachelor Party.

You keep drinking those Zombies, and I say to Alec, my arm around him, his arm around me, "We got this girl, Alec, oh, Christ is she a girl. She's got a nice rack of tits."

He giggles, and then dissolves into weeping again. "You're my best friend, you know that? You are my fucking-A best friend in the whole snatch-eating world."

"Yeah, yeah," I say, and the doorbell rings—I don't quite hear it, but you do, and you go to the door downstairs—I see you bounding down the stairs like a kid on Christmas. I decide to check out the poker game, but I can tell Alec's all hot for this stripper, and he watches the stairs expectantly.

You come up a few minutes later, the pimp and stripper in tow, and there's like dead silence—even the music stops, like the Bruce Springsteen CD knew when to end.

The stripper's changed clothes—she's in a kind of party outfit, something that Luce herself would wear, in fact, at a casual, by-the-sea kind of affair: it says glitz and glamour, but it also says throw me in the pool.

Alec calls that kind of dress a French maid's outfit, a short skirt to show off legs, and lots of poofy ruffles, and those, kind of fluffy short sleeves like the Good Witch had in *The Wizard of Oz*—in fact, she looks a little like the Good Witch, but with a very short dress and a nice rack of tits.

But she's changed more than her clothes.

I could swear her eyes had been brown when I'd spoken with her on the street, only now, they're blue, and her skin seems sort of peaches and creamy, instead of the tanned and beat look she had before. But I know a good contact lens can do a lot, and maybe with makeup—I mean, women are so into changing their faces with paints and brushes, like they're all afraid we won't want to see their true faces (and I've seen a couple of chicks without their mascara and gloss and stuff, and let me tell you, it gets pretty scary when you're prettier than your date at four a.m.).

Alec, he looked more fetching than Luce when she didn't wear a lot of makeup—I don't think I'm more into guys or anything, but give me Luce without makeup or Alec, and I'd rather see Alec's baby face down on my bone any day.

So the whore looks almost completely different than she had on the street. She looks like she could fit right in with the house and all of us, and I was thinking, boy, you did this right, you got the right girl.

I look over at you, and you wink at me, because we

know that even if this girl costs us a thousand bucks or more, it's all worth it for Alec's last night before his doom.

Her pimp, who's still dressed like one of the Beach Boys on acid, is casing the place in a fairly obvious way, and I realize at this point that you and I have made a colossal mistake. We should've just got a stripper out of the phone book, but stupid me, I wanted a girl who would, for a little extra, take Alec into one of the empty bedrooms and sit on his face.

The pimp sees me, comes over, grabs my drink out of my hand, and drinks it.

Fairly turns my stomach.

"Nice place," he says, his voice half-gravel and half-belch. "Name's Lucky. You boys gonna have a good time tonight?"

"Yeah, yeah," I say, wishing we'd wiped him off on the doormat out front.

Then he whispers, "You be careful with her, now, boy, 'cause she's one of a kind, and I don't want nothing funny to happen to her. If there's gonna be sex, it's got to only be head or hand, no tail, you got me? It ain't safe for my girl to do tail, not with everything going around."

It dawns on me, drunk as I'm getting, that in some sewer rat way, he cares for this girl.

"We will, don't worry, man. Get yourself a drink, sit down, enjoy!"

"Naw," he says, "it's time to let the games begin."

I notice he's packing something under his flappy shirt—just the glimpse of some kind of revolver. I think, well, he's in a rough business, but I know he's got to protect himself. He sees me see the gun, and we stare at each other, but he says nothing.

He's got eyes like a snake, all perverted looking and squinty—sometimes I think people with squinty eyes have squinty brains, and this pimp, if anyone has one, hell, he's got the most squinty-ass brain on the planet. I'm thinking of maybe turning the revolver into a joke, by saying, "so's that a gun in your pants or are you just happy to see me," but I know people with squinty brains aren't going to chuckle at that old standby. I keep my mouth shut.

And then the girl punches up Rod Stewart's song "Hot Legs" or whatever it's called, and she started a routine.

But you don't want to hear about how she writhed and spun, how she took everything imaginable off, lifted one leg above her head, how Alec played the Golden Shower game with her, drinking Molson Golden Ale from her pubes; how she squatted on my face and took a rolled-up fifty from between my lips just using her snatch—those are all the basics of a good party stripper.

What you want to hear about is how your fingers got on the floor in the bathroom, with you screaming bloody murder, and how she screamed even louder, right?

That's what you want to hear.

I GUESS I'm going to digress a little here, but only for clarity's sake—the night before Alec got married was one of those nights where you have to piece a few things together later on.

Like Pasco, Alec's little bro, giggling and blushing when the girl sat on his lap naked and beat his pretty face silly with her tits; or when MoJo got pissed off because she wouldn't sit on his face for a lousy ten bucks; he said, whining, "Doesn't she know any cheaper games?"—see, the girl was so hot and we were so loaded, that we were dropping hundreds and fifties on her like she was a bank.

Cigar smoke was the only veil she had around her, in the end, just that stagnant smoke that stinks and sits in the air like it doesn't have anywhere to go, and all of us, through its mist, looking like ghosts.

That's what I thought at the time:

We were enshrouded by the gray smoke and looked like ghosts or maybe old men with wrinkly, testicular skin, pale and blurry of feature. Horny bastards all, MoJo licking his lips like he was trying to taste her from three feet away, and Billy Bucknell grabbing his crotch without even knowing he was doing it.

She really had us going, that girl did. You even kept trying to get your hand up her, and she kept pushing you away, until her pimp had to come over and tell you to knock it off, that nobody, but nobody touches her kitty. That's what he called it, her kitty. Might as well have called it her flesh purse, since she was making so much money out of opening it up. The pimp and I had a nice convo about how prostitution was a victimless crime and all that; his name was Lucky Murphy, a nice Irish boy as it turned out, from Boston, who had once been a fisherman off Dana Point, and as he spoke I could practically hear someone's Irish mother singing "Danny Boy," until I looked him in the eye and knew he was a fucking liar through and through, that he was Hollywood scum and if he could, he would've been peddling all our preppie asses for the twenty bucks per corn hole he could make.

And we keep looking at her kitty, too, all our eyes drawn back to the unholies of unholy, "little pouty petals," you called it. You were pretty adamant about getting your fingers up there, weren't you, you horny son of a bitch? It was almost like a Portuguese man-of-war turned on its back.

And finally, when it was over, all her dances, she took the party boy into the bedroom, and all I can say is, he didn't come out for over an hour.

In fact, by eleven-fifteen, he hadn't come out at all, and that's when you and I decided to storm the room.

Now, I had seen this room once before—it was your folks' master bedroom, and it was a good size, with kind of a girly bed, you were to ask me, lots of silk and brass; a nightstand that looked like it was out of Versailles; green-gold wallpaper, shiny and clean like they'd just had it put up the day before; a wall that was nothing but mirrors; and two walk-in closets, the sizes of my apartment in Westwood; a bathroom, all gold-plated fixtures, something I always thought was tacky about your folks—and I told you this a few times, too—with a big round Jacuzzi bath and a window so you could take a bath and watch your neighbors at the same time.

The door is locked, of course, but you know how to take a dime and very simply unlock it. So we get in, and the bed is perfectly made; no sign of hooker or trick. You go into the bathroom to look for them, giggling as always, because we think we're going to find the two of them with her ass bent over a sink and his shlong pumping in like an oil drill. I check out the walk-in closets, but there's nothing but tons of Armani and Valentino and the smell of rich lady perfume.

As I'm about to go into the second closet, the pimp comes running in, out of breath because it's quite a hike up those stairs in your folks' house. "What you boys doing?"

I cackle—sometimes, when I'm really bombed and in a party mood, I do this laugh that's like "snort-cackle-pop," and it sounds like I hurt myself or something.

Then I notice he's got his revolver out.

Oh, shit, I'm thinking. I sober up real fast. "Looking for the party boy."

He just stares at me with the gun drawn, and that's when I hear the girl in the bathroom, kind of moaning, and you, too, still giggling, and that wet sound like rubber and lubricant.

And another sound, while the Irish pimp from hell is staring at me, a sound in the walk-in closet.

My hand is on the door.

But someone else's hand is on the other side of the door.

"Alec?" I ask the door.

The sound that comes back isn't entirely human, but it's human enough. It sounds like the noises Alec used to make when he was doing like a feeb imitation: like his tongue got cut out and his lips are shredded. So I think maybe it's some kind of setup and joke on me, so I give the door a good pull, and it opens.

Dresses and coats, hanging, rustling, in a dark closet.

The sound of slow dripping.

I can smell the pimp's breath: He's real close to me.

I can tell he's a little scared, too, and he still has the gun out.

He's pointing it at the dresses, hanging.

Something clear and dripping from the corner of a full length mink coat.

I switch on the closet light, but the pimp very quickly switches it off again.

But in that one second of light, I see something in the corner.

Something that left a trail of slime and human waste in its path.

Its ribs quivering.

Open, and quivering, like the skeleton of a boat, a slaughterhouse boat with the flesh and innards of animals dripping from its deck.

It's always through the eyes that you know someone. I once took care of a friend's dog when I was eight; and then, when I was nineteen, and had long before moved away from that friend, I was in New York, in Central Park, and I saw in the eyes of a dog an old friend, and sure enough, it was the dog I had known when I was eight, and in Orange County. It's always there in the eyes, the person, the animal, the creature, not in the skin or voice or the movements: It's in the eyes.

So I had seen in the brief light, his eyes, Alec's eyes, left in their sockets long after the skin had been torn from bone and skull to make the rest of him resemble a skinned possum.

And when it registers on my brain that it's Alec Delbanco, that this girl did something to Alec, something inhuman, I hear your scream from the bathroom, and I turn and the pimp turns, and the girl screams, too, and there's the sound of breaking glass.

The pimp gets to the bathroom first, before me, and I hear him fire two shots; I'm just behind him, and when I see you clutching your hand with all that blood coming out, I figure the pimp shot your fingers off. For just a second, I see her, too, not as she was, pretty and tall and sexy, but some small tentacled thing, like a sea urchin, dropped from between her legs, released from its empty and ragged socket, with a cut umbilical cord attached, loping on its wormlike feelers across the bathtub rim, out the broken window, into the night.

The pimp yells, "Goddamn it, that fucking bitch," then drops his gun, grabs me by the collar, "You bastards, you asked for it, you ain't supposed to get her down there, that's what she wants, you sons of bitches, you're supposed to get head or a hand job, didn't she tell you? She tricked you, and she was the best, you sons of whores!" He's weeping, and I'm thinking, *Christ, he's in love with…that thing.*

"Is that a fucking alien?" I'm screaming. "You brought some fucking outer space—"

But the pimp cuts me off, spitting a wad of slime on my face. "I fished her out of the sea, asshole, down at Santa Monica pier, she got caught on my hook and she does things to you, she gets boys like you, but not like this, it's up to you, your buddies wanting to put it there, but I told you that ain't allowed! She's the best, but you can't touch her there, it's so hard to trap her, and now, look what you done!"

But you, you start screaming again and turning blue, so the pimp lets me go and goes running out of there in search of his escaped sea creature.

That's when I figure it's time to call an ambulance.

So now I know it wasn't the pimp shooting at you after all,

but at that *thing*, that thing that you stuck your fingers up into.

It was hell cleaning up the mess in the bathroom, getting rid of her skin.

Funny thing about her skin and guts—they looked like they'd been spun with a fine silk, but they were all sticky.

You were lucky to lose only your fingers.

Think of what Alec lost, the night before he got married.

Well, not that he ever *did* get married.

He's sort of a vegetable now, living off of machines at his folks' house, and Luce got married to Billy Bucknell last year, that scheming son of a gun.

You and me, we're rooming together these days. My new nickname for you is *Fingers*.

In the morning, when you bring me coffee, it's kind of nice, just the two of us.

We get by.

I tried to do it with a girl again, after that, but what if she's up inside there, what if that girl's just spun out of her silk, what if she's waiting to take me to the Big O and rip my skin right off my back and end up like Alec Delbanco with wires and tubes all over him and his eyes all weird and sad, like he had it, that orgasm at the end of the universe, like maybe it was worth it, what she did to him, but I got to tell you, Fingers, I got to tell you:

I'm never getting close to one of those things again as long as we both shall live.

I keep seeing it in their faces, their eyes, the *It* that was the whore's core, the creature in the flesh purse, and I feel like *It*'s coming for both of us, maybe to finish off the job.

Alec, too, maybe even Billy Bucknell, and MoJo, and Pasco, and Ben Winter.

Sometimes at night, when I can't sleep, I hear Its sloppy wiping at the windows, and I pull the covers up over the two of us just to feel safe.

You and me, we'll take care of each other, we don't have to go out much, at least not till we get evicted, and then we can hide under the sewers or in the alleys.

If we see her, if we still got legs, we can run, you and I.

I will not abandon you to It, and I promise, for better or worse, good buddy.

In sickness and in health.

Only Connect

Watch the scenery awhile. It'll take your mind off the pain. I'll tell you all about him, if you'll just listen. You must never breathe a word of this to anyone, but I can tell you're an understanding sort. You won't betray me.

His name was Jim, and he worked at the train station taking tickets. He grew up in Hartford, but moved to Deerwich-On-Sparrow, called Deerwich by most, on the Connecticut coast—in his early twenties, the job had seemed good. He'd begun his career riding the rails taking tickets and cleaning the cars, but he'd moved up so that at twenty nine he could sit behind the glass and say, "Roundtrip to Boston leaves at 9:15. That'll be $49.50." His head often pounded when it rained, and he was prone to popping aspirin as if it were hard candy and just sucking on it until the headache went away. The sound of the train as it arrived in the station aggravated his condition, but Jim had begun to think of the headaches as normal. He'd long forgotten that they had never existed before he began working with the railroad.

It was the train wreck that had begun his journey toward discovery. One night, fairly late for the train—which had been due in before midnight—there was an awful screeching, from some great distance along the track. The old timers knew what this meant, and they all ran out to see the spectacle. All except for Jim, who stayed back.

He went to grab another bottle of aspirin from beneath his perch. He felt around, but all his fingers found was a completely empty bottle. He stood from his stool, stretching, yawning. Outside, he heard the scraping of metal—the train, he would later learn, went over an embankment, into the river, and some child somewhere would be blamed for playing quarters on the tracks—the shouts of onlookers as the train tossed like a restless sleeper from its bed—but Jim took the opportunity to walk across the street to the drugstore for aspirin.

Inside the store, the fluorescent lights flickered. The old man who worked the pharmacy stood up on his platform behind the white counter, measuring his nostrums and philters. Jim walked the aisles, glancing briefly at the magazine covers and the greeting card displays. Finally, he turned the last aisle and saw the large bottles of aspirin.

The fluorescent light above his head flickered in a dark way, as if it were just about to go out. As Jim reached for the aspirin bottle, he watched as his hand seemed to go through water and touch—not a bottle of aspirin, but a green tile on a bathroom wall. As the light flickered again, he sensed that he was no longer in a drugstore down near the train station in Old Deerwich, but in a small bathroom with lime green tiles and a large mirror above the toilet. He glanced in the mirror and for a moment thought he saw the aisles of the drugstore behind his reflection, but this faded, and all was green tile.

He almost said something, as if someone stood near him, but he was most definitely alone.

He turned about, facing a door. He pushed at the door, and it opened out onto a room that was all green and white and smelled of rubbing alcohol with an undersmell of urine. Flowers on the windowsill. The window looked out on a courtyard and garden, and there, as he went to look out it, were half a dozen or more patients. He knew they were patients by their bathrobes and by the nurses that pushed some of the wheelchairs, or stood beside a patient who used a walker or cane to get around. Across the courtyard, a silver metal building, probably precisely like the one he occupied at the moment.

"Mrs. Earnshaw," someone said at the door. British accent. He knew he was in a British hospital.

Jim turned, sensing others' presence in the room.

The fluorescent lamp flickered a liquid green.

Jim glanced up at the light overhead—a large brown water blotch spread like the profile of a face next to the ice tray lamps.

"It's terrible," someone said as he glanced down again.

He was in the drugstore, holding a bottle of aspirin in his hand. A woman looked up at him queerly.

"I can't imagine anyone survived."

Jim had to squint a moment to focus on his new environment. His head throbbed now. He calmed himself with the thought that the pain in his head had caused the brief and vivid hallucination of the hospital room.

The little old woman, half bent over, reached for a box of arthritis pain reliever. "Did you see it?"

"No," Jim said. Then, "See what?"

"The crash. I was in my car and driving down Water Street, and I heard it. It was terrible. It's so unsafe."

"Yes." Jim nodded.

"Travel is always dangerous. To get there from here, one must risk one's life these days," she said, nodding as if they'd understood each other.

Jim stood there a moment. Then, feverishly, he opened the jar of pills and grabbed three, tossing them down his throat.

When he paid for the bottle, the pharmacist said, "Finally found what you wanted."

"Excuse me?"

"The aspirin. I saw you standing there reading labels for nearly half an hour."

"Half an hour?"

"Bad headache, huh? You probably drink too much caffeine."

Jim walked out into the rain, feeling as if he still vibrated with his hallucination. He remembered his brief romance with peyote in college, and began to worry that this might be the flashback from that. He forgot about it for days—the hospital—and buried himself in work.

The photographs in the local papers showed all angles of the train crash. It had fallen on its side, plunging seventy nine people into the river, all of whom died. Another two hundred and fifteen people were injured.

What struck Jim most about the pictures of the fallen train was that it looked—if you squinted at the photos— like a sleeping person made entirely of metal, lying on a gray blanket.

The flashes began a week or two later.

The first time, when he tried to unlock his car, a small Honda Civic, and found that the lock was jammed. He twisted the key so hard that it broke off in his hand. Again, the headache kicked in, and he saw the aspirin bottle on the passenger seat inside the car. He felt angry suddenly—angry at the car for not opening, angry at his job for its dullness, angry at his parents for not really preparing him for the world in the way he'd wished.

Then the flash—he thought it was heat lightning. In the same moment, he was in the hospital again. This time, he sat in a wheelchair in the courtyard as a light rain fell.

"You all right, now?"

"Yes," he said, adapting quickly to his new environment. "It's only a little rain."

"A little rain." The pretty nurse beside him smiled. "Yes, that's all it is. But all the others have gone inside."

He looked about the path through the garden with its iris and hibiscus, and saw that they were indeed alone. The silver of the buildings dulled in the gray rain, but he liked the fresh smell of it.

"What's your name?" he asked her.

"Nora," she said, glancing up from her magazine. "Your reading's going to get soaked," he said, nodding.

"I don't mind. It's only a little rain, after all." She had a warm smile, and her eyes were a toasty brown. "Been feeling good today, then, have we?"

"Very," Jim said. "The pains are gone."

"A few days is what they said."

"Yes, and they were right," Jim said.

Then he bit his tongue slightly. "Where am I?"

"Holyrood," she said.

"What town?"

"Oh, you." Nora laughed. "More tricks. Is this like that dream you told me about? The one where you're a railroad man taking tickets in some little town in—where was it?"

"Connecticut."

"That's right Connecticut. The effects should've worn off by now," Nora said, glancing at her watch. "You were only on the IV for two hours before ten. It's nearly three." Then she reached over, patting Jim's hand. "All of this for just a little information. It does seem daft, doesn't it? You holding up? No more weeping at midnight?"

"No," Jim said, feeling more lost and yet extremely comfortable. "Was it the aspirin?"

"Or lack thereof," Nora said. "Do you ever read these?" She held the magazine up. It was the *London Telltale* magazine. "All these royals and celebs knocking each other up. You'd think they'd have other things to occupy them, don't you?"

"What town are we in?" he asked.

"Why," Nora shook her head, glancing at the magazine, "just look at what the Prince is up to today." Then, "What dear? Town? Does it matter?"

"Yes."

"I'm sorry, I'm not supposed to tell too much. You know that more than anyone, Mrs. Earnshaw."

Jim felt a warm salty taste in the back of his throat. He glanced down at the hand that she had just finished patting. It was the hand of a middle-aged woman, and the hospital bracelet he wore read, "Catherine Earnshaw."

When the lightning flashed overhead and the rain began coming down in earnest, Nora said, "Oh, dear, let's get the two of us in out of this nasty weather, shall we?" But then there was no Nora, and she faded, and all that was there was the Honda and the rain and his headache and a man who was not sure why he was going mad at the age of twenty-nine.

You didn't think he was married? Well, of course Jim was married—they'd tied the knot at twenty-four, almost got divorced at twenty-seven, but managed for a couple of more years because their jobs put them at opposite shifts so that every weekend was a honeymoon. Her name was Alice, and she worked at the sandwich shop on Bank Street. When she got off work at five, she went first to the library, since she was an avid reader, and then to the video shop. Her evenings, while Jim worked late, were mainly spent with the cat and a good book and a mediocre movie nine times out of ten. She'd slip into bed around midnight, fall asleep with a glass of wine, and then feel him next to her just before she got fully awake at seven in the morning. She'd cuddle with him, unbeknownst to Jim, and then get up to make a pot of coffee and begin the day again.

The movie that night was to be an old musical, and the novel, a light romance to take her mind off her worries. She slipped into the tub at about seven-fifteen, and while she dried herself off, the bathroom door opened. At first Alice was frightened, but she saw quickly it was her husband.

"Jim? What are you doing home?"

"Called in sick," he said. "I've been napping since six."

"Migraine? Poor baby."

"It's not that." But he nodded anyway.

"Come here," Alice said, reaching her hand out. Jim

approached her, his head down. She touched the back of his neck, squeezing lightly. "You're tense."

"Baby, I think I'm going nuts," he said.

"You've been nuts a long time."

"I mean it," he said, and his tone was so serious it almost shocked her.

Later, by the fire, she held him and told him it would be all right, and he wept.

Then he told her.

At first she had a hard time not laughing.

But when he told her the woman's name, she cackled.

He looked hurt.

"Oh, honey, that's a name from a book. Catherine Earnshaw. It's from *Wuthering Heights*. You must have seen the movie."

He shook his head. "Was she in a hospital?"

Alice grinned. Her grin was not as warm as Nora's, but it was familiar. "No, no. It must be some kind of dream brought on by those headaches. Let's get you into the doctor's for a checkup."

"A head exam?"

"So you're an invalid woman in a British hospital with silver buildings and your name is Catherine Earnshaw. What an imagination," Alice said, kissing his forehead. "My big baby. It's your job. It's getting to you. I told you, you needed to finish your degree and maybe get into computers or something."

Jim glanced at the fire as the flames curled and flickered. He closed his eyes, his head beginning to pound, but he was going to fight it off, the pain, the throbbing, the near blindness that the headaches brought with them when at their worst.

When he opened his eyes, he was sitting in a large white room with no windows. In an uncomfortably hard chair. In a circle, with others. Some men, a few women—nine in all. The nurses stood toward the back, sitting on chairs, crossing and uncrossing their legs, looking at their watches now and then, seeming to reach into their breast pockets for cigarettes or mints or something they needed desperately but were unwilling to give themselves.

A man sitting across from Jim chattered away, and gradually Jim began to understand what he was saying.

"It's not as if we all aren't going through the same thing. What did they call it? Adjustment?"

A woman laughed. "Mine told me to get used to it."

Someone else chuckled at this. "I was told it was a period of containment."

"Well, it's been working for me to some small extent," the man continued, his voice slight and nervous as if he were afraid of being overheard or of making a mistake in what he said. "At least in the mornings. The mornings are good. It's only about now."

"Yes," another man said, just to the left of Jim. "At about three every day. Sometimes as late as four. These flashes."

"Flashes of insight," a woman said.

"Hot flashes," another woman said, and they all had a good laugh. "Not that you can't have those, Norman."

Norman, the man who had originally been talking, blushed. He was handsome, mid-forties, and reminded Jim a bit of his father. Actually, the more he spoke, the more Jim was becoming convinced that Norman was related to him in some way. The thin tall frame, the thick black hair, the nose a bit beaky and the chin a bit strong and the teeth a bit much.

"Well," Norman said, "since we're all in this together, and since they," and he nodded backward, to the row of nurses behind him, "seem to want us to get it all out in these groups, I think we should tell everything we know."

"Not everything," another man said. "I couldn't. It'd be too much."

"All right, then," Norman said. "Whatever we feel comfortable with."

"You'll have to begin, then, Norman. Mine is rather embarrassing," the laughing woman said. "It involves me and another man, and I can't tell you what we seem to do all day long."

More laughter.

"Mine isn't that…invigorating." Norman smiled. "I'm just a little boy of ten, perhaps eleven. I live in a small village in Morocco."

"Sounds quaint," the woman said. "Unless you're employed in some house of thieves."

Norman lost his smile. "Nothing like that. I help bring water to the house, feed some animals, and run errands. I'm constantly hungry, and I can't seem to talk with others there, even though I understand them."

"Oh!" the woman gasped. "So interesting compared to mine. I'm the wife to a man who hallucinates."

Listening to all this, Jim almost laughed; something in him told him to laugh a bit. He glanced down at his hands and saw the wedding ring on the left hand. He drew it carefully off his finger as the woman told her story.

He looked inside the ring. "Cathy and Cliff Forever."

"Yes, and while he's at work in his dull job, I go have

mad affairs up and down Main Street," the woman continued, "only ... it's not called Main Street. I find this entertaining, if disconcerting. My husband really is a fool. He
surprised me a bit today, however."

Jim reached up and felt his neck. It was slender. He
drew his fingers across his throat and up around his chin—
a small slightly round chin—up to his fullish lips, his small
nose, around his eyelashes, which seemed long and
feathery.

"Dear," someone whispered behind him, "you'll smudge
your makeup."

He recognized the voice; it was Nora.

He put his hands down.

"You should listen to the stories," Nora whispered. "It
might help your condition."

Jim nodded, glancing over to the woman who was just
finishing up her tale.

"He hasn't a clue," she said. "He lies constantly himself.
It's easy to fool a liar." She looked over at Jim. "Mrs. Earnshaw, you haven't told yours, have you?"

The woman seemed to look at Jim with a special knowledge. He'd nearly forgotten he was Mrs. Earnshaw to all of
them. He began to feel his skin crawl a bit. A coldness
seeped into his voice as he spoke.

"There's not much to tell, really. To be honest, I think
I'm more there than here." Laughter across the room. "This
feels less me than the other. I know so much about him."

"Him?" The woman laughed. "Oh, Lord, you got to
change sex. Do you play with it much?"

"Juliet!" Norman exclaimed. "What a filthy mind you
have."

Jim felt slightly offended, particularly for Mrs. Earnshaw, whom he imagined to be a very circumspect and polite woman of fifty-two.

"Really," he said. He reached down, smoothing the lines of the bathrobe. "Even now, sitting among you, I feel more him than me.

"Tell us about him," Norman said.

"Yes," another chimed in.

"Perhaps I will." Jim paused a moment, wondering where to begin. "He's a nice young man in his late twenties who works for the rails in a little New England town. He is happily married, drives some kind of Japanese car, an older model, and likes rock and roll music from the 1950s. He has terrible headaches …"

After a moment, Jim continued. "Actually, I'm more convinced that I'm him than I'm sure that I am, well, *me*."

Norman's eyes lit up as he nodded. "That's how it's supposed to be, isn't it? They said you get a gleam at first."

"A glimmer," the woman named Juliet said. The smile on her face grew impossibly wide. "They called it a glimmer. It feels like … like …"

"A warm rain," another said.

"Yes, and then," Norman nodded as if feeling a religious transformation, "the warmth spreads over you."

"Like you've been rewired," another said.

The woman next to him said, "Well, Mrs. Earnshaw's certainly been rewired if she's a man now."

"He's not just a man," Jim said, and for the first time noticed that he spoke with Mrs. Earnshaw's voice. "He's a special young man. He doesn't know it yet, but he's very special."

Behind him, Nora touched his shoulder. She whispered, "I knew you'd be the first, Mrs. Earnshaw."

Jim leaned his head back slightly. "The first to what, dear?"

"The first to cross the bridge," the nurse said.

&

WHEN JIM NEXT RECOLLECTED ANYTHING, he was in bed with his wife, in their small apartment on Hop Street, the peppermint smell of the nearby toothpaste factory assaulting his senses.

Alice snored lightly, and as Jim glanced around in the scrim darkness, moonlight and the summer steam pouring in through the open window, he saw evidence of sexual abandon—the packet of condoms, open, on the dressing table, the clothes strewn about the floor in a trail, the half-empty glasses of red wine, one spilled on the carpet. Had they been animals? He wished he could remember. Because of their schedules, they didn't make love all that often, and now he had been in some kind of dream support group in a British hospital rather than in his Alice.

Then a disturbing thought occurred to him: was someone else occupying his own body while he occupied Mrs. Earnshaw's? Did Mrs. Earnshaw herself enter his skin and make love to Alice and drink his wine?

He sat up most of the night, just watching Alice as she slept.

Sweet Alice, lost in some dream world. She stirred, her fingers curled, once, her hand went to her throat, once, she seemed to weep but it was like a puppy sound—a puppy at the door to a room that she wanted to be set free from.

She awoke in the early morning, her eyes opening wide. "What are you doing?"

"Nothing," he said. "Just watching you."

"Why?" She wiped her face with her hands as if washing away a mask of sleep. "You scared me for a second."

"What was it like?"

"What?"

"What we did last night."

"Weren't you there?" She grinned, giggling.

"I'm not sure."

"Oh stop it. It's too early for jokes." She looked across the bed to the clock. "It's only five-thirty. I can sleep some more. That is," she arched an eyebrow, "if you'd quit staring."

She turned over, facing the window. The sunlight had crept up.

"Can you close the curtains?" she said. "I need some dark."

⚬

JIM WANDERED DOWNTOWN, walked along the river, along the railroad tracks, alongside the boat slips and the chemical factory—miles of walking at dawn, when the town seemed to wake like a baby, from a gasp to a full cry. When the sun was fully up, he got a cup of coffee from the doughnut shop and walked out to the pier, watching the ferry as it crossed to Newburyport.

The 7:15 blew its whistle, coming into the station, and he turned to watch it—remembering the train crash of a few weeks earlier, and the first time he remembered being in the silver British hospital as Mrs. Earnshaw.

Then it came to him. That had not been the first time. That had been the first time he'd remembered it so vividly.

Closing his eyes, he recalled an incident when he'd been four or five, and he'd been in a hospital—was it the same one? Only, it was not in England. It had been in Massachusetts, when he'd been taken to visit Grammy Evans, her drinking out of control—the white and green rooms, the silver flask she hid even there to take a nip now and then when the nurses weren't looking.

"Hold this," she'd said, passing him the silver flask. "Don't let them see it."

So he'd hidden it in his shorts, feeling the cold metal against his thighs. Then he'd wandered the halls of the hospital while the grown-ups talked and did not notice him missing. He began playing "Spy" and decided that the doctors were Secret Agents. When he came across one, he'd run up some stairs and down some others, and through double doors and hallways with words written in bright red and yellow along them. And then he'd come to a room where four men in green masks stood about a table.

On the table, a naked old woman who was probably dead.

Jim had kept himself hidden away, and he watched as the four doctors injected something terrible into the old woman so that she sat up screaming.

It had made Jim scream, too, and one of the four men turned and saw him, and before he could get out the door, someone else grabbed him.

"What in God's name is this kid doing in here? Where the hell is security?" a man said.

The woman screamed again, and then began coughing.

&

JIM, sitting on the pier, sipped his coffee, trying to remember more, but that had been all.

What he knew without a doubt was that the woman on the table had been Mrs. Earnshaw, and that she was dead when he was a little boy and that somehow this was all a hallucination caused by a traumatic incident.

The coffee grew cold as he closed his eyes.

He decided to go into Mrs. Earnshaw in the hospital.

He willed a headache to come on, he tried to simulate the pain that arrived, and the flickering lights.

After an hour, he gave up.

Several days later, while he was sitting on the toilet, he arrived into Mrs. Earnshaw again.

§▲

SHE SAT in the garden with Nora. Nora was reading one of her magazines, and Jim was doing a little needlepoint.

"Nora. Tell me about myself," he said.

The nurse glanced up.

"All right. I suppose this is good."

"It seems I'm losing bits of me," Jim said, nodding as if to the will of the universe. "I'm not sure where I fit in with all this."

"Well, that was the issue, after all," Nora said. She set her magazine aside and crossed her leg. "Mind if I light up?"

"Go right ahead, dear."

Nora drew a cigarette from her breast pocket and struck a match along the edge of the low brick wall she leaned against.

After the first puff, she said, "You're a psychiatrist from

Bristol who worked with NASA and spent a good deal of time in Belize working on the Arc Project."

"What's that?"

Nora shrugged. "I wish I knew." She said this warmly and without a trace of deception. "All I know is my end of this."

"The Arc Project doesn't even sound familiar to me."

"All of you were involved with it. That's all any of us knows." Another long drag on the cigarette. "You have the mind link to this man named Jim, as do the others, to various people. And you're dying."

"I had no idea," Jim said, setting his needlepoint on his lap. "Why am I called Catherine Earnshaw? That's obviously not my real name."

"You picked it. All of you picked names from books and movies. You liked the name Cathy."

"Do you know who I am, really?"

Nora closed her eyes for a minute. Smoked. Scratched a place just above her eyebrows. Opened her eyes. "Not really."

"Doesn't all of this seem inhuman?"

Nora sighed. "We have to trust that this is saving something important for us."

"Saving from what?"

Nora dropped her cigarette to the ground, stubbing it out with the toe of her white shoe. "From loss. The information has to be retained, and it's not like you're a computer that can just be downloaded."

"I wish I could remember the information you're talking about, but really, I can't. There seem to be great gaps in my memory."

"It's just the connection," Nora said.

She stepped over to the wheelchair and crouched down before it. She placed her hands over Jim's and looked up into his eyes. "I know that Mrs. Earnshaw is leaving us. I know that you're this other person, this Jim. I can see you when you come into her."

Jim trembled, and felt sweat break out along his neck. "Really?"

Nora nodded. She glanced about, slightly nervous. "I have to tell you something, Jim. There's someone here, an intruder from the Arc Project. I'm not sure who it is, but Mrs. Earnshaw is in danger."

Jim shivered. "What's this all about? Am I crazy?"

Nora grinned. Then she grew serious again. "Maybe. I never would've thought I'd be involved in this too. None of us really thought it would work. But someone is after you, Jim, not here, in this hospital. But the intruder's already trying to track you down."

"I don't understand. This whole 'intruder' thing."

An old man in a white jacket walked up beside them.

"Dr. Morgan," Nora said.

"Here, the rain's coming again," the doctor said. "Let's get Mrs. Earnshaw inside for another series of shots, shall we?"

As Nora wheeled Jim across the path toward the door, as the first drops of rain fell, Jim whispered, "She's already dead, isn't she? Mrs. Earnshaw?"

Nora put her hand on his shoulder, squeezing slightly. She waited until they were in the corridor before she said *yes*.

AND THAT WAS the last of it for Jim.

He returned to work the following day, sitting behind the glass, selling tickets for the train. He tried to induce the headaches, but they seemed to be gone for good. His aspirin bottle stayed full, and he had a feeling of well-being that he almost despised. Occasionally, when he didn't even realize he was doing it, he glanced at his hands, half expecting to see Mrs. Earnshaw's in their place, her wedding ring on her slightly wrinkled finger.

A woman said, "Two, plus a child, for Penn Station."

"One hundred fifty-two," he said, typing the information into the computer.

She passed him the money, he counted it out. As he passed her three tickets, he said, "Boarding on the river side. Train's delayed by ten minutes. Arrive Penn Station at 7:30."

"I wanted to get there by seven."

He looked at her. She was forty, trim, brown hair cut short in wisps.

"Sorry, ma'am. It won't happen."

"It has to happen."

"You could try the airport."

She shook her head.

"Damn it," she muttered. She reached for the tickets, grabbing them. Her husband and little girl stood back, near the benches. She turned away, then faced him again. "Is this the same Deerwich where the train crashed once?"

Jim chuckled. "Everyone asks that. Yep, it is. Just to the north, when it crossed the bridge over the river."

The woman frowned. "It's dangerous to cross bridges. I hope there aren't too many bridges between here and Manhattan. I never fly, and I don't like to cross a bridge that's already had a crash on it. Bad luck."

She and her family went to wait for the train, but Jim sat there with his mouth open. She'd said it and it felt like a secret code. *It's dangerous to cross bridges. I don't like to cross a bridge that's already had a crash on it. Bad luck.*

On his break at 9:30, he took a walk out along the tracks, trying to remember the night of the train crash when he'd first had the experience. He followed the track up to the bridge over the Sparrow River. He saw the place where it had been repaired; where the train had cut loose and gone off.

The investigation was ongoing. Maybe they'd never know what had malfunctioned about the train on the tracks.

He stood there, staring at the tracks, thinking about the woman complaining about the danger of travel, and remembering Nora's words:

The first to cross the bridge.

And then he knew, even before he found the list of names in the newspaper from several weeks earlier.

It read like a joke list of names from books and movies, the names of the dead:

Juliet Capulet, Norman Bates, Paul Bunyan, Zazu Pitts, Ramon Navarro, Silas Marner, Gregor Roche.

The list of the dead included, he believed, everyone he met in that group in the hospital room.

Every single one.

In that list, too, was the name Catherine Earnshaw.

All just happened to be in the one car of the train where all were killed.

Another name, too, that he recognized: *Nora Fitch.*

He sat down in the library with the newspaper and wept. He drank too much that night and went wandering along the docks and backstreets, as if somehow the answer would reveal itself if he searched hard enough.

Finally, after two a.m., he ambled home.

As he lay down next to his sleeping wife, he wrapped his arms around her, wanting to feel safe from a world he no longer understood, all the mysteries and strange coincidences and dreams-that-seemed-real of another world he'd somehow been thrust into, whether through madness or design.

Alice's skin was almost too hot to the touch. She seemed burning with fever. She moaned slightly in her dream.

She woke with a start, and said, "What are you doing?"

"Sorry," he said, his breath a blast of whiskey. "I just needed to touch you."

She rolled onto her back, staring up at the ceiling.

"You're drunk."

"Sure am," Jim said, wanting to touch his wife so badly, wanting to wrap himself around her and be part of her so he wouldn't feel so alone in his mind.

"Go to sleep," she commanded. "In the morning you'll be sober and we can talk about things."

"What things?" he asked, ready to fall into the coma of drunken sleep.

"Things about us. Things we should talk about. Things we need to talk about," Alice said. She sat up. Switched on the bedside lamp. He looked at her naked back, wishing it could be pressed against his chest and stomach.

"I love you," he whispered hoarsely, unsure whether or not he had really said it aloud or had only wanted to say it.

"I'm not who you think I am," Alice said, still not facing him. "Not anymore."

"Yes, you are," he said. "Of course you are. You're my wife. You're Alice."

But he hadn't said Alice, had he? As he lay there, the fear washing over him like a warm bath, he knew he had said "You're Juliet," because something within him knew it was Juliet, the Mrs. Earnshaw part of him knew, had known, and had been trying to tell him in her own way, had been trying to tell him that this was no longer the woman he loved but a woman who called herself Juliet Capulet and might not even be a woman at all or even a human being as far as he knew.

The Mrs. Earnshaw part of him let him know that this was the *intruder* in his bed.

He lay there, feeling his heartbeat accelerate as Alice slowly turned in the lamplight, a half-grin on her face. As her smile curled up and her eyes glimmered with a dark onyx that might have been shadow, might have been stone, she said, "We have to have a long talk, you and I, about what really is going on inside that mind of yours."

"Juliet?" he asked.

She smiled. "I'm Alice. Alice. Remember? Your Alice."

She sat there, watching him all night; and he stared back at her, too afraid to look away.

In the morning, she rose and went to shower.

Jim lay there, frozen, waiting for what was to come, remembering the woman on the table surrounded by doctors. He realized that in some respects he was still there in that room watching Mrs. Earnshaw—or whoever the body had been—being brought back to life, or some form of life, some kind of intelligence within the skin that had so recently been shed.

And how he had felt a presence in that room when he

was four, a presence that was not entirely human, not entirely like a middle-aged woman whose heart had given out and who now was going to have another being within her.

When the water stopped, he heard Alice sing as she toweled off, and then she opened the bathroom door and something that was not entirely Alice moved like silver liquid toward him.

But even as he felt something warm and metallic inject itself into his throat, he had the sense that he was not Jim at all, but something that lived within the skin of a nice lady sitting on a moving train as it headed down the New England coast.

YOU MUSTN'T PASS this on, because I know who you are on the inside, but you haven't crossed the bridge fully, have you, dear? You're still only halfway across, feeling the warm rain, the glimmer as it warms you, but it hasn't burst within you yet.

Mustn't make this worse than it is. It's only a train after all, and travel by rail is so safe these days.

Look at that little town we're coming to now.

Isn't it lovely?

Across that river.

Across that bridge.

Get ready, dear. Our connection's coming up shortly.

The Ripening Sweetness of Late Afternoon

S unland City was the last place in the world Jesus was ever going to come looking for Roy Shadiak.

He returned to his hometown in his fortieth year, after he felt he could never again sell Jesus to the rabble.

Something within him had been eating him up for years. His love for life had long before dried up, and then so had his marriage and his bitter understanding of how God operated in the world. He'd gotten off the bus out at the flats, and brushed off the boredom of a long trip down infinite highways.

He stood awhile beside the canals and watched the gators as they lay still as death in the muddy shallows. He'd been wearing his white suit for the trip because it was what his mother liked him to wear, and because it was the only suit of his that still fit him. And it fit Sunland City, with its canals and palmettos and merciless sunshine.

It was a small town, the City was, and they would think him mad to arrive on the noon bus in anything other than creamy white. He would walk down Hispaniola Street and make a detour into *The Flamingo* for a double shot of vodka.

The boys in there, they'd see him, maybe recognize him, maybe some women might remember him, too, and call him the King.

He'd tell them all about how he was back for good.

He'd tell them that he didn't care what the hell happened to Susie and the brats and that doctor she took up with. He'd tell them he was going to open a movie theater or manage the A & P or open a boat rental business. He'd tell them that anything you really needed, and all you could depend on in this life, you could find in your own backyard. Didn't need God. Nobody needed God.

God was like the phone company: You paid your bill, and sometimes you got cut off anyway. Sometimes, if you changed your way of thinking, you just did without a phone. Sometimes you switched companies.

Oh, but he still needed God. Within his secret self, he had to admit it. Roy Shadiak still needed to know that he could save at least one soul in the world. His feet ached in his shoes.

He had only brought one suitcase.

He had just walked out on Susie. It was in his blood to walk. His father had walked, and his grandfather had walked. They probably got tired of Jesus and all the damn charity, too. Even Frankie had walked, as best he could. All leaving before they got left.

Roy had blisters on the bottoms of his feet, but still he walked.

He passed beneath the Lover's Bridge, and the Bridge of Sighs, with its hanging vines and parrot cages. He walked along the muddy bank of the north canal, knowing that he could close his eyes and still find his way to Hispaniola Street. All the street names were like that: Spanish, or a mix of native words, like Ocala and Gitchie and Corona del Mar.

All the canals were thick with lilies, and snapping turtles lounged across the rock islets. The water was murky and stank, but beautiful pure white swans cut across the calm surface as if to belie the muck of this life.

Roy saw three men, old timers, with their fresh-rolled cigarillos and Panama hats, on a punt. He waved to them, but they didn't notice him, for they were old and half blind.

After climbing the steep steps up to the street level again, he was surprised to observe the stillness of clay-baked Sunland City.

As a boy, it had always seemed like an Italian water town, not precisely a Venice and something less than a Naples, thrust into the Gulf Coast like a conqueror's flag.

But now it seemed as ancient as any dying European citadel: It looked as if the conqueror, having pillaged and raped, had left a wake of buildings and archways and space.

It had been a lively seaport once. It was now a vacant conch.

The hurricane that had torn through it the previous year had not touched a building, but it had cleaned the streets of any evidence of life.

When he found *The Flamingo*, he kissed the first girl he set eyes on, a wench in the first degree with a beer in one hand with which to wipe off that same kiss.

A teenage boy in a letterman's jacket sat two stools over. The boy turned and stared at him for a good long while before saying anything.

Then, suddenly, as if possessed, the boy shouted, "Holy shit, you're King!"

"And you, my friend, are too young to be drinking."

❧

THE BOY STOOD UP—HE was tall and gangly, with a mop of curly blond hair, a face of dimming acne, and cheek of tan. He thrust his hand out. "Billy Wright. I swim, too."

"Oh."

"But you're like a legend. The *King*. King Shadiak."

"Am I?"

"You beat out every team to Daytona Beach. You beat out fucking Houston."

"Did I? Well, it was a long time before you were born."

"You ever see the display they got on you?" Billy pressed his palms flat against the air. "The glass cabinet in the front hall, near the locker room. Seven gold trophies. Seven! Pictures! Your goggles, too. Your fucking goggles, man."

"If they do all that for you at your high school, you should really be something, shouldn't you?"

Billy made a thumbs up sign. "Fucking A. You are something, man."

"I'm nothing," Roy said, downing his drink and slamming the glass on the bar for another. "No, make that: I'm fucking nothing, man."

"What you been doin' all this time, man?" Billy asked, apparently oblivious to anything short of his own cries of adoration.

"Selling Jesus."

"Who'd you sell him to?"

Roy laughed. "You're all right, boy. You are all right."

"Thanks," Billy said, then glanced at his watch. "I better get going. Curfew soon. Listen, you come by and see me if you got car trouble. I work at night at Jack Thompson's. You know him? I can fix any problem with any car. I'm not the King of anything like you, but I may be the Prince of Mechanics."

"Why would anyone care if his car got fixed around here?"

The boy laughed. "That's a good one."

WHEN ROY ARRIVED at his mother's house a half hour later, he was three beers short of a dozen.

"The great King comes home. You had to get drunk before you saw me. And you couldn't shave for me, could you?" Alice Shadiak said.

His mother wore khaki slacks and a white blouse. She had lost some weight over the past few years, and seemed whiter, as if the sun had bleached her bones right through her skin. A sun visor cap protected her face. She had seen him from the kitchen window, and had come to greet him on the porch.

"I suppose you need a place to stay."

"I can stay downtown."

"With your whores?"

"They all missed curfew, apparently." He attempted a light note. "Must've heard I was on my way."

His mother sighed as if a great weight had just been given her.

"Some man of God you turned out to be. I just wish you'd have called ahead. I'd have had Louise fix up your old room. Lloyd's in Sherry's old room. The house is a mess. Don't act like such a foreigner, Roy, for God's sakes. Give me a hug, would you?"

She moved forward.

In all his life, he could count the times she'd hugged him. But he knew he needed to change, somehow. He had not hit on precisely how. He would have to listen to his own instincts, then disobey them to find out how he might change.

He held his mother, smelled her saltwater hair.

When he let go, she said, "Susie called. She wants to know when you're going to forgive her."

"Never," Roy said.

"What are you going to do?" Alice asked.

Roy Shadiak said, "Mama, I had a dream. It came to me one night. A voice said—"

His mother interrupted. "Was it Jesus?"

"It was just a voice. It said, 'Set your place at the table.' Something's trying to come through me. I know it. I can feel it. Like a revelation."

"It was just a dream," Alice said, sounding troubled. "What could it mean? Oh, Roy, you're vexing yourself over nothing."

"This is my table. Sunland City. I have to set my place here," Roy said. Then he began weeping. His mother held him, but not too close.

"A man as big as you shouldn't be crying."

"It's all I have left," he said, drying his tears on the cuffs of his shirt. "You live your life and make a few mistakes, but you lose everything anyway. Everything I ever had, it all came from here. Everything I ever was."

Alice Shadiak took a good hard look at her son and

slapped him with the back of her hand. "You did it to yourself, what you are. Who you are. Don't blame me or your father or anyone else. All this big world talk and wife-leaving and crying. Don't think just because it's been twenty two years that you can just walk back in here and pretend none of it ever happened." She raised her fist, not at him but at the sky, the open sky that was colored the most glorious blue with cloud striations across its curved spine. "No God who takes my boys away from me is welcome in my house."

"I told you, I don't work for God anymore," Roy said. He went past her, into the house. He found the guest bedroom cluttered, but pushed aside his mother's sewing and the stacks of magazines on the bed.

He wrapped the quilt around his shoulders and fell asleep in his suit.

IN THE MORNING, he took a milk crate down to the town center. He set it down and stood up on it just as he would in other towns when he had preached the gospel. Folks passed by on their way to work, and barely noticed him. He spread his arms out as if measuring Sunland City and cried out, "I am King Shadiak and I have come here to atone for the murders of my brother Frankie and his friend, Kip Renner!"

A woman turned about as she stepped; a laborer in a broad straw hat glanced up from the curb where he sat with a coffee cup; an old Ford pickup slowed as its owner rolled down the window to listen.

As Roy Shadiak spoke, others gathered around him, the

older crowd mostly, the crowd that knew him, the people who had been there when he'd drowned the two boys at the public swimming pool over on Hispaniola Street, down near the Esso station, by the railroad tracks.

"No need, Roy," one of the men called out. "We don't need your kind of atonement. We been fine all these years without it"

"That's right," several people added, and others nodded without uttering a word.

"No," Roy said, pressing the flat of his hand against the air in front of him as if it were an invisible wall. "All these years I've squandered my life in service to others. I owe Sunland City an atonement."

"You want us to crucify you, King?" Someone laughed.

Others chuckled more quietly.

"That is exactly what I want," Roy Shadiak said. "Two atonements, two murders."

A woman in the crowd shouted, 'Two atonements for two murders!"

"Two atonements! Two murders!" others began chanting.

"Frankie Shadiak!" Roy shouted. "Kip Renner!"

"Two atonements! Two murders!" The crowd became familiar now. Roy saw Ellen Mawbry from tenth grade, Willy Potter from the corner store, the entire Forster clan, the Rogers family, the Blankenships, the Fowlers. As he chanted and as they chanted as the day loped forward, they all gathered—labor stopped, activity ceased, schools let out for a spontaneous holiday, until the town center of Sunland City was a sea of the familiar and the new. All turned out for the returning hero, their King, who passed among them to offer his life for their suffering.

"Two atonements!" they cried as if their voices would reach beyond that Florida sky.

It was what Roy expected from a town that God had turned his back on twenty three years before.

And then Helen Renner, her hair gone white, stepped out of the crowd toward him. She wiped her hands on her apron, as if she'd just finished baking, and went and stood at the foot of the milk crate.

Roy crouched down and took her face in his hands.

"Don't do it," she said. "Roy Shadiak, don't you do it. Neither one of them was worth it. We all let it happen. We're all responsible. It may not even fix anything, Roy. There's no guarantee."

His kissed her on her forehead. "I've got to. It's something inside of me that needs room to grow, and I've been killing it all these years. I've been killing every one of you, too. Two atonements," he repeated, "for two murders."

JOE FOWLER WAS A CRACKERJACK CARPENTER. He and his assistant, Jasper, were at the Shadiak house within an hour of Roy's leave-taking of the makeshift podium.

He stood on the porch in paint-spattered overalls, his khaki hat in his hands, looking through the screen door at Roy's mother.

"We got some railroad ties from out the Yard," he said. "They got pitch on 'em, but I think they gonna be just fine for the job." His voice quavered. "We'd like to offer our services, Alice."

Alice Shadiak stood like stone. "You and your kind can

get off my porch. I don't mean to lose two sons in this lifetime."

Roy came up behind her, touching her gently on the shoulder. "Mama, it's got to be done."

"Where is it written? Where?"

"On my soul," he said.

"Our kind has no soul," she said, pulling away from him. "I don't need God's forgiveness on my house. I don't want sweet Jesus' tears."

"It's Jesus that keeps you here."

"He doesn't even look on us, Roy," his mother said. "He doesn't even come to our churches. What does it matter? Does anyone in Sunland really believe there's a Jesus waiting to shine his light on us?"

"That's because of me."

"It's because your brother and his sick little friend were unnatural and perverted, and God cared more for them than for decency or nature or for any of us. I don't mind burning for that, Roy. I don't mind that sacrifice."

"I do," Roy said. "I saw Jesus out in the fields up north, and in the alleys of the fallen. Nobody else did. And you know why? Because Jesus was laughing at me, he was showing me that he was not going to be mine. He was going to belong to every fool who walked this earth."

Joe Fowler nudged the screen door open and stepped inside. "He's right, Alice. We ain't had Jesus or God for all this time, only those...things." He shivered a little, as if remembering a nightmare. In a softer voice, he said, "I'm getting tired of this life."

"I would advise you to get out of the light, Joe," Alice Shadiak said, sounding like the retired schoolteacher that she was. "I heard about your little Nadine."

All of them were silent for a moment, and Roy thought for a second he heard the cry of some hawk as it located its prey.

"Your boy knows what he's doing," Joe said, spreading his hands as if he could convince her with gestures. Still, he glanced briefly up at the empty sky. "We can't keep on like this." Then Joe grinned, but Roy could tell he was tense. "I'm prouder of you now, King, than I was when you won all those ribbons at the championship. Why don't we get on with this business?"

"Yes," Roy said, feeling an ache in his heart for Susie and the kids, but not wanting to retrace his steps. He glanced out on the porch, and beyond, to Joe's truck. "That's a sturdy piece of wood, Joe."

"From the old Tuskegee route, before tracks got tore up. We're going to have to balance them good. That's why I brought Jasper here." He nodded toward his assistant, who stood, mutely, on the porch. "We can get this going now, you like."

"Why wait?" Roy shrugged.

His mother retreated into the shadowy parlor. She called to him, but Roy did not respond.

Jasper suddenly pointed to the sky and made a rasping sound in his throat.

Calmly, Joe Fowler said, "Come on in, Jasp, come on, it's okay, you'll make it."

As if too frightened to move, Jasper stood there, sweat shining on his face. He stared up at the sky, pointing and shaking.

"Jasper." Joe opened the screen porch slightly, beckoning with his hand.

Roy shoved Joe out of the way and ran out to the porch. He grabbed the young man by his waist.

The cry grew louder as the great bird in the sky dropped, blackening out the sun for a moment.

THE SMELL WAS the worst thing, because they got it on their talons sometimes, from an earlier victim, that sweet awful stink that overrode all other senses.

Roy hadn't slept a night without remembering that smell. He couldn't get it out of his head for the rest of the afternoon.

"Where do they take them?" Roy asked.

Joe, who was still jittery, helped himself to the vodka. "Down to the shore. There's at least a hundred out there. And the rotting seaweed, too, and the flies, all the crawling things … it turned my stomach when I had to go down there to try and find Nadine."

"That's where it has to be."

"No, King. No. I won't go down there, no matter if it's midnight or midday."

"But how can you abandon her?"

Joe turned his face toward his glass. "She ain't her. I saw her. I risked my sanity, and I saw her. It ain't her. It's a It, not a little girl. I told her not to go out between two and four. All of us know about the curfew. All of us know to stay inside. And you ,,," Joe shook his head. He raised his glass as if to toast Roy. "You're the luckiest son of a bitch alive, you can get out, and instead, you decide to come back. You fucked up once, King, you don't need to keep on doing it."

"How many are left?"

"First, have a drink." Joe pushed the glass across the kitchen table.

Roy picked it up. Downed the remainder. Set the glass down. "How many?"

"Twenty-six, in one piece. The rest in as many as they leave us in. Some morning, you take a walk down there. Only, if any of them calls your name, you just run, you hear? You don't want to know who it is, believe you me."

Roy reached across the table and pressed his hand against Joe's shoulder. "That's where we need to do it."

"I ain't never going down there again."

"You'd rather all this continued?"

"Than go down there? You're damned right."

"I'll find someone else, then."

Joe stood up, pushing his chair back. He said nothing. He stomped out of the kitchen and went to sit with Jasper and Alice.

Roy drank some more vodka. He glanced out the bay window. On the roof, two houses over, three of them had a woman pressed against the curved Spanish tile. Their wings had folded against their bodies, and they were digging with their talons into the soft flesh of her stomach.

He was sure that one of them saw him spying, and grinned.

§

THAT NIGHT, he found the teenager working at Jack Thompson's garage on the south corner of Hattatonquee Plaza.

"Billy?" Roy asked as he stood beneath a streetlamp.

The boy dropped the wrench he was using and bounded out to the sidewalk. "Hey, it's the King. How you doin'?" He snapped his fingers several times, as if he was nervous.

"I'm doing just fine. And yourself?"

"Hey, any day you get through the afternoon here's a good day. So I heard you're going to try something."

Roy nodded.

"Let's go for a walk, Billy. Can you get off work?"

"Sure, let me just tell Mr. Thompson, okay?" Several minutes later, they were walking down along Hispaniola Street toward Upper Street. Roy had been doing all the talking, ending with, "And that's where you come in. Joe'll give me the ties, but I need someone to help."

"I don't know," Billy said. "You ever see how big those suckers are?"

"Yep. But we won't be out that late. We can do this at nine or ten in the morning. Hell, if you want, we can probably do it tonight."

"I heard the beach is really a bad scene. My dad got taken down there. I heard this guy at school say that they're like cracked eggs or they're all ripped up, only not quite dead yet. If I think about it too much, I get sick."

"It must be strange."

"What's that?"

"Well, you grew up in it. You never knew what the world was like before. You don't know what the rest of the world is like."

Billy stopped walking. "I thought it happened everywhere."

Roy shook his head. "Only here. Because of what I did."

"I don't believe you."

"Other places, you can walk around anytime of the day

or night and those things don't attack. Honest. When I was the King here, I used to skip classes at two and take off with my friends to Edgewater to the McDonald's. Didn't anyone tell you? Not even your dad?"

Billy shook his head. "Well, if God did this, why didn't he do it just to you?"

Roy shrugged. "Who knows? It may not even have been God. Maybe there's just those creatures. The way I figured it, it's not just because of me killing those boys. It's because everybody here thought it was okay, no big deal. Nobody made a fuss."

"You loved your brother?"

"I did, but I didn't know it then. I wanted him and his friend to go to hell back then. I was the King back then. I thought I was God, I guess."

They came to the end of the Upper Street, which stopped at the slight dune overlooking the stretch of flat beach.

The full moon shone across the glassy sea. The sand itself glowed an unearthly green from the diatoms that had burst from the waves.

On the sand, the shadow of slow, pained movement as a hundred or more mangled, half-eaten Sunlanders struggled to die in a corner of the earth where there was no death.

BILLY SAID, "I saw one of them up close. When they got my dad. She had long hair, and her eyes were silver. She had the fur, and the claws and all, and her wings, like a ptero-dactyl. But there was something in her face that was almost human. Even when she tore my dad's throat open, she looked kind of like a girl. Boy," he shivered, "I'm sure glad I'm up here and not down there. Down there looks like hell."

Roy said, "From down there, up here looks like hell, too. And it won't just end by itself."

Billy seemed to understand. "You swear you're not lying about what everywhere else is like?"

"I swear."

"Okay. Let's go down there. But in the morning. After the sun's up. I still can't believe it," Billy cocked his head to the side, looking from the moon to the sand to the sea to Roy. "I'm standing here with the King."

"Is that enough for you?"

"I guess. I got laid once, and that was enough. Standing here with you, that's enough." Billy pointed out someone, perhaps a woman, trying to stand up by pushing herself against a mass of writhing bodies, but she fell each time she made the attempt. "When I was little, we used to come down here and throw stones at some of them. But it's kind of sad, ain't it? Some of the guys I used to throw stones with, they're down there now. Someday, I'm going to be down there too, and if there are any girls left, they'll have babies, and they'll start throwing stones at me too. Where does it end?"

"Now," Roy said. "In the morning. You and me and a couple of railroad ties."

"There's going to be lots of pain, though, huh?"

"There's always pain. You either get it over with quick, or it takes a lifetime."

Billy rubbed his hands over his eyes. "I'm not crying or nothing."

"I know."

"I just want to get my head straight for this. I mean, we're both going to hurt, huh?"

"You don't have to. I do. I can find someone else to help."

"No. We'll do it. Then I'll be a legend too, huh? Maybe that's enough. We just drag those ties down there and set it up. One way or another, we all end up on that beach anyway, huh?"

⁂

IT WAS EASIER SAID than done, for they had to borrow Joe's truck to get the railroad ties to the beach, which was the easy part.

Lugging those enormous sticks across the burning sand, sliding them across the bodies, *the faces...*

It made a mile on a Thursday morning at nine a.m. seem like forty or more.

By the time they'd arrived at a clearing, Billy was too exhausted to speak. When he finally did, he pointed back at Sunland.

"Look."

Roy, whose body was soaked, his suit sticking to his skin, glanced up.

There, on the edge of Upper Street and Beach Boulevard was the entire town, lined up as if to watch some elegant ocean liner pass by.

The chanting began later.

At first the words were indistinct.

Gradually, the boy and the man could hear them clearly: *two murders, two atonements.*

"Roy?" Billy asked.

"Yes?"

"I'm scared. I'm really scared."

"It's okay. I'm here. I'll go first."

"No. I want to go first. I want you to do me first. I might run if I go last. I can't do it right if I go last—I mean, I'll fuck it up somehow."

"All right." Roy went over and put his arm across Billy's shoulder. "Don't be afraid, son. When this is over, it'll all change again. Atonement works like that."

"I wasn't even born when you did it. Why shouldn't one of them do it with you? Why me?"

"Now, Billy, don't be afraid. If they could've done it before, they would've. I think Jesus brought you and me together for this."

"I don't even know Jesus."

"You will. Come on," Roy lifted up one of the smaller spikes and placed its end against Billy's wrist "This one'll fit. See? It's not so bad. It's just a nail. And all a nail can do is set something in place. It's so you won't fall. You don't want to fall, do you?"

"Tell me again how you'll do it?"

"Oh, well, I set this rope up around my hand so I can keep it up like this… and then I press the pointed part of the nail against my hand and pull on the rope. My hand goes back in place, see? Like this, only I have to push a little, too."

"You won't leave me, will you?"

"No, I won't. I'm the King and you're the Prince, remember? I won't abandon you. Now, why don't you just lie down on it like that and your hand, see? It's going to pinch a little, but just pretend it's one of those things with the claws. Just pretend you won't scream, because you know they like it when someone screams. Okay? Billy, don't be afraid, don't be afraid…"

Roy spoke soothingly as he drove the spikes through Billy's wrists.

※

By sometime past noon, they'd both gotten used to the pain of the crosses.

Roy tried to turn his head toward Billy to see how he was holding up, but his neck was too stiff and he could not manage the movement.

"When's it going to happen?" Billy's voice seemed weak.

"Soon, I guarantee it. I had a dream from God, Billy. Something inside of me knew what to do."

Billy began weeping. "Just because of a couple of queers. What kind of God is that?"

"It's the only God."

"I don't believe it," Billy whimpered. "I don't believe that God would punish everyone just because of what you did. I don't believe that God would punish the unborn just because of what you did. It's all a lie. We just did something stupid, building crosses and crucifying ourselves. Look at that, look up."

Roy tried to look up, but he couldn't.

What he could see was the endless sea, and the shimmering sky as the sun crisped the edges of the afternoon.

The smell was growing stronger from the bodies.

"I don't believe in God!" Billy cried. "Somebody! Get me down! Get me down! He's crazy! Somebody help me! Somebody get me down! Jesus!"

Roy tried to calm him with words, but Billy didn't stop

screaming until an angel dropped from the sky and tore into him.

Roy remained, untouched on the cross, amid the writhing bodies on the shore of the damned.

He waited for some sign of his atonement, but only night came, and then day, and then the long afternoon set in.

Chosen

When it was over, he remembered the picture.

Because of living in the big city all his life, his first-hand knowledge of nature had come mostly from television documentaries and whatever he could recall from high school biology class.

But he'd forgotten about the picture all those years.

The caterpillar, its skin green and translucent and wet.

The wasp.

The bumps beneath the caterpillar's skin.

The caption: "As paralysis sets in, the wasp has proven her superior power."

He remembered what he thought, too, about the picture: in some awful way it radiated a beauty beyond conscience.

This was what he kept coming back to, later, when it was over, in his mind. Not his emotional life or his education or even his work, but that picture from a book he'd seen at the public library when he was only nine or ten.

How, even in his forties, it could come back to him with so
strong a memory.

§.

ROB ARLINGTON AWOKE one morning and thought he felt
something on his hand. He brushed at it but saw nothing
there. A sensation left over from a dream, perhaps. He took
a quick shower, crawled into his suit (he was so tired from
being up late the night before), and grabbed his briefcase on
his way out the door. It wasn't that he was late for work, it
was just that for the fifteen years of his life that he had lived
alone, he hated it. Not life, not work, not his loves and
losses, but just the fact of knowing he was alone in the
morning, that, at his age (forty), there was no one human
being who shared his home with him.

The hallway, when he stepped into it, was hospital
green, and smelled of paint. He locked his door, then
thought he heard a noise from inside it. As if something
were moving around in the kitchen. He looked at his door:
to open or not? Could be just an echo from another apartment. Glancing down the hall, he saw, just this side of the
fire doors, the super, papers in one hand, a dripping paintbrush in the other.

"Exterminator comes on Thursday," the super said. He
was taping notes to doors; he came up to Rob and slapped a
note to his door. The super, with his fat glasses and balding
pate with its twin sprays of hair, looked like a large worker
ant going about its business. Rob shot him a friendly grin—
never hurts to be on good terms with management—and
lifted the note off his door. It read: "Exterminator, Thursday, 10 a.m."

He wadded the noted up.

"I don't want the exterminator," Rob said, still vaguely listening for the thing that might be moving around in his kitchen. Was it a rat?

"You don't got roaches?" The super, his glasses magnifying his small button eyes to enormous disks of glare, thrust out his lower lip in a middle-aged pout that meant disagreement. "Everybody in New York's got roaches."

"None that I've noticed," Rob lied. Of course he had roaches, but he also didn't like the idea of the super and his wife going into his apartment, looking through his things. He already had evidence of their last visit when he'd been on a business trip to California, how they'd gotten in and used his tea kettle. He'd known it was the super, or perhaps Fanny, his wife, because they'd left behind a set of skeleton keys, which Rob returned to them hoping that embarrassment would be enough incentive to keep them from going through their tenants' homes again. "Look," Rob told him, "I've been fogging."

"You been what?"

"Fogging the apartment. I buy these foggers—you know —and it kills them. I don't have roaches. Or spiders, for that matter."

Then 6C opened her door. She was clunky and large, like an old piano, with hair in her eyes from just washing, and an enormous towel wrapped around her middle, barely keeping her breasts bound up. "I don't want one either," she said. "A bug killer. Don't let him into my place. Let me chance being beloved of the flies, but I don't want no bug killer coming through my place. I like my privacy."

The super looked at her, then back at Rob. "Pretty soon, everybody's gonna tell me they got no roaches. Why in hell'd I call up the exterminator if suddenly nobody's got no roaches?"

The woman in the doorway glanced at Rob. Her eyes were wide and glassy, like she'd just had great sex and was now a zombie. She was not pretty, but still looked freshly plucked, which, to a man of Rob's years was just this side of alluring. She was less overweight than stocky, and her skin was pale from staying inside too much. When the super had gone on down the hall, through the fire doors, she said, "Do you really fog?"

She'd been eavesdropping at her door, he figured. "No," he said, "I just don't like the nosy couple going into my apartment without me around."

She let slip a smile and blushed, as if she'd just dropped an edge of her towel. "They do anyway. I'm here all day, and I see them. They go through all our apartments. All except mine. 'Cause I'm here all the time."

Then she drew herself back through the doorway, hands clutching the door and frame, as if her legs weren't quite strong enough. She seemed to drag them with her, one after the other.

On the weekend, Maggie came up. When she and Rob lay after the Great Event, him feeling sticky, and her feeling exhausted, he mentioned meeting the neighbor for the first time. Maggie said, "I've talked to her on the elevator. She seems nice. It's too bad about the accident, but I guess we all get smashed about once or twice before life is up."

He moved his arm around, because the back of her head seemed to cut into it at an uncomfortable angle. "She get hit by a car or something?" Remembering his neighbor's legs, how she barely moved them.

"She told me she's agoraphobic. Stays in all the time. Lives on disability. Sad little thing."

"Sad hefty thing. How the hell does she afford that apartment on disability?"

"That's not nice, the hefty part. It's her grandfather's old apartment—he had it since the building was built in 1906. He knew the Lonsdale family, in fact, when they were designing the place. And she's sweet, even if she is strange. She's only thirty-four—can you believe it? It's life that's aged her—in that apartment, all her grandparents' things around, antiques, and dark windows, and old shiny floors, she just sits there and collects her checks and… well, ages.

"Like a cheese left too long under glass," he joked. "She claims she's beloved of flies."

Maggie was beginning to look stern; she didn't tolerate disparaging remarks about women. "Oh, stop it. She's had a terrible life. She worked at a grocer's, but her back bent or something. And then she finally works up the courage to get out, into the marketplace, as it were. She went out one day, she told me, to see her mother, who's in Brooklyn, and when she was coming up from the subway, two men took her purse and pushed her down the steps. Twenty steps, she said. She woke up in the hospital, and couldn't move for three months. She's only been back in her place maybe two weeks. She said she had terrible nightmares in the hospital. She's scared of people, I think."

"No wonder I never see her. You heard all this in the elevator?"

"You'd be amazed how much information she can fit in between the fifth and second floors." Maggie paused and looked at the wall beside the bed. "You don't think she can hear us, do you?"

"Not unless she has a glass to the wall. Hey," Rob said, rapping his knuckles along the wall, "no spying."

Somewhere beyond the wall, the sound of shattering glass.

Then, after Maggie left at eleven, he took the elevator to the basement, the weekend's laundry in the machine, and counted quarters out. He thought he heard a noise. Figuring it was a mouse, he ignored it. There were cracks in the lower parts of the walls, right where wall met floor, all along the basement. He had seen fat roaches run into these hidey-holes when he'd flicked the laundry room lights on. Always gave him the creeps; but they're only bugs, he told himself.

He put his quarters in the machine and switched it on. He leaned against it, listening to the gentle humming as water sprayed down on his clothes. Rob always took a book with him when he did his laundry—and he never left the room while his wash was going, because the one time he did, his clothes had been taken out in mid-cycle and left on the dusty cement floor. At some point in his reading, above the sound of the machine, he heard a series of ticks, like a loud clock ticking. Assuming the laundry had set the machine off balance, he opened it; rearranged the soaked clothing; closed the lid. But the ticking continued. He lifted the machine lid again, and while it turned off, the ticking kept going. He identified the area of ticking as one of the cracks along the wall. Then he thought it might be coming from over by the trash bin, down the hallway—sometimes the noises in the shafts echoed through the basement. He walked down the narrow, dimly lit hall, its greenish light humming as if about to extinguish from unpaid utilities, and looked around the trash.

Something was tapping from inside one of the disposal shafts. Rob hesitated at first wondering if a very large and angry rat might be inside it but the tapping continued, and seemed too steady to be a rat. He went and lifted the hatch up—

Something living, wriggling, wrapped in gauze and surgical tape, dropped. He instinctively caught it because he saw a bit of pink, like a human hand, from an undone section of the gauze and he knew as he caught it that it was a baby.

HE HAD the sense to call the police before he unwrapped the gauze, and was spared the sight of the dead infant.

"I think it was alive when I found it," he said. "I felt movement. Not for very long, though."

The officer, named Gage, shook his head. "Nope, she wasn't alive when you found her, Mr. Arlington. She'd been dead at least a half hour."

"I heard tapping. I think the baby was moving."

"It wasn't the baby," the officer told him.

The next morning, he read about it in the *Daily News*.

"Must be a slow week," he told one of his coworkers. In the paper they detailed the story: newborn baby, wrapped in gauze, skin chewed up by roaches, apartments under investigation, related to similar cases of babies left in Dumpsters and thrown down sewer drains, left in parks wrapped in old newspapers, covered with ants or flies or roaches or whatever scavenger insect had lucked into finding the fresh meat. There was his name: Rob Arlington. Advertising man. There was the building: The Lonsdale, Central Park West, where they refused to let the most famous rock stars live, even the ones who could pay the rent. It had another picture, older, of a man in his fifties, in the style of the turn of the century, a stern-looking man with a Rasputin beard and glaring eyes. The caption read: "The Original Lonsdale Scandal of 1917. Horace Grubb and his Theory of Nature." But nothing in the brief article elaborated on this photograph.

Maggie came by that night with wine and fresh salmon. "I thought you could use some cheering up," she said, whisking past him in the doorway with her packages. She smelled like gardenia, which he loved, and wore a bustier under a short jacket, a translucent skirt, and boots. He knew she would seduce him so that he would feel better, and he loved her for the thought.

"You heard," he said.

"Yep. Did you actually talk to the *News*?"

"What do you think?"

She didn't answer; he realized that he sounded grouchy. She opened the kitchen drawers in search of the corkscrew.

"It's in the basket on the fridge," he said. "My guess is some poor bastard junior reporter is stuck down at the precinct waiting for the dirt on a rape or riot, and he looks at the schedule of events and sees a baby-in-a-dumpster story. My name's right there. He can't file the story he's after 'cause nothing's in on it. So he ties this in with all those other dead babies left out to die stories and voila—an urban legend begins. With my name attached to the most recent one. The Man Who Found A Dead Infant In The Laundry Room Of The Famous Lonsdale Apartments Right Off Central Park West."

"You're a star," she said, pouring the Merlot into two glasses.

"I didn't know about the bugs, about how they'd been… doing that to the baby's skin," he said, shivering a little, going over to her, taking the wine, reaching around her back with his free hand, between the jacket and her skin. "You smell good. Like a garden of earthly delights."

"Yeah, I've been gargling with cologne. It's not too strong?"

"Not at all," he said, smiling, loving her little insecurities because they made her seem less perfect, more human. He drew back, sipped wine, rotated his head around to relieve tension in his neck. "God, Maggie, a baby. They said it was less than a day old."

"It's a rough place, this world," she said, and drew him to her. "You ever wanted a baby, Robby?"

He almost was going to cry, thinking of the dead thing in his arms, whatever brief and terrible life it had to endure; but he held back. Kissed her with gentleness. "I don't know," he said.

"Someday I want a baby, but—don't get that fearful bachelor look—not yet, and probably not from you, unless you play your cards right."

After dinner they watched television, and as he lay on the couch with her, he saw a roach on the wall. He picked up his shoe and threw it across the room, but missed it. The shoe made two loud thuds as it hit the wall and then the floor.

A few seconds later, the phone rang. He leaned over her head ("massive hair," he murmured, "like a scalp jungle") and lifted the receiver. "Hello?"

"Six D?"

He didn't recognize the woman's voice.

"Who's this?"

"Six C. Your neighbor. I got your number from the super. You all right? I heard a noise."

"Oh, hello. Yes. I lobbed a shoe at the wall." She seemed to accept this explanation.

Maggie looked up at him, her eyebrows knitting.

He shrugged and mouthed: *Nextdoor neighbor.*

The woman on the line said, "It scared me. After all the news."

"Oh," he said.

"It was you who found it," she said.

He felt drained. "Yeah."

"Were they hurt?"

Rob pulled his ear from the phone and looked at it. *What the hell?*

"Was *what* hurt? You mean, the baby?"

But she'd hung up the phone.

"My neighbor lady is spooky indeed," he said as he rested the phone back in its cradle.

After midnight, he had a craving for frozen yogurt. There was this place down on the corner that made the best cappuccino nonfat yogurt, a favorite spot of his. So, while Maggie slept, naked except for her panties, her breasts creamy and lovely above her small, indented belly, her dark hair obscuring one side of her face, he slipped on his jeans and tucked his cotton shirt in, stepped into his shoes, and tiptoed out of the apartment. He forgot to lock the apartment from the inside; so he stuck the key (three strikes and you're out, bubba, he thought as he finally got the sucker in the keyhole on the fourth try) into the door on the outside, and turned it so it was locked twice over. Never be too sure, even in a building like the Lonsdale, seventeen hundred a month for a junior one bedroom, even if you've been here for ten years, he thought. Babies in the garbage chute, roaches on the wall, anything can happen. He was a little drunk from the wine, and the thought of frozen yogurt, even with the October coolness outside, sobered him a bit; by the time he got to the elevator, he was standing up straight and wiped the grin of requited lust from his face.

He had to stand in line behind six others, all frozen yogurt fiends like himself, and by the time he'd gotten up to make his order, he decided on the largest size possible. He got two plastic spoons, and tasted the treat on the walk back to the apartment. He fiddled with his pockets, because he couldn't locate the keys. Had he left them upstairs? Damn it. He'd have to wake Maggie up after all. He buzzed the apartment. Three times. The last one, a long sustained buzz. Finally, she picked up the intercom.

Her voice was sleepy. "Rob?"

He giggled, high on Merlot and frozen yogurt. "Hey, sweetie pie, I locked myself out getting some dessert for the one I love and me."

As if she couldn't hear him, she asked again, "Rob?" She was still waking up, he could tell. He looked at the small black plastic of the intercom as if he could maybe see her through it if he concentrated. "Is it you?" she asked.

He pressed the button on his side. "Yeah, yeah, I got melting yogurt, Maggie, and I'm starting to feel a draft."

"Rob?" she asked again, weakly, and it sounded, for just a second, like she wasn't sleepy at all but about to pass out. About to cry, or something — something almost whimpery and breathless. Not like sleepiness at all.

And then he remembered: He'd left the keys in the door to the apartment.

Don't panic, he thought.

Pressed the button. "Maggie? You okay? Buzz me in, okay?"

He let go of the button.

Waiting for her buzzer. The intercom finally got pushed, but there was just the *ch-ch-ch* sound of dead air.

He pressed the button for the super. "It's Rob Arlington, Six D. I left my keys inside."

The super, ever vigilant, buzzed him in with no further identification required.

Rob ran to the elevator, and, luckily, it was on the first floor. He got on and pressed Six. The elevator gave its characteristic lurch. He realized that he was clutching the cup of frozen yogurt so tightly that it was all twisted, with dripping cappuccino yogurt spreading down his hand. He dropped it in the elevator. When he reached the sixth floor, he sprinted down the hall, tried the door. No keys. Locked. He rapped on it several times. "Maggie? Maggie! Maggie!"

He heard a noise, and glanced to his right.

The woman in 6C stood there, in a navy blue bathrobe. "She left."

"What do you mean she left?"

"She knocked on my door about ten minutes ago. She told me she had to go home, and she didn't know where you went off to. Here," the woman held her hand out, "she just left a second ago."

In her hand, his keys.

He looked at her, at the keys. "I just talked with her on the intercom. I came up on the elevator. I would've seen her."

The woman seemed annoyed. "She comes banging on my door at God knows what hour and tells me you left the keys in the door and then we hear the buzzer go off and she goes back to the apartment, and mister, I can't tell you what else she did, because I came back inside kinda pissed off that I now gotta wait up for you 'cause your girlfriend wants to split. If she takes the stairs or something, it ain't my business. She's a nice lady, seems like, but I can't read her mind. You want these or what?" she asked, finally tossing the keys to him. As she stepped back inside her apartment, he noticed the light blue bruises,like polka dots on her pink legs.

Maggie's answering machine picked up for three days, and then he stopped calling. He dropped by her place one night with flowers, but she didn't answer the door. Even though the lights were out in her apartment, he sensed that she was standing behind the door, looking through the peephole.

Then, on Monday morning, she called.

"It's me."

"Jesus, Maggie, I've been worried sick. What happened to you?"

"What do you mean, what happened to *me*? What happened to *you*?"

"I went out for some yogurt. You were asleep. I didn't want to wake you."

Silence on the line.

"Something frightened me."

"What?"

"Oh, Rob," she sounded close to tears, "I can't talk about it. Not like this."

"Will you meet me somewhere? Cafe Veronese?" He heard her slow breaths, as if she needed to calm down.

She whispered, "Okay. After work. Six."

When they met, she moved away as he tried to give

her a friendly hug. Her eyes were circled with darkness, and bloodshot. Her lips were chapped. Something about her skin was shiny, as if she had a fever. They sat at a booth in the back, and she, uncharacteristically, withdrew a cigarette from her purse and lit it. "I didn't know where you went. The door was wide open. The lights were off. Someone was inside with me. I knew it wasn't you."

He noticed that she kept glancing down at her fingers; and then he knew why. She was afraid to look him in the face.

He said nothing.

"I was just about naked, and scared. I reached for my jacket, but…it…it grabbed my arm."

"A man," he said.

She shook her head.

"A woman?"

Maggie laughed once, bitterly. "None of the above. It crawled up my arm."

He looked at her face, thinking it was a joke. "It was a bug?"

She glanced up, saw his grin. "Fuck you," she said.

"Sorry. But you got scared by a bug?"

"It wasn't just a bug, Robert. I knew I couldn't talk to you."

He sipped his coffee, she smoked her Camel. Her fingertips were yellow-brown from smoking.

As if suddenly inspired, she rolled the sleeve of her sweater up and thrust her arm under his face.

Dark bruises, in a diamond pattern.

He touched along them and felt thin blisters.

"It attacked me," she said.

"Jesus," he gasped, "Maggie, you've got to see a doctor. This isn't just some bug."

"Exactly," she said, triumphant. Tears shone like jewels in her eyes. "It's like a disease. It feels like a disease. It's taking me with it. Whatever it is. Inside me. It did something. But this," she nodded toward the diamond bruise, "this was only where it held me. The others…"

"Others?"

Maggie's expression turned again to stone. "You don't believe me."

He said nothing.

She said, "They opened me up."

❧

"She doing okay?"

Rob was checking his mailbox. He glanced around the corner, and there was the woman from 6C. It was eight o'clock, and he had walked Maggie home, put her to bed with a stiff drink, made her promise to see a doctor in the morning, and then walked home. He was hoping to just go to bed early, himself.

The woman said, "Your girl. I heard from the super she got attacked. He said it was a spider from South America or something. He started talking exterminating again— sounded like Adolf Hitler, you ask me."

"Better," he said, "she's doing better. I haven't talked with her since Monday, though. I think maybe she just needs to be alone for a while."

"You think she imagined it, don't you?"

"I don't know."

"She seemed nice. I don't think she'd make it up. I

mean, I seen spiders big as birds at the museum. She doesn't seem like the lying type, your girl."

"I didn't say that. Something definitely happened."

"You was thinking it, though. Hard for guys to deal with things like that, I don't know why, happens every day in this city—bugs and thugs. You probably don't believe about the gators in the sewer, but I know two cleaning women who swear by them. Guys, they never believe it till it hits them butt first in the face. But you ain't like that, right? You half believe her, don't you?" The woman gave a hopeful smile. "I got attacked in the subway three months ago. My hip still ain't too good. You give me a choice between getting bit by a spider or jumped by a hoodlum, I choose spiders every time."

He managed a smile.

"My name's Celeste. Celeste Pratt. We talk a lot in halls and junk, but we never been introduced." She extended her beefy arm. She'd dressed all in black, which somehow brightened her face. "I didn't know she got bit that night. I'm sorry I ragged on you so much. I was tired. Friends?"

He nodded. "Sure."

"Glad to hear she's doing better. You think it was a black widow or something?"

"I don't know. She won't see a doctor."

"I don't like doctors neither," Celeste said, shaking her head. "I believe in homeopathy and stuff like that. The mind, Rob. The power of the mind. And nature. It's weird to believe in nature when you live in a city like this, ain't it? But I always lived here, all my life, and you look for nature where you can find it. The law of nature, way I see it, is we got to sometimes give ourselves up to it, like we're part of this big system, and your legs—like, say, mine—get bashed, but you just let the pain of healing take over, you let nature run its course. It's like Grubb's Nature Theory, about survival and adaptation. Know what I mean? You tell your girlfriend I hope she gets better, okay? Do that for me? She's always been so nice and friendly to me, I hate to see nice people get hurt, but in this city, you know, it happens every day, but better some spider or something instead of a guy with a butterfly knife, right?"

Rob stared at her as if he could not quite believe she existed. He blinked twice.

"What's wrong?" she asked.

"Nothing," he said, then headed for the elevator. Celeste got on with him and smiled, but didn't volunteer another river of conversation. On their floor, he let her off first, then got off, stood just on the other side of the elevator door, and watched Celeste go to her apartment.

When she had put her key in the lock and turned it, he said, "Excuse me, Celeste."

She turned to him, beaming.

"Downstairs, did you mention something about someone named Grubb?"

"Grubb's Nature Theory. Yes."

"Is that Horace Grubb?"

She nodded, blushing.

"My grandfather," she said.

CELESTE INVITED him into her apartment to show him her grandfather's books. Rob accepted out of curiosity, as much to see the large apartment as the texts. The apartment had three bedrooms, "although it was once this entire floor, a fourteen-room affair, but it was divided up in late '29, when everyone with anything lost it. My grandmother, she was from New Orleans. She redecorated like crazy," Celeste pointed out the French touches, "and the apartment, what's left of it, is pretty much the way she wanted it. She was off the deep end, you ask me. 'Course, she ruined the floor, the beautiful wood floor, what with her wheelchair scraping along. It's why I got all these fancy carpets and runners all over the place, to cover up the damage. My mother never wanted to live here ever since she married back in '48, but Grammy left it to me. Who else? She knew I'd take the right kind of care of it. But I ain't much of a housekeeper. The bedrooms, you should see, all disaster areas—I do all my crap in them—but, here, come over here, we can have a nice martini at the window." She led him to the kitchen, which was dark like the rest of the place; the floors were thick with layers of dust and crumbs, as if she never cleaned up after herself; the windows were painted black, supposedly because her grandmother, at the end of her life, could not handle light because of eye problems. Celeste pressed a small latch to the left of the pane, then pushed open the larger of two windows.

The view was of the nearby park, shrouded in night, and was not blocked by the Cavanaugh Building, as it was from Rob's small apartment

After making the martinis, Celeste sat down opposite him and raised her glass. He clinked his to hers and sipped. *Strong.*

He said, "I saw a picture of your grandfather. In the papers."

She rolled her eyes and flapped her hand in a gesture of dismissal. "Oh, God, my grandfather, twice as nuts as

Grammy, and all that business. Grampy's book was called *De Naturis* and it basically was nothing but his theory, which always sounds loony-tuney in the light of day. Oh, right, right, you want to know about it, don't you? It was like something about how man's role in Nature was to be a farmer. That kind of thing. We ain't here to control nobody's nature, he said, but 'cause we got to do stuff, ease the birth he said, so nature can keep on keeping on, or something like that"

"How'd he get in trouble over *that*?"

"Different time, you know, back then, nobody liked the message. World War One just started, and it had something to do with soldiers going to France, and some papers Grampy gave out. He got attacked. Terrible. Would've killed him, too. Things worked out eventually. But it made the news here for about ten minutes before the war took over. Grammy used to tell the story like he was some kind of saint. Which he most definitely was not. Put the Lonsdale on the map, though."

"Was he anti-war?"

"Oh, no," she said, her breath strong and gin-soaked, "not by a long shot. He loved war, he said, 'cause it meant more human flesh got put in the ground, which was good for crops. Crazy I know. Genius but crazy. He believed the best use of human beings was as compost or incubators. Imagine thinking that. But is sold newspapers. And his book. But that's really where the trouble was, in his big fat mouth. He thought dead people was the best food nature's got. He had people, you know, who agreed with him, listened to him and stuff. Wrote a lot of pamphlets. They called themselves Grubbites. He was definitely a class-A weirdo. He wasn't a cannibal or nothing like that, even though they all thought he was. Got arrested five times, just for causing a ruckus. He was a...what do you call it?"

"Misanthrope?"

"Yeah, in a big-ass way." She drank down the rest of her martini and went to get another. Her back to him, she said, "Maybe something different, too. He had this whole spiritual side to him, like he believed there was a god in everything alive. Trees. Birds. Even the air."

"Sort of a pagan transcendentalist then," Rob said.

She was drinking her martini at the sink, half turned to him, looking out the window.

"Everything. Even unto the smallest," she whispered.

Rob noticed that a trail of ants running from a crack near the top of the kitchen wall, all the way down beneath the sink. *No wonder she leaves crumbs and scraps everywhere.*

Celeste was watching the ants, as well, but made no move to kill them. As he followed the trail from its highest point he noticed that the ants went down to the corner of the shelf at the sink and trooped across shiny tile to within an inch of her hand.

⁊❧

HE LAY in bed that night with a reading light on. He thought about Maggie, about her gardenia smell, a garden of earthly delights—and somehow this reminded him of the ants in Celeste's apartment, for he wondered what kind of urban garden they made their nest in. Finally, he turned out the light and fell asleep.

He awoke sometime in the night hearing the sound of a woman moaning from nearby.

Through the wall.

Celeste. Having a very loud nightmare. The moaning continued, escalating to muffled cries, and he guessed it was not nightmare but a private pleasure. He heard the humming buzz of what could only have been a vibrator, and he thought: *good for her.*

Strangely, it aroused him, and the more he listened, the less aware he was of his own left hand slipping down beneath the elastic of his Jockey shorts.

Just as he was closing his eyes, dreaming about a faceless but beautiful woman, the moaning from the other side of the wall turned into a scream.

He threw on his bathrobe and dashed to the hall, but by the time he knocked on Celeste's door, it was silent. The hallway light flickered and buzzed; the bulbs would need replacing. He stood there, looking around at the other apartments, wondering if anyone else had heard the woman's scream. He started knocking again, and this time he heard her moving around, as if drunk, knocking things over as she made her way to the door. Maybe she'd had another martini or two after he'd left; she'd certainly gulped them down fast enough.

He saw her shadow beneath the space between the floor and the door. She was standing on the other side of the door, looking through the peephole at him.

"Celeste? Are you all right?"

She must've been scraping her nails on the door.

"Celeste?"

The shadow beneath the door vanished; he heard noises as she moved back down the corridor.

From within the apartment, the chime, of a clock.

Two a.m.

He turned to go back to his apartment, shaking his head. Had he imagined the scream? Was it a cry of pleasure?

As he climbed back into bed, he thought he heard the buzzing of her vibrator again, just at the wall. A little louder than before. He closed his eyes, wondering if he should investigate further. Maybe she'd just tripped on something and screamed, maybe she was drunk, maybe she didn't even scream with pain, maybe it was the way she climaxed — who the hell knew?

He was asleep, probably dreaming, but he imagined that an enormous cockroach was riding Celeste's ass, its feelers stroking the back of her neck, and its face turning slowly to look at Rob as it diddled his neighbor, its face all brown and callused, with flecks of dirt across the broad platform between its eyes, and its eyes looking just like the Rasputin eyes of Horace Grubb.

The phone rang, both in the dream and out of it; in the dream, Rob went running down a long corridor in search of the phone; in reality, he awoke with a groan and reached to the table by the bed.

"Hello?"

He heard static on the line.

Then: "Help me."

A woman's voice.

Its very weakness shocked him awake.

"Celeste?"

"Help me," she said, and then a sound like high-pitched humming, like the Vienna Boys Choir humming one note without taking a single breath. The hum filled the phone, and it felt like a needle thrust in his ear.

He dropped the receiver.

THE DOOR to 6C was open.

The sun was still not quite up, although the honkings and screechings of morning traffic had already begun outside.

Her apartment was lit with red lights, like a bordello, and he thought of Celeste's grandmother decorating the place with her New Orleans touches. The furniture seemed bloodied by the light, and it made him queasy as he walked through the front hallway. He had a sense that there was movement all around him, just on the periphery of his vision, but every time he glanced at the red-shrouded furnishings, nothing seemed out of the ordinary.

The phone, off its hook, lay in the kitchen.

A smell, too, like clothes that had been sweated in and discarded on a heap to rot for months. The window that had formerly held the view of the park was blackened over with dark cellophane.

Again, he sensed a slithery movement, and scanned the floor, but saw nothing. He glanced down the slim hallway that led to the three bedrooms.

"Celeste?" he asked.

A sudden noise, as of someone rushing to a door and throwing herself against it, sliding down to the floor. Sobbing. Muffled, as if a mouth were taped over.

His first instinct was to walk back to the door, go to his apartment, and call the police.

He took one step back, and stood still when he heard another sound: a repetitive vibrating sound, like monks chanting *aum* over and over.

But it was a woman; it sounded like a synthesis of a

woman and a machine, for the vibration of her voice seemed to increase beyond what a human might be able to, and he felt the vibrations in the floor and walls.

Someone threw herself at the door again.

Door Number Three.

He could not bring himself to turn around and run for cover.

He recognized the voice. It was Maggie's, humming louder. It made him want to cover his ears.

Then it was as if he were being swept along with a tide, for he found himself moving toward that door, that dark red-stained door, moving smoothly straight forward, moving his feet, not one after another, but together, as if he were in a dream and not in contact with the ground at all. His heart was beating like a vibrating drum; or it was not his heart, but her humming; his mouth had dried up; he swallowed dryness.

When he reached the door, he twisted the knob, opening it.

The room was dark.

The stench came at him in waves of heat; it smelled like a compost pile.

He stepped inside and reached for the light switch.

The switch was low, as if made for someone in a wheel-chair (*her grandmother had been in a wheelchair, she'd said, and had left tracks all along the floor*, he thought as if explaining away what bothered him).

The light came up, also red, from the solitary bulb dangling from its thin chain at the center of the room.

The room itself was small and its floor was covered with dark earth and wet leaves.

Maggie lay in mud just a few feet in front of him.

She was naked.

She stared at him, and he could see the vibrations of her lips as she hummed.

Bruises, too, all along her arms, stomach, breasts, legs.

Her humming increased to a shattering pitch.

There was a twitching, almost, no, a wriggling of skin along her arms and belly, too, and as he leaned forward to touch her…

As the humming seemed to vibrate the entire building …

He felt the edge of an antenna stroke featherlike down the back of his neck.

Celeste whispered in his ear, "Isn't she beautiful?"

He turned around, and Celeste was dressed in a gown made entirely of wasps, all with wings twitching, diamond heads, their thousand legs clinging to her. "I am their chosen, Rob. For what my grandfather did for them, his many kindnesses, I got chosen as their midwife. They won't hurt you, Rob, I wouldn't let that happen, as long as you don't try to hurt me, you're gonna be fine."

The wasps moved along her shoulders, over her breasts, her living clothes shimmering in the light.

He gasped, "What did you do? What in God's name?"

"Nature is God," Celeste said, "we only live to serve. People build cities like this, and what, you think it's all for us? It ain't. It's for them. We're just part of a big-ass colony, Rob. God's a maggot, turns the flesh to earth. We're less than maggots, don't you get it?"

"What about Maggie? What did you do to her?"

Celeste shook her head, clearly disappointed that this was his interest. "It ain't like she's in any pain, you know, one of the mothers paralyzes her while they lay their eggs under her skin. I ain't gonna make anybody go through pain. Not what's not natural, anyways."

The scream on the other side of the wall.

Maggie's scream.

Maybe. Maybe.

Maybe it was Celeste, maybe she was mating with a wasp, maybe the scream was pleasure, maybe it's her eggs inside Maggie's body.

It was then that Rob felt his mind leaving his head, as if it were leaking out of his ears and drifting in a cloud of smoke, to dissipate in the hall. Something short-circuited for him; he could not easily remember words or how to make his arms or legs move right; for a moment, he wondered if he knew how to breathe.

Celeste reached out and took his hand in hers. He watched her do this and felt like an infant, unable to make sense out of the world in which he'd found himself. She stroked his hand. "If I want, they'll choose you, too, to help. I want you to help. I feel like you're a friend," she said, drawing his hand to her bosom. "It's so lonely sometimes, being chosen. It's so lonely sometimes being the one to do this."

He watched the wasps travel from her hand to his, then up his arm, sometimes biting, but it didn't bother him, he didn't mind, he didn't mind. He felt them everywhere, all over his skin, and when he listened carefully he began to understand what they were saying, all of them at once, through their vibrations and feelers and bites.

🜨

THE SEASON WAS A HARD ONE, for the earth needed turning, and there needed to be others; for, once these young came up, the mothers would need to lay more eggs after the mating time.

When it was over, he remembered the picture.

He remembered the picture when he looked at Maggie as they were coming out.

The caterpillar, its skin green and translucent and wet.

The bumps beneath the caterpillar's skin.

Beauty beyond conscience.

The cruel face of nature.

But as he watched it happen, Maggie's eyes on him, her humming at a pitch, he knew it was the most glorious and selfless act that any human being could ever perform and he wept with the intense and silent beauty as her shiny skin ruptured with conquering life.

Damned If You Do

Calhoun was sweating up a storm, and it was only ten, but this was La Mesa in summer, and he actually found the talk radio soothing while he worked.

He could hear, beyond the chattering radio, the children in the schoolyard across the street, all yelling and pounding the blacktop while they played dodge ball.

He could smell the jaw-aching sweet stink of the fat lemons in the trees that Patsy had planted when they'd first moved into the bungalow ten years before.

The old shepherd, Vix, was chawing on a lemon, which made the dog whine with sour hurt as the juice got into his gums—and still, he wouldn't let go of a lemon once he got hold of it.

Cal's beard itched, too, another annoyance on a particularly annoying day, and his shovel struck the flat rock again, or maybe it was a pipe this time—the sewage system ran this way and that across the back of the property, and who the hell knew why since the toilets were always backing up and the garbage disposal ran rusty brown nine times out of ten.

"Mother—" he began, then held his tongue, laughing because Patsy didn't like strong language or strong drink in her house.

Her house.

It's my house as well as yours.

He had been digging for twenty minutes—the ground was dry and hard, and there weren't many places left.

Not that he'd left any markers, but he had a memory like a trap, and once he saw something, he always remembered it.

I remember you, you, and you, he thought, blinking his eyes in the sun, looking from one patch of garden to another, or there, in the mulch pile.

He went back in for a soda pop and one last piece of apple pie—she had baked it the night before, and he had had one too many pieces, but he loved her pies. The radio was louder in the kitchen, echoing, and a man was on it talking about his problems with his wife, and how he wanted to leave but couldn't because he loved her.

The call-in DJ, who claimed to be a therapist, although she doled out advice about as bad as any Cal had ever heard said, "Love is not just a state of being, but an active, everyday thing, you know—know what I mean? Like you maintain your house and your car, you also have to every day maintain your relationship, like a tune-up…"

Patsy always had that thing blaring, always talk radio, from morning till night till morning.

The Radio Lady jabbering, nattering, bantering.

He wanted to turn it off, but if he did then they'd know.

The neighbors.

They'd know.

Old Broad over the high wall with her arms of beef and face of jug, always leaning over and saying, "Whatcha doin'?"

Or that brat of hers trying to get over to pick lemons, looking in the windows, trying to slide through the casement windows into his wood shop.

Mr. Erickson, whom Patsy called Ear-Ache, complaining about the volume of the radio, wouldn't he think it strange when the radio went off? Ear-Ache once came over to be neighborly, and asked Cal, "So, you're retired now, what was your business, anyway?"

And Cal had told the truth, although he sometimes lied because he hated when people pried. "I used to be a principal of a school down in Dauber's Mill, back before they consolidated. I liked teaching better, more hands-on work, but they needed a principal more than they needed a wood shop teacher, so I had at it for a good fifteen years."

Ear-Ache and Old Broad, eyes, ears and mind on him all the time, wondering if they were looking, if they were watching.

He never did his work at midnight or in the wee morning hours, because he had learned in his sixty-three years that you could do anything you wanted in life as long as you did it in broad daylight, when nobody believed what they saw anyway.

He took a bite of pie and a swig of soda, and looked out across the lawn at the shallow trench he had begun.

Maybe I'll just put her with that pig-tailly girl, in the mulch.

The problem with the mulch pile, or with any mulch

pile, is you couldn't put anything salty in it or you'd ruin it for sure. No bacon drippings, no skin, nothing that had a high salt content. The pig-tailly girl was easy enough to scrape, and even though she still had plenty of salt in her, he just had to bury her deep and hope for the best.

Dead mice you could put on the mulch, and even dead birds, but nothing too much larger or you had a pile of shit that was just a pile of shit.

Cal set the can of soda down, stroked his walrus mustache, scratched his chest through his sweat-stained T-shirt.

Can't scrape Patsy, though. Can't do it

Take much too long, and then I'd have to flush too much scrapings. More backup in the toilets, maybe too much, and maybe they'd have to come out and dig up the lawn to check on the sewage pipes, and then what?

"No more wood shop, for sure," he said aloud.

He whistled for Vix to come inside, then he turned and went down the narrow hallway with its family pictures tattooed on the wall, all the kids they'd had in all those years.

The radio noise got louder, this time just a commercial. He hated the way on TV and radio, how they made the commercials louder than the shows.

They were advertising for *Squeaky Kleen*, a deodorant. Cal didn't use deodorants, although he made an excellent natural soap in his wood shop, using an old recipe he'd found in a book from the turn of the century. It was a little bit of lye and a little bit of animal fat, and it got skin so clean it practically took the hair right off, with a fresh smell, like children on their birthdays.

He went into Patsy's room—they had separate rooms,

ever since he'd retired, because she wouldn't put up with his night fears anymore. So he had the little guest room, what used to be the nursery off the second bathroom, and she kept the master bedroom, which looked out over the back-yard. She was simple in her tastes, which is what he always liked about her anyway, and difficult in her emotions.

She had a bed, a table with a reading light, her mother's rocking chair, and the radio. It was an old one, a big jobbie that she'd had since the fifties, hell, it took four big fat batteries to run it, and like his old Royal typewriter she had it repaired constantly rather than replace it with something newer and easier to use.

On the radio, a woman began crying, and the DJ lady said, 'It's all right, it's good to cry, hey, I'd cry, too, if that happened to me. But you do have a choice, sweetie, you can walk right out that door and get a life! It's the thing to do, get...a...life. It's easy. When you do it, you'll see. You'll call a friend, or a family member, and see if you can't stay with them for a while, until you've got your feet on the ground, and then you'll get a life. Sound good?"

The woman on the line said, "I guess. I thought this was my life."

"What you described is not a life. I know it hurts to hear this, but it's why you called in, isn't it? It's not a life, I repeat. A life is something you participate in and draw some satisfaction from. All right?"

Cal wanted to shut that damn radio off more than anything, but he knew if he did, someone somewhere nearby would think something, would wonder about some-thing, might even look in a window somewhere.

Patsy's eyes were wide, but the tape had held on her mouth. The wire around her ankles had cut into the flesh, but not too far, and they held well, strung around the frame of the rocker.

She'd exhausted herself all night rocking back and forth, trying to get over to the window; he'd had to pick her up twice between eleven and two when she'd spilled forward and slammed her head into the parquet.

He'd wiped the blood from her nose, and kissed at her tears, and used his heart to try and unscramble a message to her, to help explain what he was doing and why he had to, but she was too busy listening to talk radio.

She never got the messages he sent from his heart, but he always followed his heart and tried to get her to understand the direction it took him.

It was no use talking to her, because she only understood normal everyday problems and emotions, not the kind that made a man do what he had to do, a place beyond words, a territory of pure obligation.

Maybe if she still went to her job downtown, she wouldn't have even noticed.

But she, too, had retired; the retirement party had taken place at the Sportsman's Lodge down on Edison and Fourth the previous Friday night. He was going to wait until she went to run some errands—and maybe if she hadn't given up liquor so suddenly, and gotten religion in one lightning bolt of revelation, maybe she would've missed what he did.

What he'd been doing for twenty-five years.

He remembered his mother's words, so many years back, on her deathbed. Her advice, her comfort. He repeated them, whispering, although Patsy would not hear them, she would hear the radio, radio, nothing but radio. "I know it's terrible to watch your mother die like this, Cal. But far worse is it for me to go to my glory without knowing that you are taken care of. I want you to be happy, but I know the pain life brings. We've all had it visited upon us. Happy is the man who buries his own children, for in his pain, in his burden, is the care and comfort that he laid them to rest before their spirits could be crushed."

The sunlight burned the windowsill, beneath the translucent shade, and he heard old Vix whining from the kitchen—still chewing that lemon.

Patsy smelled, and her face glowed with sweat.

Nine children in twenty-five years.

Someone was bound to find out, one day, but he never imagined it would be his wife. She had used the soap, she had used the candles, she had blown on the whistle he made out of bone, the whistle with the little sparrow carved into the side, the whistle like ivory.

She had stood by him when he spoke with the police about each one running away, about the troubles boys and girls like that faced, not feeling that their biological parents had claimed them, not feeling at home, not feeling safe.

Not feeling cared for.

On the radio, a teenaged girl giggled and talked about not having her first period until she was sixteen.

He had promised Patsy, too, that he would care for her until death. Perhaps this was Providence stepping in and making sure he was as good as his word, although he didn't believe in fate or God or karma.

Soon, he'd have to stop old Vix's breath, too, for what would a dog do if his master were to die?

I've been dying for years, Patsy, his heart said, and I've cared for my own.

It wasn't fun, never, he wasn't one of those who enjoyed

doing his duty. It was like being a soldier, shooting his brother, but the weight of his obligation was great.

His mother, too, he had taken care of her in her last moments.

He had no choice back then, when he was sixteen, because she had been the one with the gun in her hand, and it had taken a good half hour to wrestle it from her.

Mother was trying to take care of him, but Cal had known, even then, that it was a man's job. He knew he was damned, but it was a damned if you do, damned if you don't sort of proposition when you came into this world.

Patsy's eyes were bulging, and he never liked to see her worried or in pain, but he had wanted to give her time to think it over and make her peace. Life is meant to work out the way it works itself out, and maybe Patsy, maybe she would die within the next decade anyway, and if something happened to him, who would care for her?

The weight of duty was heavy, for sure.

The Radio Lady said, "We are given free choice when it comes to our own behavior, and we can only change someone else insofar as we can change ourselves, you know?"

He looked around for her needles, the long thick ones.

He didn't like to prolong pain, and he remembered how peaceful his mother had been, how the gasp from her bosom, and the stench, and the relief in the act itself, were like opening a sewer pipe of flesh to release gas and what was trapped inside the gutter of the body.

It was noon before her heart stopped, and nearly one when he'd taken her down to his wood shop. He laid her across the bench, her neck in a vise because it helped keep the rest of the body stable if the spine held.

Then he went to work, and he cried, as he always did, and he drowned out the sound of talk radio with his instruments.

The sky clouded over by two-thirty. The children were let out of school, and he had to wait until the last yellow bus took off, and the last child had finished walking home, peeking over the wall to taunt Vix into barking, before he could go out and dig some more. He went to the mulch pile, which was still moist and humid with dead grass and sour milk and the fish heads from Tuesday's supper. Vix lay down beside him and let a lemon roll from his mouth. The old dog looked at the lemon and pawed it. Cal noticed there were ants crawling across it. He bent over, his back hurt, picked it up, was about to toss the rotting, chewed, ant-cursed lemon into Old Broad's yard, when he figured, what the hell, and dumped it down beside him. Then he pitched the shovel in deep, trying to keep in mind where he'd buried the pig-tailly girl from two years back. When he felt he had dug down far enough, he went and got several of Patsy's parcels, and plopped them in, and then checked the wall for a spy, saw no one, and went and got the rest.

Vix sniffed the hole he'd dug, but the dog was more attached to lemons than anything else out in the yard. "Find another one, Vix, this one," Cal nudged the rotting lemon by his foot, "this one's all wormy. Good boy."

He took the radio, too, shut it off, finally, and dropped it in, kicked in the wormy lemon and some fish heads, and covered the whole mess up.

Then he went into the kitchen, sat at the small glass table, and actually missed the sound of talk radio for once in his life. He went and turned on the little radio he'd bought for Patsy, the one she'd never used. He turned it to the talk radio station and kept the volume up.

"I just loved that last call—didn't you?" the Radio Lady said. "It's a day brightener to hear something like that in these times. Imagine, rescuing a cat and someone's grandmother in the same hour. Gosh, sometimes life is difficult, but it's always fascinating, isn't it?"

Cal looked at the telephone hanging from the wall.

At the radio.

Wonder if Patsy ever called in.

She wasn't one for discussing her life.

Miss her, even so.

The Radio Lady announced the number to call in, and Cal went and dialed it.

After seven rings, a man picked up, and Cal hung up quickly.

Then he dialed again, got the man who mentioned he was screening calls, and asked Cal what his problem was.

"It's about my wife and kids. I have trouble, sometimes, taking care of them."

The man on the phone told him he'd be on in about two minutes.

Two minutes turned to four, when the Radio Lady came on. Cal had to turn the radio down to hear her. "What can I help you with?"

"Well," he said, then thought he might hang up.

"Don't be shy," she said.

"I've been listening to you for a long time. Years."

"Well, I've been here four years so far, so thanks for the compliment."

"Hmm. I thought it was longer. Well, it's about my wife and my kids."

"Is it good or bad?"

"Neither. Just about life. What I've learned. I'm sixty-three, you know."

"Congratulations. Hey, isn't it great that you people still call in?"

"My wife, I miss her, and the kids. Most of the kids."

"How many do you have?"

"Nine."

"Holy cow, nine kids. And you raised them all?"

"I cared for each and every last one of them to the best of my ability."

"Well, you deserve a pat on the back for that. These days, too many people are abandoning their children."

"That's right," Cal said, "most of my kids were like that. Foster kids. But my wife and I took them in. Loved them. Gave them a home. And I fulfilled my obligation to them, too."

"I wish I could meet a man like you," the Radio Lady said. "I'll bet a lot of women in my audience would. So what are you calling about, you catch?"

Cal paused. "I'm tired of burying them. I miss them."

The Radio Lady said nothing.

Cal said, "Oh, they live on, in things, in day-to-day objects, when I wash sometimes, I can smell their skin. Fresh. So fresh, the way only a child can smell."

The Radio Lady said nothing.

And then Cal realized why.

She was crying. "Oh, you poor wonderful man. God bless you, God bless you."

"Thank you," Cal said, and hung up.

He went and turned off the radio. He couldn't cry anymore. Except for taking care of Vix, he had fulfilled his obligations. He just couldn't take care of Vix, not yet.

In the morning, the roses needed hosing down because he had been hoping it would rain and had left them dry for days. He washed with the sunken-eyed boy soap, and remembered the tight little curl to the child's fingers (although he couldn't for the life of him remember names much anymore). Then he went outside, turned the hose on, and sprayed down Vix while he flooded the roses. Ants came out from the soaked earth, and crawled up the garden wall. Old Broad emerged in her yard wearing a muumuu and barbed-wire curlers with her Yorkshire terrier, getting the ball of stringy fur to yap, yap. Before he could take cover, she'd spotted him and called out, "Your wife—is she all right?"

Cal pretended not to hear.

She thinks I'm ancient, so being deaf isn't much of a stretch.

Old Broad and her Yorkie toddled over to the wall, and he smiled and then dropped the smile.

She said, "I don't hear the radio. The talk shows."

"Radio broke. Wife won't listen to any other radio. She's a peculiar woman. Thirty-five years of marriage."

"I'm not surprised it broke. Good heavens, she played it night and day. You must be happy it broke."

He scrunched up his face angrily. "Not at all, woman. I was used to it."

"Well, it's nice to have the quiet so I can hear my wind chimes."

"Doesn't get too windy," Cal said, stepping as far from the wall as he could without getting too muddy in the puddles he'd created with the garden hose. Vix put his forepaws up on the wall and began barking at Old Broad and her Yorkie, so the neighbor retreated.

He went and checked the bougainvillea, which hadn't been growing well this year, although the trumpet vine was in full bloom, with hummingbirds darting in and out of its blossoms.

I take care of my own. My family, my garden.

My obligations.

Oh, but he missed them, their kisses, their hands, their love.

Even his mother, with that friendship of blood that transcended all others.

It's over, he thought. It's done.

Someone, in another yard, somewhere, he thought, just beyond Old Broad's, turned up their radio loud as if to fill the void left by Patsy's blaster.

He could faintly hear the Radio Lady say, "You're on the air, caller? You're on the air." A child's voice said, "Hi… um… I don't know if I'm s'posed to call you … but I listen to you all the time."

The Radio Lady said something, although Cal couldn't quite hear it.

The boy said, "I ain't—I mean, I guess, I haven't ever called in. Not like this."

Another voice, a girl's said, "Hello? Wow. This is cool. Hello? Is someone there?"

"You're talking with the Radio Lady," the other voice said, and although faint, Cal recognized it. It was Patsy.

He went and called Old Broad back over to the wall. She came over, shuffling like she was all bound up inside that oversized dress, and curled up her nose at him like he stank.

"You hear that?" he asked her.

"What?"

"Listen." He held a finger to his lips.

Old Broad was silent for a moment, cocking her head to the side like she was trying to roll that last marble right out from her eardrum.

Another boy, about six, said, "I scared."

The girl, the pig-tailly girl, Cal was sure, said, "Don't be scared. We're all taken care of. Aren't we?"

Old Broad interrupted Cal's listening. "I don't hear nothing. Is it a siren or something? If you tell me what I'm listening for, maybe I can hear it."

Cal was angry that she was talking so much while the talk radio was going on. "No," he said. "I won't tell you. If you don't hear it, I won't."

"I hear things sometimes," Old Broad said, nodding. "Maybe you're hearing a ghost."

Cal looked at her sharply. "I don't believe in ghosts."

"I don't mean that kind, I mean like on TV when you have a ghost image. Or now that your wife's radio broke, you're so used to hearing it that you still think it's playing." But the woman saw that Cal was paying no attention to her, so she tramped across her own pansy bed to reprimand her son for leaving his bicycle out in the driveway.

Cal listened, and noticed that Vix, covered with mud in the garden, seemed to be listening, too.

He couldn't fall asleep. He went to Patsy's room and rocked back and forth in the chair, smelling her smell. He pulled the curtains aside and looked out at the backyard. The radio had gotten louder, just a bit, but still not to the volume it had been up to when Patsy had been around. He listened to each of his nine children talk with their mother, and he listened to her words of comfort, but he was still very sad.

At least I have one comfort, he thought, at least I can hear them.

And then, around three a.m., just as he was nodding off, he heard a voice on the radio that did not belong to any of his children, nor to his wife.

It was a woman with such an impediment to her speech, it sounded like a toad was sitting beneath her tongue. "Ca-hoo, Ca-hoo, heh-up mee, Ca-hoo."

He got out of the rocker and went to the window. He rolled the side windows open wider.

"Mother?" he asked, peering out into the dark.

"Cay-uh, cay-uh," she said, and then was lost in the static of the radio.

She had said "care," he was sure.

Even though she wasn't buried in the yard, but in a cemetery twenty-five miles away, she had traveled through the ground waves, through the sewage pipes of the dead, to speak to him.

He knew why her voice was strange, because of what he'd had to do to her mouth.

He wished now he hadn't. He would like to understand her better, for she was a person of enormous wisdom.

He watched the darkness, listening for her voice again on the radio, but all was silence.

He drank several shots of whiskey, not his style at all, and slept late. He dreamed of the sound of machines roaring and dogs barking, and awoke at nine-thirty when someone tapped him on the shoulder.

He smelled mud and flowers, and looked into the empty eyes of his mother, her face dripping with mud and sewage. She opened her scarred mouth, the one that had burned so well when he stretched the electric cord across her lips, between her teeth, and switched on the juice. The scars took the form of a star pattern, and when she parted her lips, dry leaves and dead grass dropped out.

She took his hand and led him to the wood shop, where the sound of talk radio drowned out the other sounds, the sounds of the care one human being shows for another.

The Hurting Season

The wind had a taste to it.

Leona hung out the wash on the rope strung between the willow and the sapling, down by the river, with the smell of shad, dead on the water's surface from running, and the clean of soap powder and bleach; the Sack was strung up and bounced with each wind-blow; and Mama was boiling meat in back before the flies would be up to bother her; and it was a rough wind, a March wind even in late April, coming ahead of a storm.

The river was high, threatening flooding if the storms kept up, which they were wont to do, but Theron had done all the clearing, and the chairs and table from the levee were already in the springhouse, the old springhouse that no longer flooded, and he was almost to the shed now, because the horses were kicking at the stall.

The sky was its own secret blue, unnatural, with blue clouds and blue winds and blue sun, all signaling a squall coming down from off-island.

Theron could see the oyster boats rocking across the bay,

two miles from the house, just like mosquito larvae wriggling, and he wondered how it was on Tangier, and what about that girl he met at Winter Festival—he was fourteen, and she was nearly seventeen, but he had seen it in her eyes, those flatland island dull eyes, a flicker of what could only have been fire when she had let him touch her the way Daddy touched Mama.

The horses, prophesying storm, kicked the wood, and the shed trembled.

Mama cried out at the noise, surprised, but Leona, in her earthly wisdom, just kept hanging sheets and shirts as if the impending storm mattered not one whit, for it would come and go quickly, a final rinse for the laundry. Theron kept buttoning his shirt; the screen door banged with the wind; the blue sky turned indigo and then gray, with flashes of lightning between. First drops of rain, sweet and cold.

He ran like a horse himself, back to the shed, for he loved the horses and could not bear their distress. The ground was damp but not muddy, and he galloped across it barefoot in spite of the biting chill. He could feel the rain spitting at his back as he got there, to the door, which he drew back. The smells of the horses, the manure, the cats, too, for they roamed among the piles and hay for mice and snakes, strong but not unbearable.

His father was there, at the mast that centered the shed, around which the horses were knocking and frenzied. The mast had a great length of chain hanging from it, and the leather strops of discipline, too, wrapped about its middle. Carved notches marked the days of the season, from Winter Festival to May Day, the days when Daddy did his penance, the hours of his atonement for a sin long ago forgotten. His father wore no shirt; his chest was covered with kudzu hair that sprawled across his shoulders and connected to his belly like inflamed moss; trousers were caked in filth; boots, too, with blood near the toes for they were tight and he would wear them all during the hurting season.

"You got Naomi upset," Theron said, not meaning to scold, but it was hard to avoid. Naomi was not yet a year, and needed gentleness; the old horse, her sire, Moses, was used to the season, the frantic pain that Daddy put himself through, but Naomi was barely more than a foal.

His father's eyes were not even upon him, but gazing through him, beyond him, to some richer meaning, listening to the words, but decoding them. The man's face was yellow jaundice, and the hunger was showing in the sunken cheeks; the thin blond hair, cut short like a monk's, Theron thought, was slick and shiny, the sweat, pearls of mania. "That's not good," his father said, "you take her out, then, take her out, boy."

Theron nodded, glad, and ran around the mast to grab Naomi's bit. He tugged at her, but her eyes were still wild. Theron looked around the shed. "It's the chain, Daddy," he said, for he knew that a horse, unless tempered to a rope, would take fright at anything that resembled one; the silver chain swung lightly about the thick wood. On its end was a rusty hook, from one of the oyster trawlers that had dry-docked over in Tangier, and there was blood on it. He registered this for a moment, wondering what his father did with the hook that drew blood from him. It was frightening, sometimes, the hurting season, at least to him; he was sure it frightened Mama, too, for she was moody during those months; Leona, older than Daddy or Mama, didn't seem to notice or care; and Milla, being so young, accepted it the way Theron had up until he'd become aware that it

was only his daddy who did it, that when he went to Tangier, nobody else had a mast or the chain and strops, nobody
else had a daddy that slept with the horses from February
to May.

The boy brought the horse out of the shed, into the
slapping rain; the smell of bleach and soap stronger, and he
looked up to see the wash swimming in the wind, but their
stays holding tight to the rope; Naomi tugged away from
him, but he kept his grip, watching for the horse's teeth. He
spoke to her, calmly, and led her over to the springhouse. It
would be small for the horse, but she'd be safe and fairly
dry, and the darkness of it would calm her.

He tied her to the upturned patio chair and wiped at
her forelock and nose with the red bandanna the girl over at
the Festival had given him, smoothing down the horse's
mane and then her withers to settle her.

The horse had the thick hair of the island horses—it was
said that they could be traced back to the Spanish ships
wrecking off the islands, and his father had told him that
the harsh winters in the wild had developed the breed to the
point of hardiness and hairiness. Something Theron had
learned in school, too, a phrase, "survival of the fittest."
That had been the island horses, for they swam every spring
around the time of May Day from Tangier over to Chite
Island, which was here. Centuries of horses coming to mate
on Chite in the spring, and to swim back in October when
winter came too harsh here first.

Chite was a small island, although the river that ran
through it connected it through the wetlands to the
Carolina Isthmus, so it had not been a real island since
sometime long before Theron was born. Old Moses, he had
been a Chiter, and his dam, a wild horse that had never

been tamed on Tangier, had died and left the one foal, Naomi. The horse had a bad fetlock, the back left, and she raised it a little, so he squatted down beside her and massaged it. The wind through the cracks in the old gray wood bit around his ears, but the whistling sound it made seemed to steady his horse. "Good girl," he said, and wrapped the bandanna around his neck the way the girl had. It smelled of horse now, and perfume, and fish, as all things on Tangier smelled of fish.

Theron waited out the storm in the springhouse, and when it was over, in just a few minutes, he led the horse out to the rock pile road that spanned the wetlands to the west of the house, and took her at a canter.

The horse slowed toward the middle of the rock pile, for it became less smooth here, and there were small gaps in the rocks. The sky cleared, but the sun was still not up in the middle of it, but back in the west, over Tangier. A red-winged blackbird flew up and out from the mesh of yellow reeds and dive-bombed at Theron's hair.

"Hey!" he shouted. "Didn't do nothin' to you!"

He flapped his hands at the descending bird, and dug his heels into Naomi's side until she galloped some more. His butt was sore from the pounding, for he didn't have his seat yet, at least not with Naomi, for she was an erratic bounder, but he rose fell rose fell with her, his leg muscles feeling stronger, and he tried to pretend that he and the horse were one animal, just like his daddy had taught him.

The bird left him alone once he was out of its territory, and he guided Naomi down to some fresh water for a drink. He saw their reflection, the horse's long neck, its thick shaggy mane hanging down, and then his own face in the cold brown water—the red bandanna tied smartly just under his chin, and some whiskers on his upper lip. He smiled at himself; she had liked him, that older girl in Tangier, the pretty one. She was brown eyed just like everybody else on the islands, and brown hair, and freckles. Her hands were like little brushes on his, for they scratched and tingled and smooth when she had slid them across his palms.

"Look," she'd said after she'd done it, and he had looked at his hands.

At the palms of his hands. All red, the palms, like they were blushing and warm.

"You got skin like water," she said. "See-through hands. I can see you through your skin, boy. Boy." She said "boy" like it was a dare, so he had kissed her behind the booth, where nobody could see them.

He had known what the other boys did, the ones in school, even over in the Isthmus, for they bragged about girls in a way that disturbed him. But he had felt lightning in his body, and her lips felt like fire and sensations had gone through him that words could not even describe, for it was his first kiss ever, and she had seen his excitement when she drew back from him. She had whispered, "I guess you like me."

Embarrassed, he had dropped a hand in front of him and clasped it with the other, "Huh?"

"It's nature," she had said, the teacher of his flesh. He leaned forward and kissed her again, but she pushed him away this time and said, "Nuh-uh." But it led him, this feeling, just like the boys had told him it would, it led him without a thought in the world to anything else.

᪲

THE HORSE LEANED DOWN, disturbing the water, and Theron's reflection whirled and broke in the water. She had liked him, that girl, that day. He had changed since then, he knew it.

He was a man now, even if the others called him boy.

The rock pile road ended at the Isthmus Highway, rising out of reeds and swamps and trees like an altar of the true religion. Theron wasn't supposed to take Naomi up on it, for even though few cars traveled it until summer, when the summer people from the cities came down, and when Daddy blocked the rock pile road to keep them off his property, the highway could be dangerous, for an occasional truck roared through in nothing flat, and a girl's mother got hit a long time ago trying to push her daughter out of the way and to safety. But Theron, a man now, and cocky, rode Naomi up the brief, steep hill, batting back the sticks and dead vines that had not yet greened since the winter, and clopped up onto the potholed blacktop. Naomi was faster on the highway, riding down the centerline, for it was completely flat, and where it dipped could be seen, and avoided, for several yards.

As he slowed her down at a bend in the road, there was a car stuck in mud on the shoulder.

THERON WAS NOT big on cars, not like the other boys, but this one was pretty and sporty, a two-seater.

A man stood beside it, kicking the bumper and cursing to high heaven. He was a lot younger than Daddy, but maybe only Mama's age. He wore a tan suit, and had rolled his slacks up almost to his knees, which were black with mud.

He was soaked head to toe, caught, no doubt, in the storm.

His eyeglasses were fogged up.

Theron dismounted, and led Naomi up to the man.

"Mister, 'scuse me, but what kind of car you got?"

The man looked at Theron as if he could not hear. Almost like his father in the shed. Then he said, "Right now it's the kind that breaks down."

"Pretty nice. Never seen one like that before," Theron nodded. "You're stuck."

"You must be the local genius," the man said, and then grinned. "Sorry, but you ever get so pissed off at something you can't see straight, kid?"

"I guess."

"So, kid, you live nearby? You got a phone or something?"

"Yeah, only we don't let strangers use it."

"Okay. Anybody else around here? A drugstore?"

Theron chuckled, and covered his mouth to keep from making the man feel too bad. "Sorry—sorry— don't mean to laugh. Don't mean to. But you're twenty-five miles from town center." He pointed toward the direction that the man must've already come.

"That piss hole? Christ, kid, that's a town? I thought it was a mosquito breeding ground. Nothing the other way? You sure?"

Naomi whinnied, and Theron patted her nose. "She's shy. Just shy of biting, sometimes, I think."

He tugged at the bandanna around his neck, self-consciously.

There was something about this man he didn't feel comfortable around.

The man said his name was Evan, and he was from Connecticut, and that he wrote magazine articles and was supposed to meet his wife up the shore, but he was doing some kind of article on lost byways of the South.

"You write," Theron said. "That's wild. *Wild.* Me, I barely read. I watch TV. Anything you write ever get on TV?"

Evan shook his head. "Yeah, I once did write for the TV news."

"I can't watch that. My daddy thinks news people make stuff up, but Daddy thinks anybody on TV's a big fat liar."

"Well, kid, I definitely I hated the work. I hate what I do now, too. What a way to make a living, huh? Get up in the morning, not liking your work? The rat race."

"You do what you got to do." Theron shrugged. "Survival of the fittest, I guess. Even rats got to eat."

The wind, which had died, picked up again, rattling the dead reeds, shagging at the budding trees, dispersing the petals of those that had blossomed early.

The boy could smell honeysuckle already, up here on the Isthmus, and it wasn't even May.

The man had a kind look to him, a wrinkled-brow honesty, and Daddy had always told him that when someone needed help, there was only one thing to do.

"Look, mister," Theron said after watching the man pace his car, "if you don't mind walking down there," he pointed down the gully past the wetlands to the stand of trees that separated Chite from the mainland. "It's about two miles. I'd let you ride her, but she wouldn't make it easy on you. Look, my daddy's got a phone and nobody's supposed to use it, but I don't know what else to do. Only I got to warn you about one thing."

Evan said, "What's that, kid?"

"We keep to ourselves most of the time. I go to school up in Isthmus, but we don't really mix. My baby sister, Milla, she never even seen a mainlander."

The man named Evan seemed to grasp this immediately.

"Let's go," he said.

Evan got a camera and a tape recorder out of the back of his car and strung both of them around his neck like ties. His shoes were brown and would be uncomfortable for the trip; Theron smiled when he thought of crossing the land on the other side of the rock pile road, where the mud would surely suck him to his ankles if he wasn't careful.

As they descended from the highway, down to the road between the wetlands, Evan asked, "are there snakes down here?"

"Too cold still. There'll be plenty by June. I once saw a man from Tangier bite the head off a cottonmouth. You ever see that? He just chomped, and spit it out like it was tobacco."

Theron rode Naomi, but walked her slow so the man could keep up with them.

He wasn't sure how Daddy or Mama, or even Leona for that matter, would take having a stranger over; Daddy was normally friendly with outlanders, but this was the hurting season, and it might be embarrassing for someone to walk right into the middle of that.

Theron assumed that other fathers had their own hurting seasons, although he'd been too awkward to ask any of the boys over in the high school, both because they always seemed smarter than him, and because he was already teased enough as it was for being so different.

The sun was just past noon when they reached sight of the house, and the wind had pretty much died. The sky was white with cloud streaks, and the earth was damp, the moss that hung from the trees sparkled with heaven's spit, as Mama called rain when she was feeling poetic.

Naomi tried to pick up speed as they neared the shed, but he kept her slow out of courtesy to the stranger.

"How you doin'?" he asked Evan.

Evan wagged his head around and said, "Hey, kid, can I get a picture? You and the horse and the house and that thing—what is that? Some kind of bag?"

Theron looked in the direction where Evan indicated, as the man unscrewed his camera's lens cap. Dangling from the willow, with the wash, was the Luck Sack.

"It's for good luck," Theron said. "It keeps away hurricanes and floods in spring."

"How's it work?"

"So far, so good."

The boy posed for a picture, sitting up proudly on his horse, keeping his chin back so the man could get a clear shot of the red bandanna that girl in Tangier had given him.

Theron wished he had a hat—his father had a hat, and now that Theron had crossed the border between boyhood and manhood, he would've liked something brown with a broad brim to keep the sun out of his eyes, to make him feel like a horseman.

"So," Evan said, snapping several pictures, "you have other good luck charms?"

Theron struck pose after pose, attempting a masculine look for this one, a shy look, a rugged, tough pose. "We're not much into good luck. It's what we call tradition. Say, how much film you got in there?"

"Lots."

Snap–snap–snap.

"What's in that sack, anyway?"

"One of the cats. We got seven. Kittens on the way," Theron said. "I love kittens, but cats I ain't so fond of. You gonna put my pictures in a magazine or something?"

"Maybe," Evan said, lowering the camera. He let the camera swing around his neck. He reached beneath his glasses and rubbed his eyes.

The man's face glowed with sweat—the two miles had been hard on him, because he was a Yankee. He seemed to be taking in the house and the river, maybe even the bay if his eyesight was any good with those thick glasses. "Are you people witches or something?"

Theron straightened up and grunted, "Nahsir," his pride a little hurt by such an assumption. "We're Baptists."

"Ronny, honey," Leona said, her eyes lowering, not even looking at the stranger; she kept the screen door shut, and her massive form blocked the way. "I don't think you should be bringing people home right now."

"This's Evan. He's a Yankee," Theron said. "He needs to use the phone."

Leona looked at Evan's shoes.

Theron saw the squiggle vein come out on her forehead, like when she was tense over cleaning.

"Mister, our phone's out of order." She said it lightly, delicately, sweetly.

Then she looked him in the eye.

Evan blinked.

"That's okay," he said, patting Theron on the shoulder.

Leona arched her eyebrows and stared at the small tape recorder and camera around his neck.

"You a traveling pawnshop, mister?"

"Nah'm," Theron butted in. "He writes for magazines. He's a famous writer, Leo, he used to write for Dan Rather."

"Not really," Evan said.

"I'm sorry, sir, but you can't come in the house. The little girl's sick, and like I said, the phone's not working. We had a big storm this morning. Always knocks out the power lines and such." She kept her hands pressed against the screen door as if the man would suddenly bolt for it. And then, to Theron, "Now, Ronny, why'd you bring this nice man all the way out here when you knew the line was down?"

Theron said, "'Cause I thought it'd be up by now," turning to look up at Evan, who kept staring at Leona. "It's usually up in a hour or two," and, as if this were a brilliant idea, he clapped his hands. "I know, Evan, you can stay and have some sandwich and pie, and then maybe the phone'll be up."

A groan from the shed out back, and Evan and Theron both glanced that way. It was Daddy with his hurting. Leona groaned, as much to cover up the other noise as anything, and she clutched her stomach. "I tell you, mister, what little Milla's got, we all seem to be coming down with. You'd be wise to get on back up to Isthmus."

"Some kind of flu," Evan said.

"That's right. That one that's been going around." She nodded, looking pained.

Evan grinned, as if this were a game. "Had my flu shots, ma'am. And anyway, even if I hadn't, I'll survive it."

Leona lost all semblance of pretend kindness. "Just get

off this property right now, and Ronny, you take him back up to the highway." She stepped back into the gray hallway and shut the big door on both of them.

"She always this sweet?"

Theron shook his head. "I don't know what's wrong with her today. She's almost a hundred, but all age done for her is make her ornery." He went and tied Naomi around the sapling.

"I thought you had your marching orders," Evan said, following him.

"I don't listen to Leona. She's just the hired help. You take orders from servants, my daddy says, and you end up a shit frog. We got them in the spring house. You ever see a shit frog? They go from the stable to the river, but they still can't get it off them." Theron grabbed the laundry rope with both hands and clung to it, letting his knees go slack. "You gonna take more pictures?"

"I don't know," Evan said, but he lifted his camera again, snapped some more of the boy, and then of the river, and the house, and the tire swing, and the Lucky Sack hanging on the willow. He looked all around, through his camera, as if trying to see something else worth photographing, when he seemed to freeze. He lowered the camera and turned to face Theron.

Theron shivered a little bit because of the man's look, all cold and even angry, maybe.

"Where are the lines?" he asked.

"Huh?"

"Kid, if you got a phone, where's the pole? Where're the lines? If the line's down, you got to have a line in the first place, kid. What kind of game is this?"

Theron didn't have an answer, not yet anyway. He said, "Dang."

From the shed, a series of shouts, cusswords as strong as Theron had ever heard from the boys at Isthmus.

The stranger named Evan turned around at the sound, took in the whole landscape, the house, the river, the shed, the springhouse, the laundry rope, the bay, the boats, the way the grass was new and green and damp. He walked over to the Lucky Sack, and Theron shouted, "Mister! Evan! Hey!"

But the man had already opened the sack, his face turning white, and he looked at Theron, his eyes all squinching up, and Daddy began screaming at the top of his lungs from the shed, and Old Moses, the horse, started thumping at the wood.

"You sick fucks," Evan said, weeping, "you sick fucks, you said it was a cat, you sick…" But the sobbing took him over, racking his body, the convulsions of sadness shaking him.

Theron blurted, "It's bad luck to look in the Sack, mister."

"Who is it, you sick fuck, what is this?"

Theron tugged at the red bandanna around his neck. "It's private."

"Listen, you." Evan raised both fists and brought them down on the boy, knocking him to the ground.

Theron was angry, and knew he shouldn't, but told him anyway because he hated keeping the secret. "It's the first girl I ever kissed. It's the part of her that's sacred. It's the part that made me a man!"

But then Mama was there, behind the man, and hit him with the back of the hoe, just on his skull, and the glasses flew off first, and then his hands wriggled like nightcrawlers, and he crumpled to the ground.

MILLA HELD on tight to Mama's skirt, her brown eyes wide, her hair a tangly weedy mess.

She looked like an unmade bed of a baby sister; when Theron got up from the ground, he went and lifted her up.

"It's okay, it's just fine, Milla-Billa-Filla," he said as he bounced her around. She was only three, and she looked scared. Theron loved her so much, his sister. He had prayed for a brother when the birthing woman was in their house, but when he had seen Milla in the shed, lying there in his mother's arms, while the birthing mother screamed as Daddy tied her to the mast, he knew that he would love that little girl until the day he died, and protect her from all harm.

Mama said, in her tired way, "Ronny, why'd you bring him down here?"

Theron kissed his sister on the cheek and looked up to his mother. He was always frightened of his mother's rages, for they, like the hurting season, came in the spring and lasted until midsummer. "I—I don't know."

"That ain't good enough. And don't lie to me, or you shall eat the dust of the earth all your days and travel on your belly."

"All right. I guess because I wanted Daddy to stop hurting for a while. I want us all to stop hurting for a while, Mama," and then he found himself crying, because he didn't like the hurting season, and he didn't completely understand the reason for it.

For a moment, he saw the temper begin to flare in his mother's eyes, and then she softened. She bent down, dropping the hoe at her side, and gathered him up in her arms, him and Milla both, hugged tight to her bosom. "Oh, my little boy, you may be a man now, but you will always, always be my little boy." She threatened to weep, too, and Theron figured they'd be the soggiest mess of humans in the county, but Mama held back. Daddy was silent in the shed, no doubt exhausted.

THERON THOUGHT it might be the right time to ask the question he'd had on his mind since he first discovered about the hurting season. "Why, Mama?"

"Ronny?"

"Why does it have to be us?"

"You mean about the season?"

"Not just the season," he said, drying his tears, "but us here, and them," he looked across the bay to Tangier, "over there. We don't mix."

His mother reached over to his forehead and traced her finger along the brand that had been put there, a simple X. He felt her nail gently trace the lines of the letter. "It's our mark," she said, "from the beginning of creation. Passed through the fathers to the sons." Theron looked at Milla. "What about the daughters?"

"Uh-huh, that, too, but no birthing, no creation. Our womb must not bear fruit. You remember the scripture."

He did: "And your seed shall not pollute your womankind, but shall be passed through the women of the land to bring your sons and daughters into lesser sin. And of your daughter, the fruit of her womb shall be sewn shut, and neither man nor beast may enter therein. Behold, you and your seed shall sin that the world may be saved."

But when he told the lines to one of the boys in Isthmus, the boy laughed and said he knew the Bible by heart and that wasn't in it. But in the hide-covered Bible that Leona kept above the bread box, it was right there, in Genesis.

The man on the ground began to stir, his hands twitching.

"I'm gonna take him to the shed," Theron said, pulling away from the warmth of his mother's arms.

THE MAN WAS HEAVY.

Dragging him through the mud was made more difficult because of the way he was moving, for his legs kicked a bit, and Evan was groaning, but the blood had stopped from the wound on the top of his skull. Theron felt muscles in his arms and legs begin to plump with this effort. He was sore from riding, too, which didn't help. He smelled the spice and meat from the stewpot and felt crazy hungry, but dinner would wait until after the important work.

When he reached the shed, Evan looked up at him, although the glasses had fallen somewhere along the way. Theron could tell by the way he was squinting that he wasn't seeing much right in front of his face.

"It's okay, mister," the boy said, "don't worry."

Evan, scrunching up his face, not quite sure where he was, coughed up some spit, which dribbled down the side of his chin. "Uh-awh," was the noise he made.

Theron rapped on the shed door, not wanting to let go of the man's shoulder with his other hand.

"Daddy," he called, "open up, Daddy!"

The door opened inward, and his father seemed to know what to do. He bent down on one knee, cradling Evan's face between his hands. His father's face was slick with greasy sweat, and there was blood around his eyes where he'd driven the fish hooks beneath the lids. He brought his face close to Evan's and kissed the sputtering man on the lips.

Theron knew then that he had done the right thing, for it would mean that Spring would come fast now, and that Daddy didn't have to suffer through the hurting season alone. While he kissed the man, Daddy brought the oyster boat hook with its length of chain down beside their lips, and began pressing its rusty point into the man's forehead to carve the X of their mark upon him so that the transfer of hurting could begin.

༄

LAUNDRY DRIED BY THREE, with Leona taking it down, and laying it out across the basket.

Milla was playing on the tire swing, head first through it, her small fingers clutching desperately at the black sides as she twirled around.

Mama was napping, and the horses had calmed after the first wave of screeching.

Theron sat out on the dock, twiddling his toes in the icy water, and soon, Daddy came and sat down beside him.

"Give him some rest," Daddy said, but the pain was gone from his eyes, for the first time since Winter Festival.

"No more storms, I reckon," Theron said, feeling the weight of his father's arms around his shoulders. A bird was singing from one of the trees, and there were ducks bickering out on the river. Across the bay, the solitary Tangier, so close, so distant.

"You may be right."

"Daddy?"

"Boy?"

"Why does it have to hurt?"

"What do you mean?"

"This life. Why does there have to be a hurting season?"

His father had no reply.

That was what disturbed him about life, the very mystery of it, the deepness of its river, where on the surface all was visible, but beneath, something tugged and grabbed and drowned, and yet the current flowed, regardless.

"Look there." His father pointed off toward Tangier.

Theron squinted but could see only the island and the emptiness beyond it.

"The curvature of the earth," his father said. "Why does it go in a circle? Who knows? It's for God to decide. But we have our task here. We follow the rituals so the circle remains unbroken."

Theron was fourteen, a man now, he had been kissed, he had helped his father with the serious work of life, he had the mark, but he thought, looking at the eastern horizon, that one day he would go beyond Chite and Tangier and even Isthmus, and see the places that the Yankee had seen, in some yonder springtime.

He would take what he knew of his task, of his mark, and show the world what it meant.

I am Infinite, I Contain Multitudes

A NOVELETTE

I got a peek at both their files. Joe's *and* the old man's.

I bribed a needy psych tech with all kinds of unpleasant favors, but I got my grubby mitts on those folders.

Here's what I found out about Joe:

He had murdered, sure, but more than that, he had told his psychiatrist that he wanted only to help people.

He just wanted to keep them, all these lost souls, from hurting themselves.

He wanted to *love*.

Remember this.

It makes sense of everything I've been going through at Aurora.

I found out things about the old man, as well, but it was all too late by then, wasn't it?

LET me tell you something about Aurora, something that nobody seems to know but me:

It is forsaken. Not just because of what you did to get there, or how haywire your brain is, but because it's built over the old Aurora.

Right underneath it, where we do the farming. I heard this from Steve Parkinson, right underneath it is the old Aurora.

I saw pictures in an album they keep in Intake.

It used to be a dusty wasteland.

Yes, the old, ancient Aurora once existed smack dab underground. Back then they believed it was better, if you were like us, to never see the light of day, to be chained like animals and have your food shoved to you in a slot at the bottom of your door.

Back then, they believed that nobody in the town outside the fence wanted to know that you were there. But that's not why it's forsaken.

You will know soon enough.

There was a town of Aurora once, too, but then it was bought out by Fort Salton, and 'round about 1949 they did the first tests.

I heard, from local legend, that there were fourteen men down there, just like in a bunker at the end of the war.

They did the tests out at the mountain, but some people said that those men in Aurora, underground, got worse afterward.

I heard a story from my bunkmate that one guy got zapped and fried right in front of an old-timer's eyes. Like he was locked in on the wrong side of the microwave door.

The old-timer, he's still at Aurora; been there since he

was nineteen, in 'forty-six. Had a problem, they said, with people after the war.

He was in the Pacific, and had come back more than shell-shocked.

That's all I ever knew about him, before I arrived. You can safely assume that he killed somebody or tried to kill himself or can't live without wanting to kill somebody.

It's why we're all here.

He's about as old as my father, but he doesn't look it. Maybe Aurora's kept him young.

He was always over there, across the Yard. He knew everything about everyone. I knew something about him, too. Actually, we all pretty much knew it.

He thought he was Father to us all. I don't mean like my father, or the guy who knocked your mother up. I mean the Father, as in God The.

In his mind, he created the very earth upon which we stood, his men, his sons.

He could name each worm, each sowbug, each and every centipede that burrowed beneath the flagstone walk; the building was built of steel and concrete and had been erected upon the backs of laborers who had died within the walls of Aurora; the sky was anemic, the air dry and calm; he could glance in any direction at any given moment and know the inner workings of his men as we wandered the Yard, or know, in a heartbeat, no, the whisper of a heart-beat, where our next step would take us.

There was no magic or deception to his knowledge.

He was simply aware; call it, as he did, hyperawareness, from which had come his nickname, Hype.

He was also criminally insane by a ruling of the courts of the state of California, as were most men in Aurora.

I watched him sometimes, standing there while we had our recreation time, or sitting upon the stoop to the infirmary, gazing across the sea of men.

His army, he called them, his infantry: they would one day spread across the land like the fires of Armageddon.

The week after Danny Boy got out was the first time he ever spoke to me.

"Hey," Hype called out, waving his hand. "Come on over here."

I glanced around. *Me?*

I had been at Aurora for only four months, and I'd heard the legends of Hype. How he called on you only after watching you for years. How he could be silent for a year and then, in the span of a week, talk your head off.

I couldn't believe he was speaking to me. He nodded when he saw my confusion. I went over to him.

"You're the one," he said, patting me on the back.

You couldn't help but look him in the eye, he was so magnetic, but all the guys had told me *not* to look him in the eye, not to stare straight at him at any point. They all warned me because they had failed at it. They had all been drawn to his presence at one time or another.

He was pale white. He kept in the shack at all times. His hair was splotchy gray and white and longer than regulation. His eyes were nothing special: round and brown and maybe a little flecked with gold. ("He milks you with those eyes," Joe had told me.) There were wrinkles on his face, just like with any old man, but his were thin and straight, as if he had not ever changed his expression since he'd been young.

"*I'm* the one? The *one*," I said, nodding as if I understood.

I had a cigarette, left over from the previous week. I offered it to him.

He took the cigarette, thrust it between his lips, and sucked on it.

I glanced around for an orderly or psych tech, but we were alone together. I didn't know how I was going to light the cigarette for him. They all called me Doer, which was short for Good-Doer, because I tended to light cigarettes when I could, shine shoes for one of the supervisors I'd ass-kiss, or sweep floors for the lady janitors.

I did the good deeds because I'd always done them, all my life. Even when I murdered, I was respectful. But since there was no staff member around, I couldn't get a light for the old man.

Hype seemed content just to suck that cigarette, speaking through the side of his mouth.

"Yeah, you know what it means, but you're it. Danny Boy, he would've been it, but he had to pretend."

He drew the cigarette from his mouth and held it in his fingertips, "He is of a certain breed of sociopath, you must've recognized that. He had to perform for his doctor and the board. He studied Mitch over in B–the one who cries and moans all the time. Mitch with the tattoos?"

I nodded.

"He studied him for three years before perfecting his technique. Let me tell you about Danny Boy. He was born in Barstow, which may just doom a man from the start. He began his career by murdering a classmate in second grade.

It was a simple thing to do, for they played out in the desert often, and it was not unusual for children to go missing out there. He managed to get that murder blamed on a local sad little man.

"Later, dropping out of high school, he murdered a teacher, and then, when he killed three women in Laguna, he got caught.

"The boy could not cry. It was not in him to understand why anyone made a fuss at all over murder. It was as natural to him as is breathing to you."

Hype paused, and drew something from his breast pocket.

He flicked his lighter up and lit the cigarette. Although we weren't supposed to have lighters, it didn't surprise me too much that Hype managed to keep one. As an old-timer he had special privileges, and as something of a seer, he was respected by the staff as well as by his men.

It's strange to think that I was suitably impressed by this, his having a lighter, but I was. It might as well have been a gold brick, or a gun.

He continued:

"Danny Boy is going to move in with one of the women who work in the cafeteria. She's never had a lover, and certainly never dreamed of having one as handsome as Danny Boy. Within six weeks, he will kill her and keep her skin for a souvenir. Danny Boy would've been it, but he wasn't a genuine person. You are. You know that, don't you?"

"What, I 'cry,' so that makes me real?"

He shook his head, puffing away, trying to suppress a laugh.

"No. But I know about you, kid. You shouldn't even be

here, only you come from a rich family who bought the best lawyer in L.A. I assume that in Court Ninety, he argued for your insanity and you played along 'cause you thought it would go easier for you in Aurora or Atascadero instead of over in Chino or Chuckawalla. Tell me I'm wrong. No? How long you been here?"

"If you're so smart, you already know."

"Sixteen weeks already." He grinned, shaking his head. "Sixteen weeks of waking up in a cold sweat with Joe leaning over your bed. Sixteen weeks of playing baseball with men who would be happy to bash in your head just for the pleasure of it. Sixteen weeks hearing the screams, knowing about Cap and Eddie, knowing about how all they want is the taste of human flesh one more time before they die. And you, in their midst."

He seemed to be enjoying his own speech.

"You're not a sociopath, son, oh no, you're just someone who happened to kill some people and now you wish you hadn't, and maybe you wished you were in Chino getting bludgeoned and raped at night, but at least not having to deal with this zoo."

The bell rang.

I saw Trish, the rec counselor, wave to us from over at the baseball diamond. She was pretty, and we all wanted her and we were all protective of her, too, even down to the last sociopath.

"Looks like it's time for phys ed," Hype said. "She's a fine piece of work, that one. Women are good for men. Don't you think? Men can be good, too, sometimes, I guess. You'd know about that, I suppose."

"What am I 'it' for?" I asked, ignoring the implication of his comment.

He dropped the cigarette in the dust. "You're the one who's getting out."

IN THE LATE AFTERNOON, I sat beside Joe on the leather chairs in the TV room after we got shrunk by our shrinks.

I said, "I don't get it. If Danny Boy wasn't it, and 'it' means you get out, why the hell am I it?"

Joe shrugged. "Maybe he means 'you're next.' That old guy knows a shitload. He's God."

Joe had spent his life in the system.

First, at Juvy, then at Boys' Camp in Chino, then Chino, and finally some judge figured out that you don't systematically kill everyone from your old neighborhood unless you're not quite right in the head. But Joe was a good egg behind the Aurora fence.

He needed the system and the walls and the three hots and a cot just to stay on track.

Maybe if he'd been in some strict religion or in the army, with all those rules, he never would've murdered anybody. He needed rules badly, and Aurora had plenty for him. He had always been gentle and decent with me, and was possibly my only friend at Aurora.

I nudged him with my elbow. "Why would I be it?"

"Maybe he's gonna break you out," Joe whispered, checking the old lady at the desk to make sure she couldn't hear him. "He broke another guy out awhile back, through the underground. That old man's got a way to do it, if you go down in that rat nest far enough. I heard."

Joe grabbed my hand in his, clutching it, his face inches

from mine. "He knows where the way out is, and he only tells it if he thinks your destiny's aligned with the universe."

I almost laughed at Joe's seriousness. I drew back from him. "You got to be kidding."

Joe blinked.

He didn't like being made fun of.

"Believe what you want. All's I know is the old man thinks you're *it*. Can't argue with that."

And then Joe kissed me gently, as he always did, or tried to do, when no one was looking, and I responded in kind.

It was the closest thing to human warmth we had in that place.

I pulled away from him when a psych tech strolled in with one of the shrinks.

I WANTED to believe that Hype could break me out of Aurora. I

I spent the rest of the day and most of the evening fantasizing about getting out, about walking out on the grass and dirt beyond the fence. Of getting on a bus and going up north where my brother lived.

From there I would go up to Canada, maybe Alaska, and get lost somewhere in the wilderness where they wouldn't come hunting for me.

It was a dream I'd had since entering Aurora. A futile and useless dream, but I nurtured it day by day, hour by hour.

I could close my eyes and suddenly be transported to a glassy river, surrounded by mountains of pure white, and air so fresh and cold it could stop your lungs; an eagle would scream as it dropped from the sky to grab its prey.

But my eyes opened; the dream was gone.

In its place, the dull green of the walls, the smell of alcohol and urine, the sounds of Cap and Eddie screeching from their restraints two doors down, the small slit of window with the bright lights of the Yard on all night.

Only Joe kept me warm at night, and the smell of his hair as he scrunched in bed, snoring lightly beside me, kept alive any spirit that threatened to die inside me.

I had never been interested in men on the Outside, but in Aurora, it had never seemed homosexual between us.

It was survival.

When you are in that kind of environment, you seek warmth and human affection if you are at all sane. Even if sanity is just a frayed thread.

Even the sociopaths sought human warmth; even they, it is supposed, want to be loved.

I knew that Joe would one day kill me if I said the wrong thing to him, or if I wasn't generous in nature toward him. He had spent his life killing for those reasons.

Still, I took the risk because he was so warm and comfortable, and sometimes, at night, that's all you need.

The next morning I sought Hype out and plunked myself right down next to him.

"Why me?"

❧

HE DIDN'T LOOK up from his plate.

"Why not you?"

He had that stoned look of one who could see the invisible world. His smile was cocked, like a gun's trigger.

"Why not Doer, the compassionate? Doer, the one who serves? Why not you?"

"No," I said. "It could be any one of these guys. I've only been here four months. We don't know each other."

"I know everybody. I am infinite, I contain multitudes. I know all. Nothing is beyond me. I see the you within you. Besides, I told you, you don't pretend."

"Huh?"

"You don't pretend. You face things. That's important. It won't work if you live in your own little world, like most of these boys. You've got the talent."

"Yeah, the talent," I said, finally deciding the old fart was as loony as the rest.

"I saw what you did," he said.

As he spoke, I could feel my heart freeze. In the tone of his voice, the smoothness of old whiskey.

"I saw how you took the gun and killed your son first. One bullet to the back of the skull, and then another to his ear, just to make sure. Then your daughter, running through the house, trying to get away from you. She was actually the hardest, because she was screaming so much and moving so fast. You're not a good shot. It took you three bullets to bring her down."

"Just shut up," I said.

"Your wife was easy. She parked out front, and came in the side door, at the kitchen. She didn't know the kids were dead. All she knew was her husband was under a lot of pressure and she had to somehow make things right. She had groceries. She was going to cook dinner. While she was putting the wine in the fridge, you shot her and she died quickly. And then," Hype shook his head. "Then, you took the dog out, too. Who would take care of it, right? With everybody dead, who would take care of the dog?"

I said nothing.

"Who would take care of the dog?" he repeated. "You had no choice but to take it out, too. You loved that dog. It probably was as hard for you to pull the trigger on that dog as it was to pull it on your son. Maybe harder."

I said nothing. I thought nothing. My mind was red paint across black night. His words meant nothing to me.

He patted me on the back as my father had before the trial.

"It's all right. It's over. It wasn't anything anyone blames you for."

I began weeping; he rubbed his hand along my back and whispered words of comfort to me.

"It wasn't like that," I managed to say, drying my tears.

Although we had been left alone, I looked across the cafeteria and felt that all the others watched us.

Watched *me,* anyway.

But they didn't; they were preoccupied with their meals.

"It was…" I stumbled over words in my mind.

"Take your time," he said.

I wiped my face with filthy hands. I felt so dirty. I just wanted to be clean. I fought the urge to rise up and go find a shower.

"I wanted it to be me."

"But you wanted to live, too. You killed your family, and then suddenly–"

"*Suddenly,*" I repeated.

"Suddenly, your life came back into focus. You couldn't kill yourself. You had to go through all of them before you found that out. Life's like that," he said. "The bad thing is, they're all dead. You did it. You're a murderer. But you're not like these others. It wasn't some genetic defect or some lack of conscience. Conscience is important. You couldn't kill yourself. That's important. I don't want to get some fellow out who's going to end up killing himself. You need to be part of something larger than yourself. You need God. Tell me, boy: How do you live with yourself?"

I couldn't look him in the eye. I was trying to think up a lie to tell him. He reached out and took my chin in his hand. He forced me to look at him.

I remembered a warning: he milks you with those eyes.

"I don't know how," I said, truthfully. "I wake up every morning and I think I am the worst human being in existence."

"Yes," he said. "You are. But here's the grace of Aurora. You're it. You will get out. You will live with what you did. You will not kill yourself or commit any further atrocities."

He let go of my chin and rose from the table. "You love your friend?"

"Joe?"

"That's right." He nodded. "Joe."

'Two guys can't love each other," I said. "It's just for now. It's surviving. It's barely even sexual."

"Ah." He nodded slowly. "That's good. It would be hell if you got out and you loved him and he was here. You must be careful around him, though. He is pretty and warm. But he has the face of Judas. He will never truly love anyone. Now, you, you will love again. A man, perhaps. Or a woman. But not our friend Joe. You know what he did to the last man he shared his bed with? He ever tell you?"

"No."

"Ask him," Hype said.

He walked away. From the back, he didn't seem old. He had a young way of walking.

I believed in him.

&

"TONIGHT. LATE," Hype said to me later on, during our recreational time. "Two-thirty. You must first shower. You must be clean. I will not tolerate filth. Then wait. I will be there. If your friend makes trouble, stop him any way you can."

&

JOE COULD BE POSSESSIVE, but not in the expected way.

He wasn't jealous of other men or women. He simply wanted to own me all the time.

He wanted me to shower with him, to sit with him, to go to the cafeteria with him.

Our relationship seemed simple to me: we had met about the third week in, when he caught me masturbating in the bathroom.

He joined in, and this led to some necking, which led to a chilly week or so afterward when I felt strange from all that.

Then I got a letter from my mother in which she severed all connections with me, followed by one from my father and sister.

I spent two days in bed staring at the wall.

Joe came and took care of me until I could eat and stand and laugh again.

By that time, we were tight.

I had been at Aurora for less than two months before I realized I could not disentangle myself from Joe without being murdered or tortured – it was a Joe thing.

I didn't feel threatened, however. I'd grown fond of his occasional groping and nightly sleepovers.

In a way, it was like being a child again, with a best friend, with a mother and lover and buddy all rolled up into one person.

That night, when I rose from my bed at two a.m., Joe immediately woke up.

"Doer?" he asked.

"The can." I nodded toward the hallway.

Because Joe and I weren't in the truly dangerous category, we and a few others were given free rein of our hallway at night. Knowing, of course, that the Night Shift Bitch was on duty at the end of the hall.

"I'll go, too," Joe whispered, rising. He drew his briefs up. He had the endearing habit of leaving them down around his ankles in postcoital negligence.

I tapped him on the chest, shaking my head.

"Doer," he said, "I got to go, too."

The two of us quietly went into the hall.

In the bathroom, he said, "I know what's going on."

HE LEANED against the shiny tile wall. "It's Hype. Word went around. This is the night. Are you really going?"

I nodded, not wanting to lie. He had been sweet to me. I cared a great deal for him. I would be sad without him, for a time.

"I'll miss you, Joe. I really will."

"I could kill you for this."

"I know. But we're okay, buddy? You and me?"

"If you leave I'll be lonely. Maybe it's love, who knows?" He laughed, as if making fun of himself. "Maybe I love you. That's a good one."

"No you don't."

I imagined then that Joe was fairly incapable of something so morally developed as love, not because of his sexual leanings, but because of his pathology.

"Don't go," he said.

"For all I know, Hype is full of shit"

"He's not. I know things. I've seen him do this before. He gets people out. But don't go, Doer. Getting out's not so terrific."

"I want freedom," I said. "Plain and simple."

"I want you." Joe seemed to be getting a little testy.

"Now, come on, we're friends, you and me," I said, leaning forward to give him a friendly hug. "You're my buddy."

I didn't see the knife right away.

All I saw was something shiny, which caught the nearly-burnt-out light of the bathroom.

It didn't hurt going in – that was more a shock, like hearing an alarm clock at five a.m. waking you from a sound sleep.

Coming out, it hurt like a motherfucker.

He pressed his hand against the wound near my chest. "You can't leave me."

"Don't kill me, Joe. I won't leave you, I promise. You can come too." I gasped although I wasn't sure if the words in my mind formed from my lips or if I just imagined I said them as I slid downward.

He caught me in his arms and brought me down to cold tile.

I felt light-headed. The burning pain quickly turned to a frozen numbness.

I coughed, and wheezed, "get help, Joe. Please."

Joe pressed his sweaty body against mine.

Had he drawn his underwear down? I could feel his flesh against mine.

He murmured, a moan followed by softly whispered words that I couldn't make out.

I began to see brief tiny explosions of light and dark, as my vision faded.

Joe kissed the wound where he'd stabbed me, as blood pulsed from it.

"I love you this much," he said.

I AWOKE in the infirmary three days later, barely able to see through a cloud of painkillers.

I stared up at the ceiling until its small square acoustic tiles came into focus.

When I was better, months later, I went looking for Hype in the yard.

"I TRIED TO MAKE IT," I said.

He seemed to look through me.

"You know what he did to me," I said. "Please, I want to get out. I have to get out."

After several minutes, Hype said, "Love transformed into fear. It's the human story. The last man Joe befriended was named Frank. He grew up in Compton. A good kid. He tore off another man's genitals with his bare hands and wore them around his neck.

"His only murder. Sweet kid. Twenty-two. Probably he was headed for release within a year or two. He had an A-plus evaluation. A little morbid. Used to draw pictures of beheadings. Joe latched on to him, too. Took care of him. Bathed him. Serviced him. Loved him, if you will. Then rumor went around that Frank was getting some from one of the psych techs. Totally fabricated, of course. Frank was taking a shower. Joe knocked him on the head. Strapped him to the bed, spread-eagled.

"Don't ask me how, but he'd gotten a hold of a drill–the old kind, you know, you turn manually and it spins. He made openings in Frank. First in his throat to keep him from screaming. Then the rest of him. Each opening..."

"I know," I said, remembering the pain under my arm. Then something occurred to me. "Where did he get the knife?"

Hype made a face, like he'd chewed something sour.

"The knife," I repeated. "And the drill, too. Everything's locked up tight. You're supposed to be God or something, so you tell me."

Without changing his expression, Hype said, "Joe gets out."

The enormity of this revelation didn't completely hit me. "From here?"

Hype nodded. "It's not something I'm proud of. I can

open the door for about three hours, if I use up all my energy. Joe knows it. He was the first one I took out. But he didn't want to stay out. He only wanted out to get his toys. Then he wanted back. He's the only one who manages to get back. Why he wants to, I couldn't say."

For the first time ever, I watched worry furrow the old man's brow.

He placed his hand against his forehead. A small blue vein pulsed there, beneath his pale skin's surface.

"I created the world, but it's not perfect."

"*Joe* knows how to get *out?*"

"I didn't say that. I can get it open. I just can't keep him from going back and forth. It something he does what nobody else seems able to do. And then the door closes again."

I wasn't sure how to pose my next question, because there was a mystery to this place where men got out.

I had figured it to be down in the old underground, where Hype would know the route of the labyrinthine tunnels.

"Where does *it* go?"

"I can't tell you," Hype sighed. "Never been through it. I just know it takes you out."

BACK IN MY own bed that night, trying to sleep, I felt Joe's hand on my shoulder. He slipped swiftly between the covers to cradle my body against his.

"Doer," he said. "I missed you."

"Get off me." I tried to shrug him away. He was

burning with some fever. A few drops of his sweat touched the back of my neck.

"No." He tucked himself in closer to me. I could feel his warm breath on my neck. "I want you."

"Not after what you did."

He said nothing more with words. His mouth opened against my neck, and I felt his tongue heat my sore muscles. All his language came through his throat and mouth, and I let him. I hated him, but I let him. Afterward, I whispered, "I want out."

"No, you don't."

"Yeah, I do. I don't care if you stab me again. I want out. You going to get me out?"

I waited a long time for his answer, then fell asleep.

I was still waiting for his answer a week later.

ॐ

I CORNERED him in the shower, placing my hands on either side of him. I could encompass his body within my arms. I stared straight into his eyes.

"I want out."

He curled his upper lip; I thought he would answer, but first, he spat in my face.

"I saved you. You don't even care. Out is not where you want to be. In here's the only safe place. You get fed, you got a bed."

He leaned closer to me. "You have someone who loves you."

I was prepared this time. I brought my fist against his face and smashed him as hard as I could. His head lolled to the side, and I heard a sharp crack as his skull hit the tile wall.

When he turned to face me again, there was blood at the comer of his lips. A smile grew from the blood.

"Okay," Joe said. "You want out. It can be arranged."

"Good. Next time, I kill you."

"Yeah." He nodded.

As I left the shower room, I glanced back at him for a second. He stood under the shower head, water streaming down–it almost looked like tears as the water streamed in rivulets across his face, taking with it the blood at his lips.

§.

AN HOUR LATER, Hype found me out by the crude baseball diamond we'd drawn in the Yard under the shade of several oak trees that grew just beyond the high fence.

"Your lover told me we're moving up the schedule. Shouldn't do this but once every few years. You should've gotten out that night. Joe shouldn't have stopped you. Any idea why he did?"

I kicked at home plate, a drawing in the dirt. Aurora was a funny place that way – because of things being considered dangerous around the inmates, even home plate had to be just a drawing and not the real thing. The real things here were the fences and the factory-like buildings.

"No," I said. "Maybe he's in love with me and doesn't want to lose me. I don't care. He can go to hell as far as I'm concerned."

"I once tried to get out all by myself," Hype said, ignoring me. "It was back in the early fifties. I was just a kid. Me and my buddies. I tried to get out, but back then there was only one way – a coffin. Not a happy system. I didn't know then that I'd rather be in here than out there."

"Make sense, old man," I said, frustrated. I wanted to kick him. The thought of spending another night in this place with Joe on top of me wasn't my idea of living.

"A little patience goes a long way, Doer," he said. It felt like a commandment.

He continued. "Then they started doing those tests – bombs and all kinds of things, twenty, thirty miles away. Some closer, they said. Some this side of the mountain.

"We lived below back then. Me and Skimp and Ralph. Others, too, but these were my tribe. We were shell-shocked and crazy, and we were put in with the paranoid schizophrenics and sociopaths and alcoholics – all of us together. Some restrained to a wall, some bound up in straitjackets. Some of us roaming free in the subterranean hallways. Skimp, he thought he was still on a submarine. He really did. But I knew where we were – in the farthest ring of hell.

"And then, one morning, around three a.m., I heard Skimp whimpering from his bunk. I go over there, because he had nightmares a lot. I usually woke him up and told him a story so he could fall back to sleep.

"Only, Skimp was barely there. His flesh had melted like cheese on a hot plate, until it was hard to tell where the sheets left off and Skimp began. He was making a noise through his nostrils. It was like someone snoring, only he was trying to scream.

"Others, too, crying out, and then I felt it – like my blood was spinning around. I heard since that it was like we got stuck in a microwave. The entire place seemed to shimmer, and I knew to cover my eyes. I had learned a little bit about these tests, and I knew that moist parts of the body were the most vulnerable. That's why insects aren't very affected by it – they've got exoskeletons. All their softs parts are on their insides. I felt drunk and happy, too, even while my mouth opened to scream, and I went to my hiding place, covering myself with blankets. I crawled as far back into my hiding place as I could go, and then I saw some broken concrete and started scraping at it. I managed to push my way through it, farther, into darkness. But I got away from the noise and the heat.

"Later, I heard that it was some test that had leaked out. Some underground nuclear testing. We were all exposed, those who survived. Never saw Skimp or Ralph again. I was told they were transferred. Back in those days, no one investigated anyone or anything. I knew they'd died, and I knew how they'd died. There were times I wished I'd died, too. Every day.

"That's when I learned about my divinity. It was like Christ climbing the cross–he may or may not have been God before he climbed onto that cross, but you know for sure he was God once he was up there. I wasn't God before that day, but afterward, I was."

HYPE WAS A TERRIFIC STORYTELLER, and while I was in awe of that ability, I stared at him as if he were the most insane man on the face of the earth.

"So I found a way out," he concluded.

"If that's true, how come you don't get out?"

"It's my fate. Others can go through, but I must stay. It's my duty. Trust me, you think God likes to be on Earth? It's as much an asylum out there as it is in here."

I was beginning to think that all of this talk about going through and getting out was an elaborate joke for which the only punch line would be my disappointment. I decided to hell with it all: The old man could not get me out no matter how terrific his stories were. I was going to spend the rest of my life with Joe pawing me.

I went to bed early, hoping to find some escape in dreams.

I awoke that night, a flashlight in my face.

JOE SAID, "Get up. This is what you want, right?"

His voice was calm, not the usual nocturnal passionate whisper of the Joe who caressed me. He hadn't touched me at all. I was somewhat relieved.

"Huh?" I asked. "What's going on?"

"You want to get out? Let's go. You've got to take a shower first."

I felt his hand tug at my wrist.

"Get the hell up," he said.

THE SHOWER WAS COLD.

I spread Ivory soap across my skin, rubbing it briskly under my arms, around my healing wound, down my stomach, thighs, backs of legs, between my toes. Joe watched me the whole time. His expression was constant: a stone statue without emotion.

"It doesn't have to end like this," I said. "I'm going to miss you."

"Shut up," he said. "I don't like liars."

After I toweled off, he led me, naked, down the dimly lit hall.

The alarm was usually on at the double doors at the end of the hall, but its light was shut off.

Joe pushed the door open, guiding me along. The place seemed dead.

Hearing the sound of footsteps in the next ward, he covered my mouth with his hand and drew me quickly into an inmate's room.

Then, a few minutes later, we continued on to the cafeteria.

He had a key to the kitchen; he unlocked its door.

I followed him through the dark kitchen, careful to avoid bumping into the great metal counters and shelves.

Finally, he unlocked another door at the rear of the kitchen.

This led to a narrow hallway.

At the end of the hallway, another door, which was open.

Hype stood there, frozen in the flashlight beam.

"Hey," I said.

Hype put a finger to his lips. He wore a bathrobe that seemed shiny purple in the light.

He turned, going ahead of us, with Joe behind me. I followed the old man down the stone steps.

WE ENTERED THE OLD AURORA, the one that stretched for miles beneath the above ground Aurora. We walked single file down more narrow corridors, the sound of dripping water all around.

At one point, I felt something brush my feet—a large insect, perhaps, or a mouse. The place smelled of wet moss, and carried its own humidity, stronger than what existed in the upper world.

For a while it did seem that Hype had been right:

This was the deepest ring of hell.

But I'm getting out, I thought. I'll go through any sewer that man has invented to get out. To go through. To be done with all this.

JOE RESTED his hand on my shoulder for a brief moment. He whispered in my ear, "You don't have to do this. I was wrong. I love you. Don't get out."

I stopped, feeling his sweet breath on my neck. Even though I had been in Aurora only a little over four months, I had begun getting used to it. If I stayed longer, I would become part of it, and the outside world would be alien and terrifying to me. I saw it in other men, including Joe. This was the only world of importance to them.

"Why the change?" I asked.

"You don't want to go through. I want you here with me."

"No, thanks." I put all the venom I could into those two words. I added, "And by the way, Joe, if I had a gun I'd shoot your balls off for what you did to me."

"You don't understand." He shook his head like a hurt little boy.

Hype was already several steps ahead. I caught up with him while Joe lagged behind.

"I'm going out through that hiding place you talked about," I guessed.

"No," he said. When he got to a cell, he led me through the open doorway.

A FEEBLE LIGHT emanated within the room—a yellowish-green light, as if glow-worms had been swiped along the walls until their phosphorescence remained.

It was your basic large tank, looking as if it had been compromised by several earthquakes over the past few years.

Joe entered behind me. "This is where Hype and his friends lived. This is where it happened."

He waved the flashlight beam across the green light.

I shivered, because for a moment I felt as if the ghosts of those men were still here, trapped in the old Aurora.

"Tell him, Hype. Tell him."

Hype wandered the room, as if measuring the paces.

"Ralph had this area. He had his papers and books – he was always a big reader. Skimp was over there," he pointed to the opposite side of the cell, "his submarine deck."

"Tell him the whole thing," Joe said.

In the green light of the room, as I glanced back at Joe, I saw that he had a revolver in his right hand.

"Tell him," he repeated.

"Where the hell did you get that?" I pointed to the gun.

"You can't ever go back," Hype said. "Once you're out, you can never go back. I won't let you back. Understood?"

I nodded. As if I was ever going to want to return to Aurora.

§

"TELL HIM," Joe said to Hype. This time he pointed the gun at Hype.

Then, to me, he said, "The gun was down here. I get all my weapons here. We get all kinds of things down here. Hype is God, remember? He creates all things."

'To hell with this," I said, figuring this bad make believe had gone too far. "You can't get me out, can you?"

Hype nodded. "Yes, I can. I am God, Joe. Those underground tests, they made me God. They were my cross. I'm the only survivor. The orderlies, the doctors, the patients, I'm the only one. That's when I became God."

"You want to get out, right?" Joe snarled at me. "Right?" He waved the gun for me to move over to the far wall.

Hype turned, dropping his robe.

§

BENEATH THE ROBE, he was naked, the skin of his back a festering sore.

The imprint of hundreds of stitches all along his spine, across the back of his rib cage.

To the right of this, a fist-sized cavity just above his left thigh.

"Tell him," Joe said.

The old man began speaking, as if he couldn't confess this to my face.

"Inside me is the door. The tunnel, Joe. To get through, you've got to enter me."

The must vulgar aspect of this hit me, and I groaned in revulsion.

Joe laughed. "Not what you think, Doer. Not like what you like to do to me. Or vice versa. His skin changed after the tests. Down here, it changes again. Look–it's like a river, look!"

At first I didn't know what he was pointing at–his finger tapped against Hype's wrinkled back.

Then, before I noticed any change, I felt something deep in my gut.

A tightening.

A terrible physical coiling within me, as if my body knew what was happening before my brain did.

I watched in horror as the old man's skin rippled along the spine. A slit broke open from one of the ancient wounds. It widened, gaping.

❧

JOE CAME CLOSER, shining his flashlight into its crimson-spattered entry.

It was like a red velvet curtain, moist, undulating. A smell like a dead animal from within.

The scent, too, of fresh meat,

Joe pressed the gun against my head. "Go through."

My first instinct was to resist.

· · ·

SECONDS LATER, Joe shot a bullet into the old man's wound, and it expanded further like the mouth of a baby bird as it waits for its feeding.

JOE KISSED MY SHOULDER. "GOODBYE, DOER."

He pressed the gun to my head.

THE OLD MAN'S back no longer seemed to be there; now it was a doorway, a tunnel toward some green light at the end of a long red road.

His body had stretched its flesh out like a skinned beast, an animal-hide doorway.

WITH THE GUN against my head, Joe shoved me forward, into it.

I pushed my way through the slick red mass and followed the green light of atomic waste.

Once inside, the walls of crimson pushed me with a peristaltic motion deeper, against my will.

Tiny hooks of his bones caught the edge of my flesh, tugging backward while I was pressed into the opening.

❧

WE ARE ALL IN HERE, all those who got out through him.

Only, "out" didn't mean out of Aurora, not officially. We're out of our skins, drawn into that infested old man.

When I held the reins of him for an afternoon, I got him to go down and bribe the psych tech on duty.

I pulled up both of their files — Joe's and Hype's.

Joe was a murderer who had a penchant for cutting wounds in people and screwing the wounds. This was no surprise to me. Joe was a sick fuck.

I knew it.

Everyone who's ever been with him knows it.

Hype was a guy who had been exposed to large amounts of radiation in the fifties.

He had a couple of problems, one physical and one mental. The physical one I am well aware of, for the little bag rests at the base of my stomach, to the side and back. Because of health problems as a result of the radiation, he'd had a colostomy about twenty years back.

The mental problems were also apparent to me once I got out, once I got through.

He suffered from a growing case of multiple personality disorder.

I pulled my file up, too, and it listed:

Escaped.

I had a good laugh with Joe over these files.

Then God took over, and I had to go back down into the moist tissues of heaven and wait until it was my turn again.

THERE ARE PRISONS WITHIN PRISONS, and skins within skins. You can't always see who someone is just by looking in his eyes.

Sometimes, others are there.

Sometimes, *God* is there.

"I am infinite," the old man said. *"I contain multitudes."*

Afterword

Dear Reader,

I want to thank you for reading this collection. I hope you'll let others know about if you think they might be interested.

Next up, here's a listing with notes on the collections gathered in *Lights Out*, but be sure and go to the *Story Copyrights & Publications* page for more information on dates of individual stories if this interests you.

THE COLLECTIONS

The Nightmare Chronicles, published 1999, Leisure Books/Dorchester Publishing, originally had a frame story around the whole thing I've since discarded about a kidnapped boy who turns out to be more than he seems. If you want to read the frame story, you'll need to check with secondhand dealers for the old mass market paperback edition of *The Nightmare Chronicles*, the one with the cemetery in the moonlight on the cover.

The book won a Bram Stoker Award and an International Horror Guild Award in its category.

The Machinery of Night, published 2004, by Cemetery Dance Publications. I did not reprint everything that's in that collection here, partly because I didn't feel *Lights Out* needed those stories, some of which I've still held back for a future collection.

Yes, I'm planning one.

The Machinery of Night can be found from secondhand dealers now and then. Only in hardcover. Beautiful edition, signed.

Wild Things: Four Tales, published in 2006. First published as a Cemetery Dance hardcover, later in ebook and paperback by Alkemara Press.

Night Asylum, first published 2012 by Alkemara Press although its current iteration was 2014 in paperback and ebook.

Lights Out first came out in 2014 from Alkemara Press, but this book you are now reading is the more recent edition (2019) that includes this *Afterword* and the *Story Copyrights & Publications*.

Keep turning the page (or scrolling) to hit that section, if interested

And thank you again.

— Douglas Clegg, Connecticut, March 3, 2019

Story Copyrights & Publications

A BIBLIOGRAPHY OF SORTS

These are the original publication and story copyright dates, as accurately as I can give them. All copyrights are held by me, Douglas Clegg, for the year in which the story was first published.

"People Who Love Life" - 1991 - *The Scream Factory,* Bob Morrish, editor.

"Where Flies Are Born" - 1991 - *Tekeli-Li!,* Jon B. Cooke, editor.

"Damned If You Do" - 1993 - *Cemetery Dance* Magazine, Richard Chizmar, editor.

"The Hurting Season" - 1993 - *Deathrealm,* Mark Rainey, editor.

"Ice Palace" - 1994 - *Little Deaths,* Ellen Datlow, editor. Dell Publishing.

"The Rendering Man" - 1994 - *Cemetery Dance* Magazine, Richard Chizmar, editor.

"White Chapel" - 1994 - *Love in Vein*, Poppy Z. Brite, editor. HarperCollins.

"The Night Before Alec Got Married" - 1994 - *Palace Corbie*, Wayne Edwards, editor.

"Chosen" (originally titled "Celeste, of the Chosen") - 1995 - *Deathrealm*, Mark Rainey, editor.

"O, Rare and Most Exquisite" - 1996, *Lethal Kisses*, Ellen Datlow, editor. Millennium.

"The Five" - 1996 - *Twists of the Tale*, Ellen Datlow, editor. Dell.

"The Fruit of Her Womb" -1996 - *Phantoms of the Night*, Martin Greenberg and Richard Gilliam, editors. DAW Books.

"The Ripening Sweetness of Late Afternoon" -1996 - *Dante's Disciples*, Peter Crowther, editor.

"Underworld" (originally mistitled in print "Underground") - 1996 - *Phantasm #3*, J.F. Gonzalez, editor. Iniquities Publications.

"I Am Infinite, I Contain Multitudes" - 1997 - *Palace Corbie*, Wayne Edwards, editor.

"Fries with That?" - 1998 - *Cemetery Dance* Magazine, Richard Chizmar, editor.

"265 and Heaven" - 1998 - *Imagination Fully Dilated*, Alan Clark and Elizabeth Engstrom, editors. Cemetery Dance Publications.

"Only Connect" - 1998 - *The Conspiracy Files* - Martin Greenberg and Scott H. Urban, editors. DAW Books.

"The Wicked" - 1998 - Shocklines Website, Matt Schwarts, editor.

"The Little Mermaid" - 1999 - *Palace Corbie*, Wayne Edwards, editor.

"Becoming Men" - 1999 - *Subterranean Gallery*, Richard Chizmar and William Shafer, editors. Subterranean Press.

"The Machinery of Night" - 1999 - *The Psycho Ward* - Victor Heck, editor. Dark Tales Publications.

The Dark Game - 2004 - *Flesh & Blood* Magazine, Jack Fisher, editor. Also same year, *The Machinery of Night* (collection), Richard Chizmar, editor. Cemetery Dance Publications.

"A Madness of Starlings" - 2004 - *Cemetery Dance* Magazine, Richard Chizmar, editor.

"Subway Turnstile" - 2004 - *The Machinery of Night* (collection), Richard Chizmar, editor. Cemetery Dance Publications.

"The Skin of the World" - 2004 - *The Machinery of Night* (collection), Richard Chizmar, editor. Cemetery Dance Publications. (NOTE: there may have been a very slightly earlier publication in a magazine, but I can't find it or recall this right now.)

"Why My Doll is Evil" - 2004 - *The Machinery of Night* (collection), Richard Chizmar, editor. Cemetery Dance Publications.

"The Wolf" - 2006 - *Wild Things: Four Tales* (collection), Richard Chizmar, editor. Cemetery Dance Publications.

"The American" 2006 - *Wild Things: Four Tales* (collection), Richard Chizmar, editor. Cemetery Dance Publications. (NOTE: Written originally for an absinthe-themed anthology to be edited by author/editor Joseph Nassise, this was released when the anthology was delayed. A more accurate copyright would likely be 2003 or thereabouts.)

"Belinda in the Pool" - 2012 - Alkemara Press.

"The Stain" - 2012 - *Cemetery Dance* Magazine, Richard Chizmar, editor.

"Funerary Rites" - 2014 - *Dark Discoveries*, Aaron J. French, editor, JournalStone.

Acknowledgments

Throughout the years in which I wrote these stories, certain people made contributions to their success, mostly by buying the first publication rights to these stories for their magazines or anthologies. I'm only putting a few here because otherwise this would be an endless bray of thanks to far too many people.

Special thanks go to Ellen Datlow who taught me more about sentence and meaning through her editorial eye and red pen than nearly anyone else.

To Richard Chizmar who enthusiastically published my fiction…and did it beautifully.

To George Clayton Johnson who, on a sunny afternoon in Westwood in Los Angeles many years ago, taught me more about plot in ten minutes while scribbling a diagram on a napkin than I'd learned from studying about it.

To Chelsea Quinn Yarbro who once told me what a short story was, at least from a writer's point of view, and this advice made all the difference.

To Matt Schwartz who opened my mind to so many

stories, writers, and aspects of examining story that it always feels like a master class in the art, craft, and business of story whenever we get together.

I already dedicated this edition to my husband, but I have to reiterate: thanks to Raul Silva, who has been vital to my sense of "a good life," and instrumental in supplying the stability and hard-won *excelsior* necessary for someone like me to spend a lifetime creating stories.

About the Author

Douglas Clegg is the *New York Times* bestselling and award-winning author of *Neverland*, *The Priest of Blood*, *Afterlife*, and *The Hour Before Dark*, among many other novels, novellas and stories. His first collection, *The Nightmare Chronicles*, won both the Bram Stoker Award and the International Horror Guild Award. His work has been published by Simon & Schuster, Penguin/Berkley, Signet, Dorchester, Bantam Dell Doubleday, Cemetery Dance Publications, Subterranean Press, Alkemara Press and others.

A pioneer in the ebook world, his novel *Naomi* made international news when it was launched as the world's first ebook serial in early 1999 and was called "the first major work of fiction to originate in cyberspace" by *Publisher's Weekly*, covered in *Time* magazine, *Business Week*, *Business 2.0*, *BBC Radio*, *NPR*, *USA Today* and more. His book *Purity* was the first to be published via mobile phone in the U.S. in early 2001.

He is married, and lives and writes along the coast of New England.

Find the Author Online:
www.DouglasClegg.com

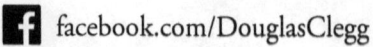 facebook.com/DouglasClegg

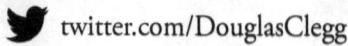 twitter.com/DouglasClegg

BB bookbub.com/authors/douglas-clegg